FOX DEN
BOOKS

Oregon

Miranda Mayer

A Beast With Silver Eyes

THE Beast
WITH SILVER EYES

A fantasy by

Miranda Mayer

The Beast With Silver Eyes

Miranda Mayer

www.mirandamayer.com

Cover Art by:

Christian Bentulan

www.coversbychristian.com

Photography:

Stephanie Robertson-Maier

Model:

Chloë Rossman

Costume:

Mt. Hood Creations

Dedications

To Dan, Alex, Stephie, Molly, Shea & Aelfgyva. You are everything.

Chapter 1
The Crownless King

Edrick of Bethranorn glared into the bleakness of the night. His thoughts were grim and convoluted as his body swayed with the motion of the vehicle on the precipitous seat of the bouncing carriage. He was more than reluctant to supplicate himself before the enemy that had caused his empire's fall one hundred and eighty years ago, but he had been the one chosen to do so. It was hoped that by sending someone of his bloodline would be sufficient enough a gesture; enough of a demonstration of what his people were willing to forgive, in order to beg the assistance of the Farkas.

He had no idea what to expect coming face to face with his people's former enemy. To look into the eyes of the nation that had torn down and destroyed a millennium-old birthright and shattered his state. The Farkas had reduced much of his royal family to scattered paupers, sending them fleeing and hiding for decades in fear of imprisonment for the crime of being highborn.

He had no idea what to expect from this meeting, for he had never truly encountered the enemy before. He had glimpsed a party of them in passing as they traveled through the country now and again, but he had never looked into the eyes, or spoken to a Farkas. Inside him, resentment still boiled beneath the surface. He had feared it would ruin their chances, this lingering hatred.

Nobody could prepare him for what he was about to do, because hardly anything was known about the Farkas, even after all these years. The tremulous truce between the once-great nation of Yvrem and the Farkas was a snarled weft shuttled across a warp of scattered delegates from various states, tangled and disordered; some never even communicating with others. But peace had been somehow woven nonetheless. It was fragile and expectant, as if at any moment the Farkas would surge forward again and bite back at the Yvremi nation, which were only just starting to thrive again after the complete devastation of their former government. The Farkas had been brutal. Why they withdrew their occupying armies, nobody really truly understood. A peace had been negotiated somehow, with all the shattered city states together. The Farkas had backed off but had never quite gone away.

Edrick emitted a groan as the sound of raindrops began to batter the brim of his hat. The downpour was quick to follow; so heavy, it drowned out the sound of the horses' hoofs on the ground and the rattle of the wheels. He wanted out of this rain, to be in a fine parlor, drinking port and enjoying the warmth of a fire. Instead, he was headed towards Farkas territory.

The Farkas still held great estates scattered across the broken empire, even managing some boroughs, but cut off from the rest of the countryside, withdrawn, closed and secretive. They were known as the *Sentely*. Some of the Yvremi-controlled estates around them regained some standing, and had begun to flourish again, as if the Farkas weren't really there. The government had struggled to rebuild itself, stumbling and rising again and again. Finally, after over almost eighty years, it appeared that stability was within reach. The Farkas remained a shadowy presence, quiet, likely watchful, perhaps biding their time. But Yvrem no longer had the option to fear and resent.

Not now. Not when everything they had worked so hard to rebuild was on the brink of ruin again. Their only hope was the Farkas.

Edrick had been summoned to the Senate where he was placed into the wide-armed embrace of a crescent bench facing a semi-circle of white-haired old men. He had already heard whispers of the Akravani massing troops. It was a rumor circulating about the upper crust of society, the mutterings of it heard at various social visits and parties Edrick had attended over the past few months.

Edrick never took much seriously, except perhaps his lineage and his dislike of the Farkas for the ruination of his royal line and those of countless other noble families. Everything else was just noise in the background of his idle existence. He was a man of leisure and gratification. He attended assemblies and traveled with parties throughout the countryside pursuing pleasures and vices. However, he did take cards seriously. And drinking. And the pursuit of women. Whispers of possible invasion, war and other such unpleasant things were best ignored. At least until he was summoned to the Senate.

They had managed to track Edrick down on the hunting excursion he was partaking in with several other rich layabouts. "It is only a matter of time. Your idle pursuits will end. Society as we know it will cease to exist if we do not face this threat head-on." The senate's envoy told him when the silver-haired, graceful man arrived at the hunting lodge. "Yvrem still struggles for stability. The absence of the Farkas from most of our city states has only made successful invasion more attainable for the Akravani."

Edrick grudgingly parted with his friends, who seemed quite put out for having their sport interrupted, and their best companion removed from company. Edrick pouted all the way to the Capitol of Kireen as the agreeable sensation of drunkenness faded into dreaded sobriety. The unpleasant things only continued to compound upon him as he arrived at the capitol.

9

"*You* must go. You are a Bethranorn. Your family legacy, your birthright of rule, was shredded by the invasion. For you of all people to request their assistance, the Farkas would understand the significance of our need; the depth to which we are willing to humble ourselves to save what remains of our precious nation. You must go, Honored Edrick."

"To where?" Edrick snapped in return, dubious and indignant. His head throbbed and his mouth was dry and tasted of old cheese. He didn't want this task. For one, though he would scarce admit it to anyone, he loathed the idea of responsibility of any kind. Secondly and more importantly, he feared he would be an impediment rather than an incentive for the Farkas to come to their aid. He was afraid he would not be able to put away the ire and disgust that filled him anytime anyone even uttered their name.

"The great house that was once Heddritch Peak Hall, but is now called Eyome. It is just north of Ullach."

Edrick stiffened. That estate had once belonged to a branch of his family, a duchy. It had been taken during the war with the Farkas.

"Word is," the Senator continued, "the resident of Eyome is of the highest consequence among the houses under Farkas rule. We are uncertain who this landlord is, but we are told that they hold great influence with their homeland and would be the best option."

"Why go to the highest order to start? Wouldn't it be prudent to find someone of lower rank, or someone connected to the Farkas estates to introduce our need with more care and decorum based on their own protocols? How do you know our striding up to the door of the highest ranked Farkas stronghold in our nation will not offend them?" Edrick was determined to find fault with this plan. But he could not add more fault where there were already so many uncertainties and flaws. It was a stab in the dark to send him to this house, the resident of which was largely an unknown factor, without the slightest idea of how even addressing them after all these years would affect them. They were desperate.

"We have no time to stroke the egos of the connected people, Mr. Bethranorn, and hope they will send the message up the line, if at all. We must go directly to the source and hope for the best. We choose you because you are a living embodiment of our desperation. We will not hide the exigency of our situation from you. Our nation is in peril, and you must set aside your anger and do what you can for your nation. You may no longer be entitled to a throne, Bethranorn, but you still have an obligation to Yvrem. To its people. You *are* royalty."

Edrick chuffed and leaned back in the tall, creaking wood chair. His eyes painted his bemused gaze upon each wizened, exhausted face. Each one had sunken, watery eyes— reddened from fatigue and duress. Shaking, papery-skinned hands rested lightly on stacks of papers on the table that had once been the meeting place of the ancient royal council. It now it hosted the top seven of the Senate; known as the Eldren. They were the tie-breakers and the voice of the present interim government—the fourth version of government to take power since the end of the Farkas occupation. So far, this one was free of power-mongers and madmen, which presented an optimistic start. Edrick, however, believed that the monarchy ought to be restored as long as it wasn't incumbent on him to rule. He much preferred his life of idle pursuits

Edrick had the option before him to leave the old men to find another to speak for the people. He could return to his sport with his useless friends. But he felt the weight of his legacy upon him, and knew it was his burden to bear. He might not have a throne to sit on, but indeed, he was royalty of Yvrem. He was the rightful King; the crownless king of Yvrem.

So he was sent north only moments after the meeting to gather some items from his town home. He began his journey not in the comfort of a closed coach, but on a towering, lurching curricle with wheels almost taller than he, and a suspension that had lost its rigidity years ago, causing the assemblage to oscillate madly, sometimes sending the seat feet up and down for the smallest potholes.

Hunched underneath an oiled leather greatcoat, and a wide brimmed hat, he wedged the flat of his boots on the angled footboard, while the ostensibly mute driver managed the barely tame team that pulled the teetering device. Thus they drove toward Eyome, The great house now occupied by the invaders that refused to go away.

Edrick expected to be turned away at the gates of Eyome, but the great road merely split off into a small, picturesque dorp where the estate bordered Yvrem land. The curricle trundled unimpeded, through a pair of monolithic stone pilasters marking the border. The road quality changed instantly—from rutted, muddy disrepair to a neat, extraordinarily well-laid and neatly paved cobble. The effect of it was jarring, to go from being jostled about to the sudden smooth rattle of the iron wheel on the flat stones. The bouncing of the coach leveled itself out shortly thereafter. The horses even seemed less agitated and their trotting hoof beats almost synchronized.

The names of the towns were no longer the same, if they were within a Farkas estate. The Yvremi, as an act of defiance, often refused to print the new Farkas names on modern maps, leaving great swaths of the countryside blank as if they did not exist. But there were still Yvremi within those borders, living their lives, farming, trading, and going on without the rest of their world. They were merely eaten up by the blank spaces on the maps, and considered a loss to the rest of their countrymen.

This was Edrick's first venture into a Farkas-run enclave. This one was vast, having once been a small duchy. It contained many towns and villages around it, even a city or two. Many of the Yvremi Sentely contained smaller versions of this annexed country estate, and the senators that represented the regions acted as if the Farkas held lands were not there. But here it was. And it was idyllic.

12

The first village Edrick set eyes on was devoid of dirt and muck. It had no detritus in the streets. The air smelled clean with no reek of sewage. The roads were paved. The people, although quiet and suspicious, were clothed in fine garments. Edrick's gaze wandered to the guttering systems on the common houses and the bizarre appearances of grates on the sides of the road into which the runoff from the early morning rain that had soaked the curricle's occupants now flowed.

The Capitol of Kireen was considered to be the pinnacle of Yvremi culture, and it was a vile mess in comparison to this Sentely. The village centers here were tidy and green, the houses dripping in hanging plants from window boxes, even the herd of sheep that at one point blocked the curricle while being shepherded into a nearby pasture between villages, seemed whiter and cleaner and healthier than anything Edrick had ever seen.

There was the Farkas influence of the past one hundred and eighty years evidenced all over the landscape and towns. Although many of the buildings were of the old familiar Yvremi styles, there were newer constructs, buildings and infrastructure that was markedly in the style of the Farkas; a heavy, ghostly line to things with sweeping arches and cantilevered building faces. Stone more than wood, intricately carved corbels and posts, hideous medallions on buildings carved with the faces of Farkas myth; ravens and wolves, strange gaunt looking harts, and bizarre gargoyle faces.

There was also a marked presence of Farkas animals and some types of trees growing he'd never seen before. Feathery hoofed Hellas horses were everywhere, from a deep grey to black, with a strong draft-like shape and size; and shekas that were like cats, but not quite; longer, thinner, with lengthier snouts. They slinked between buildings and glared at the curricle as it passed. He even spotted some coal-colored sheep under the shade of a large walnut tree, balls of raven wool atop four squat legs with double-pronged, elegantly curled horns protruding from their high-foreheads. Farkas animals were often dark in color, as were the people; pale faced and black haired. The reason for the swarthy coloring was unknown, but being shadowy was a Farkas trait no matter what sort of creature, or so it seemed.

There were orchards of osteal trees that looked like gnarled hands, flocked in tiny bright green leaves, just budding for spring and already covered in a riot of tiny pink flowers. They emanated a unique herbaceous scent that tinted the air as they drove past. Fields of unfamiliar grains were beginning to rise up from the soil. What appeared to be vineyards—covered in knobby vines—were sprouting new leaves the color of the setting sun, which one would imagine in autumn but not at the cusp of spring. These were all crops his people knew nothing about.

The clothing styles, however, did not diverge too greatly from that of the rest of Yvrem, which was interesting to Edrick. Although the seaming and the manufacture seemed more sophisticated, the silhouettes were largely the same. The fabrics looked of superior quality, but he wasn't really able to stop and take a closer look. The idea of better materials intrigued him. As a renowned dandy, he was drawn to such things as fashion and fine clothing. He worked hard to appear at the forefront of whatever was in mode, with the trendiest silks and most competent craftsmanship. He prided himself on his eye. It was that peacockery that won him the attentions of so many elegant ladies. So he watched.

It still continued to shock him to see the tranquil nature of the country. As they drew between a small village towards what looked like a larger town, a group of young ladies drew his eye. Four girls, probably around fourteen years or so, were walking along the road, each one in the whitest of gowns, the most delicate of muslins. One girl had on a hat that was one of a cheese maker; a broad straw oval with the ends drawn in and fixed into wings to frame her face. It was not the most prestigious of occupations. The curricle slowed as the girls drew aside, and he peered down at them, as they watched him.

14

A cheese maker, he scoffed to himself. She was idling with some other girls whose manners, although decent, were not refined. He could scarce believe a cheese maker and other common girls could afford such elegant clothes. Their common, ruddy faces simply did not fit with their accoutrements. They did not look away; they showed no deference or respect. They gawked openly and suspiciously at him.

He wondered why the Farkas coddled the lowborn. He pondered this only briefly before he was overcome with guilt for wondering such a thing. He then considered how lazy and entitled they must be to be so well cared for. Certainly they must not be half as productive for the estate. Surely if the girl was larking about the countryside in a flowing gown nobody of her station should rightfully afford instead of at home making cheese, she must be a great cost to her immediate society.

He set aside his silent grumblings as they exited this village, and made their way along a road between two large fields towards a much larger town. As they passed through it, the curricle was noticed more acutely by the villagers. There were also more Farkas faces mixed in with the Yvremi. Their wan faces and black hair were anomalies amongst the ruddy, pink cheeks and ginger, blonde, and chestnut-haired natives. Well-groomed tradesmen in the doorways of their workshops straightened up from their work and narrowed their eyes at the sight of the passing strangers, their untrusting glares holding fast to Edrick and his driver until they were out of sight.

Edrick's spine tingled. *Would former Yvremi be so suspicious of their own countrymen? Why? Do they not despise the Farkas for taking away their empire? Enslaving them to serve a Farkas household instead? No, not if they were treated so well, coddled so well. Allowed to be lazy...* Edrick paused, and his brow darkened. He could suppose all this to his heart's content, but he saw no evidence of laziness. No evidence of enslavement or fear. He saw a country that was idyllic and peaceful, productive and healthy. He was annoyed that it peeved him. It made him feel like a bad person; and the Farkas had always insisted that the nobility of Yvrem were bad people. That is why they scattered and persecuted them.

The curricle finally cleared the town and took a sharp right onto a smaller road that continued on for some miles. The driver was following what barely passed as a map, depicting roads that existed almost two hundred years before. There was no predicting if those might have changed. They were still there so far. They had not been forced to stop and ask anyone anything yet.

They passed other villages, but within sight of the road, not on it. More hours passed, and once again darkness fell. They had not stopped for any substantial amount of time since the evening before, except to change horses before the border of Eyome enclosed them. The horses were tired, but the pace was slow to accommodate them. And they'd stopped at an old mill briefly to eat bread and cheese from their basket and let the horses drink from a trough. Nobody disturbed them.

As night drew fully over them, they arrived at the great hall. It was everything Yvrem was in before the invasion. A material maniefestation of hubris. Overstated, unnecessarily imposing and austere. A pile of coursed, squared and pitched face stonework with tall mullioned and transomed windows with weeping stains dripping down like old tears from the corners, which even at night, were like black streaks against the soft sandstone. There was light emanating from several of the windows, which in spite of the task ahead, Edrick was relieved to see. He desired a respite. Edrick dismounted to a pair of shaky legs and an overwhelming surge of nervous energy as the great door opened before he was able to reach it. There stood a tiny little crone who peered in puzzlement at him.

"Zhedra el di metranem?" she asked.

Edrick did not speak Farkas. He shook his head. "I'm here to speak to the master of the house. It is of an urgent matter."

"Oh," the old lady paused. "You are of Yvrem. I see. I do not think the Navray will speak to you." She began to close the door.

"He must. He simply must. You must tell him that I am the heir of Bethranorn. And I have come to speak to him of a matter of great importance. I simply cannot be turned away." Edrick strode up the four stairs to the large door and faced the old woman head-on.

She studied him with her watery eyes, and pursed her lips. "I make no guarantees. Come in. I will ask." She stepped back and let him move past her.

He stalked into the large foyer, and looked about him, waiting for the old woman to shove the great door closed. He followed as she ambled with exasperating slowness across the polished marble floor. She led him to a door where there was a small sitting room. It was empty of people.

"Wait here," she said. "I will return."

Edrick studied the room as he waited. It was graceful in a way he had never seen before. Lit by a chandelier with at least forty candles and festooned in glass droplets. The light poured out over the space with sparkling warmth.

The furniture was neither weighty nor imposing, but it did not diminish the richness of the room despite its lightness and delicacy in shape and form. The chairs looked nearly spindly, the tables too—the legs curving like the hips and waist of a beautiful woman. The woods were smooth and polished with intricate inlays. Nothing overdone, nothing gaudy, nothing gilded. The carpets were piled, not woven, and utterly astonishing in detail and richness of the sapphires and soft blues. The wall panels were painted the color of a robin's egg given a wash of gold by the candlelight. They were hung with oil paintings; all placed artfully about the space instead of cluttering the wall in volume to prove the owner's wealth. Although the room was small and lightly furnished, there was no doubt of the wealth and consequence of its owner. It was understated, and subtle, but affluence was well demonstrated in the restraint rather than the glut. It was quite beautiful, he had to admit.

He sat down in a velvet-covered wing-chair by the modest white stone hearth, and waited in silence, feeling like a lump of coal in a snow bank. He was there for at least half an hour. Finally the little old woman in her exquisitely tailored black gown of polished cotton appeared and gestured for him to come. He stood and followed her out of the winter room, back across the foyer to a long passage. He was led to the very end. There, she pushed open a set of double doors and stepped aside.

"The Navray will see you. Please, be respectful," she warned him in a low voice as he passed her. As he entered, she retreated, pulling the doors closed behind her.

Edrick was struck utterly dumb. Before him stood a woman of such considerable beauty, she did not look real. She could have been a painting drawn from the imagination of a skilled artist. Such beauty could not truly exist, thought he. I must be dreaming.

She held a sheaf of papers in her pale hands. Her gown, a snowy white, was trained out behind her in a long, elegant line beginning at the middle of her back and draping down to the floor in a graceful pool of rumpled translucent gauze. Her arms were covered in sleeves so sheer they looked almost bare. The same gauze encircled the inner neckline of the gown, enhancing her long, smooth neck.

Her eyes were ice blue; almost white. Sharp and penetrating, bordered by lashes as black as raven's feathers, and fine arched brows of the same hue. Her jet hair was lifted off her neck and into a wrap of curls on the back of her head, adorned with but a single silver diadem. She wore a tiny pendant necklace on her delicate décolletage and two small pearl drop earrings. Everything she wore was white except for a pair of sapphire satin slippers with matching ribbons twined around her perfect ankles over white stockings with blue clocking, which could be partly seen peeking from the slightly shorter petticoat beneath the wispy gown. She hung like a pale tulip against the grey granite of a heavy fireplace and dark wood panels of the walls. Poised at her feet were two Ney wolves. One stood beside her like a black cutout against her gown, the other laid upon the floor with its head up and ears and eyes pointed towards Edrick,. He had heard of them but had never seen them in all his days.

Like all Farkas creatures they were dark, but these dogs were like the absence of color and light itself. Two moving silhouettes shaped almost like the wolves of the wild. Something was unusual in their shape, something intended. They were also extremely large; larger than any of his wolfhounds. The perked triangular ears, the sleek raven coats with the slightly ruffed hackles, the sloping back and noble shape of their heads; they were dog and wolf. But it was the pewter eyes that unsettled him. A burnished silvery gaze punctuated by dark, bottomless irises, both sets fixed on him. He felt the weight of their gaze, and the undeniable intelligence behind them.

They were a sight indeed, but nothing to compare to the lady beside them. Her gaze was just as cool and calculating. Her hand holding the papers lowered against her leg, and she angled her shoulders to face him. In perfect Yvremi, she said:

"It isn't every day I get a visit from a crownless king. Why have you come?"

Edrick bit back his words, his thoughts muddled by the striking effect of her beauty, the forthrightness of her question and the tone of irritation at his presence. Her pale eyes looked almost bored, but in her aloofness there was a measure of hackling and distrust prickling off of her being. He did not want to stammer or fumble his thoughts, but he knew if he responded he would. He was unsure how to speak to a woman who represented greater authority than he. There was no precedent for it in his world. Women did not hold power. He counted by tens in his head, collecting his wits about himself, trying to remember the narrative he'd practiced in silence during the long trip.

Instead of finding the thoughts he'd so carefully collected, he found only the reasons why he *must* hate this woman. His posture shifted in part; from befuddled to cross, in less than a silent count to sixty. She was Farkas. Beautiful or no, her people had destroyed his family's legacy, torn down a government that had stood in dignity for centuries, erased hundreds of noble lines and stole the great houses many of Yvrem's high born families had raised from the soil, brick by brick.

It was almost two hundred years ago, but that did not matter right now. He was standing in her house... his house; a house that had belonged to an ancestor. "I will not apologize for upsetting the peace of your evening, Madame. I suspect that out of the two of us, the one that has been most inconvenienced is *not* you. I have, however, been charged to speak to you by the Yvrem Senate, and as disinclined as I am to be standing here before you, irritating you with my presence, I must," he snapped. It was only then he came to realize there was a third person in the room. A man that was unmistakably Yvremi of birth. He was sitting in a chair that was angled towards the fire; the high back had largely concealed him. He leaned into view and the face peered 'round at Edrick in curiosity. He seemed intent on seeing this interaction as well as hearing it.

The Farkas woman did not acknowledge the presence of this third person. Her eyes remained impassively upon Edrick, whose bluster faltered under the weight of her unnerving stare. With liquid grace, she folded the paper with the telltale creases of correspondence, as well as a broken bit of emerald-colored wax seal with ribbon hanging from it still clinging to the back of the page. She faced him squarely, calmly toying with the letter as her gaze swept over him. The wolves shifted as well, but their eyes remained fixed upon him.

"Do go on," she said. He thought perhaps he saw some amusement flash through her eyes. He glanced briefly at the wheaten-haired man in the chair who, too, stared at him expectantly. Edrick then straightened his back and pushed out his chest a bit, toying with his hat as he spoke.

"The Senate has sent me. As a sign of their... need. You see, there has been a developing issue in the southern isles."

"Yes," the Farkas woman said, lifting up the letter. "You speak of the Akravani; their naval forces amassing there. The invasion of Hellebos, which is now occupied. I have been recently informed of this. What does this have to do with me?"

"They are aiming north, my Lady. They endeavor to invade Yvrem."

"And?" she asked.

Edrick had to pause to keep his temper in check. Her indifference was infuriating. "You are also part of Yvrem, all of the remaining Farkas Sentely…"

"The Akravani know better than to harm a blade of our grass, sir. I see no reason to be bothered by this news." She tossed the letter onto a small side table and glided to a sideboard where she served herself from an amber snifter of what smelled like a biting apple brandy. She did not offer her visitors any. She then turned to look at him, draped her left arm across her chest and rested her right elbow on her wrist as she sipped languidly from the round, stemless bulb of glass. The brandy coated the interior viscously as she swirled it. Her gaze rested calmly upon him.

"Do you really think Akravani occupation surrounding yours would be a benefit to your people?" Edrick demanded.

"A benefit?" she asked, her dark brow arching. "No. Not a benefit. I think it will make little difference as to which type of animal is sniffing at my threshold, Mr. Bethranorn. It's still merely an *animal*."

These words were meant to rankle him. He was amazed he managed to keep his countenance. He snorted out a laugh through his nose, and walked to the window looking out into the darkness. The fire snapped and popped.

"Don't be obtuse. It would certainly make a difference if that animal sniffing at your threshold is the timid golden fox, or a slavering ice bear," he replied matter-of-factly. "Are ice bears not known for their unpredictable behavior? The most skilled hunters have something to fear in them." He turned and looked at her. She had dropped her left arm to her side; the other with the glass was poised before her.

He continued, using her silence to press his point. "But the fox," he lifted his finger. "You've lived alongside the fox long enough to count it as a known element: to understand its ways. You've appropriated its finest... dens.... as your own; and you've adapted your ways to align with his. Am I right?" he asked. She did not respond, but her unflinching gaze never left his face "The fox in turn has accepted this. It lives its life with you in its midst and takes nothing from you; demands nothing. He understands respectful coexistence." Edrick left a long pause there, hoping the unspoken words would drive home as well as the spoken ones that preceded them. He finally continued, this time in a voice imbued with wonder. "You must admire *something* about Yvrem and its people to keep this Sentely as yours after all these years despite the distrust between our people. I saw your villages. Yvrem is not completely lost to them."

Again, she remained keenly focused on him, but pointedly silent. Edrick cleared his throat and crossed his arms, his hat dangling from his fingers. "Is it not wise to foster the presence of the animals you are already adapted to, rather than invite another capricious, wild beast to replace it?" he asked. He then tilted his head and furrowed his brow. "Is it true that the Farkas name for the Akravani translates to The Savage?"

As if she had lost her patience with his missive, the lady blurted out: "I have received news of the invasion; I don't see the point of your standing before me to inform me something of which I am already aware."

"You *know* why I have been sent. All the clumsy allegory aside, I don't think I've been unclear, have I?" Edrick directed that question to the onlooker, who sat in his chair gaping. He shook his head once in reply with a curious smirk on his lips. The woman looked back at her companion dismissively and sighed.

"What makes you believe I of all the Farkas estate holders in Yvrem, am the one to help you?" she asked.

"I did not choose you, Lady. The senate did. I am merely carrying out their orders. And that is to ask the help of the Farkas people to avert a violent and devastating invasion." He said it plainly. There was a pall that fell over the room for a moment, and then the Navray stepped toward him, stopping at arm's length. Her perfume of rose oil was subtle but tantalizing, her skin as smooth and perfect as it appeared at a distance. Her icy eyes bore into him, and she glared at him unspeaking for a moment. Then she laughed.

"There is such delightful irony in this moment," she declared, breaking into a radiant smile. "My father would have laughed and laughed if he could have been here to see this." She put her glass down on the small table and picked up the letter again, unfolding it, studying it. The wolf dogs' eyes followed her as she paced about before the fireplace. Her Yvremi companion, whoever he was, remained tightlipped and observant. She dropped the letter on the small table again and turned to Edrick.

"I will do what I can," she concluded.

"Forgive me Lady, but that is no answer. I must have a response to give to the Senate."

"I cannot speak for my government, crownless king. I can only present them with what you brought me today. It is up to them to decide. I am only a messenger. Much like you." She leveled a gaze at him that ordinarily would have· frozen him. She was so extraordinarily beautiful; he could barely stand to look directly at her. Her hardness melted momentarily and she blinked. "I will do my best to forward your concerns," she assured him. She plucked the letter from the table and tossed it into the fire. She then retrieved her glass of brandy. "You may go." She said this with a bit of a mischievous smirk, as if it amused her to say such a thing to a deposed monarch. He accepted the dismissal as he knew it was the only answer he was going to receive.

Leaving the great estate was as jarring as entering it had been. The roads turned back into a rutted, mucky nightmare, and— as if to compound upon the insult— the sky decided to open up and pour more rain onto them. At the lake town of Hardorp the nearest city to Eyome, they stopped for the night and Edrick made the decision to send the curricle back to its home livery and make his own way home. He dismounted, paid the man an extra fee to rest the horses in Hardorp before leaving.

He then grasped his small traveling trunk by its two worn handles and melted into the rainstorm. He slogged through the mucky street and waded between the carriages, drays and foot traffic. The noise, the stink, the filthy roads, the things he had so accepted as part of his life suddenly seemed quite savage in comparison to the Farkas Sentely. At first glance, it seemed the Yvremi were less civilized than their former occupiers; and it rankled him to know this.

Edrick located the nearest relay office and stepped through the door. His soaked greatcoat dripped puddles at his heels as he carefully wrote out a letter to the senate. A few coins tossed on the counter, explicit directions, and he watched the relay office clerk roll up his dispatch and stuff it into a water-proofed leather cylinder. After tagging it for delivery, he gave a bell cord strung above his head several hard yanks. A horse and rider arrived at the front door only moments later, and he handed it off. . When the letter was gone in a clatter of hooves, Edrick asked the clerk which were the best lodgings in town, and once he got his answer, he swaggered out onto the street into the rain to seek them out.

Harcastle Hall was a surprisingly fine establishment in what seemed to be a rather dingy little town. It was an archaic fortification house built off the lake shore on a small man-made foundation isle. The old fort was connected to land by a graceful stone bridge. The keep had been remade into a superior inn with large, comfortable rooms and an ample common space and dining hall for tenants and visitors to enjoy.

Hardorp, it turned out, was a hub of sorts for merchant traffic, since the larger part of the canals webbing the countryside converged on the lake. Many a merchant came here to buy and sell from the markets, warehouses and silos that lined the shore.

The fortification house was separated from the rest of the lake by a low harbor wall that encircled it. Small openings in the back allowed rowboats access to the waters outside the enclosure. On either side of the harbor wall the shore bristled with wharfs of stone and wood. Hugging those wharfs in rows like logs, so closely one could walk from one onto the next, were barges large and small from all corners of Yvrem. Some were merely houseboats of the water-traveling clans. Others were loaded with tarped piles of goods. One barge moored to the nearest pier was covered in great big wheels of cheese that Edrick could smell from underneath their large oiled leather tarps. The overwhelming smell of cheese overpowered the reek of sewage and animal droppings that rolled off of the city towards the hall. It all faded as he crossed the bridge to the house.

In the harbored waters inside sea wall a few small boats were paddling towards the opening, headed out in the eastward direction of Aken Island. Several boats were already well out into the water, their lanterns lit and visible in the fading light.

Aken Island was a largish landmass about a half mile out into the lake on which was built was a small extension to the town. It was where most of the finer homes were located. At present, in this late afternoon, the rain had stopped, but the mists were rising and Edrick could scarce see the island from where he stood.

He walked across the bridge, passing a group of men and ladies climbing down the steep steps on the side of the bridge leading to the small stone dock underneath it where several rowboats were tied. The ladies were dressed in high-waisted gowns of gauzy silk over bright petticoats, studded in beads and pearls. Hair curled to perfection, silken slippers on their dainty feet, they crept down the stairs gingerly; the gentlemen in elegant frock coats with soaring collars and crisp white cravats; with splashes of jewel tones in their waistcoats. He thought perhaps there must be a great ball or gathering on Aken Island to explain the boats moving steadily towards it. He bowed in silent greeting and kept walking towards the great doors of the house. He was tired, and wanted to have a good night's sleep in warmth and comfort.

His two nights at the inn had grown into a unique form of torture only he and a few of his relatives would ever know. Someone somehow had discovered his identity and word spread rapidly through the town. He was barely there two hours when he began to experience the typical deference and cowing by the hordes of well-to-do travelers passing through the inn to attend the many social delights of the season on Aken Island. He suspected the innkeeper must have whispered that the uncrowned king was at Harcastle. By the next morning, there were six invitations to events on the island waiting for him at the breakfast table.

Even with the absence of a monarchy, the people clung fast onto the fantasy of it. They still revered the nobility that remained and sought out a connection with them as surely as they would have before the occupation of the Farkas. As it was whenever anyone sniffed out royalty, even deposed royalty, the pretentious rose out of the woodwork like scrabbling bugs. So he was driven to his room instead of the comfortable common space with its wonderful library and broad hearth bellowing out its heat. He had hoped for a quiet stay, one of undisturbed quietude shared with the company of kind souls. He was sorely disappointed. Even in his room, the servants would bring him new correspondence and cards every few hours or so. He immediately tossed them into the fire before sitting back down glumly.

He slumped in the one comfortable chair—a sagging squashy wingback which he'd moved to face the large window overlooking the water and the island in the distance. He rested his heel on the stone sill and crossed his other boot over that foot. With his chin on his chest, he simply stared out into the fading day until there was nothing but a faint sprinkle of lights from Aken Island. Edrick had convinced himself that he bore this kind of isolation well, but he did not. He felt it even when surrounded by his peers.

Edrick was a lonely man. Who he was, what he was, left him little chance of meaningful friendships. He could say with certainty that he had only one or two true friends, one of which was his sister, lately married and moved to Kireen. He was barely thirty, neither married nor involved in any courtship. He lived on a sizable estate, quite comfortably, but quite alone, with only the company of his few servants and housekeeper. His closest confidante aside from his sister was his man, Maddin, who was left behind when Edrick climbed aboard the curricle. A common born man, Maddin was loyal and kind; but lacking interest or knowledge in anything much beyond his duties. He was the closest thing Edrick had to a friend, and even he knew how pathetic that was. With his frequent travels with the hordes of people that called him friend, Edrick was still lonesome and remote. He warmed to nobody. He was a mask of laughter and good spirits, while inside, he felt hollow. He knew that if his royal lineage were not in play, they would find him as tedious as he found them.

Edrick lived off of the proceeds of his family's many concerns. Edrick's great, great, great grandfather; King Dannot, thanks to the shrewdness of his brother, the former Duke of Hakastell, had managed to liquidate much of the family's personal assets during the Farkas invasion. The land and properties were taken away by the

Farkas, as well as the family's legislative power. But they had protected their money. The family had lived humbly for the one hundred and eight years of occupation, but when the Farkas withdrew seventy two years ago, it was put to work and it grew exponentially.

All this was done with the intent of preserving the bloodline. The King and the Duke believed that the family's deposition was temporary. Over the years Edrick's grandfathers invested in businesses or put the money in foreign banks to gain interest. It saved several generations of his immediate family from complete ruin, and now provided for many of them to this day, including Edrick.

The family was happy to endow Edrick with a living because he was the heir to the throne—in spite of his status meaning absolutely nothing to anyone else. He had freedom and was unencumbered. The idea that he was now burdened with the responsibility imposed by the senate, goaded him. He desired to escape it. He did not like to answer to anyone—which in and of itself was a sign of his great privilege. He'd done what they asked. His duty was met.

He would have stayed longer if the grovelers had not hounded him into his room; left him sitting in his chair by the window, bored out of his skull, sinking into his own thoughts. He fell asleep in that chair on the second night, woke up before dawn to the smell of fizzled candlewick, and discovered he had a sore neck. He was through here, he decided. It was time to move on. He had already paid for the two nights, so there was no need to wake anyone.

He wanted to leave early so nobody would see him go and report back to anyone, including the senate who he suspected were expecting more out of him than what he provided. He hurriedly packed his belongings into his trunk and was hauling it down the steps when he was intercepted by the innkeeper who immediately proffered a communication with the heavy seal of the senate in gold wax. Edrick irritably put the trunk down, took the letter from the man's thick fingers, and pushed past him to the empty common room. He sat down under a lit sconce and hastily cracked open the letter. It had the relay stamp on it, and a mark for urgent reply.

His answer was not what the Senate wanted, as he had suspected. They wanted him to go back to the Navray, and request a more definitive answer than what she had given him. Edrick knew to hound them would serve nobody. He suspired deeply and frowned. Rising, he went to the desk of the proprietor's office and scratched out a hasty reply with the tidily trimmed quill.

I have done what I could. Returning to the Farkas will not speed their response. I believe it would only hinder it. They have been communicated with. The answer was clear; the Navray will do what she can. What that means I don't know, but it is the reply we have been given. The request must reach their hierarchy before we can know if they will assist us. There is nothing more that can be done.

Walking out of the inn, Edrick realized that he was so bent on leaving that he hadn't thought about *how* he was going to get home. He was nine days by coach from his villa in Amaronna; a bustling town a half a day from the capitol. He was in no desperate hurry to get home, and after the long ride in the curricle he was not particularly eager to repeat the same experience for nine days. As he stood in the middle of the bridge and ruminated, a narrowboat slid gracefully in between two cargo barges. He watched the owner lithely hop from the prow of his narrowboat onto the shore and tie it fast, moving then to attend to his draught horses. The vessel was small next to the long commercial barges, but it was a neat little boat. With a resolved set to his mouth, Edrick made for the market district where the canal was broadest and visiting narrowboats could pull alongside the shore to take berth while their occupants shopped for supplies. He was determined he would go home via canal aboard a narrowboat. He would not be easy to find if the senate came searching; it would take a good long time, too. Hopefully long enough for the Farkas to provide the senate the answer they needed, without involving Edrick anymore.

Chapter 2
Keela's Obligation

Keela's laugh was as pure and earnest as a laugh could be. And it rang ebulliently into the rafters of her humble home. It was answered in a tone of incredulity by her mother, Alara:

"They were doing what?"

"Rolling great big rocks off the side of the hill into the trees trying to fell the smaller ones. They did this for no bloody reason that I could see. And they lent the activity such hilarity, just laughing wildly. Especially when the rock snapped the trunk of a sapling and sent the birds flying. It was plain odd." Keela crossed her arms and shook her head in bewilderment.

"And you're surprised?" Alara picked up a piece of wood and poked the low-burning, sleepy embers. Her intrusion caused a crackling, hissing protest as the flames awoke. She then fed the flickering, grumpy fire the kindling she'd used to rouse it. It welcomed it by wrapping itself around the wood and growing brighter. "I'm an old woman," She assured the younger girl "and I've seen much in my days. One inevitable truth I discovered is that all men, and believe you me, *all* men—from ditch digger to scholar (although I'm sure the latter would scarce admit it)—absolutely adore acts of destruction. It's fascinating to them—they are powerless against this impulse. Men will delight in things breaking, falling, rotting, crumbling, burning, exploding into splinters and, mark my words, if *they're* the ones doing the destroying, well, that's almost as high on their list of life's pleasures as what goes on between the sheets," she declared smugly, tossing a few more sticks onto the flames before brushing off her hands. Keela's ears burned hot red and her eyes dropped.

"Mother..."

"Oh, Keela, no need to hide behind your shyness. You should never be stuffy or prim. We aren't the sort of people that have to worry about those things. We are common folk. Don't forget that. Hanging about with the highborn shouldn't make you think otherwise." She straightened herself with some difficulty, and grunted a bit as she did. She saw Keela's expression, and frowned momentarily. She then shook her head.

"I'll promise you, if you have something that needs destroying, there will be no shortage of men happy to oblige. They volunteer when there is no apparent need at all—hence what you saw today. So if they're loafing about, bored as anything, and there's a hilltop with lots of rocks on it, odds are, they're going to start chucking them over to fell trees, mark my words." She exhaled in resignation. "They're all oafs... even the smart ones, few of those as there are," she exclaimed. "They just never grow out of those grubby little boys they once were."

"They build things too," Keela said in the defense of man-kind.

"Only so they can have something to destroy later on," the old woman grumbled, picking up her heavy pot. "The trick is to keep them busy... otherwise they would be mucking everything up all the time everywhere."

Keela chuckled. She bent down and grasped the stained hem of her worn, much repaired day gown, and hoisted it up over her knees. Her stockings were rumpled, messily-darned and had lost their tensility long ago. They were saggy and rumpled at the ankle. What should have been embroidered ribbon garters were two lengths of common twine holding her stockings up at the knees. Her boots were worn and the brown leather scuffed and shabby, as well as caked in muck from her many excursions out into the forest.

Keela's features were dark and pale at once. She had raven hair as smooth as silk, with an almost blue undertone to it. A humble widow's peak decorated her forehead, and her arched brows—shadowy and decisive—made for dramatic feature on a young face. Her eyes were the deepest of grey, almost the tone of hematite. People, mainly the youngsters of the town, made fun of her pale, fair skin against the starkness of her hair and eyes. They said she was Farkas, and they spat at her sometimes.

Her lips were almost unnaturally rosy pink and full. By all standards she had a beautiful face; deep, lovely eyes rimmed with thick lashes, a perfectly proportioned nose, unblemished skin. Her figure was petite, but she well-shaped, if perhaps a bit too rounded and curvy compared to some of the slimmer girls.

She swung her leg ungracefully over the bench, straddling it before lowering her bottom down onto the smooth surface. "Do you need help?"

"No. I'm fine; you just sit there and keep me company."

Keela complied, and watched the old woman go about her tasks with an air of purpose. Keela sat in the warm single downstairs room of their little cottage on the outskirts of the city of Veros. Her adoptive mother, Alara, was a jewelry-maker who had raised Keela from very young. They both lived in the one-room cottage with a little loft for a shared bedroom. There was a workshop in the yard where they did their work.

Keela thought of herself as a simple girl. She was however, afforded some special privileges thanks to her patron, Lord Xanett.

She was permitted to school with the highborn; and she had learnt to ride a horse. She enjoyed significant freedom for a young woman, because of her particular circumstances. As a wanderer by nature, this worked out well for her. She had just returned from one of her frequent jaunts, and her stomach was roaring. Alara was preparing leek soup, Keela's favorite.

Keela's thoughts returned to the idiots on the hill, laughing riotously when one of their stones collided with an old tree, causing a great noise and making the whole thing sway; scaring a flock of small birds out of it. They all laughed and laughed. Adarnoth, his hands on his hips, chortled away.

Adarnoth irked Keela. He wasn't necessarily attractive—not in the way that made most girls all-a-giggle. He wasn't beautiful like some of the other men in town, but this large fellow was never want for people surrounding him. He had a wide chest and a bit of a belly, with narrow hips and lean, powerful legs. It gave him a triangular appearance. He kept a goatee beard of ruddy red in spite of the fashionably shaved faces of his peers; and had sparkling blue, intelligent eyes. He was not lacking in wit; that was certain. He had no problem engaging strangers and have them laughing and interested in no time. His charisma was potent. Girls flocked around him; his male companions sought him out. They would walk around in a huddle after a long day's work and do stupid things, like throw rocks and boulders from hilltops just to knock trees over.

Keela was embarrassingly aware of her own desire to be part of the group that followed this magnetic character and found herself angry for being left on the outside. All she could do was to pretend to not care at all—to want the complete opposite of everyone else her age—and have nothing to do with him, or the people who revered him so much. She wasn't funny enough. She wasn't pretty enough, or whatever it was that was a requirement to make her fit into this group. She just wanted to be part of the laughter, even if it was the inexplicable hilarity they found in throwing rocks off of hills.

She had heard them from half a mile away. The noise had disturbed her quiet hike into the forest and had forced the massive bear she'd been watching from afar to disappear into the brush. She glowered at the sight of them, knowing not to approach them as to be seen; or she would likely become the object of their ridicule. Instead she stamped away, finding solace in a woman who was her adopted mother. Better to laugh at them with her than to admit that their indifference; nay, their dislike of her wounded her pride.

She sighed loudly, and lifted a leg, stretching it along the length of the bench. The older woman glanced at her, and pursed her lips. "Bored again?" she asked. Alara wore a gown of rusty red stripes on ivory which was quite shabby. It was slightly old fashioned with a lower waistline than was currently in fashion. There was a large diamond shaped patch of a solid fabric rumpled into the folds of the heavily pleated back skirts. Over this gown she wore her cooking apron. Her neckline was filled with a simple white cotton fichu with the ends pinned to the front of her gown, and her head of silver hair was adorned with a ruffled cap with lappets that drooped onto her shoulders. She had a simple chatelaine of her own creation pinned to her waistline. Little bits and bobs dangled from it: a key to the workshop building about back, some tiny scissors, an eyeglass and other sundries. They rang pleasantly together as she worked.

"No, I'm fine" Keela lied. She knew never to admit to Alara that she was bored, because the woman would fly off the handle at the slightest complaint from a young person about being bored. To her it was impossible for a young person to claim boredom when they were blessed with youth, energy and vitality—there was no excuse for it and all young people ought to use their gifts to the very extent of their potential

Other than her angry outbursts at the criminal waste of youth on the young, Alara was a wonderful woman. Keela credited her with the foundation of who she was. Alara had been caring for

Keela for most of her life; taking her in when Keela's own mother was tragically taken by illness when Keela was two. She did not know who her father was, and neither did Alara.

Alara had never married, nor did she have children of her own. She was a woman who in youth had enjoyed a powerful wanderlust, and had a life full of rich experiences. She was just thinking of settling down a bit when Keela came into her life. She took her in, and imparted her philosophies and worldly knowledge to her the moment Keela was old enough to learn. Keela loved her for that, and loved her free spirit and blunt manner. She also loved her leek soup.

"I was talking to Vianca today," Alara ventured. Her knobby fingers were plucking the leaves off of some fresh parsley she'd plucked from the garden. Keela saw her take a surreptitious glance at her from the corner of her eye, and knew at once this was going to be a bad conversation. Keela offered absolutely no reaction, allowing her adoptive mother to continue, even if she didn't want to hear a word of it. "She said that she needs someone to go with her to Calabras—to help her watch over the child."

"Calabras, eh? That's nice." Keela was carefully ambiguous in her response, mindful not to find herself being inadvertently volunteered for the job by uttering the wrong word. One had to walk gingerly when Alara was up to no good

Keela simply despised Vianca. She was one of the girls who'd made Keela's life miserable as a young child and now she was married a well-to-do landlord who was twenty two years older than his remarkably beautiful young wife. She lived in a large, elegant manor, had a young son already, and boasted her great happiness to all those people that Keela would never be friends with. She heard these stories third-party and rolled her eyes at them accordingly. She always found it suspicious that Vianca enjoyed such happiness that she felt it necessary to prove this to everyone.

This wasn't the first time Alara had tried to get Keela to do something for Vianca, and it probably wouldn't be the last. The lord was Alara's patron after all, so she tried to make a good impression—but it was nearly always at Keela's expense. So far, she'd managed to escape various situations that would put her in direct contact with Vianca. She'd managed to avoid being drafted as a governess for the baby, which was proposed when Vianca was still with child. The Lord also tried to have Keela come work at the great house a several times a week working his ledgers for the home and his various concerns. That was something he seemed to think was still in negotiation, as he had mentioned it again to Alara not even four days ago. He seemed bent on having Keela in his household one way or another; and Keela would have nothing of it. Not with the shadow of Vianca looming about like a specter.

She did not want to work for the young woman. It would be the highest of all humiliations. The common girl was criminally bullied by Vianca and her peers, including the charismatic Adarnoth, or Dar as he was called sometimes.

Vianca would undoubtedly spend the whole voyage to Calabras lording her superiority over Keela. It was just the kind of person she was. *Smug whore.* Keela seethed behind a mask of indifference.

Alara was growing visibly frustrated by Keela's willful silence. "She doesn't want to travel alone. She wants someone who will keep her engaged. She also wants to travel with someone who will mind her son well and can be trusted with him."

"Oh, she has no end of friends from school to do it for her, I'm sure."

"I thought so too, but things have changed since she was married. Her friends have strayed... out of jealousy or who knows. She has nobody left from that circle to rely upon. You would think they'd be stumbling over each other to be her companion—and part of the household," Alara said in wonder.

"Oh, the poor little thing." Keela was careful to inflect each syllable of those words with as much sarcasm and contempt as she could muster. "I don't feel the slightest bit sorry for her. She made her bed." She reclined on the bench—one foot still on the floor— rested the back of her head on her hands, and stared at the ceiling, noticing a host of cobwebs and dust amongst the beams and plaster. She reminded herself to clean that when she had the chance.

"I always thought you had matured enough to put those infantile prejudices aside," Alara bristled, grasping three large leeks that had been soaking in a large bowl of water, and chopping them up with a large knife at the small wooden work table in front of the kitchen hearth

Keela did not take that bait. The immediate thought, which she kept to herself, was: *that's rich coming from you, mother.* Alara of all people had no right to be indignant about holding grudges; the woman had several rivals in town that she would neither speak to nor acknowledge, so Keela was able to laugh off this hypocrisy in quietude. There was one woman in particular that overtly disapproved of Alara's devil-may-care lifestyle, and in turn spent a goodly portion of her time spreading gossip about Keela's mother and citing all the things she did wrong to anyone willing to listen. These were nasty things—a wide swath of sweeping generalizations and untruths, much like Vianca had done to *her* when they were young girls.

Alara did not only refuse to address, look at, or affirm the existence of this woman publicly, but she also was guilty of childish acts of sabotage. Like dumping the contents of the night's chamber pots over the fence into the woman's meticulously kept gardens. Alara was rigidly unapologetic about it, and did not deny having done it when accusations and anger resulted from her actions. Even when confronted, her actions did not cease. It was an ongoing war.

As an example of righteous, mature behavior, Alara was not exactly the strongest mentor. Keela felt a bit self-satisfied about it as she lay there on the narrow bench. She steepled her knee, and rested her other ankle on it. She took a deep breath of the fine aromas that filled the air as Alara tossed the leeks and other complementary vegetables into the pot, sweating them all in a buttery glaze before pouring in her tasty chicken stock, which was sumptuous all on its own. Usually, Alara would groan about Keela's unfeminine and ungraceful position and fuss about the sight of her exposed bottom when she loafed like this on the bench. But Alara wasn't in that frame of mind. She was pursuing another mission.

"Well, you're going to have to put those puerile thoughts aside," she said. "I've told Vianca's husband that you'd be going with her."

Keela's eyes widened. She screamed: "*What?*" and promptly fell off the bench in a tangle of limbs. She got onto her knees, and then onto her feet, brushing herself off with an angry haste. Her tight lips and furrowed brow expressed exactly how she felt about this declaration.

"You haven't been doing much lately. I can't get you into the workshop for more than a few hours a week at best. Frankly, you need to get away from Veros for a while."

"I don't think that the decision is yours to make, mother!" Keela was angrier than she'd ever been with her adoptive mother. So much so, her eyes stung with tears. She hated that when she felt anger; tears came instead of the ire that was truly required for the occasion. This problem with tears had caused her no end of trouble when she was younger—never able to truly defend herself against the bullies and rapscallions that made her childhood a living misery. She felt just like she had back then; ganged up on by her only true ally. Betrayed. "You would force me to spend time with someone who treated me no better than dog shit on her shoe all through our younger years? How could you?"

"She's grown up. Obviously you have not." The older woman was just being mean now.

"Those things don't go away. Just as the vile, sour words that Ledri spread about you still cause your hackles to puff up and chamber pots to be dumped in her garden... How *dare* you hold me to a standard you yourself cannot maintain?"

"Keela, sit down and shut your mouth this instant!"

"I won't," Keela screamed.

"You will, or I shall disown you and have you out of this house immediately!" The words stuck hard, and it felt like the rest of the world had gone silent in order to make the impact of her statement stronger. Keela's knees felt weak. She fell onto the bench ungracefully, her face a mask of incredulity. Hurt took all the wind out of Keela's lungs, and made her want to cry harder. Why would Alara treat her so ill—and threaten the thing that Keela feared most?

Keela had always feared that she would do something to make Alara not want her anymore; ever since she was a little girl. Alara would assure her again and again that there was nothing she could do to make Alara stop loving her; but Keela's fear of being cast out alone into the world never went away. Alara finally let her shoulders fall, and she hobbled over, sinking down next to Keela with an apologetic look on her face. She wiped her hands on a cloth, more a nervous wringing than a purposeful action. She looked at her adopted daughter with eyes filled with regret.

"I'm sorry, sweet child," Alara whispered. "I'm angry about it myself. It made me speak too harshly."

"I don't understand…" Keela's confusion was complete. How could Alara be angry about something in which she was complicit?

"It's Vianca's husband, you see. He's pushing for this. It was he I spoke to, not Vianca."

Keela immediately understood. Lord Xanett owned their house, as he did nearly the entire town. He was the landlord. He was not a lord by the traditional meaning. He was merely the richest man and owned everything. Everyone called him Lord—even if lords weren't supposed to exist anymore.

Alara's place in the community existed by *his* good graces alone. She was an unmarried woman with no fortune. She was a magnificent jeweler, a trade she'd learned on her travels; bringing back a unique style from foreign lands that made her work especially desirable. Lord Xanett, Vianca's husband, traded Alara's work as a product of his estate—and therefore provided her the space to live and work in return. He paid her for the items, and that money was what allowed them to eke out a comfortable existence. She'd taught Keela this trade as well; however Keela had never met Alara's standard of excellence—even if she was rather good, her work was never quite as striking as Alara's.

Keela's head dropped, and she stared at her pale hands in her lap.

"Apparently, Vianca has been impossible," Alara continued. "He is at wit's end. He came to look at some pieces and rattled off about the whole thing. His wife has been a scourge—miserable and cantankerous ever since the child was born. He wants her out of his house for a spell; for her health, as well as his. The child is to accompany you. He desires that Vianca have the option to be away from him and not be burdened with his care all day. He asked about you—and then all but threatened to cut off our income; making an intricate act of how these pieces he was inspecting were sub-standard and probably wouldn't sell for much more than what they cost to make; and how that could spell trouble for our situation unless we produced better work. He then suggested that perhaps you weren't applying yourself because you, too, needed some time away, and he recommended that it might be good for his wife and yourself to become friends, and to perhaps go together. He offered to pay for all your expenses. There wasn't a hint of kindness in his tone, only a weary resignation; and perhaps a bit of regret for having to blackmail an old friend for something as trite as a temperamental wife. I'm sorry, Keela. I really am, but we have no choice."

Keela's lower lip trembled. She had hiccups from weeping.

"I hate her, mother. She's simply awful. She was always the spearhead of all the horrid things the others did and said to me."

"It should give you some comfort to know that she's not so

perfect that her husband wants her around then, eh?"

There was a pregnant pause, and Keela chuckled, sniffing at her runny nose and wiping her eyes with the back of her hand. "I suppose it is sort of funny, isn't it? She's so annoying he is willing to ruin a good trade relationship to get her out of his house."

"And that she has no friends any more to help." They laughed sadly together. Alara looked at Keela with a gentle smile. "Don't ever think I don't know the hurt that girl and the others imposed upon you. Don't ever think I didn't understand, or care."

"I've never thought that, mother." She leaned her head on Alara's shoulder, and the woman handed her the cloth she had in her hands to wipe her nose. Keela's hiccups subsided, and they stayed together like that for a few moments—Alara rubbing her back affectionately.

"I do love you, you silly girl." Alara patted Keela's back. "But I need to go and stir that soup."

Keela righted herself, and let the older woman get up. Alara shuffled to the pot and put her much worn wooden spoon in it, stirring the contents with a thoughtful expression. She quietly stirred her soup, releasing another gust of the aroma into the room.

"You know, what you do is so valuable. Why can't we just set up another trade situation like this one with another lord who isn't married to a vile wretch?" Keela said. "We could, you know. They'd probably offer far better consideration for your work. They would understand the value of your skills, and not be predisposed to take you for granted like he does. And you could move away from your horrible neighbor…"

"Ai, child," Alara sighed, shaking her head. "If only things were that simple. I have a contract with our wonderful landlord. A mistake? Maybe. But I had nothing but this skill when I arrived in Veros. It is the bargaining chip that got me this wonderful cottage, even if it *is* so unfortunately situated next to that reeking, steaming heap of a woman. It provided me with the security I needed to care for you."

"Maybe it would have been better if you continued to travel, and took me along."

"My traveling resources are gone. Whatever I had, I'd used up along the way. All I had was the hope that a prior acquaintance would remember me, and be generous enough to take a chance on me. Lord Xanett is a decent man—and I'm sure the only reason why he did this to us is because he doesn't trust anyone else with the details of his bad marriage. But he also fears that our comfortable relationship would have allowed for me to say no on your behalf. So he used what leverage he had. I cannot fault him for it. He needs help."

Alara added some fresh green herbs to the soup. Their fragrance blossomed, filling the room as soon as they hit the hot stock. Keela took a deep draught of the delicious air, and instantly felt heartsick at the thought of being away from these comforting things.

"I know. I wish he'd just asked. But he didn't want to risk my saying no." Alara's tone was disappointed. Keela had no idea they'd been friends, not to the measure she witnessed here.

"That's not what I meant," Keela waved her hands in annoyance. "It's a domestic problem; and more importantly, not our problem. I don't know why he just can't handle it himself," she said sulkily.

Alara sighed, and stirred the soup again. She reached for the two earthenware bowls she had sitting on the proofing shelf of the cooking hearth. She lifted the unfinished edge of a kitchen cloth made from an old flour sack covering one of them. The size of the dough must have satisfied her, because she pulled the bowls down and put them on the table, flicking the kitchen cloths off and tossing them into the growing pile of laundry items she had in a basket by the door. She took a wooden pallet with a short handle down from its peg on the wall, sprinkled some roughly ground grains on it, and turned the contents of the first bowl onto the pallet. A quick slice of the knife made a large asterisk on the top of the round, shining loaf of leavened dough. She picked up the pallet and slid the loaf into the bread oven. She repeated the steps again with the second bowl. Moments later, the aroma of the leek soup was intermingled with the scent of baking bread.

Keela stood and shuffled to the washing urn and knelt to look inside the little oven beneath the stone bowl. The fire had gone out. She reached for some kindling, and started a small fire inside, adding wood as it grew. The kitchen was warm already and more heat rose into the combined chimneys, and radiated off the river stones and granite that made up the kitchen's entire east wall. The assemblage included an open hearth with two hooks and a shelf made of flat iron grate, two ovens, a proofing shelf, and the laundry corner. The fire burned always; day and night. In the height of its workday, it would heat the whole house, fading into a cooler temperature come morning when the embers had burned down during the night. But morning brought new flames, and more work.

Their home was comprised of a large single room. The cabin was over a hundred years old, one built of the old style, with no separate spaces except the loft. The main space downstairs comprised of the large cooking and washing area, the dining table and two short benches, a sitting area clustered around the smaller hearth on the opposite wall and a bookcase full of used, worn looking books that Keela read at least ten times each.

Upstairs in the large loft area, two beds and some old padded chairs comprised the private sleeping area. Keela never had much of a problem with the lack of privacy or the rustic furniture. She loved her domicile. It was shabby, but it was cozy and it was home.

Keela plugged the drain with the leather-covered stopper, and pumped water into the urn, throwing in her adoptive mother's special recipe of soap made from hearth ashes and rendered animal fat. She'd also included some essential oils that made all of their linens smell nice. Alara's skills were boundless—her travels had brought her many more skill aside from jewelry making, and had gathered along the way a host of skills few in Veros shared. Keela then picked up the wooden lid and let the water heat inside the urn, adding logs as needed.

They worked quietly together, words spent. Keela had questions, but didn't want to hear the answers, so she didn't ask them. She felt that, perhaps, if she delayed them, it would postpone this ridiculous endeavor with a girl she couldn't stomach. She knew the answers would inexorably be imposed upon her anyway, so she stirred the dirty linens into the hot, cloudy white, clean-smelling emulsion, watching with a sense of accomplishment as little globules of melted grease and dirt came to the surface of the milky water. She been doing this work for a long time and had strong arms from it. She had a fairly large scar on her upper arm from a scald when she was eight. She did this task with an automated air about her, pulling clothes and linens out, and wrapping them around the wooden bar that stood at the rim of the washing urn. She put a well-worn dowel through another loop in the roped fabric, and began to twist the water out. When it was done, she loosened it, tossed it into the basket, and picked out the next garment.

By the time the whole load was washed and wrung, the bread was cooked and the soup was ready. Keela picked up the basket and took it to the back yard where the workshop—a small building made of river stone with a slate roof—hunched in the far corner, with a short span of herb and vegetable beds, just freshly tilled, and seeded, Strong laundry lines hung between the house and the workshop.

She draped the linens over them with a practiced hand; efficient and fast, anticipating the soup. She would even miss this drudgery, she decided, looking at her pruned fingers. She walked inside, rolling down her sleeves, and sat down just in time for Alara to place a bowl of the green potage in front of her. She sliced off a piece of the hot bread for Keela to slather butter on as she so much liked to do when it was warm enough to melt it. This was her favorite meal of all. And she realized why Alara had made it for her. It was a gesture of indemnification for what she was about to do to her adopted child. Keela savored it, not allowing her pride to keep her from enjoying something she knew she would miss very much.

Chapter 3
Magpie

Deyran was a tolerable sort of fellow. Soft-spoken, deliberate in his movements, kind eyes nestled in folds of papery skin, it was hard not to like him just from his air and appearance. In spite of being a native of the boating clans, he was articulate and polite. Serendipitously, he was looking for a paying passenger and he was going through Amaronna to Neyat, so it was no inconvenience to him to take Edrick as a passenger. He habitually carried travelers aboard his stylish, beautifully crafted little narrowboat. Painted in bright reds and blues with a buttery yellow trim, the boat stood out from the others which were a bit drabber and more beat up than Deyran's boat. His two horses were also extremely well tended to, which was a good sign. He called the boat the *Stonesthrow*. The grey haired eccentric seemed almost eager to show the boat off to his passenger.

"Here's your berth." He pointed to a broad bed in a nook between two walls. "It ain't much, but it's comfortable," he went on. They'd descended into the belly of the boat via narrow, steep steps

47

and Deyran gave him the perfunctory tour. Edrick put his trunk on the bed and then followed Deyran. The interior of the narrowboat was brightly lit by the long row of wooden windows on either side of the vessel. The long, slender space was segmented into several parts: a little cabin through which one descended from the deck, the sleeping berths—which were surprisingly commodious—set one beside the other with sliding doors for privacy, and the common area. When closed, the sliding doors created a tight little corridor from the entry cabin to the common area.

The common room was a simple space with two built-in banquettes facing each other. An ingenious collapsible table was bolted into the floor. There were some useful storage bins under the seats and shelving on the walls of the berth. The kitchen was adjacent. The stove that heated the main room was also used for cooking, and it was designed to open from both sides, with one side furnished with metal plates for the pots and pans that hung from hooks above the stove.

There was also a tall cabinet with a hanging water urn and a basin for cleaning and washing, along with space-economic shelving built into the cabinets and the door to store food. There was a flour sifter hanging over the one small marble countertop that capped the wider base of the cabinet, two drawers, and myriad notches and hooks to hold knives, utensils, plates, bowls, dried meats and more. That was all there was to the kitchen.

From there, a set of steps led up to a small cabin where the tiller was located. The space was merely a slightly sunken portion of the rear deck with a roof and an enclosure of windows that provided a full circular view, including over the low, curved roof of the residence. Seeing that these boats required a great deal of skill to steer, it was important that the person in charge of it have a good prospect from prow to stern. The state of the run-down chair by the tiller made it clear where Deyran spent most of his time. The fabric was filthy, the padding flat; shaped to his narrow body. He had rigged a little hardwood table to the bulkhead and there were four mugs in various states of dirtiness crammed on it.

Next to the helm was a strange little angled door with one step leading to it that allowed access to the deck. The boat itself was mostly hull, roof and window, with a narrow walkway all around and only a small area on each side of the tiller cabin where trap doors opened to store goods and feed for the horses. This was almost entirely a residential boat. Most narrowboaters both lived on their vessels and used them to carry cargo, but Deyran seemed quite at ease, and carried no cargo, sacrificing no space to it. He carried mostly passengers if he could find them.

"Now those are lovely," Edrick muttered, pointing to some skillfully carved wooden plates with delicate inlays of brass and hardwoods, hanging on the wall above the windows.

"Thank you," Deyran beamed. "I make those to sell, for extra funds if I need them." Edrick was impressed. Deyran squatted in front of the stove facing the common space and threw in a wedge of hardwood. The greedy, orange-glowing mouth swallowed it hungrily. He stirred up the embers with a poker and slammed the little iron door closed. The chimney rose up straight through the roof and the smoke puffed out over the canal.

"You settle in, sir. We'll be off before dawn. I like to leave before everyone else does. Less traffic, and gods forbid we get stuck behind one of those big fellas. They clog up the works." He referred to the cargo barges across the way, jabbing his chin towards them.

Edrick wasn't planning on going anywhere. He intended to kick off his boots, and settle down on one of the benches near the fire until dinnertime. He'd paid Deyran good money for his place as a guest aboard this ship. Edrick smiled wanly at his host, and moved aside so Deyran could squeeze out the front of the ship and make his way to shore. With his pockets full of coins for Edrick's passage, he was impatient to go and spend it on good things.

When the old man was gone, Edrick returned to his berth and

deposited his trunk. He wrestled his outwear off and hung his greatcoat from a peg. Taking off his boots, he stowed them in the storage area with his hat. He lit the lamp in his little nook and sorted through his belongings, packing what he could away in the drawer underneath his bed, and on the small shelves at the ends of it. As he did, he heard someone call his name.

"Edrick of the Bethranorn." The voice was a soft, feminine singsong.

He straightened, and turned to look out the windows to the bank where he spotted a young lady peering in at him. Behind her, a large man waited holding a sizable hardwood box.

Edrick threaded his way through the tight boat and exited at the prow, climbing up the steps onto the thin little walkway. He braced himself with one hand on the rooftop. "I'm sorry, you called me?" His gaze took in the lady. She was no more than fifteen years old and, unmistakably, Farkas. Her companion as well. Both dark haired and pale; she gazed at him with dark eyes.

"I am to deliver this to you, sir," she replied sweetly. She gestured to the box. "The Navray has asked that you take it to Calabras."

"Calabras? I'm on my way home; I have no intention of going all the way to the coast. I'm sorry, but I understood that she had taken my request and would seek assistance through her channels. There was no mention of…"

"If you would please fulfill this request, it will serve to aid you in your mission. You will be given more information upon arrival at Calabras," she instructed him. "There is a guest house at the center facing Aliborne Park. You will go there and wait for further instruction." The large man reached across the gap and placed the box in Edrick's arms. He took it, bewildered.

"How did you find me," he asked.

The girl did not reply. Garbed in a long cloak with a train, a blue like the last light of dusk, she merely gave him a nod and slid away, her companion in tow. The box he held shifted in his arms, as if something inside stirred. He then noticed that the millwork on the top was open and he could actually see whatever it was moving about within. He put the box on the rooftop and lifted the lid.

He was confronted by a pair of pewter eyes and the sight of shining black fur. A little Ney-wolf puppy of no more than six weeks of age—barely weaned; jet as midnight, peered up at him from inside the box with an astonishing air of calm. He reached in and caressed its precious face. "Well then," he muttered, confused and shocked; unable to even begin to interpret what this meant. Calabras was past Neyat, by the ocean. About six days from his home. He frowned. There was no indication there would be new terms to their so-called agreement. What could bringing a dog to a coastal city signify? This just made him angry. To leave him without the slightest explanation was even more infuriating. His eyes fell again onto the dog, and his hackles lowered a bit. He lifted the little dog out of the fine box and studied her.

There was one strange thing about her that made him question her breed for a moment. The pup had a white mark on her chest. It looked like a bird with its wings spread in flight. Ney wolves did not have markings like this. Everything else about her was as anyone knew of the breed; the silvery eyes, the jet black fur, the shape of her head. Even in its blunted, rounded puppy stage it was unmistakable. Some Ney wolves had copper eyes. The silver eyed wolves were rarer from what he understood. He was holding an oddity.

"You are an uncommon sight, aren't you? A little Ney pup with a magpie on her chest..." he said to her. She lapped her lips and gazed at him impassively, dangling from his hands; her rear legs slack, her forelegs sticking out from where his hands clutched below them. He tucked her under his arm, picking up the box with the other hand. He gingerly made his way back down into the boat and put the dog on his bed. It looked at him and yawned with a high-pitched whine. The dog then plopped down onto the blankets, rested its head on its paws, and drifted immediately off to sleep.

Edrick drew deeply of his ale, thankful for the old man's consideration. Beside him, on a small decorative table, was a wedge of hard cheese, a sliced apple and a round, crusty bread roll on a thick clay platter. Although he had thoroughly enjoyed the rustic yet tasty fish stew his host had made for supper, it had been hours since, and they had decided to partake of a little snack and a nice beer before they retired. The old man was looking at the fine box Edrick had given him—admiring the workmanship— the delight of owning it quite evident on his wrinkled brow.

On Edrick's lap, the puppy had managed to sink into every dip and curve of his legs, one back leg drooping off the side like melted wax. She took a long, tremulous sigh and made a little snorting sound. Her belly was round and warm, full of some left-over roasted chicken from the old man's lunch. Outside it was raining and the sound of it on the roof was mesmerizing. Deyran was not put off by the sudden presence of an unexpected puppy. He found her charming; for looking at this raven-black, pewter eyed beauty, how could one not find the striking thing delightful? Even Edrick, who had never cared much for the idea of having pets, could not resist the sweetness of this little infant dog.

Deyran had confirmed with his passenger that he was not going as far as Calabras. He would take the easterly canals towards Ellyth and avoid the briny waters as much as he could. "This ain't a seagoing vessel, I'm 'fraid," he said.

"There aren't many places to supply oneself in the prairielands, so I'll be making a nice long stop in Neyat. You and the pup can disembark there. Besides, at Neyat I'm usually lucky in finding passengers who want to cross to the eastern cities," he added.

Edrick didn't argue. He figured he could find his own way once he got to Neyat.

There would be a nice leisurely time to enjoy the quiet in between, if the Farkas were finished with their unexpected visits. His hand slid down the shining fur of the puppy as he thought on it, still bewildered by what her significance was. He wasn't sure if it was an honor to be bestowed with such a precious gift, or if it was a test. He concluded that it must be a test of his capacity for responsibility; and he would be judged by how well he would care for this little wolf. These were important creatures to the Farkas. Almost all Farkas were rumored to have at least one per household. After only the fourth day on the canal, he was dreading Calabras for one reason and one reason alone: he was afraid they would take little Magpie from him when he got there.

Travel was slow. The horses plodded on the canal path, unbelievably well trained and responsive to Deyran who clicked and barked at them occasionally from inside his cabin, one of the many panes of his windowed space opened just for that purpose. Traffic was dense leaving the city, but after a few days it thinned out as boats took different routes that branched off the main waterway. Edrick watched with fascination the cooperation and kindliness with which the bargers treated one another. As the *Stonesthrow* passed a rather immense cargo barge, he watched the family that crewed it work to lift up the tow-line connected to the horses over their ship so the little boat could get by. The child riding point for their team of three horses ducked under the line as the *Stonesthrow's* two beasts wove around them. A few clicks and the horses trotted just long enough to get the boat ahead of the larger one, and there was an exchange of calls of gratitude and greeting from both ships—Deyran working the tiller and adjusting the horse-line expertly all the while, navigating the ungainly vessel with a smooth hand.

He would stop periodically during the day to jump off the boat and provide the horses rest, grazing and water. Edrick used that time to let little Magpie toddle about in the grass of the bank and take care of any business she needed to. Mornings were mostly rainy, or cool and foggy; but afternoons were warmer, and Edrick liked to stretch his legs with the puppy. While Deyran brushed down his horses and tended to things, Edrick knelt in the grass by his dog and looked about the countryside appreciatively. The lines of windbreak poplars were everywhere in this farming country. Great walls of them divided the land. Crops were neatly laid out in patchwork. Some stone-walled areas contained sheep and cows. Farmhouses made of stacked stone hid beneath stands of old oak, chestnut and walnut trees. Avenues to fine houses lined in ancient trees led off of the canal towpaths, which so often were used as throughways for local traffic.

There was little sign here of the unrest that often befell the city states. Edrick sometimes ran into skirmishes on his many travels. Graveyards for fallen fighters, ranks of mercenaries marching in file to the next battle, Yvremi fighting Yvremi for no other reason than a shambles of a government that allowed for rich men to squabble over land and power. Here, he had yet to see any of it. It was refreshing. The countryside was quieter, cleaner. It was almost as nice as the Farkas Sentely, except for the particularly shabby appearance of the peasantry that reminded him that it wasn't.

Small bergs popped up here and there accompanied by the smell of cooking food and the laughter of children playing by the canal. He sighed deeply. On this eighth day of travel the air was warm and bees hummed over a sprinkling of daisies and buttercups along the water banks. It was a rare spring day when the sun was shining and the air was warm. There was a well established avenue of trees here, all along the horse path. Magpie was rolling around, most likely on something dead, and he reached out to stop her. As he did, he heard hoof beats coming from behind them.

He looked up the lane and saw two stylish young ladies riding a pair of dapple grey hacks, their skirts hanging elegantly from the mounting side. They slowed at the sight of the barge, and eyed it warily. Deyran ignored them as they approached, but the ladies—both fair and golden—watched the men with great suspicion. Edrick picked up his puppy and stepped further back from the horse path, as if to indicate that the ladies ought to pass safely.

The eldest of the two noticed the dog and she reined her horse to a stop. "That is a Ney wolf!" she declared, her voice imbued with wonder and delight.

The other woman, who was undoubtedly her sibling for their strong resemblance, gasped and then made a little squeal of glee. "Oh, it's so precious. May we see him, sir?"

"It's a her," he muttered. He lifted her up for the ladies to see.

"Oh, I must have her. How much?" the eldest asked.

"She is not for sale," he replied.

The second girl tilted her head. "That's no common accent. You're wellborn," she concluded.

"He would have to be to get his hands on a dog like that. The Farkas cling closely to their creatures. They don't sell them to the likes of us," the eldest replied.

"What's your family name, if I may ask?" the younger of the two girls inquired.

This was a question he did not want to answer, but he also wanted their deference and respect so he could make them go away. "I am Edrick of Bethranorn," he replied.

"Oh," the eldest half-whispered. "Well, I am Annik," she said. "And this is my younger sister Reeta. We are ClanEthim."

"Enchanted," the word fell from his mouth before he realized it, and he was already in a shallow, graceful bow. His flirtations were a habit, and it often created more problems for him. He watched them both flush, and he mentally kicked himself for it.

"How long are you to be here?"

"We are only stopping to rest the horses. We'll be on our way shortly," he replied.

"You will be stopping for the night at Ezley?" she directed this question to Deyran who merely nodded and stuck a pipe in his mouth. He lit it and puffed on it, watching the interchange.

"Then by the time you reach there this evening, you will be able to join us for supper, your grace," she offered.

Edrick frowned. The painfully familiar sense of social obligation possessed him. To refuse them when asked in person would make him seem unkind and proud; things his family frowned upon. But he had no desire to dine with middling gentry. He felt trapped by the request. He had nothing against the young women, they were much like the throngs of ladies he encountered in many a parlor. He could sense their glee at meeting this infamous, unattached royal, and the intentions behind their invitation.

"You simply *must* join us. Our house is close to town. It won't interfere with your travel. Just dinner. And bring the precious little cub with you! We'll have a man fetch you with the coach. My father is a great admirer of the Bethranorn dynasty. He will be so delighted to meet you."

"Oh, he'll be there. I'll make sure of it," Deyran said. "I'll have him in the square by sundown."

The girls smiled at one another with satisfaction and trotted off with a nod to the men. Edrick spun about to give the old man a glare, only to find him smirking at him.

"Ah, don't be cross with me, sir. I can't imagine anyone would want to miss a fine meal in a fine house across from fine ladies like that. Even you, great *Bethranorn*!" He laughed.

Edrick shook his head and grumbled. Clutching his dog, he strode across the horse path and vaulted onto the boat. As he clambered down into the cabin, Deyran still chuckled behind him.

Edrick had not furnished himself with too many good clothes for his trip to Eyome. He did not expect to be there long, which had turned out to be true, and so he had only brought one presentable set of garments; the rest were mostly made for travel. Deyran had kindly brushed his breeches and frock coat clean. He washed his shirt himself in a bucket on the deck of the ship, leaving it to dry on the tow line. The waistcoat of deep, conifer green with tiny stripes of gold was in decent enough shape. He spent the better part of the afternoon as they traveled toward town polishing his worn boots; for the one thing he did not have were slippers. He was thankful for that, for all of his stockings had developed some dye staining at the ankles from his boots.

Deyran ironed Edrick's cleanest cravat to a state of near respectability, and he dressed below deck while Deyran maneuvered the vessel into one of the few free spaces along the town's west bank.

The canal broadened as they often did when going through a town. Here, there was a livery facility for horses. So while Deyran settled his animals in the cozy stalls for the night; Edrick prepared to set off. Deyran returned just as Edrick was leaving. He was carrying a large round of bread under his arm and had a little sack of fragrant smoked sausage that made Edrick's mouth water. He wished immediately he could stay and partake.

"Glad we berthed here tonight. It's starting to rain. Horses will be dry. That's good. Wear your hat. You takin' the little pup?"

"Aye, I am," Edrick replied.

Deyran assented with a faint grunt. "Kind of makes me want one. So many boatmen have dogs. They make good guardians. The bargemen keep them without fail. It is almost a requirement on a barge. All that merchandise should be protected. But it's the company that I think would be nice. And this little lady has reminded me of that," Deyran mumbled. "I'm not sure what time you'll be back, but I'll leave a lamp burning if I'm asleep. And some ale for you, if you want it."

Edrick assented with a nod. Deyran was an excellent host and an even better boatman.

He set off down the towpath, past the stables, to where the cobbled paving widened to a plaza. There were still a few carts selling goods in the dwindling daylight and some people lingered around a fountain, talking. Boatmen and townsfolk alike. The coach arrived to collect him with a great noise. It was a small town, not bustling, and the coach did not belong in this subdued little scene. It was an ostentatious, gaudy looking thing with a showy chestnut pair pulling it. One of the young ladies waved out the window at Edrick and offered him a welcoming smile as the coach drew to a stop.

"I'm so glad you agreed to join us. Do hop in, Your Grace."

Edrick bowed his head, biting back his embarrassment to be addressed as such. The footman had hopped down off of the rear perch and held the door open for him. He joined the young woman in the coach and greeted her with a nod as he collected Magpie's gangly legs and balled her up before sinking down onto the seat with her on his lap. The lady's eyes fell to the large-pawed pup and she sighed whimsically. The coach lurched into movement and rumbled loudly on the cobbles.

"I thank you again for the invitation," Edrick said politely. She dipped her chin, looked up at him with her lovely eyes, and blushed.

She extended her hand for him to take, and let it fall into his. He bowed over it. She withdrew. "Would it be forward of me to ask to hold your little pup?"

"No, of course not." He handed Magpie over to her, and she bundled the noodley creature into her arms, clucking and cooing at her. The dog took her in with shining eyes and wagged her tail lazily.

"Where oh where did you come upon this little thing? I have longed for one since I was a little girl when I saw a Farkas family traveling in from the coast. Such beautiful animals they rear there. Such an affinity for the dark colors too. Look at her eyes. Are they not utterly beguiling?"

"They are indeed. She was given to me," he said.

"Oh. How fortunate for you. What must one do to be gifted such a dog?" she asked half-jokingly, half seriously. He shook his head and did not reply. The lady fussed over Magpie until the coach drew up before a large house. It was a simple late Aurian stone box with a slate roof that slanted in from each side, with a ring of stacks protruding near the apex. There were large divided light windows painted a cheerful white on each face and a porticoed entryway at the top of three broad steps leading to a door the color of pine needles. There was a nice little park around the house, and an avenue of poplars led to the circular drive. It was well kept and a fine home.

Nobility was still surreptitiously regarded as nobility in most Yvremi circles. Noble names still garnered more respect than the powerful, rich common men that now claimed equal purchase. Although some families managed to reclaim their wealth and status after the invasion, a host of common-born opportunists were quick to fill in the vacancies they left behind, and the rich became much like the peerage of days past.

But the flood of common blood did not eradicate the influence of the peerage. The Farkas may have deposed the rich elite ruling class, it was impossible prevent the slow and subtle return of those old patterns; where nobility was still cherished over those who came from common stock. And the ClanEthim family seemed to be one of those.

Edrick estimated by the trappings of the coach and horses, the quality of the lady's gown and the size of the estate, that this family was perhaps the equivalent of a Baronetcy. It wasn't nobility; a baronetcy, but it was still a title. The patriarch of the family awaited the coach with his younger daughter and his spouse standing just behind him. Edrick reclaimed his dog and waited for Lady Annick to descend before following her out. Introductions were made.

"Your Grace, this is my father, Bester ClanEthim. My mother, Jannad, and you've met my sister, Reeta," Lady Annick said.

He bowed gracefully to each in turn, and took the ladies' hands.

He was then ushered into a stuffy little hall where his coat and hat were taken by a mousy little chamber maid. All the while he could scarce keep the girls' hands off of Magpie. The mother, Jannad, cooed over her as well.

They led him to a comfortable parlor where he was invited to sit. There, a pair of smallish house-hounds idled by the fire. Loud and not particularly useful or appealing in Edrick's view, house-hounds were not what he would ever choose as a companion. They were a miniaturized version of the hunting hound with the same floppy ears and the same single-mindedness that was counterintuitive to an animal that was meant to provide comfort and companionship. They barked in deafening howls at anything and were renowned for running away to follow whatever scent they came upon, sometimes disappearing for good.

The family's two dogs lifted their heads and yowled stridently at the newcomer, but in a strange turn of events, they then sniffed the air and began whining and growling. Then they scurried from the room with their tails tucked and hackles raised. Magpie watched from her comfortable nest of arms and sniffed after them suspiciously.

"It seems the scent of Ney wolf does not agree with your house hounds," Bester ClanEthim said with good humor. The girls were momentarily bemused, but quickly returned to fussing over Magpie. He relinquished her to their custody and they moved to another sofa to adore her, the little black dog floating away in a rustle of silk. Mrs. ClanEthim offered Edrick a glass of port, and he turned his attention to the parents.

"I suspect, Your Grace, that you must be in this country for a purpose. I've heard rumors about a Bethranorn being sent up to a Farkas settlement. In regards to the problem brewing overseas," ClanEthim ventured.

Had the council been so careless as to let details of this mission to escape the chambers? Edrick found that astonishing. He did not expect to be found out so quickly.

"You must not look so surprised Your Grace, but I am particularly attentive to what goes on in the senate chambers these days. Especially when my trade contacts talk of the imminent threat. I have a family to protect; holdings we have struggled to maintain since the peerage was stripped of its powers."

"Understood," Edrick replied.

"And may I ask if your mission was successful?"

"Hard to say, Sir ClanEthim," he said.

The man seemed gratified by the appellation. He puffed up a bit being addressed as Sir. Edrick was correct in his assumption of the man's status. Something like a Knight or a Baronet. He did not care to ask.

"The Farkas have always been enigmatic in their interaction with us. I passed on a message. It was received; whether it gets to where it must go, that is the question. But this little creature your daughters are fawning over, I believe might be a gesture of goodwill. I am on my way to meet with another representative of the Farkas interests. I may know more then," he said with a conclusive tone, indicating that this was all he was willing to say about the matter.

"Interesting," ClanEthim replied, pinching his chin. A round man, he had the air of a contented soul. Large bushy sideburns of peppery grey overtook the sides of his face; his hair on his head, the same color, was cropped and artfully curled forward towards his face. He had a barren spot on the top of his skull which shone like a teapot. His cheeks were ruddy red and he had a large nose with a spidering of gin blossoms on it. He clutched his glass of deep amber sherry in his pudgy fingers. The bottom of the stem rested on the swell of his round belly, which dawned from under his frock coat in a shining waistcoat of red silk. "I suppose there is one benefit to this imminent threat of the Akravani, and that is a cessation of virtually all infighting amongst the city states," he said.

"Really?" Edrick asked, his brows rising. This was unexpected.

"Yes. I think that maybe there is still some sense left in the government and leadership of Yvrem, even if the senate and parliament is peopled with commoners and fools. There was a call for cessation of hostilities throughout the nation last week—all troops have been recalled for training and refitting in case of invasion. The landlords can tousle over borders and farmland another time—more important matters are afoot. I myself have sent a portion of my land's young fellows out to be outfitted and trained by the lord Metrim's guard. We must do what we must," Sir ClanEthim muttered.

"I'm glad there's some measure of coordination between states at least. There's been so little consensus and cooperation these past years. If it takes an invasion to bring us together again, than I suppose it is an advantage we cannot ignore." They both fell still, and the older man stared into nothing speculatively while his wife took up the conversation.

"You travel by boat, I understand sir," she asked.

"Yes," Edrick replied, sipping from his drink. "I decided to take a restful journey back after a rather uncomfortable one out," he said.

She smiled and tilted her head.

"I've often wondered what it would be like to travel in those little ships. I have always imagined they would be close and uncomfortable."

"Oh it's not *so* bad. However I'm the sort of person that is comfortable with small spaces. And as I am not a lady, my needs are simpler. I am happy to sit by the little stove with Magpie there on my lap, a simple mug of ale, and the quiet. I must say, the sound of the rain on the roof is most soothing, and I am fortunate to have a boatman of particular quality. He's an admirable host and he takes exceptional care of me and the little pup."

"She is lovely," the Lady said. The daughters had let Magpie down to explore the room. She bandied about the space, gawky on her long legs and her astonishingly large paws, her gracefully pointed muzzle pressed to the floor where she traced the steps of the domicile's resident dogs. She wound up at Edrick's feet, and whined to be picked up. He did, petting her gently.

"I remember once hearing a tale being wound by a brewer at Fairkeep who spoke of the Ney Wolf," Sir ClanEthim suddenly blurted. "It was about fifteen years ago, when Annick was just a wee thing. I was traveling up to Fairkeep for some business or other, and I stayed there. I was in the common room of the inn with other gentlemen and some merchants. As we sat and drank, he rambled on about the ale that we'd been served.

"A party of Farkas passed by the window on the main road, heading to goodness knows-where. It was the usual contingent. A lady and a lord, six pole men; all on those monstrous horses. And invariably, a pair of those dogs. Grown of course. Two of the copper-eyed ones, who are smaller than the silver-eyed ones. Those are large dogs, those silver eyed ones. They were taller at the shoulder than Annik's first pony, I do not jest.

"The whole tavern in the inn fell silent as they went by. And then the brewer started telling a story about how his great-grandfather had seen a Ney wolf transform into a person right before his eyes. 'They're shape shifters, mark my words,' he insisted. 'We haven't seen the like of shape shifters in Yvrem for a thousand years,' I told him. 'The olden folk have moved on, left it all to us,' I said. The brewer shook his head. 'The Farkas *are* the olden folk,' he declared. 'They have the old powers as the ancients did.' Shape-shifters. You could have one right in your lap," Bester joked.

"Perhaps the Farkas have furnished you with a little spy to watch you," Annick laughed.

"If that's the case, then they have given me an infant, for she is not two months old, this pup," Edrick said, laughing quietly. He looked down at the pup's wide, earnest eyes, and smirked at her. Her tail slapped his knee twice. "I hope not, eh girl? Because that would mean I cannot keep you."

As he spoke the door opened and a tired-looking butler slid into the room. "Dinner, my Lady."

"Let us eat then! What a delight to have a Bethranorn under our roof!" Lady ClanEthim declared. She rose and patted down her gown. "Will you accompany me, your Grace?" He put the pup on the floor. "She can follow and sit under the table. Nobody will mind," she assured him.

He took her arm and she guided him to their cozy dining room where a blissfully simple and delicious meal awaited them.

Chapter 4
The Beautiful Beast

The details of the much unanticipated voyage with her childhood enemy did indeed follow for Keela. She would have only a few days to relax and enjoy her home before she was to leave with Vianca. The gossip that reached them was as expected. Vianca wasn't too pleased with the arrangement herself. Keela heard from Alara that she wasn't happy to be traveling with Keela, or her own child. Keela thought that was the most selfish thing she'd ever heard.

Alara received a pouch of gold to pay for the provisions and clothing Keela would need for the journey, as well as a little allowance to cover various unexpected expenses. Alara was methodical about the preparations, and made sure that Keela was supplied for all occasions, social or expeditionary. Keela on the other hand spent much of her time loafing around the town she'd grown up in, trying to soak up as much of it as possible before she left for the summer.

Keela went out to the old watchtower a good deal, and climbed the spiral staircase to the top. It didn't stand out cleanly from the forest anymore; the growth had long since surrounded the tower and blocked off the view off to the east. It had lost its usefulness when the Farkas invaded, and remained a crumbling testament of a different time. It belonged to the wilderness now. The hillside sloped away on the west side and the tower's watch just cleared the tops of the pines. There, Keela could sit in the crenel look out over the forest valley below. There was a wide platform to sit on, and room for her to fold herself up and press her feet against one merlon tooth while her back rested against another. From her pocket she produced a little book, which she opened, but did not immediately read. She idled in this quiet place, the wind playing with her long black hair.

She spent many an hour planted in that spot, staring down at the narrow Dekka River which wound its way sinuously through the valley bottom; flush and noisy in the cool months, and lean in the summer; with freshly revealed rocky banks and water-tumbled wood and stones piled up along the bends.

There was always something to see there. Wild creatures emerged from the trees to drink of the river. Deer, foxes, common wolves, and Een cats. And her favorite: a bear of absurd size with a ruddy, reddish brown coat and a streak of black fur that blazed from his snout, between his white-tipped ears, to the top of his hunched shoulders, spreading out into what was almost a saddle shape on his back. He was unusual, and nobody else spoke of such bears existing in the forest outside of Veros. She felt especially privileged to witness the lumbering thing as it idled along the valley floor and sometimes stood up like a towering man. It would point its head toward the tower to sniff the air for the scent that undoubtedly announced her presence there. Her ursine friend was not there this particular day. Instead, there was a fog that hung low, filling the valley beneath her. Treetops pierced the fog like ghostly bristles. She could hear the river roiling and churning at full strength. The rain of the past few days had made it turbid and frothy, and it carried with it new bounties of tree limbs and other flotsam shorn from the mountains.

Keela was graceful when she wanted to be, or wasn't thinking about it. But often she made herself coarse in some eccentric act of self protection. She took little care in her toilette, something her mother complained about a great deal. She wore shabby clothes in company and sported muddy boots and hems almost all the time. She had been conditioned by the cruelty of her childhood tormentors to not recognize her own loveliness, and to make herself unnoticeable; to give herself no special importance or to be deserving of care.

Her attractive features did not invite the boys to pursue her—or the girls to overtly envy and praise her loveliness as they did one another. She was treated like a pariah by her peers. From the first moment she could remember, she had been reviled and bullied. The monikers they assigned to her were contemptible. Farkas whore-child, peasant scum, black-haired witch.

When she arrived at Veros with Alara, her different colorings set her apart from them immediately. Even while she grew from an innocent toddler into a child, she was aware of her differences. Her status of outsider never changed as she grew older and blossomed; the youths too proud to take back their unjustified judgments of her. By that time, she was so beaten down by their rebukes and hatred, she didn't even bother to try to make friends anymore—she was a taciturn, introverted soul. They used that—amongst her other differences—to keep her distanced from them. She had no friends in this place except her adoptive mother, a hermit farmer named Ejesh who was afraid to speak, and an old man she occasionally helped with daily chores. He too was full of wise words and advice for Keela—but not the kind of companionship a young person ought to have—not a friend close to her age that she could relate to. She had no equals, no confidants. Keela never complained to her guardian about it, or to Loralo, the old man; or the farmer who sometimes caught himself gazing with longing at her; but inside, it hurt terribly that her that her peers hated her so. Because of all this, Keela had become quite adept at being alone.

She would miss this place. She especially loved it in summer. The fireflies and the dragonflies, the buzz of the weeping bugs. It was the first time she would leave Veros since she arrived as a child of two. The idea discomfited her.

She wriggled around on the cool stone to make herself more comfortable, the wind playing with the pages of her book—it was noisy today—the birds quite vociferous as they gamboled in the trees. The brisk, cool breeze and the fog made them frisky. The little ones were already learning how to fly.

"Gods, what are *you* doing here?" Adarnoth's voice startled her, but she didn't react. Keela didn't even look at him; she could see his shape out of the corner of her eye. He started off the sentence with his usual snide bravado, but it petered out, as if he realized he was being an idiot and it was too late to fix it. He stood in the hole where the stairway vanished, shoulders and head poking out.

"I come here almost every day," Keela said calmly. "You know that as well as anyone—stop pretending to be surprised. What do you want?" Her tone was imbued with displeasure. She felt his coming here somehow tainted her favorite place. Most of the others were too lazy to climb the hill, or too frightened of the darkened interior, saying the tower was overrun with bats and other creepy crawlies.

Keela was delighted they believed this because it left the space for her alone. Most of the time. Sometimes someone would come on a dare, or sneak up on her with to prank her. It was rare, but not entirely unexpected. That Adarnoth had come surprised her, but part of her expected someone from the delegation of idiots would not be able to contain their curiosity about this impending voyage with Vianca—the reigning queen of her tormentors, and would show their face before she left.

He climbed the remaining few steps and walked to the crenel

directly across from hers, his back to the wall of trees that loomed over the east side of the tower. He pushed aside a bough, scooted onto the ledge, and sat there in silence for a while. Watching her read, she imagined.

"Calabras, right?" He didn't beat around the bush. The group needed information to feed their gossip.

"Yes." It was a simple, monosyllabic response which was usually her method of communication with the people who were so apt to treat her badly. He crossed his arms and nodded. There was a long silence, and then he sighed. He seemed oddly contrite—in his posture and his mood—as if being alone with her made it safe to be so. And then he spoke.

"I used to really like Vianca," he confessed. "I used to like you too."

"You are a boy. You like anything with *tits*." She flipped to the next page of her book with a brusque movement.

"Look. You know how these things work…"

"Only too well." She was unable to contain the resentment in her tone. It came out like an evil hiss. Keela couldn't believe it. He was trying to apologize to her in his own stupid way.

He winced, and chewed his tongue, making his jaw ripple, unable to meet her black glare. He flushed, and shook his head. "You're entitled to whatever you're feeling; I'm just trying to help. She's not perfect, and never was," he offered.

"It doesn't take a genius to see that. About any of you," she added acidly.

"Look, let's call truce for just a moment, if we could. Because I think you ought to be watchful with Vianca."

"I can be nothing but. Our history is all the warning I need.."

"Yes, but it could be worse. She is in a state. A terrible state. My sister saw her and Vianca is worse than she ever was. Distilled and concentrated anger. And she's not happy about you going."

"I didn't imagine she would be," Keela mumbled. "Would

69

anyone who knew our history be stupid enough to believe that Vianca would suddenly be delighted to spend a summer with *me*?"

"No. But... just please, approach her with care," he said, as if unable to put into words what he really wanted to say.

"You think I'm in danger from her? That she would actually harm me?"

"I don't know. My sister described her as volatile. It made me ... worry. For you."

"Why do you feel the need to warn me now? You never warned me before when you stood beside her and hurled your hateful bile at me at her bidding." She could not wrap her mind around this. She felt like he was doing this to get her guard down and manipulate her somehow. There simply was no reason for Adarnoth to be considerate of her feelings. Not after years of teasing, cruel mischief, false rumors and no end of other abuses he and the others had heaped upon her.

"We are no longer children." That was a flat truth. "Things happen to us that make us realize how stupid we can be."

"What happened to you?" she asked.

"I'm to join the Jaratoom. My father's punishment for some ill choices I've made of late," he said. With a regretful look he stood again, and made his way to the stairway. "Just watch yourself. Please."

"I plan to do nothing but," she retorted. "But thank you for coming up here to state the obvious."

"I just thought you should just be prepared for anything when it comes to Vianca."

"Believe you me... I know," Keela said; a touch of dark humor in her voice. He smiled wanly and then looked down at the darkness below him. He descended a few steps.

"Adarnoth," Keela called. He paused, his head still visible, and turned to look at her. "Thank you."

He smiled sincerely, and his head vanished. She heard his heels clattering all the way down. Keela was confused, but somehow heartened. Part of her wanted to scream down to him as he left: *Too little, too late!* The other part of her suspected he was up to something. But the admission that he had been drafted into the Jaratoom by his angry father was a good reason to make amends to people in your life.

The Jaratoom was a military force that had been assembled by the second interim government withdrawal. It was made up of young men from the various city states of Yvrem. Faced from the start with incursions by other nations and tasked with putting down inter-state rebellions by a great number of civil forces, the Jaratoom saw a great deal of action. With the rumors that Alara had spoken of—of an invasion by the Akravani—this was not good news at all for Adarnoth.

Keela was well versed on many subjects, but was only lightly educated on the Akravani and who they were. She knew they were a war-like people from the Effen Mainland; and that they had raped and pillaged their way through history, spreading their violent culture brutal religion throughout Effen. Effen was a backwards nation because of the constant war and the barbaric ideologies they followed. They were thought by most other nations to be uncivilized savages. But the sheer numbers and the violence of the armies were renown. And now they had taken to the sea, and successfully overthrown nations that were far more advanced than their own.

Yvrem was now vulnerable because of its instability, even over 70 years after the Farkas withdrew. Keela was unsure, with the Yvremi city states always locking horns, if they could pull themselves together enough to offer a proper defense of Yvrem. The Jaratoom was an asset on that end, but that meant that Adarnoth would possibly face battle against the vicious Akravani.

Adarnoth's father was a regional recruiter for the Jaratoom. It was astonishing to Keela that Adarnoth hadn't foreseen this probable sentence long ago and curbed his bad behavior. Perhaps

71

he'd grown too comfortable in his skin, too smug to think himself subject to the possibility.

It was difficult to focus on reading after his unexpected visit. Her mind was abuzz with speculation. She did not look forward to the impending voyage.

Keela snapped her book closed, and hopped down from her perch. She ran down the dark stairs, comfortable with the drooping treads, worn from hundreds of years of use. She had once dreamt of taking this place as her home and dividing the cylinder into five sections, each one a comfortable room. She even had a plan to install a chimney that would provide hearths to all of the rooms. There were once floors here, evidenced by the holes that had contained large supporting beams, now a rotting pile of splintered wood at the bottom of the tower and on the five landings along the spiral stairs. One day, perhaps. She would ask Lord Xanett if she could. Maybe by granting him this favor, he would be more disposed to allow it. She smiled at the prospect of something positive coming from the journey with his ill-tempered wife.

She tramped down the steps in her hand-me-down boots and her sodden hems. As she jumped down the last three that led out of the tower, she was confronted by an astonishing and terrifying sight: the enormous bear was only a short distance away from the tower entrance on a small, jutting shelf, sniffing fervently around the base of a tree.

She stopped short, frozen completely still. She was so close she could hear the soft *uung uung* sounds it made as it roved, its black, moist snout hovering over the ground. Its body was impossibly large. Like an animated boulder, it hunched about; following a scent away from her. For a moment she was worried it was following Adarnoth, whom she could see far down the path almost to the valley floor, but the scent trail that the bear followed led off the edge of the shelf where the tower stood, and the great creature vanished down into the ravine. It soon disappeared into the dense vegetation. When she felt safe enough to move, she picked up her hem with one hand, clutched her book to her breast, and scampered down the path.

As she reached the riverside path, she heard a frightening roar far in the distance. Exhilarated and thrilled, she thought that this close encounter was a parting gift from Veros. For soon, she would face a much, much worse creature than a gargantuan bear.

Keela's trunk hunkered by the main door. It was a rather nice one made of fine wood, but simply constructed and held together by elegantly scrolled brass straps. It closed with a delicate looking clasp and matching lock. Alara had made sure she had everything she would need, but didn't go entirely cheap with the purchases, making sure she wouldn't be embarrassed by the low quality of her possessions compared to those of the rich lady that she traveled with.

She stood in the dormer, the window panes partially obscured by moss that drooped from the edge of the thatched roof. The Crone's-Hair moss got out of control in the wet spring, and it was usually her job to go up on a ladder and tug it off the thatching. It was soft moss, and when it was dried it could be used to pad things or make wonderful kindling cakes. It also served as an excellent substitute for hay if one ran out during the winter—horses and other hoofed creatures loved to devour it. She often gathered what her mother did not want, stuffed it into an empty sack, and brought it to Ejesh, her farmer friend, to give to his sheep and goats. He would smile broadly at her in gratitude; keeping his words to himself; fearful she would laugh at his flawed speech.

Keela realized it was one chore she would have to do before she left because Alara's arthritis made it hard for her to climb the steps to the loft, let alone a ladder. Keela went out the back door into the yard and picked up the ladder, leaning it against the back of the house. She pulled the moss down in colossal wads, letting them plop to the ground in a fluffy, damp pile at the base of the ladder.

Practice made her work quickly, and made her brave on the ladder. She leaned out far, avoiding having to move the ladder more than she needed to.

When she squeezed through the narrow alley between their house and their neighbor's, Alara's arch-nemesis, Ledri, poked her head up above the high stone and wood wall that separated their properties. Her double-buns on her cap-less head, looking like bear's ears, could be seen bobbing along as she scurried along the length of the wall, eager to catch Keela before she reached the front of the house. Ledri hissed through her teeth and coughed and ahemed, but Keela ignored her, letting the woman suffer. Finally, she heard her name in a raspy whisper.

"Keela. Child."

Keela stopped and righted the ladder, leaning it against the short side of the house. There was moss there too, but not in the quantities that it was on the cut ends of the thatching. She climbed the ladder regardless, looking down over the fence at the old woman. Ledri gazed up at her, hand shielding her eyes against the bright, morning sun.

"What is it?" Keela said impatiently.

"You're leaving today. You shouldn't be soiling your nice new clothes."

Keela glanced down at her simple, forest-green gown. It was the first gown in a long time she could recall wearing that was not pieced from the fabric of Alara's old gowns; or handed down—patched and repaired—from someone else. The simple day gown she wasn't too concerned about. She was more careful with her brand new, soft kidskin ankle boots of slate blue. These were the first boots she ever had that fitted her properly, and that didn't look like four people had worn them well, before she had. She was besotted with her new boots. Alara gave them to her the night before, along with eleven pairs of pristine, brand new stockings in a variety of colors with attractive clocking over the ankles.

"Nobody else is going to do it. I'm going to be gone for three months, at least. Do you want to do it?"

"Don't be silly..." Ledri admonished. "I hear from the household servants that Lady Vianca is most displeased and upset to be traveling with you."

"I've heard that too. I expected no less. I would be disappointed if it were not the case. Besides, the feeling is *quite* mutual." Keela stretched precariously up onto her tip-toes on the rung of the ladder. She grasped a bare-looking string of moss that was entangled with larger pieces, making the harvest worth the risk.

"Well, it won't be easy for you."

"I'm sure it will be a challenge—but I don't quite understand—are you concerned? What point are you attempting to make?" Keela asked.

"Oh, I'm greatly concerned. She's a fine lady, but a young creature. And oh, the things I hear about their fiery, unhappy marriage. Such rages and tempers, you would be shocked. I've a theory about the journey. I am almost convinced that she's leaving and she will not return. Perhaps there will be a convent or a respite house awaiting her at Calabras, and she was never meant to come back!"

"Ledri... I would ask you what inspires these mad speculations, but in all honesty, I am just not interested in hearing them." Keela's patience was wearing thin. She threw the next clump of moss right into Ledri's side-yard. The woman ignored this little act of spite.

"Well," she went on, "I've been thinking on this whole business. I've come to a worthy conclusion about it. The Lord is looking for a new wife, of course. And the Lady, she knows this, of course. You're young, pretty and the very opposite of Lady Vianca. He could find nobody more to the opposite of her as you are. You're going along, I suspect, because he wants you to get to know his son, and grow attached as you journey to return the child to him, after Vianca's been delivered to her destination."

"I'm to be gone three months, I'm fairly certain that doesn't work with this scheme you so imaginatively created."

"Oh, that's all simply part of the scheme, you see," Ledri said. "Gone long enough to give people time here to forget her. And then you come back to him with his son."

Keela let out an exasperated groan and clomped indelicately down the ladder, lowering it again. The woman was actually wringing her hands in delight as she imagined all these things. Such amusement she seemed to derive from dreaming up gossip to spread about her troublesome neighbors..

"Gods, woman, you imagine such nonsense. Do you have nothing better to do with your life than fill your head with wild assumptions? This is a colorful one, I dare say. And I think you might have achieved the pinnacle of nonsensical blather this time. You've outdone yourself." Keela was beginning to see merit in living in a large city where people cared nothing about the lives of their neighbors. This woman was positively fanatical. She actually believed Keela was being groomed as Vianca's replacement, and going along with Vianca on her permanent departure. That she would return with the Lord's son and—*and become his what? Concubine?* She shook her head incredulously, and hoisted the ladder. Walking around to the front of the house, Keela lifted the ladder.

Ledri persisted, calling over the wall:"There's no other reason why you would be chosen to go. I'd wager on my own head that he's got something illicit in mind. All I have to say is: mind yourself, young lady."

"Your warnings are anything but original, believe me. I've heard those exact words already today from another unsavory source. Your imaginings make no sense, you mad old bat," Keela called down as she worked.

It was no wonder Ledri was determined to undermine every aspect of Alara's social standing in the community—and so obviously jealous of the travels and the experiences of Keela's mother. It was because her life was so empty, lonely and meaningless. It wasn't hard to deduce, seeing how much time and energy she expended on stupidities like today's. Keela moved the ladder farther away from the edge of the property, centering it on the house. Alara appeared in the doorway as Keela climbed the ladder, faced immediately by Keela's lovely booted feet, her clean hem and petticoats and the ladder.

"What are you... oh." Alara's question was answered before she could finish it by a shower of stringy, pale green moss that plopped down into tangled messes all over the cobbled walkway and the muddy, unkempt front garden. "I thought I heard voices."

"Ledri was sharing some of her inventive theories about this journey I'm taking," Keela said from above, another wad of moss falling down onto the ground.

"How does she know about the excursion to begin with? Gods, it's like everyone in the village is more informed about this thing than we are." Alara grunted as she bent to pick up the moss. She then slipped out from behind the ladder, collecting the piles Keela had left.

Ledri hadn't heard their conversation and was still on her side of the wall, coming up with more things to say. "Lady Vianca will surely suspect this as well, I wager. You should prepare yourself for her to treat you *very* badly; for who would tolerate being accompanied to a confinement by one's replacement? Nobody, nobody indeed! She will be cruel and hard, I warn you!" The woman's voice rang shrilly from behind the wall Alara had paid to have erected when their sour relationship began.

"As if that would be different from any other day," Keela grumbled under her breath.

Alara's head rose up like a predator spotting prey, and her eyes widened with anger at the sound of Ledri's intrusive voice. She straightened, and with hands full of moss, she scurried towards the front door, fists clenched around the helpless moss, her jaw set in a hard, angry line.

"Keela, did you empty the chamber pots already today?"

The carriage arrived at length. Leaving the manor required more time than planned, especially since it looked like the thing was about to buckle under the weight of the trunks, bags and other paraphernalia heaped on top, which included something with large spindly wheels that protruded from below the tarpaulin. One footman had already set to loosening the leather cover to incorporate Keela's humble trunk into the teetering heap. They hoisted it up and managed to strap it down amongst the other clutter. Keela bade her farewells while they covered everything in the oiled leather. Alara was trying hard to be strong, and was extremely apologetic for forcing her into this.

"It wasn't you doing the forcing, Mother."

"Just don't let the wench get to you. Let it roll off your back like water off a duck—promise?"

"I promise, mother," Keela said, her throat tight. She looked at the little stone cottage, the walls cross-sectioned by beams dark with years of reapplied creosote solution. The door was open, and she could smell the bread for the next few days baking in the oven. Smoke rose from the chimney and then was carried out over Ledri's home by a rather strong wind that had blown away the fog.

Keela's heart hurt. Behind her, the squall of a young child made her skin crawl. She had yet to set eyes on Vianca. She'd caught a glimpse of Vianca's pale face and wheaten hair as the coach arrived, but she'd sunk back into the darkness within the coach and Keela forgot her for the time being. When she was done bidding Alara farewell, she turned to Mr. Loralo who'd made the long, difficult walk to her home to say goodbye. She hugged his bony frame tightly. Unlike Alara, he felt like a sack of sticks, and she half-expected him to rattle when she hugged him. Alara was solid... her arthritis had slowed her down, but she was still as strong and vital as she'd always been. Loralo was frail, and gaunt. Keela feared she was looking into his deep blue eyes for the last time.

"I'm going to miss you." They both said this at exactly the same time. She smiled, and hugged him tighter, tears burning in her eyes. "I won't be gone for long. Alara will come by in my stead to help you."

"Be good, my girl. I'll look forward to having you back soon." Keela pushed him away to arm's length and felt as if she was about to lose control. She looked once more at Alara, and then at Loralo.

"Take care of each other until I get back." She bit back her tears, and stepped away.

Alara reached for Loralo, and looped her arm under his. They steadied one another as Keela turned away, waiting for the footman to open the carriage. Keela stepped up into the carriage and ducked inside. It was dark. Vianca had drawn most of the little curtains. She sat there, peering at Keela with a strange detached look, and waited for her to settle in.

They stared at one another while the footmen readied the coach for travel. The conveyance swayed under their weight, and the horses shifted restlessly.

A little baby was in a basket between the two wide, comfortable bench seats. Vianca followed Keela's gaze to the wriggling form under the knitted blankets. Her face was impassive. "He thinks if I spend lots of time with it, I'll learn to love it or something. But he doesn't quite trust me either. That's why you're here." She turned her head and looked out the one open window, her eyes glazed and sunken.

Keela was surprised. She had never seen Vianca look so terrible. She'd always been a girl of consequence, and had always had the best that her father's money could buy. Her hair coiffed to perfection, her skin soft from special scented tallow, her face perfectly enhanced with colors, jewelry, lovely gowns—she had always been perfection; save for her sour character. Now she looked thin and drawn. Her skin was sallow and her lips pale. She wore a frumpy walking dress and her hair was carelessly tied into a bun on top of her head.

Keela had heard so much rumor and speculation about why *she* was chosen to accompany this wreck of a person on her trip. Keela finally decided she understood the truth. In spite of Vianca's so-called friends abandoning her in her married state, she still cared what they thought. She was in a phase of pure self-loathing. It was as clear as day, and she didn't want them to see this side of her. Her baggy, shapeless garments; her depressed, morose face—complete with blemishes and ruddy skin; her listless, slumped posture. Keela was the only one whose opinion was completely irrelevant and unimportant. Keela was a non-entity in Vianca's world, and even if Keela spent the years afterwards telling everyone every detail of Vianca's horrible condition, nobody would believe her. They would call her spiteful. It made much sense indeed. This *had* to be the reason she was sitting in the coach with the loathsome wretch of a girl.

The coach lurched forward with a click of the coachman's tongue, and Keela lurched with it. Vianca, facing the front, didn't even turn her head. She watched Alara and the old man as they waved goodbye. "Must be awful to live in a hovel like that. Your guardian has no pride to rent such a dodgy old shack from my husband," she said with a curl of her lip. The baby gurgled.

"At least the people in that hovel are sad to see me go. I can't think of anyone who cares that you're leaving," Keela muttered, crossing her arms and her legs.

Vianca turned to look at her, but Keela looked down and away, at the poor, unloved child in the basket. What sort of person called their child an 'it' and spoke of the child as if it were but a pebble in her shoe? Then Keela remembered it was Vianca who was sitting there, and then came the sharp memories of her taunting smile as she purposefully tipped a muddy glass of paint water over Keela's desk and onto her gown. The delighted arch of Vianca's brow as she gracefully turned her back to the prefect to hide the fact that she'd stolen Keela's cup and was spitting into her tea. That was the kind of person that would call her own child an *it*.

The road changed as the coach left the edge of the town behind and entered the farmland that encircled Veros. Alara's cottage was on the last street in town before the fields and forest appeared.

"You are such rubbish," the blonde girl snarled.

Keela snorted and laughed, glancing back up at the girl who'd always been so cruel to her. There was nothing to intimidate in her air now. She just appeared wholly pathetic. "If I am such rubbish, why did you waste any of your time even deigning to speak ill of me?" Keela smiled sardonically, her arched eyebrows demanding a reply. "What is it about me that threatens you so much?"

Vianca twisted in her seat so that her shoulder turned towards the window, and she glared at the trees going by, and the livestock in the fields rather than look into Keela's eyes. That spoke volumes.

What a coward.

"Nothing about you threatens me, except that you breathe my air, and offend my eye."

"Ooh, I'm so wounded." Keela feigned hurt and sorrow. "My entire being is balanced upon your opinion. I don't think I can go on." She then laughed and leaned forward so that her face was only a short distance from Vianca. "I'm not sure what your ultimate motive has been all these years, Vianca—and frankly, I don't care. I'm going to make something clear to you before we get into the meat of this trip. I'm stuck with you, and obviously, you're stuck with me. I was given no choice on the matter myself. Whatever motivated the decision to have me here, it's *your* burden to bear, not mine. I suggest you treat me respectfully for as long as we're mired together. I cannot predict how I will react if you do not. However, I won't quail if you keep pushing me, because I've been looking for a good excuse for a long, long time. Give me an excuse, Vianca."

81

"For what?" Vianca spat, shrinking away a bit.

"Why don't you keep pressing my limits, and find out? I'm certain someone of even your limited imagination can dream up what twenty years of swallowing unchecked torment can stew up in a person." There was a good minute or two where this standoff lingered, and then Keela said: "—am I making myself clear enough?"

Vianca didn't answer. She only turned and looked out the window again.

Under her breath, a few moments later, Vianca said: "Uncouth and crude, just as I expected. As unladylike and ill-mannered as any common rubbish."

Keela glared at Vianca as she pulled off her black wool redingote and draped it over the bench at her side. She took a book from one of the large pockets. She'd packed a few, but thought it prudent to have one on hand. She reached over to the window on her side, and shoved the curtain aside quite violently. She challenged every glance Vianca shot her way, and kept her spine straight, her bristles up. Keela was personally and secretly surprised at her own reaction—she had no idea she'd be on the offensive so.

Vianca had usually made her feel weak and victimized. Keela would stand there and listen to the abuse, or suffer the indignity Vianca's pranks, and say nothing. She would go home and cry. But something happened since Vianca's marriage. Something had made Keela unafraid of the consequences of being disrespectful to a person of higher caste than she. She wasn't quite able to find the reasoning behind this newfound fearlessness—but she embraced it. Maybe being infinitely rude and insufferable would get her out of this arrangement.

Vianca hardly uttered a word. She only groaned when the baby cried, and sometimes wept herself. Keela, who was not exactly deft with child rearing skills, was good enough at it to know not to ignore the whimpering of the child. She reached down and picked up the baby.

"Why didn't you just bring a nurse with you?" Keela asked. Vianca was slumped in her seat, hands lying at her sides, palms up, eyes languidly following the landscape that rolled past. "This baby has soiled himself, and he's hungry. Can you sit your worthless self up enough so that he can eat?"

Vianca ignored her. Keela sighed and stood as best she could in the carriage, rummaging through the number of bags to find a new nappy, and the other things that were required. She found the bag, likely prepared by careful hands of a servant, and set up a place to change him next to the baby's mother on the bench. She found a bottle of antiseptic water and used it to soak a rag with which to clean the baby's sore bottom. She was careful, and made sure he was as clean as he could be before wrapping him up in a fresh cloth—mimicking the technique of the one she'd just undone as best she could. She was fairly successful. She reapplied the baby's bunting, and set him in his basket for a moment while he returned to squalling.

She stumbled over to where Vianca sat, and grabbed her under her arms, hoisting her up into a better position. "Unpin the stomacher," she commanded the indolent thing.

Vianca did so, and loosened the drawstring around the neck of her shift, all the while giving Keela an acid glare. Vianca reached down into the cup of her stays and lifted a breast out of it. Once it was exposed, she slumped back and glared at Keela. Keela shook her head and picked the baby up, forcing Vianca to position her arm properly to hold the baby while he ate. The baby latched on hungrily, and Vianca's revulsion was immediately expressed in an air that astounded Keela. Her lips disappeared into a line, and she convulsed twice as if she was about to vomit, her eyes even swimming. Her whole body looked as if it had curled away from the small person, and she looked at the baby as if it were the most repulsive thing she had ever seen. Keela furrowed her brow.

"Do you really *hate* this child?" She sank down in front of Vianca's head nodded in disgust, her mouth pressed closed as if she were still fighting the urge to gag. Keela had heard of women becoming forlorn and sleeping frequently after giving birth. But hating the child? She'd never seen that before.

Vianca took in a breath that sounded like a sob, and then bit it back. They remained silent until the baby fell asleep, and then Vianca leaned forward and handed him off to Keela. She held the child, staring down at his peaceful face.

"Why?" she asked finally.

Vianca shrugged, and returned her breast to her stays, tightening her shift's neckline again and fastened stomacher flap on her gown with a pin. She watched Keela with the baby for a while, and then turned to look back out the window. "I cannot stand the sound of him… the smell… I can barely tolerate his mouth on my breast. Every day I wish I'd never had the child. He destroyed my soul, sucked the life and beauty right out of me. He robbed me of any respect my husband had for me. It's like when he was growing inside me, he was consuming my life, and when he was pulled out of me, my whole life left with him. If people didn't force me to feed him, or take his care into their hands, I would just let him die. His birth has made me capable of that. He's turned me into this." Her voice wavered as if she realized she was talking to Keela. Vianca clapped her mouth shut and fought back her vulnerability in front of the other girl.

Keela shook her head incredulously. It was hard to imagine feeling that way about something innocent and so defenseless. "You were never one for compassion. Maybe you've always been this way and you just blame him because you're too weak to assume responsibility for who you are." Keela said.

Vianca's chin trembled. "You know *nothing* about my compassion," she hissed. "You know *nothing* about me."

"I can easily say that as well, however it never stopped you from judging *me.*"

"I was doing many things, but I wasn't *judging* you." Keela laughed out loud at this response

"...whatever you choose to believe to absolve yourself," Keela muttered. "How selfish you are to sit there and list all the things this innocent child has taken from you." She was purely disgusted. She put the child into his basket, and sat back, looking down her nose at this dismal shadow of the hellion that once was.

"And you're so perfect..." Vianca continued in a falsetto, "...little Miss Keela of the dark hair; prancing around with all her smarts and her freedom; nose in a book, following us all around like a worthless dog. A little Farkas orphan, little pauper, thinking herself grand and equal, all because my husband took pity on her. You make me ill. You made us *all* ill." Why they thought her Farkas was beyond Keela. There were lots of Yvremi with dark hair and dark eyes.

"I think I reached my limit with you when Dar started getting all soft on you. It made me want to *retch.*" Vianca said 'retch' as if she were gagging. "You filled out and got your curves and bosom, and took advantage of your freedom to wear immodest clothing. You pretended ignorance of the effect you had on men, throwing your assets about. Tempting the attentions of men away from worthier women. Fortunately most of them saw through your manipulation and wouldn't soil their thoughts on you. But Adarnoth; he was drawn in—it made me lose him forever... and I married a man old enough to be my father instead."

This was all news to Keela. She never saw herself as alluring... at all. She laughed at the absurdity of Vianca's words, and shook her head. "Please... Immodest gowns? I wore what my guardian could afford, and believe you me, there isn't a single gown that I have owned that has done anything for my figure or enhanced my form. They are all threadbare, patched and unfashionable as could be. And even if what you say is true, you wouldn't have been permitted to marry Adarnoth. He's too low-born for your father's tastes. Xanett was meant to take you as his wife from the moment you were born. Everyone knows that."

"I *did* have the choice!" Vianca screamed. "I *had* the freedom to choose, but *you* took it from me! And then your existence only continued to pollute my life, even after I was married…" Her eyes were wild, and her passionate exclamation drew the attention of the coachmen.

"My lady?" the driver called. Her mad expression melted, and she looked up at the ceiling.

"We're *fine!*" she spat. Her embittered eyes rolled down to look at Keela, and whispered, "You are a bane. A thief. A dark-haired ghoul."

Keela's eyes grew soft and she dropped her shoulders. She suddenly was overwhelmed with pity for Vianca. Keela had been her outlet to direct her rage against herself and her limitations.

"I've dreamt of murdering you, you know."

"Oh, Vianca." Keela slumped back onto her bench. Sympathetic tears filled her eyes as she glanced out the window. "How sad."

Vianca seemed unprepared for the pity. Her brow furrowed up into patches, and she withdrew a bit, eyes darting about in confusion.

"How very, very sad." Keela reached out and took Vianca's hands into hers. The girl didn't pull away, she only looked down as if the touch burned her; her expression startled and confused. Her hands were trembling, and her whole body seemed taught, and fragile, like a rope before it snapped.

"I had no idea," Keela continued. "It never occurred to me that you might feel trapped by your life. I always thought that you treated me so ill because you enjoyed it, because it made you appear more interesting to your friends. I understand everything now." A tear fell onto her cheekbone, and rolled down her cheek to her chin. Vianca's eyes followed it manically, her trembling body in suspension, her mouth partly open in bewilderment. "I'm sorry that your life's direction made you so miserable. But I never, ever, advertently took anything from you—or even tried. All I wanted to do was be accepted by some of you—it didn't matter who. I wanted so much to be part of all the things that you laughed about and talked about—and nobody ever let me. As for Adarnoth, I had no desire to take him from you. I had no feelings for him aside from just wanting to hear his jokes and be part of the circle that still shadows him around now. It wasn't necessarily the intelligence or content of the conversations that drew me… just the fun they all seemed to be having. It was awful being left out of everything. Awful." Keela paused, her gaze locked onto Vianca's own. She looked like she was about to explode. For the better or the worse, Keela did not know. She only knew she felt horrible for Vianca suddenly.

"I suppose I did have many more freedoms than you did, and I've never had the burden of a family legacy on my shoulders. I have never been told I would be cast into a certain marriage or life defined by someone else. I think I was one of the very few that didn't have some obligation or other awaiting me when I came of age. Maybe that's why you all hated me."

"You have no idea, do you?" Vianca whispered hauntingly.

"No, I never did. I'm sorry, Vianca. It's not as if I could have changed your attitude towards me by understanding it back then—I could not have changed what happened with Adarnoth either. I never suspected once that he had… gone *soft*… over me. He never showed it. He was just as cruel as you were."

"Oh, he was soft all right," Vianca muttered. "Tempting them all away…" She pulled her hands from Keela's, but gently. She leaned away again, her gaze trailing out to the view again. The trees had given way to open fields, and beyond that, the occasional glimpse of the ocean. They could even hear gulls somewhere over them. "You don't know."

Keela reached down for her bag, and put it onto the seat beside her. She withdrew a leather bottle, a bag with several rolls in it, and two small clay pots, each with a wax seal on it. She put each item along the bench seat before pulling out a largish bread roll. With a knife, she sliced it open, and put the bag of the remaining rolls back. She used the knife to pry the fragile wax seals off the top of the pots. Beneath one was a compote of berries, sweet and rich. The other was butter. She smeared butter on the bread roll first, and then the jam. She reached out and offered the first piece to Vianca, whose pale fingers grasped the bread. Keela ate the second, watching Vianca. Her nemesis sat across from her in silence, nibbling on her bread while tears dripped from her beautiful eyes.

 **Chapter 5**
Runaway

Edrick could hear Deyran cursing as they drew up behind a barge that was almost as wide as the canal. "That's a sea barge, it has no business this far inland. Look at the size of that thing! That'll slow things down," he grumbled through the open window of the steering house.

Deyran climbed out of the tiny door and stomped along the roof deck to the small mast from which the towline hung. He pulled in the line to bring the horses closer and clucked loudly with his tongue. The horses slowed and let the boat catch up a bit. The narrowboat was not quick by any means. How much slower a cargo barge moved seemed negligible in comparison, at least to Edrick. Deyran seemed quite put out by the presence of the wide interloper.

Edrick and Magpie sat on the roof of the boat at the prow, above the steps to the cabin. He was in his shirtsleeves, writing in a journal he picked up infrequently. The puppy sat beside him, her little body resting on its belly, her back legs folded tightly beside her. Magpie's front paws were hooked over the edge of the roof, and her eyes intently watched the barge ahead with interest. The barge had two dogs of its own; a pair of scruffy fawn-colored bull hounds. Not much of a barker as a breed, these two instead stood at the stern of the barge silently gazing back at the Ney wolf pup, their huge heads and tankish bodies bulky in comparison to Magpie's lanky, clumsy puppy limbs. Every now and again, she'd whine towards them.

"Look at those things. Beady little eyes…" Deyran grunted, startling Edrick who hadn't heard him approach. Both he and the pup looked up at Deyran. "They're quiet like, and they look harmless enough, but they'd tear your little girl up to pieces given the chance," he snarled. "Don't belong on a boat, those dogs. They belong on a cattle farm. Not the kind of dog I'd want."

"The boatman might find them useful. If he's carrying valuable loads, he might want dogs that can tear intruders to pieces," Edrick said. Deyran grunted at that response, so Edrick changed the subject. "You thinking about the kind of dog you want?"

"Aye, I've been thinkin' about it. Not one of them hounds. Maybe a dog from the winter lands. Like a deerhound of some sort." There was a moment of silence as he thought on it. Then Deyran blurted: "Hang this dolt in his whopping boat. We're stopping at the next town. This time of day these half-wits will likely move through without taking berth, so it will give him time to get far enough ahead to not be such a bloody hindrance. I think the town is only about an hour further, going at this intolerable speed. We can refresh our stores—we are low on ale—the little one can run a bit. Let's do that," he decided.

Edrick nodded blandly and turned to look at the barge again. The two dogs continued to glare at Magpie, who seemed only curious and full of yearning to play.

Although Deyran could have attempted to pass the barge where the canal widened, it would have been a difficult task as both banks of the canal were stacked with narrowboats and barges, two deep in some cases. With the masts and the various boats emptied of their crews, it wasn't likely they'd be able to get their towline over all the short masts with ease. So Deyran steered the vessel up to a barge and, with the captain's permission, he tethered his narrowboat to it. They had to cross over the boat to get to shore, but it was no real inconvenience. Soon the two men and the dog were ashore and headed towards a bustling market.

Magpie vanished sometime when Edrick was having a late lunch at a covered pavilion surrounded by food vendors. She had been comfortably tucked beneath the bench where he sat, happily accepting scraps from his boiled beef stew; and then she was gone. Where she went, Edrick did not know. His meal abandoned, he leapt to his feet.

"Has anyone seen my black pup?" he barked.

A few people responded, some pointing towards the square. He threw a coin on the table and broke into a run, his heart racing. It was impossible to know what alarmed him more; that he would fail whatever test this was in protecting this wolf, or that he had possibly lost his Magpie.

As he scoured the town for his dog in an increasing state of distress, he was directed by a merchant towards the friary of Assilan which was but a few minutes' walk from the periphery of town at the edge of the canal where it narrowed again. The merchant said that the friars would often take in lost and wayward animals and would keep them, even if never claimed. Edrick broke into a jog, arriving at the plain, single door on the face of the featureless edifice. He pulled the long bell cord, which was answered by a chorus of barks and howls. He waited. The barking was shushed, and at length he heard the approach of shuffling feet, accompanied by the click of a hundred dog-nails on stone pavers. The door was unlocked and pulled open.

A veritable cascade of dogs poured from the widening gap. They flowed around his legs in a roiling sea of wagging tails and wet noses. Behind them was a man in his fifties wearing a typical Assilan friar's habit.

The Assilan friars were an ancient order of world worshippers. They believed that the world was a living, intelligent entity that created and sustained all life upon it. The entity they believed in was called Raia, and she was known as the mother of all. It did not surprise Edrick that this would be the place where the stray dogs were collected. The Assilan cherished all living things. This friary cherished dogs most of all, it seemed.

The friar's habit was pale blue with a deep red hooded scapular over it. As with most of the order, the decoration was minimal on the overlay. A sacred friarly sister had likely applied the straightforward tamboured edgework in a buttercup yellow that adorned the friar's otherwise simple garments.

His most notable feature besides his softly smiling, clean-shaven face, was the bulbous heap on his head. Forbidden from cutting their hair, the Assilan friars hand-rolled skeins of their hair into ropes. As the hair grew longer, they wound it into a turban of sorts on their heads. Over this they would wear the large hood that hung from their shoulders—the tail of which swung to their calves—adorned with a string of tiny brass bells.

Friarly sisters—who likely occupied the other half of this abbey—were identically attired. There were never more than twenty of each in every friary. The population of this friary was well above forty for certain; as the dogs made up the majority of it. They milled about his legs and jumped up in attempts to lick his face.

"Down, down, you shaggy horde!" the friar exclaimed cheerfully. "Give the visitor a chance to say hello."

"Sacred Brother of Assilan, I wonder if anyone might have brought you a Ney wolf pup. She ran away from me in town, and I am eager to find her," Edrick said.

The friar's brow arched in interest, and he shook his head. "A Ney wolf you say? How did you come about getting one of those?"

"It's a long story," Edrick said. "She is unusual in that she has a white patch shaped like a bird in flight on the front of her chest."

The friar pursed his lips. "I would know if we had one of those here, and so would our dogs. None of our brothers or sisters have returned with one today, nor has anyone brought one to us, I'm afraid. But if they do, where can I find you?"

"I'm traveling by narrowboat towards the coast. I am aboard the *Stonesthrow.*"

"Very well. I will keep an eye out for your wolf, and if she comes, someone from the friary will bring her to you."

"I thank you," Edrick replied, defeated. He left the friary, and its many dogs, and spent another three hours searching the town and leaving directions with various merchants and city folk, should the missing Magpie be found.

Deyran was thoughtful and sympathetic and concluded that they had no other choice but to remain until Magpie was found. They spent the remaining afternoon and evening searching fruitlessly, and stopped only when it became too dark to carry on. Edrick and Deyran took pause at a tavern to have a late supper and a few ales, and to commiserate before going back to the boat. As they quietly consumed their generous portions of cabbage and ham, they overheard some patrons talking about a brutal attack.

"Throat torn out, arms ripped to shreds," one fellow said. The group of four men—who appeared to be local tradesmen and farmers—were huddled in chairs by the fire, clutching large mugs of hoppy beer. The others shook their heads slowly and muttered quiet words of incredulity.

"Metcoff said it was likely a wild dog or a wolf. He's gone to the friary to see if it could be one from their pack of hounds."

"Nobody we know then?"

"No. Nobody local. We expect someone will come looking for them. Must have been a big dog. The man was not a frail thing."

"Bull hound…" Deyran muttered under his breath to Edrick. He nodded with certainty. "I would wager ten gold erthings it was bull hounds."

"I hope Magpie didn't go looking for them," Edrick grunted.

The two men, slightly drunk, staggered back to the boat when the moon was high and full in the sky. They were astonished to find Magpie tied to the deck by a string of baling twine fastened around her neck. She whined and wriggled at the sight of her companion and Edrick felt a surge of stinging relief. He tore off the rope and cuddled her in his arms.

"Do not run away again little one," he whispered into her fur. He had allowed himself to imagine she had been killed by some savage dogs. He wondered at how she was returned, and figured it was the friars that had come upon her. Happy again, he climbed down into the cabin to ready for bed.

He lay there, staring at the moonlight-dappled wall of his berth, the dog snoring by his ear. Her body stretched along his chest, her head resting on his shoulder. He was struck by how strong his feelings were for this dog. He couldn't remember once in his life feeling that powerless and that emotional over anyone, dog or person. The prospect of her loss had filled him with a despair he had never felt before, and it shook him deeply. He reached up and stroked her soft fur with a sighed. He smirked in the darkness. *Stupid dog.*

The next morning as Deyran maneuvered the boat and horses from the town, they passed by the friary. The dogs were all out bounding along the banks beside the friar that Edrick had met. He was throwing sticks as he walked and the pack of dogs loped after them with tongue-lolling alacrity. Edrick climbed up onto the deck to thank the friar, but was surprised when he spoke first. "Oh, ahoy there, I hope you have found your lost dog! I cannot think you would leave without it," he called.

"She was returned to us. I thought it was by you. Am I mistaken?" Edrick asked.

The friar, with the great hood sagging over his ball of hair, looked strange and comical to Edrick. He also looked quite surprised.

"She never came to our friary, I'm afraid. Someone else must've found her. I'm glad you are reunited. They are precious, these dogs," the friar called from the shore, coming up behind the horses with his pack. The horses ignored the horde of canines coursing around their legs along the tow path. The friar gave a last smile, and his face vanished inside his hood as he made his way past the horses, ducking under the tow line.

Edrick's tried to remember if he had told anyone other than the friar what ship he was on. He was sure he had not. He merely told the people that asked to bring her to the friary if she was found. He looked up at the monk, who was now ahead of the horses with his dogs, and moving back inland to a broad, freshly ploughed field; the dogs along with him. Edrick furrowed his brow and shook his head. *Ah, never mind. I got her back, is all that matters.*

Chapter 6
The Leap of Faith

The sky opened up that day, and the rain didn't stop for four days as the coach traveled for what seemed like an endless journey along the coast. The bright colors of spring were washed with the ghostly tint of grey that had concentrated in the sky and banished the sun. The constant hammering sound of the rain and the wheels cutting through it was grueling. The humidity made everyone cold and uncomfortable, and the wet wind seeped in through the windows and the cracks, chilling the passengers to the core.

There was, thankfully, a scheduled stop that evening that would give the party a good full day of rest at a fine establishment; according to the coachman. Vianca had gone stone silent and barely responded when Keela prepared her for breastfeeding. The task of caring for the baby fell entirely on Keela otherwise. She would see to the laundering of his soiled nappies and clothing. She let the child huddle on her chest when he was restless for affection, and she hummed tunelessly to him at night until they both succumbed to utter exhaustion. His little sighs were tremulous and haunting. It was as if he knew he wasn't wanted or loved, and he clung desperately to anyone that offered anything remotely akin to those things. This was deeply saddening to Keela.

She sent a letter back home each chance she got, detailing these things to her mother, expressing her sadness and frustration as best she could. She felt that if she did not, she would be at risk of succumbing to the same despaired stupor that consumed Vianca.

Vianca often wept at night, when they were stopped to take rest. She remained remote and in a state of desolation. Keela could not help but wonder what this voyage would accomplish, if anything. Did Lord Xanett truly believe that it would perk up her spirits to be in a garden city? Or was it a way for him to escape the enveloping cloud of wretchedness that emanated from his wife; one so deep and dark that it felt as if one's soul was being drained of its vitality and caring? Keela might never know. What she did know was that the voyage so far was having the opposite effect. Vianca was getting more despondent and more detached with each passing day. The further they drew away from home, the lower she slumped into her seat, the less she cared about her toilette, and the more invisible her child grew to her.

Vianca went straight up to the rooms they had reserved upon arrival at the inn that evening. She remained there throughout the night and refused to open the door when the baby needed feeding. The coachman—with the help of the innkeeper—was able to find a wet nurse to provide the child nourishment, while Keela continued her efforts to persuade Vianca to eat.

Keela stared out to the whitecaps on the ocean, awed by it. They were close to the city of Calabras. Only a day away. She'd heard a little about the seaside town and its lovely sights. There was a great park in its center, and a famous collection of gardens strung together along the main coastal road. It was a place where many rich people sought refuge against the summer heat.. She was both elated and filled with dread. The idea of an end of being confined to the coach was appealing, but there was now the prospect of long months mired in a guest house with Vianca that chilled her. The inn where they now rested was situated on a bluff high above the rocky shore, overlooking the ocean. It was beautiful, but she did not have the luxury of enjoying it. She was burdened with a madwoman and the responsibility of a child. And Vianca was of such despairing spirits that even the coachman who oversaw their care was growing concerned.

He arranged for the child to remain in the care of the wet nurse for the remainder of the journey, and asked Keela to oversee the nurse. She agreed, glad the child would have more capable care.

The next morning as they were to leave, Keela—the baby in her arms—knocked on Vianca's door. Vianca appeared, a mess in all aspects—from her wild hair to her rumpled clothes—and declared she was going nowhere.

"Go back home. Take the coach, and that *thing*... I'm not going home. I'm not going to that insufferable city either. I'm staying here."

Keela frowned. "If I go back, then you should come back with me, Vianca. Your husband would never accept that we left you here alone."

Vianca glared malevolently at Keela, and suddenly, brusquely, grappled the baby into her arms, hugging him roughly to her chest. He began to cry. "Shut up, shut up!" she hissed at him, pacing in the corridor in front of her room. She abruptly pushed past Keela and trampled down the steps in a flurry of wrinkled skirts passing the footman as he managed Keela's trunk, and the wet nurse, who was sorting through the baby's bags in preparation for travel.

Vianca strode outside, and holding the baby, stopped in the yard. She looked utterly feral; her eyes filled with confusion and madness. Keela's stomach turned to ice. She was swiftly overcome with a sense of dread, and she knew that Vianca was about to do something foolish. She looked like an untamed beast. She held the child firmly against her, her fingers white from holding him so forcefully. Keela approached slowly, like one would approach a wild animal, her hand outstretched, her steps ginger and tentative. She was so close, she could smell Vianca's nervous sweat.

"Give me the child, Vianca. I'll watch him. I know it's hard. You're frightening him, and that's why he's crying. I'll quiet him…"

"Shut up, shut up, shut up!" Vianca replied, her mad eyes flashing. Vianca's grip on her baby tightened, and her strange, lost expression melted into something deeply sinister. She gave Keela a look that struck her cold. With a wicked smile crossing her lips, she said: "So stupid. You don't even see what you are. Farkas bitch. I hate you. Watch me ruin your future. My husband will have your head for this…" She then broke into a run towards the cliff, her skirts ballooning out behind her and whipping wildly in the wind. Keela took off after her, only a step behind, clawing out to catch hold of her or the baby. Vianca launched herself off the cliff only a fleeting second after Keela had miraculously gained purchase of the baby's lower arm, which had been hanging against Vianca's upper shoulder. The mother fell, careening down to the rocky wash as Keela landed hard on her stomach, knocking the wind from her. Her chest and upper half hung precipitously over the edge, her hand desperately clutching the dangling, wailing child.

She felt hands grappling at her legs as she was and pulled back from the precipice. She clutched the baby tightly to her chest as she wheezed and gasped for air. Her arms were scraped terribly from the gravely earth. The one that had held the baby had taken quite a beating. The nursemaid could barely pry her fingers from the baby's arm; for they had locked so tightly onto it that they remained clawed and taught for some time. Keela's breath was ragged and she was sobbing and shaking as the people from the inn, the coachmen and the wet nurse flocked around her and the baby. Keela's eyes were wide, the image of Vianca's body dashed upon the watery rocks below still burned into her mind.

Chapter 7
Calabras

They'd arrived at Neyat during the night, and Deyran insisted Edrick stay until morning. After a hearty breakfast shared with his boating friend, Edrick set off to find a conveyance to Calabras. It had been a challenge and at last he decided on a horse. The pup could ride in a saddle bag. He had sought out a livery and found himself a nice, reliable heavy breed steed, a used saddle and bags, a bridle, and a large travel bag to exchange for his trunk.

He then went off to find a few articles of new clothing in anticipation of meeting with Farkas representatives in the near future. There was something comforting and pleasurable in the idea of adorning himself in a gentlemanly fashion again. He looked forward to returning to the standard of living he was accustomed to, however much he did enjoy the narrowboat.

Edrick gave his host a generous gift of fifty gold erthings as a parting token. He had also given Deyran his trunk. It was too cumbersome for travel by horseback. The old man was beside himself with gratitude. He shook Edrick's hand vigorously, and he saw Edrick off. He bade the pup a farewell, too.

"Travel well young man," Deyran said with a smile.

After his horse was loaded and ready to go, he mounted and turned toward town in search of the much-used Seward Road leading out towards the coast. It was a pleasant journey accompanied by the recurrent traffic of riders, coaches, curricles, phaetons, carts, chaises, fancy barouches and several hands in four. He also encountered a tired-looking cohort of Jaratoom moving with a less-than-enthusiastic shuffle towards the merchant city Neyat, where Edrick had just left the narrowboat behind. They were led by a small group of cavalry officers who tipped their hats at Edrick respectfully as they passed. It was a long, seemingly endless line of men; two abreast, almost five-hundred souls. He imagined they would garrison somewhere outside the city.

He arrived at the garden town of Calabras in early afternoon. Understanding that it would not be too challenging to find the guest house at the park, he decided he had time to run some errands before he located it. First he had to make a stop at a banking concern to trade in some of his notes for coin currency. The notes weren't always trusted by many merchants no matter how official the crisp, crinkly papers appeared. He had spent almost every last coin he had on his person at Neyat.

He secured a purse of coins and lodged his horse at a stable. He made several stops at a few shops for incidentals. He then sought out the inn in question. He found the place at the town center, which was built like a great crescent, which enfolded a portion of the massive park that faced it. It was called Aliborne Park, and it was a piece of wilderness enclosed by a sprawling, beautiful town. He hoisted his bag onto his shoulder, and his dog under his arm, and approached the attractive townhouse.

Built of smooth sandstone, the building towered up four stories; it was wide, and was wedged between two houses of similar style, but made of different, darker stone. Tall windows peered out over the street and towards the park. The face was adorned with delicate architectural details added in marble, including two stately columns holding up a portico over the apple-red doors.

A simple marble plaque was embedded in the short half-wall that edged the street, by the entrance. It read: Aliborne Guesthouse. This was lodging meant for the highborn and the rich. It looked the part. And Edrick felt too coarse and dirty to walk through the doors, but he knew a bath and some clean clothes would solve that sense of inadequacy right away. With all the unknowns awaiting him, he had at least that to look forward to.

He was greeted at the door by the owner—an ample, formidable looking woman with a hard face and narrowed, critical eyes. She gave him a once over and glowered without subtlety.

"I've been traveling a ways, dear lady. I do hope you don't mistake me for a vagrant. I am no such thing. I do, however, require your finest rooms if you have them. I am exhausted and hungry, and I could certainly use a tub full of soapy water," he said to her in his most patrician accent.

She glanced at him again, and then down at the dog. He lifted his purse, heavy with coins, and shook it. She relented at the pleasing jingle of coins and gestured for him to enter. "I am called Mrs. Bellham," she informed him. She grasped her chatelaine from the high waist of her gown, and removed a key from one of the many chains that dangled from it. "Follow me, sir," she said haughtily.

She led him up the stairs—two fights—to a rather large apartment with a full sitting room and a separate sleeping room. There was also a bathing chamber with a hefty brass tub beckoning to him.

"Dinner is promptly at the sixth hour. The clock will chime. It is downstairs through the white doors. There are other guests. I do hope you will be considerate of them and be punctual, sir," she said. He assented with a nod.

"We will worry about your payment and your registration when

103

you are settled. You have a couple of hours until mealtime. Use it to your advantage. I will send hot water up for your bath immediately," she declared. She placed the key in his hand and he watched her sail out of the room. He put Magpie down on the floor and his bag on the chest at the foot of the bed. He began to peel away his outer layers, which were still slightly damp from the brief rain that had fallen that morning and made the road muddier than it already was.

As promised, a trio of young men marched in succession for a good quarter of an hour, bringing large basins of steaming water up to fill his tub. Shavings of scented soap were mixed into the water like spices to a broth. When the tub was a little over half filled, they ceased their march and left Edrick to his soak. He stripped down and steeped himself in the fragrant water until his fingers and toes wrinkled. Satisfied and relaxed he rose out of the tepid water and dried himself off.

He shaved off the grizzle of a beard that had grown in over the past few days, and trimmed around his sideburns. He then put on some of his recently acquired stockings, and a pair of slippers he purchased the day before. He next donned the lighter breeches, a shirt of snow white with a crisp collar, a thin waistcoat and a silk frockcoat. He styled his hair, and then took the little Miss Magpie out to the edge of the park for a brief stroll.

He returned in time to see Magpie to their room, and to write his name in the registry under the supervision of Mrs. Bellham, who was astonished by the transformation of her newest guest. He paid for the night, with the option to extend. "I'm not sure how long I will be here. I do hope this isn't inconvenient to you, Madame."

"Oh, no Mr. Bethranorn. No indeed," she assured him, whispering his name. Unlike previous inn keepers, this lady was aware of who he was, and was the kind of person who respected discretion.

With that, the sixth bell rang and the sound of feet pattered about the house, doors opening and closing. Mrs. Bellham gestured for him to precede her into the parlor where the guests would enjoy an aperitif before dinner. She poured him some port, and invited him to sit. Before his backside could meet the sofa, the door opened and a young woman entered.

Like the lady he'd met at Eyome, this creature took his breath and his senses away. Although her traits were much like the Farkas woman, her mannerisms were not. He straightened his posture as she moved into the room. She was tentative and restrained, her gaze never meeting anyone else's for more than a flash. Her eyes looked completely black at first glance, but upon closer scrutiny, he saw that the black contained flecks of luminous grey which were revealed in certain light, like raw shards of iron ore. She wore a simple arrangement, like most ladies did these days: White muslin gown over a tulip red petticoat.

"Miss Keela, may I introduce you to our most recent guest, Mr. Edrick," the hostess intoned, using his first name to respect his privacy. He liked the imposing woman, he decided. He bowed shallowly to the girl, unable to tear his gaze from her heart-shaped face and dark, bottomless eyes. Keela curtseyed clumsily, her shadowy eyes flashing up to look at him. "Miss Keela, would you care for a glass of port?" he asked.

"No thank you," she replied gently. Her sleeves were elbow length, and on the bottom side of her right arm was an immense bruise that ran from her wrist up to her elbow, possibly beyond. Her other arm had scrapes along the underside that had scabbed over. The bruise, however, was startlingly dark and painful looking. She also had a little scratch on her delicate chin.

"The other two guests will be arriving soon. In the meantime, I will see to the child and the wet nurse, miss," Mrs. Bellham said with a nod to Keela before exiting the room.

"So much for being prompt," Edrick said jokingly.

Keela offered him a brief glance and an uncomfortable smile. He had at first thought that this young woman was perhaps the person he was supposed to meet, but it could not be. Not with her reticence and her timidity.

"If I may be so forward to ask? Your injury... I hope it isn't serious."

She looked at him squarely, and then shook her head. "No, I am not badly injured. Just some bumps and bruises. I took a bit of a fall."

His brows rose, his gaze still lingering upon her. "Where do you hail from?"

"Veros," she replied shortly. Her accent had the lilt of a commoner, but her words also the unmistakable enunciation of a well-educated person. It was intriguing to Edrick.

"I see. I don't often encounter new mothers traveling with their babies. It is most unusual."

"He is not my child. I am looking after him until his father arrives," she replied. She was growing progressively anxious. She was wringing her hands and glancing about, her jaw rippling from chewing her tongue. Edrick's curiosity was too strong to relent.

"You're a governess?" he asked.

She paused for a second. She then turned and looked at him straight-on. "No. I was a travel companion for his mother. She threw herself from the cliffs at Enyesh two days ago and died a horrible death. The coachman brought me and the child here to wait until the child's father could come and collect us."

Edrick's blanched and he felt unexpectedly mortified for forcing the conversation. "Good lords, I apologize sincerely for that. I would never have..."

"It's fine," she said irritably. Her shoulders relaxed and she shook her head slightly. "Honestly, I thought I'd shock you into silence by telling you, but felt awful the moment it came out of my mouth. I don't know why..." she groaned for a lack of words.

"I know why," he admitted. "It is perfectly understandable. I was being dim-witted and brash. I apologize again."

She peered at him in earnest and sighed in relief. It was a tremulous, broken sigh.

"Sounds like you've been through a great deal these past few days," he said. "I imagine you will be glad to go home."

"You couldn't have said anything truer," she muttered. He could only nod, his eyes lingering on her arm. She caught his stare, and gave another little sigh. "She tried to jump with the baby. The bruise is from grabbing the child and nearly falling behind her with him."

He gaped at her for a second. "You're a bloody hero," he blurted, his eyes widening.

She scoffed and then shook her head, her mannerisms slipping into the easy ways of a common girl. "Don't be ridiculous…"

She was cut off as the parlor door opened and the two other guests entered followed by the visibly irritated hostess. "This is Miss Kamb and her brother, Mr. Eddle Kamb," Mrs. Bellham declared with forced kindness in her tone. She completed the introductions and served up a glass of sherry for each of the newcomers.

There was idle chatter, and then the dinner announcement was made. It wasn't long before they were all seated around a large oval table eating a robust meal in a restrained and awkward silence. The sound of forks and knives ringing on plates was the only sound. Mrs. Bellham attempted to fire up some discourse, only to be answered with nods and grunts of agreement.

The group then retreated to the drawing room after dinner. Mr. Kamb asked Edrick if he wished to play billiards, to which Edrick declined. "I would rather stay here with the ladies. I've been traveling with a boat captain for many days, and am starved for gentle company."

Mr. Kamb bowed shallowly and left the room. Edrick remained next to Miss Keela, who was reading from a book she produced from a pocket hidden in the side of her skirts.

"At risk of irritating you, I wonder if I might engage you in a few words, Miss Keela. About your journey. I am curious. But if you do not wish to speak of it, I understand," he said.

Keela dropped her book to her knee and smiled sadly. "I don't mind. My mother would probably tell me it is good to talk about the difficult things. What questions do you have?"

"The girl who died, was she your friend?"

"No. Not even close. She was not my friend at all. I wasn't too fond of her, either. We knew one another from childhood. She never liked me." Her words were short and forthright.

Edrick continued expectantly. "But you accompanied her?"

"Her husband is my mother's patron. I didn't have a choice." Keela's eyes flashed with hurt and anger. "It was torture to begin with. Now I have the consequences and memories to carry."

"She was *that* awful?"

"I don't like to speak ill of people with mere acquaintances," she retorted. But then she suspired. "But there's also the benefit of your not knowing me or her, so I suppose I can be frank. Yes. She was a harpy." As she said this, Mr. Kamb returned to the room and sat with his sister. The siblings smiled at them wanly and then stood to look at the options at the game table. Keela and Edrick waited until they were settled before they continued their conversation.

"Was she overtly cruel to you? Or the kind of cruel that is insidious and passive?" Edrick asked.

"She was a contemptible, selfish, angry person from the moment we met until she flung herself off that cliff. She made no effort to hide her disdain, or to be clever in her delivery of it." Keela paused as Mrs. Bellham entered and offered a round of drinks.

She asked Miss Kamb to play the pianoforte, and Miss Kamb delightedly agreed to. She got up and began to stumble her way through the March of the Swans. Keela gave Edrick a sidelong glance that embodied her displeasure at this horrendous music, and he actually snorted with laughter.

He was so curious, he could barely stand it, but they respected the protocol and remained respectfully quiet until Miss Kamb finished murdering the piece of music. She returned, glowing, to her brother, who congratulated her on a job well done. Keela clapped affectedly, and then, angled her body back towards Edrick with a look of relief on her face.

"Tell me about this woman."

Keela's brow knit in the most appealing fashion. She proceeded in a whisper, leaning in towards him. The Kambs and Mrs. Bellham were taking up a game of cards and were quietly playing. "Her name was Vianca. She was, without a doubt, one of the angriest people I've ever met. Even when she was being magnanimous and seemingly kind to others, there was still an inner layer of ire. Her resentment... it ate her up inside. The older she got the more malignant she became. It wasn't uniquely towards me. But it was focused often on me.

"In the short time with her these past days before she died, I discovered that her awfulness towards me was more about her. That it was something about herself that she hated, and she merely transferred that odium onto me because I was different. But her husband and the other people in her life were not immune to her hateful character. She even despised her own baby."

"Good gods!" Edrick exclaimed.

Keela frowned grimly. "She called her child an 'it'. And I still don't know what his name is. She never told me. He was always just 'it'." She glowered and her shoulders tensed. "That poor child will know deep down his mother didn't want him. Poor thing was starved for her affection. He's so unnaturally quiet and watchful for a baby. He knows even now that he was not loved by his mother. I am sure of it." Edrick watched her eyes darken. "I know she is dead. And I know that her dislike of me wasn't motivated by anything real or honest, but her cruelty still stings me, in spite of my understanding. It still sticks with me. It makes me feel harder for the baby—knowing that he, too, has been the object of her resentment. Growing up with her criticism and her unkindness, it still colors how

I perceive everyone…" she paused, thoughtfully. Edrick shifted on the sofa, scooting just a bit closer to Keela, admiring her face and the animation of her dark, dark eyes. She tilted her head—a whimsical smile crossing her lips.

"Ejesh is a friend of mine," she continued. "He's rather a bit of a recluse, and he doesn't come out much. He lives near an old man whom I care for at Veros. Ejesh has a little farm on the edge of town. He is a strong, burly fellow. He's handsome in his own right, but he's quite conscious of an impediment he has when he speaks. He cannot say the *s* sound. It comes out more like *sh*. He was mocked for it relentlessly as a child and it has made him reluctant to participate in conversations with others, or make friends.

"A few weeks before I left home, a traveling merchant arrived and set up shop. He was a seed trader and he positioned his cart outside of town only a few streets from Ejesh's home. Ejesh went to buy seeds from him. He walked with me since it was on my way home. I stopped to wait for him to buy seeds. And next thing I know Ejesh and the seed seller were both exchanging blows and rolling in the muck of the street, fighting like animals.

"It took two bloody noses and some bruised knuckles for them to discover that they both possessed the same impediment," Keela explained, a smile creeping onto her lips. "Each thought they were being mocked by the other, imitating them as other people had so cruelly done to them for years. The realization that this was a coincidence only came to them after they threw some blows. Neither of them stopped to think that someone had to speak first. That neither of them knew the other. They were so keyed to be angry and to expect mockery."

Edrick could not help but laugh softly.

"It made me realize how deeply the unkindness of others can bury itself into people. And people are unkind all the time, sometimes without even realizing it. How just a passing snide remark can stain a person's entire life…" she turned the book in her hand, gazing down at her fingers. "I don't know what poisoned Vianca. Or why she was the way she was. I know there was something there that made her so awful. But it doesn't stop me from feeling the pain she inflicted upon me, sometimes by her own hand and sometimes by the hand of others."

"Is it too forward to ask how she was cruel? It what way?" he asked.

Keela shrugged. "In every way. I was spat on and called Farkas rubbish. I had droppings thrown at me. I was shoved to the ground, locked in a closet at school, tripped, shoved, kicked, punched… those things mostly happened as a child. When we got older, it became more personal. Gossip of the most malicious kind, which would end in shunning all over the city. She just couldn't stand that I was there, breathing and existing. It was too much for to bear. It was like my very being was an offense to her. I think it reminded her about something about herself, I suspect. I may never know the source of it now. And now, I feel only pity for her. And her poor, poor baby." Her voice trailed off. She stared off into nowhere for a second or two, and then straightened, looking at Edrick squarely. "I now only have to wait for her husband to come. And I fear that he will be angry at me for failing to watch over her. Before she threw herself off the cliff, she taunted me. She told me that her husband would punish me for this."

Edrick's brows rose in incredulity. "He could not blame you for what she did. You saved his child. He will be grateful to you for that."

She shrugged. "I hope so. My mother's livelihood depends upon him. If he is angry, it could upset a great deal for her. I'm young, I have options. She is not so young, and too old to keep traveling as she used to. I can only sit by and wait. I will not speculate any further because it only creates unnecessary anxiousness." Despite her words, he could see she worried about it.

Edrick watched her as she shyly twisted her lip into a helpless smile, and cracked open her book again. He let her continue to read, but he remained seated beside her. This unlikely creature now occupied his thoughts entirely.

"You know, you are accused of being Farkas… perhaps you should accept it and make friends with a Farkas dog," he suddenly said.

Her brow furrowed, and she looked up at him in puzzlement. He held up his finger and got up, excusing himself from the room.

He scurried up the stairs and unlocked his door where Magpie pined and wiggled in delight at the sight of him. He picked her up and carried her downstairs, barging into the room with her in his arms. Keela's mouth dropped open and then spread into a girlish grin.

"Oh my goodness!" She stood up and immediately took possession of the puppy. The other guests looked on in astonishment. Magpie's reaction to meeting Keela was one to be remembered. She squealed and squirmed and licked Keela's face as if she were being reunited with a long-lost sister. Edrick was staggered by it.

"A Ney wolf! A *real* Ney wolf!" Keela whispered, trying to cuddle the wiggling puppy and kiss her face. "Look at her chest… there's white on her. That's so remarkable. I wonder if she was branded or wounded and the fur grew back white…" She touched the pup's skin, her eyes filled with inquisitiveness.

"I don't know. It is unusual isn't it? That's why I called her Magpie. Sort of looks like a bird doesn't it? And she's black with white."

Keela agreed with a delighted smile. "Where? Where did you find her?"

The light in Keela's eyes was enthralling, the joy in her expression magnetic. Edrick knelt where Keela had sunk to the floor with the puppy writhing on her knees. He caressed the dog's head, and that calmed her a bit. She still tried to wriggle in Keela's arms.

Magpie found a comfortable spot to rest, laying her head in the crook of Keela's arm. Magpie exhaled happily and slapped her tail on Keela's knee.

"She was given to me. To care for. I hope to keep her. I've become quite attached."

"How could you not? She is perfection." Keela's eyes were misty. "Absolute perfection," she whispered. "Magpie." She ran her free hand along the puppy's silken, raven fur, and admired the pewter eyes that gazed at her adoringly.

"Who gave you this beautiful creature? Oh, she will be a beast when she's grown. She's got paws the size of saucers," she giggled, picking up the large, ungainly paw. Keela kissed her head again.

"A Farkas girl. I was to bring her to Calabras. Those were my instructions. I am now here waiting for what's next. Not to be insulting, but when I saw you, I thought perhaps you were the person I was to meet."

Keela snorted at that and shook her head. "No. But I wish I were. I'd happily take her off your hands." She grinned. "I never had a dog." She then rose to her feet and sat properly in the chair, with the puppy on her lap.

The other guests looked on still, but said nothing. They sipped their drinks and returned to their cards. Edrick sat down next to the girl and the dog, and watched them. He, too, wished it was Keela he was supposed to meet, for he wanted an excuse to continue their acquaintance. He watched her pale, gentle hand caressing the dog into a quiet contented cuddle.

"You are not a conventional young woman, Miss Keela," Edrick observed.

She glanced up at him with her dark eyes. "I was raised by an unconventional woman. I call her my mother, but she is not. She traveled a great deal, and has seen much of the world all on her own. She gave me a different perspective of the world, I think. I had tremendous freedom. Far more than any of the other young people in my village. I have not lived richly, but I have lived with a privilege many have not enjoyed."

"Yes, I can see that. Perhaps that was what your poor tormenter resented about you."

"It was one of the many things. She admitted as much." She petted Magpie sweetly, and rubbed her ears. "This wolf is perfection," she said wistfully.

He smiled at her, and for a moment, they gazed at one another. There was an understanding that somehow passed between them at that moment. Keela's cheeks flushed and Edrick, unfamiliar with this sort of infatuation, was scarce able to control himself. He had not employed a single ploy from of his arsenal of flirtations upon Keela., yet for the first time he knew of, he actually desired to flirt with her. Somehow he knew that his usual advances would seem like a joke to her. She was too clever; too honest. He wasn't sure exactly what would work with Keela. It was maddening.

"You are welcome to cuddle her as long as we are here. I'm not even sure *I* can keep her, so I could not offer her to you even if I wanted to," he teased. She laughed through her nose.

"I was only jesting. I would never ask to keep her in earnest. I adore her, but you do too, I can see. I am not so cruel as to take away something you so very much love." Keela's hematite eyes sparkled at him, melting Edrick's soul. He offered her a slightly lamenting smile, sad that he would not know her for much longer. He was even further irritated that he lacked the ability to express his interest in a way that would not make this intriguing creature laugh at him.

Keela liked Edrick. She found his quiet, easy air endearing. In her eyes, he was a gentleman without airs. She liked his dog even more.

She glanced up again to catch a glimpse of his face. His walnut colored eyes were deep and thoughtful, set below a brooding brow.

His hair was also the same shade of brown with a devil-may-care tousled curl in it, falling onto his forehead and temples; his sideburns, well manicured and running down onto his jaw. He wore the fashions of a rich man. His shirt the whitest of white, the collar high against his jaw line, his cravat crisp and starched.

He was the sort of young man that she would think well out of her reach. She would see him from afar and simply acknowledge his handsome looks and move on. She never would have imagined him to be so approachable, so warm and kind. She was, in all honesty, shocked and confused by him. She could not recall any young man unconnected to her, and so markedly above her, treating her so kindly. She flushed at his attention. She wasn't sure how to feel about it, but she knew that she welcomed it. How her mother would laugh if she knew that Keela were blushing over a fellow. She could not think of any other young man she knew who made her feel quite so charmed and flustered.

She held the precious pup for a while longer, and then Mrs. Bellham prompted everyone to retire, and the guests rose from their quiet groupings.

Edrick took the puppy and bowed elegantly to Keela before scaling the steps to his room. Keela followed, entering the small set of apartments that she shared with a hired nanny and the baby. The baby was asleep already, and the nanny was nodding off in the chair in the sitting room. Keela's entrance woke her. She helped Keela out of her gown and into her night clothes. It was strange to have someone assist her in what she had always done on her own.

Keela slid into the plush bed, one finer than she'd ever slept in before, and nestled down into the pillows. Thoughts of Edrick filled her head. With a frustrated sigh, she rolled onto her side and closed her eyes. Lord Xanett would be there soon to fetch her, and this nightmare turned dream would end. She would be back to her ordinary life soon enough.

First thing at breakfast, Edrick sidled down to the dining room, choosing not to sit until Keela arrived so he could find a spot beside her. She looked a bit drawn and tired, but her cheeks and ears flushed at the sight of him, and a shy smile spread over her face.

"Good morning, Mr. Edrick," she said quietly.

"My surname is Bethranorn," he whispered to her. "I thought perhaps you might wish to join me, and more importantly, Magpie on a nice walk after breakfast? I know it's unseemly to go about without chaperones. Perhaps your nanny and the baby can accompany us? But the poor pup should not be confined to the room as much as she is, and as long as I'm here with no direction, I thought perhaps I could do something pleasant in the interim. What do you think?"

Keela bowed her head and smiled a bit, and then turned to look at him, her fork resting on her plate.

"I think that's a grand idea, Mr. Bethranorn," she replied, her cheeks burning.

He set to eating, a cheerful look on his face. They did not speak much as they ate, and instead listened to the other guests—a new one had arrived early that morning—chatting about the state of the roads and discussing the possible war and the movements of the Jaratoom and city-state armies. The new guest was an older man of about sixty years with fine features and an aristocratic air about him. He peered at Keela with suspicion as he spoke to the Kambs.

Keela was accustomed to the looks she got for appearing so Farkas, and ignored them. She realized that Edrick was the first person she ever met who simply embraced her appearance rather than treating her differently because of it.

"I heard the girl call you Bethranorn before," the new man barked across the table to Edrick. "Are you a one of *the* Bethranorns?"

"I *am* the Bethranorn, actually," Edrick retorted with an uncharacteristically condescending tone. The man immediately bowed his head, and fell silent. Keela didn't know what this signified, but the man's bold, confident manners were subdued afterwards. Mrs. Bellham smirked quietly and served Edrick more tea. When they had eaten their fill of ham, eggs and toasted bread, Edrick stood and bowed to Keela.

"Shall we meet in the drawing room in half an hour? I imagine you will require time to change into a walking dress and to make arrangements for the child to accompany us?"

Keela stood and curtsied, exiting before him. She heard the new guest asking Edrick politely if he was courting a Farkas lady. Edrick did not reply and exited shortly after, only to catch Keela's eye as she climbed the stairs. He gave her an amused grin and she returned it.

She changed into her nicest walking dress, a trained cotton gown in a burnt red. She donned the pale ivory bonnet that her mother had gotten for her, a tasteful hat with a square top and twisted box crown that ended in a round, narrow brim that encircled her head. It had a handsome cockade of gold with sapphire feathers arched over the top in a mound of billowing, white ostrich feathers. Her soft leather walking boots adorned her feet. She minced down the stairs, feeling like an impostor, and entered the drawing room to find Edrick waiting in a fine blue coat, with Magpie wriggling at his feet.

She curtsied. "The nanny will join us out front," she told him. He bowed and gestured her to precede him out the door.

Outside, they met with the plump, sweet-faced girl who had been selected to care for Lord Xanett's baby. Her own baby was nestled next to the lord's child in a shell-shaped pram. The coachman, who had arranged everything for Keela and the baby, was at present just finishing assembling the parts of this unusual device.

"My goodness, that's an intriguing contraption," Edrick blurted to Keela.

"It was packed with the many things the Lady was bringing along. I didn't even know what it was when I saw the wheels. It is a strange thing, is it not?" Keela replied.

The nanny picked up a long, tiller-like handle with which she would pull the device. Keela had never seen anything like it. *Only the rich*, she sighed to herself. The nanny tucked a blanket over both babies, who were cooing and kicking their little feet—her child a little smaller than the Lord's—and began to walk ahead, pulling the babies in the spindly, four-wheeled, shaded basket. Edrick and Keela followed; Magpie running gleefully at their feet.

"What comes next for you, Miss Keela?" Edrick asked.

"Back to my old life of making jewelry and taking care of my mother and Loralo," she replied. "That is, if the Lord doesn't blame me for what happened."

"You said she was a troublesome lady. I imagine he might be a bit relieved to be rid of her if that's the case."

Keela laughed sardonically and shook her head. "I confess, if I were he I would have hated being married to her, too. If she behaved like she was with me all the time, the marriage must have been untenable. I'll know what he feels in time. He should be arriving soon. He's on horse, so it'll be faster than the coach. And I doubt he'll stop as much as Vianca made us stop."

"I hope to still be here so you have someone to stand beside you if the situation becomes difficult," Edrick offered.

Keela blushed again, and felt the unexpected burn of grateful tears sting her eyes. It was the first time she could ever remember someone other than her mother, Ejesh or Loralo show concern about her welfare. She bowed her head and hid her emotion, her heart glowing warmly inside her chest for the attentions and kindness of this handsome, strange man.

"Thank you," she croaked.

 **Chapter 8**
Foraging the Wild

Being rather unfit, the nanny quickly grew tired from pulling the pram. They had at that point reached the distant trout pond in the park. On its grassy banks was a fine, old walnut tree that cast its canopy out over the thick, velvety grass. A few sheep grazed nearby, cropping the long grass into a soft, dense pile. It was a nicely treed area where nobody else was to be seen. Keela suggested they stop and rest.

They laid out the quilted blanket that the babies were sitting on, and the nanny and two babies were deposited in the shade where the nanny could tend to them and feed them in peace. Keela then picked up a stick from the ground and goaded Magpie into a growling tangle of puppy limbs, playing tug of war and chase.

Edrick laughed openly and heartily as Keela giggled and cavorted with the dog. Her hat tumbled off her head and rolled off into the grass. He, too, then shucked his frock coat and joined in, and they ran and played by the water until they fell to the ground laughing, desperate to catch their breath. Magpie threw herself across Keela, grinning with her tongue lolling, as happy as any

119

playful pup.

Edrick plunked down beside Keela and looked down at her. Her eyes were trained up at the sky. "This is the first time I've ever left Veros since I was little. I hate that it had to be under these circumstances that I finally got to get out and to see the world," she declared. She rolled onto her side and propped her head on her hand, leaning on her elbow.

"I'm sorry I'm not ladylike. They always made fun of me because of it; because I climbed the watchtower, and went hunting for crawfish in the river. Vianca called me a Farkas savage more times than I can count, because of my muddy hems and the burrs in my hair. I never quite understood her logic, since the Farkas are far more sophisticated and civilized than we are. But that was what she decided I should be."

"All those things sound perfectly lady-like to me," he replied. "I was never much permitted to forage about like that when I was a child. I did enjoy it when I did have the chance. Most of the time I spent outdoors was in the gardens of my family's home where there was nothing wild. Every shrub was trimmed and every leaf raked. But I would hide under then great domes of rhododendrons and pretend they were great forests in the wilderness."

"You must have been born to a rich family, then," Keela concluded. It was utterly unheard of to raise the question of money and riches in idle conversation, but Edrick did not even flinch.

"Yes. I would be a highly ranked member of aristocratic society if the Farkas hadn't dismantled the government. My immediate family was careful to protect its assets and to invest wisely. We hardly stumbled at all, really. For the lower ranked relatives, it was a completely different story. People who knew nothing but comfort and ease were cast out of their ancestral homes and made paupers."

Keela sat up, and Edrick could not help but drink in the way her hair caught the light, and how her flyaways made a halo around her beautiful face. Magpie was still lying across her legs, her head now resting on her front paws. Keela was petting her unconsciously.

His memory was suddenly thrown back to his journey through Eyome, and how he had frowned upon the cheese maker girl and her friends. How he had thought so little of them. He knew this was pride instilled in him from childhood. It never felt wrong until he climbed aboard the *Stonesthrow* and met a commoner he liked. It felt even more awful now that he found himself slightly besotted by this strange girl. To him, her common behavior did not seem common. It just seemed easy and likeable. He felt comfortable with her in a way he only felt in the company of his youngest sister, Dayna. Keela did not cower or simper because of who he was. She really didn't care even now that he alluded to his status. He felt badly for thinking ill of those girls, and for frowning on the commoners as he had. Keela came from that same stock, and he found her fascinating and beautiful.

"Don't we make a pair? A wild, ostensibly Farkas orphan, and what? A fancy fop?" she said.

He chuckled and shook his head. "A crownless king," he corrected her.

"Well lah-dee-dah," she cried, pretending to bow to him from her partly reclined position. "Your Highness, King of Wolf Pups!"

Edrick had never considered himself a romantic man. He had enjoyed the company of women in a temporary sense for most of his life; flirting overtly with ladies, dancing and sometimes even half-heartedly courting some to please his family; all to no end. He had left a string of broken hearts in his wake, never quite interested in anything lasting. It was too complicated for his wayward life. He liked the freedom to go where he wished without worrying about upsetting someone. He wasn't prepared to commit to rearing children and such things. His now deceased father had badgered him relentlessly to cease his philandering and to settle down. His father had always had something to say about Edrick's uselessness and idleness, his irresponsible and selfish nature. He reminded Edrick continually what a great disappointment he was to his family.

But Edrick was so greatly drawn to this common girl. All he wanted to do was to lean forward and kiss her. She was the antithesis of everything his family hoped for in a wife for him—and something he had never imagined he'd find himself entangled with. But he did not care. This was the first time in all his life he'd ever felt this kind of attraction for anyone. He could not stop thinking of her when she was not with him, and he could not get enough of her when she was.

He resolved that this was the woman for him, regardless of his family's preferences. He wasn't beholden to bloodlines anymore. Not officially. He watched her talk about how she and her mother's occupation was to create beautiful jewelry for people of his breeding, her fingers finding a tiny daisy as she spoke. She plucked it, and poked it behind her ear. He wrapped his arms around his knees, propped his chin on them, and listened intently, his heart growing fonder with every beat.

The nanny returned the babies to the pram—now fed and sleepy—and began folding up the quilt. Keela groaned and got to her feet, stamping gracelessly across the grass. She bent to scoop up her hat, her train slithering across the grass behind her elegantly. She brushed the dirt from her bonnet and sauntered back, Magpie trailing her all the while. Edrick followed suit and got to his feet, picking up the rumpled pile of frock coat, shaking it and pulling it on.

"Where to next?" she asked. "Shall we explore this whole park?"

"I suppose it depends on how far our companion wishes to go," he replied.

The nanny, who was just approaching, furrowed her brow. "I hope you don't mind, but I'd like to make my way back, Miss. The babies both need to be changed." Keela looked at Edrick with apprehension.

"I can't see why not," she said when he merely smiled at her.

"Are you comfortable going on your own?"

The nanny curtsied. "I was born at Calabras. I know the paths well." She turned the tiller on the pram and hauled it back the way they had come. Edrick shrugged and proffered his elbow, which Keela accepted.

"How awful of us, wandering about without a chaperone," she said in a forced, haughty voice. "Let's go to that old folly that I saw from my window. I think it's atop a hill that way." she pointed down a path that led into a tunnel of trees.

He thought on it and bowed low, gesturing with his arm for the Miss to proceed. She did, putting on her bonnet and smiling broadly. He watched her stride ahead, her skirts with the high back billowing out gracefully behind her, the feathers on her bonnet flouncing.

The path did, indeed, lead upwards. He followed Keela, who seemed to possess an endless fount of energy for exploring. He remained a good length behind her, watching her head swivel about. She reached out to touch the velvety leaves of a foxglove growing on a steep bank, and threw back at him a succession of smiles which he returned.

Abruptly, out of what seemed like nowhere, two black streaks emerged from the shrubbery on Keela's right, and pounced on her. Keela screamed and fell underneath two silver-eyed Ney wolves that both attacked her viciously. Her arms went up to protect her face and her scream echoed out into the trees. Magpie, who'd been running back and forth between them before the attack, jumped into the fray, and yelped as she was bitten. Edrick had already begun to run towards them, but stopped cold.

He watched transfixed as Keela, upon Magpie's yelp, roared out in fury, and rose to her feet with almost preternatural fluidity. Her back hunched with a lurch and her dark eyes flashed, and then turned bright, shining silver. What followed was impossible.

Right before his eyes, Keela transformed with incredible swiftness into a wolf. Her body slipped right out of her clothes.

She threw her massive, dark lupine body at the one of the other wolves in a violent tousle. She bared her teeth—white and sharp—champing and snarling. Once she grounded the first dog, which let out a painful, she turned on the second. She assaulted the creature brutally, tearing at its ears and biting at its throat.

They wrapped themselves into a growling, snarling ball that rolled along the path until one of the canines—Edrick could no longer determine which one it was—cried out. It scuttled off into the trees whimpering. The first attacker limped after it. The remaining wolf—which he now saw was significantly larger than the others by a good measure—was now standing with its head lowered, growling in a resonant, bass rumble and snarling after the other wolves. Its jowls were wrinkled up to reveal a fearsome set of razor sharp teeth. Its hackles bristled into a thick patch on its shoulders. Magpie cowered between its legs as if seeking protection.

When the attackers were out of sight, the wolf pivoted its head to peer at Edrick, who was frozen in horror. With a slow blink of its pewter eyes, it gazed at him. Then it looked away, padded a few steps from Magpie, and unexpectedly crumpled onto the ground into a heap of bare, smooth, beautiful human limbs.

Keela snapped to alertness again at the sensation of her face being licked. She winced. Her forearm had a fresh scattering of scrapes on it, and she had a rather deep gash on her hip that hurt tremendously. She was disoriented. Uncertain of what she just experienced. Unsure if it was real.

Edrick's familiar face appeared before her as he laid his frock coat over what she realized was her naked body. She sat up quickly and balled herself up beneath the spare garment. Edrick's face was waxen, his expression both frightened and concerned.

"Here, let me help you get your gown back on…"

"What happened?"

"Do you not remember?"

"I think I do, but what I remember seems like the imagining of a lunatic," she blurted.

"You did not imagine it," he said with grim certainty. "It happened."

She started to mist up, and shook her head in puzzlement. He knelt in front of her, and gathered up the bundle of clothes that was her gown and underpinnings. Even her stockings and boots. The only thing that was missing was her hat.

"I already saw it all, so no need to be bashful now," Edrick added, smiling stiffly.

She glanced at him and stood. Handing him his frock coat, she drew her shift quickly over her head. She winced as her hand brushed her hip, and she noticed the fresh blood dripping from a cut right on the bone of her pelvis. Edrick gave her a kerchief from his waistcoat pocket and she used it to press onto the wound, hissing through her teeth from the sting.

They heard voices calling out far off, and she looked at Edrick in panic.

"Get dressed quickly. Someone must have heard your scream."

She then leaned on a fallen log to pull on her stockings. She tugged on her boots not bothering to lace them. Her short stays followed, and then the thin petticoat. Edrick helped her fasten the assortment of hooks and tighten the various drawstrings. The last layer was her walking dress.

They'd scarce gotten her fully clothed when a group of young men in militia uniforms appeared 'round the bend of the path carrying muskets.

"You there! Did you hear a cry for help?" the man in front called out.

Keela had picked up Magpie to check her for injuries, and she turned to look at them. "I'm afraid that was me," she blurted. "My little dog and I were just attacked by…"

"Bearhounds. A pair of them," Edrick interrupted. "They ran

off after she screamed. They went that way…" He pointed to where the wolves had run. "They were after my little Ney wolf pup," he lied.

The militiamen trotted into the brush in the direction of the wolves.

"Why did you not tell them it was Ney wolves?" Keela asked, stumbling after Edrick, who had grasped her arm and begun to lead her back out of the park.

"I suspect that the attack probably has something to do with me. And I don't want to create problems between the Yvremi and the Farkas as long as I can avoid it. Not when we need their help," he said.

"I'm sorry." She stopped. "But you think they had something to do with you? They attacked *me*… and look what happened!"

"Yes. I'm still trying to understand what I just witnessed."

"You're not the only one," Keela murmured. His haunted, stricken eyes took in her disheveled state.

"You truly know nothing about this? You've never experienced it before?"

"No. Never." Edrick's gaze was confused. He looked shaken and a bit frightened to Keela, which filled her with dread. Not only had something inexplicable and terrifying happened, but it stood to possibly drive the only young fellow she liked away.

"The fact that they attacked you does present some complications. But there have been attacks before. As I was traveling. I think it has to do with Magpie. I think your…" he paused, "…response to the attack was unexpected."

"They attacked me, not Magpie. She only jumped in to help me." She caressed the pup's head. Magpie's ears were tucked back meekly and she trembled and whimpered a bit from the experience.

"It's lucky your gown is the color it is. Look." He pointed at the small, spreading dark blot of blood on her hip.

"Oh bother," she hissed. "Let's get back."

126

They scuttled hastily along the path, across the grassy area by the pond, and back towards the road and village.

"What are people going to think of you keeping company with a mess like me? I lost my bonnet and my hair is loose everywhere. Here, hold Magpie." She passed the puppy to Edrick and reached up, gathering up her luxurious raven locks, and wrapping them into a bun, which she knotted on her head. The bruise on her arm looked even worse now, and the other arm had great, big scrapes and scratches on it.

The inn came within view just in time to see Lord Xanett dismount from his horse with a flare of his greatcoat, and stalk into the building. She groaned at the sight of him. By the time they arrived, the Lord had already been situated in his room and was not there to see them. Keela slipped away, relieved.

Edrick was filled with questions and bewilderment, but he was more concerned for Keela. Her injuries aside, he saw her ice over when she spotted the Lord, and her anxiousness was more acute at the sight of the man than it had been after she'd transformed into a colossal Ney wolf and fought off two attackers.

He was denied the chance to sit with her and discuss what had happened, to settle his mind, and perhaps help settle hers. He could not help but think back to the conversation with the ClanEthim gentleman. The tale of the shape shifters. Was Keela indeed Farkas? Was she what ClanEthim described? And this Lord that Keela dreaded, he did not know anything about him, but he did know she feared the Lord would punish her for his wife's act of self-harm. There was so much to wonder about, and the fact that Keela was so attractive to him only made it more confusing to Edrick.

Edrick only saw her again at lunch the next day. She had remained in her room that morning and the night before under the pretense of feeling unwell. Now, at the table, she was anxious and afraid. He could relate to some degree, to the sense she was not in the least bit in control of her fate at this moment.

"Keela," Edrick murmured to her across the table. She glanced up at him, and her eyes, full of worry.

"I'm sorry, Edrick. I've been remote. I'm a little overwhelmed," she replied. He smiled reassuringly at her. The little gesture melted her reserve, and he could see her eyes warm to him, and she beamed affection towards him across the table. Just then, the Lord Xanett arrived to join them for lunch, twelve minutes tardy, much to Mrs. Bellham's irritation. He bowed indifferently to the guests, and moved with purpose to sit next to Keela. His harsh, icy gaze immediately focused on the quiet exchange between Keela and the young fellow that he had yet to name.

Lord Lessander Xanett was introduced by Mrs. Bellham, since he had not bothered. He was a tall, lean man of about forty. He had a face that was severe in its natural state, and his hard, steely blue eyes, straight, serious brow and thin lips made him even more austere. His face was bony and angled with a broad, sharp jaw and chin and a narrow, hawkish nose. It was how he looked at Keela that disturbed Edrick the most. The moment he stalked into the dining room, his pointed gaze fell upon her and her eyes dropped when she curtsied in her graceless way. His regard towards Edrick for looking at her was one of possessive jealousy. Edrick gave the man a nod, and watched him sit. Mrs. Bellham shrank back the sight of this harsh looking character.

Edrick surmised that he must be a descendant of aristocracy or landed gentry by the sight of him. He was not one of the newly made men. There was an innate superiority to the way he moved and looked upon the others, and a refined breeding about him.

"Miss Keela." The resounding, bass nature of his voice resonated into Edrick's bones.

Xanett proceeded to serve himself some food, and then everyone else began eating. Keela, however, was not hungry. She pushed some peas around on her plate with her fork and stared at her food as if she were a child that had just been freshly castigated.

"I saw my son this morning, Miss Keela. He looks well," the man said in as low a voice he could muster. Keela bowed her head contritely. His eyes then fell onto the bruises along her arm, which had gone from dark reddish blue to purple, with a sickly yellow spreading out along the edges. The fresher ones only made the old ones look worse. "The coachman explained to me in person what happened. I am most grateful," he muttered. Keela nodded stiffly and smiled forcedly.

"We will be returning to Veros this afternoon," he said, reaching for the mustard pot. He made the sentence somehow hang, as if there was something he left unsaid. "I understand you have not been feeling well, but I hope you are recovered enough to set off today."

Keela assented mutely. He loudly tapped the rich, tart mustard onto his plate and then cut up some of his roast pork, quickly spreading a bit of mustard on each bit before forking them gracelessly into his mouth. He chewed and ate as if it were merely a function. He cleaned his plate quickly, and then looked impatiently about as everyone else ate at a reasonable pace. His gaze fell again on Keela.

Edrick knew avarice when he saw it. He was a rich man, surrounded most of his life by rich men. And Xanett's gaze, when he looked at Keela, was painted with desire and greed. Even his cold eyes could not hide it. Edrick was immediately awash with jealousy, as in spite of Keela's deference to him, there was an air of familiar that passed between them that Edrick envied.

Keela's dark gaze rolled up to meet Edrick's. He gave her a fleeting, friendly smile, but what he saw in Keela's glance was anything but encouraging.

"I would warn you to take care on the road returning home, my Lord," Mrs. Bellham said, startling everyone. "There has been a violent attack on the trade road leading out towards Enyesh only last night. Someone was killed. Perhaps it would be wise to hire some men to accompany your coach and horses."

Edrick looked up in mid chew and his brow wrinkled. "Attack?"

Mrs. Bellham assented with a grave nod. "Constable Neth said it looked like a large animal. There's been talk about bearhounds, but there is no evidence of that. The person's horse had a great gash in its shoulder. And Constable Neth said the person who died …" she paused, and lowered her voice. "He had his throat torn out!"

Edrick's gaze fell and he frowned in thought. Keela was looking at her peas, and did not move.

"Well. If our gracious host doesn't object, I will excuse myself from the table. I have to make arrangements with my coachmen for the child and the young lady to travel home," Lord Xanett articulated. He did not wait for leave. He simply unfolded himself from his seat and stood to his lofty height. "Miss Keela, the nanny has been packing your things. You should be ready to be on your way in about an hour." He strode out without any further ado. Edrick, first consumed by the talk of a murder, was then overwhelmed with the idea that Keela was leaving. He caught her gaze and he could see she was upset. But she drew her hands from the table, stood, curtseyed, and half-ran from the room in a flurry of skirts.

Chapter 9
Departures

Edrick waged an inner battle as he watched the coachmen load the trunks onto the conveyance. His first instinct was to follow Keela. He knew that his feelings for her were true no matter what he witnessed. No matter how much the supposedly rational side of him feared what he had seen. He could not stop from reliving that moment in the sun—the halo of gold around her head, the shine on her lips, and the way she looked at him, her cheeks just a little flushed like a besotted teen. She was so beautiful, and such a pleasure to be with. He missed her already and she had not yet left the inn.

He had his obligation to the Farkas to fulfill. He'd brought Magpie—who was at present whining and scratching at the door to get out—to this city for a purpose, though it had yet to reveal itself to him. He was beginning to feel that somehow Keela was part of it all, no matter how impossible it seemed.

Meanwhile, he was also concerned about the intentions of Lord Xanett who was at present standing outside the coach, hollering at the coachmen about something. Edrick watched from his window above. Xanett glanced up by chance and caught his eye. Edrick wasn't sure if there was a challenge in his gaze, but that is what it felt like. Xanett then drew one of the footmen aside and spoke to him. The man glanced up at Edrick and then bowed to the Lord, moving away from the chaos towards the servant's entrance of the guesthouse.

It was not long before the nanny and the babies appeared, with Keela in tow. She stood patiently behind the nanny as she and the babies were installed inside the coach. Keela clutched a small travel bag in her mustard colored gloves. She was enveloped in a long-sleeved sage travel gown and the dirt-stained bonnet over her hair, which had been recovered by the militiamen and returned to her at the inn the evening before.

She did not turn around or look back when she boarded the coach. Edrick's stomach fell. He watched Lord Xanett—in a long garrick with stacked capelets on the shoulders and broad brimmed hat much like his own—sweep up onto his great bay, and bark at the coachmen, who climbed aboard. The carriage lurched forward.

Magpie howled, whined and cried, scratching at the door vehemently. Edrick shook his head, confused—utterly lost. He felt like a rudderless ship the moment the coach rumbled out of his sight, with Lord Xanett following closely behind it on his horse.

After an evening meal where there was much gossip and rude speculation about the baby, Keela and the enigmatic Lord Xanett, the guests gathered in the drawing room. Edrick ignored the pleas for him to partake in the activities. He was again subjected to the terrible musical talents of Miss Kamb. He had gone to fetch the pup after dinner to take her outside to stroll. Magpie, who had been insistent on getting out, sniffed at the door of Keela's room, and when discovering she was no longer there, grew despondent and listless and remained so.

They sat together now, Magpie at his feet, limp and morose; he in a similar state, lost inside his own head. Miss Kamb ululated shrilly at the pianoforte. He reached down and gathered the puppy up, pulling her onto his lap.

He realized that in the short time between his receiving her and now, she'd grown quite a bit. She'd sustained a small cut from the fight on the hill near the folly. He sighed again, his memory brought back to the smooth, stunning transformation he'd witnessed.

The image of her smooth skin changing before his eyes filled his mind again. The fur growing out into a silken raven coat, her limbs stretching into the long, sleek, leggy slice of wolf she became. And then his mind fell back to the moment when she collapsed back into her own body, and his heart skipped a beat. The rise and swell of her pale curves resting on the leafy ground, it was like a sculpted masterpiece.

Edrick was surprised at how much he'd taken the event in stride. To discover that the myth of shape shifters were real, it was humbling to know that he had been party to it; witness to such a miraculous thing. He thought back to the tale told to him by Sir ClanEthim—about the ancient people. Were the Farkas the ancient people? Were they indeed shape shifters? Were those two large wolves at the heel of the Navray, and the ones that attacked Keela actually people?

There was no doubt the two attacking wolves had gone straight for Keela, whatever he'd pretended. This was so confusing to him. Firstly, if they were the same creatures… well, almos the same. Keela was a much larger wolf than the others. And why would they attack her? And also, what did she have to do with anything? Was it more than coincidence that she was in Calabras when he was? There was the trail of attacks that followed him from Hardorp. These could certainly be connected to the wolves. If so, then why were they attacking people? Was Keela indeed the person he was supposed to meet? If she was, she was southwest, inland towards

Veros at that moment—away from him. Was he failing his objective by remaining here? Was *this* the test?

He sighed and threw his head onto the back of the wing chair. He crossed his legs under the droopy dog, and unconsciously caressed her silken coat. If Keela was here intentionally, for him to meet; that meant Lord Xanett had to know something of what was going on, for it was he that sent her to Calabras, was he not? Edrick looked down at his companion, who had become so remote since the departure of her new friend, and his brow wrinkled.

The night was spent in fitful sleep. He felt deep down that he was doing something wrong. In the morning he woke up groggy and ill-tempered. He threw his legs over the bed, and planted his bare feet on the floor. He looked at Magpie, who was lying by the door with her nose almost beneath it, her tail slack, and her food plate untouched. She had not slept in her usual spot behind his knees in bed. She shuddered out a great big sigh and sniffed under the door, whining once.

"Hang it," he muttered. "I'm not going to wait around for anyone here anymore. It's been long enough." He was worried about the pup. She was so forlorn. She was important. *And if the damned Farkas wanted to find them, they could. They found him on the narrowboat easily enough.* He got to his feet. "Well then, girl," he said to Magpie, who only rolled her eyes to look at him. "Let's go."

Keela was relieved to see the crenelated crown of the old watchtower on the hill. The grueling trip was over. She resolved to avoid coach rides like this again. They were tedious. Without the task of caring for the child, whom she now knew was named Mennick, and without the undercurrent of Vianca's hatred towards her filling the coach like a cloud, it made for a boring ride. Lord Xanett rode behind every day. She would peer through the little window behind her head now and again to find his prickly gaze resting on her. She felt the sear of it on the back of her head for the duration of the journey.

He spent most of the evening stops with Mennick. He asked Keela to join him in the sitting rooms before bedtime, where the baby mostly sat on the floor grappling at objects he put there: a spoon, a little rattle he brought him, and a small smoothly carved porpoise. Or he'd play at Keela's feet, or on her lap where he toyed with her hair and kicked his legs.

Lord Xanett did not say much to Keela, but seemed to only want her for company. She had sat for several nights at different inns quietly reading or minding the child while the Lord read a periodical or smoked, staring into the hearth with a far off gaze.

The final night, he lowered his pipe, and peered squarely at Keela. "You're a quiet, even tempered thing, aren't you?"

She turned her eyes up at him, not responding to his observation. He gazed at her quite boldly, studying her face and her bruised and cut up arms. His eyes lingered there. She felt her cheeks heat up, and her heart quickened. She looked away.

"You did a remarkable thing. I cannot think that many people would have even tried to do what you did," he said mournfully. He paused, and his brow furrowed. "Tell me… did she go quickly?"

"I imagine instantly," Keela replied. "It was a bluff over rocky, water-washed shallows." Her voice cracked. "It's a clear image in my head that will likely never go away."

He pursed his lips, "I knew she was… *ill*. I did not realize to what extent. I am sorry that this happened to you, Miss Keela. I would not have wished it upon you for the world. If I had even suspected she was capable of such a thing, I never would have done what I did to force you go."

Keela wanted to ask him why he chose her. But instead she put forth another thought. "I often wonder if putting me in that coach with her is what pushed her over the edge," Keela ventured. "I feel responsible. Her hatred of me was so complete, and overpowering."

"No, Miss Keela, you must never blame yourself. Vianca was broken like that from the beginning. So filled with anger and resentment of everything and everyone. I am sad to say that it is Mennick here who pushed her into earnest madness. Of course, I will never tell *him* that. He doesn't need to know that his mother was so resentful of him. No child should know that."

Keela agreed most wholeheartedly.

"He will know motherly love. I think he already has felt what it is to be cherished when he is in your arms."

Keela's stomach flipped a little bit when he said this. *Was the old bat, Ledri, right about Lord Xanett's ultimate intentions toward me?* That was the first question that popped into her head. Again, she became flustered. She did not like this feeling at all. She hoped with all her might that he was just being kind and not making a pointed statement.

She chose not to respond. She merely gave him an uncomfortable half smile and then returned to reading. Mennick squealed with the joy of a baby, and waved his arms, rattling his rattle, a bit of drool slipping out of his mouth. The doting attentions of the nurses, of Keela and now his father, that the child had received since his mother's death had an immediate effect on his countenance. He seemed like a happier baby already. Keela felt sad for him that his mother had to die for him to be content. She could feel Lord Xanett's eyes on her long after the conversation ended.

The coach drew homewards, but rather than stopping at her cottage, it made its way instead to the manor house. Lord Xanett lived in a great old house in the center of Veros. It was a towering town house that was quadruple the width of the other adjoining buildings. It also had a long, narrow yard in the back that butted up against the Enith canal. The street was only a few steps from the portico, with a small iron gate separating the walk from the servants' stairway to the basement. There was a large archway with a wooden door leading into the livery and coach house, which were annexed off the yard area. The coach drew right into it, clattering loudly in the tunneled passage, stopping when the light brightened again in the small, cobbled stable-yard.

Lord Xanett rode in behind them, jumping off his horse and landing with a thump. He handed the reins to a stable hand and strode to the coach.

"I thought you might want to rest a bit here, and freshen up before you returned home," he told Keela the moment he opened up the little door. He extended his hand and waited for her to take it, helping her down the step to the ground. "Come, let me show you to a guest room. You can change into something comfortable there, and I'll have a basin brought to you." He ignored the nursemaid and the baby; who were left to their own devices.

Keela, anxious and speechless, let him put her hand on his arm as he led her to the rear entrance of the house. They entered opposite the front doors, beneath the staircase to the upper floors. Keela was suddenly conscious of what she realized were subtle caresses of his thumb on the back of her hand. She was overwhelmed with a rush of confusion and inexplicable emotion, and she stopped cold in the lobby on the way to the stairs.

"You are so considerate of my wellbeing sir, but I am eager to see my mother, and my mother is probably eager to see me. I think it would be best if I went straight home," she said, her cheeks and ears burning.

He frowned and shook his head. "I can't in my good conscience merely throw you back to work after what you have endured. The least I can do is provide you some comfort. And Mennick will miss you if you just vanish so abruptly." His eyes were soft, and sincere, and his strange, harsh face seemed almost handsome to Keela, which discomfited and bewildered her at once.

"I would gladly visit in a day or so. To be truthful, the trauma of this whole thing has taken its toll on me, and I seek the comfort of familiarity, sir. I want to go home." Her voice wavered with emotion, and she saw his resolve falter.

He glared down at her with his intense eyes, his jaw muscles rippling. He bowed abruptly, and relented. "I'll see to delivering your trunk once it is offloaded. If you wish to go now, please feel free. If you are too tired to walk, you are welcome to stay until the coach is ready."

"I can walk. After so much sitting, I am looking forward to it." She offered him a little reassuring smile, which he received with a look of befuddlement. "Thank you, sir. Thank you." She picked up her skirts with her free hand—her travel bag clutched in the other—and followed him to the front door, which he opened. She gave him a final grateful smile, a clumsy curtsy, and skipped down the steps to the street, crossing it at a run. She scampered down the main throughway to the market area, and cut through the bustling merchants and the flow of people towards the brewer's square, where the road led to her home at last. The misting rain cooled her flushed skin, and soothed away her angst. She would be home soon.

Alara was, indeed, pleased to see Keela home and in good health. She was eager to know what had happened since Keela's last letter. Keela filled her in over a bowl of freshly made leek soup. She kept many details to herself, namely Edrick. And the suspected advances from the husband of her recently deceased *friend*. She was just happy to be home, Happy to put the trauma behind her. The only regret she had was leaving Edrick behind. But she tried not to dwell on how much she missed him. She had probably disgusted him anyway with that nightmarish thing that happened, and she hadn't even taken the time to process that bizarre occurrence. She had been confronted with the looming Lord Xanett, who was like a great shadow hovering over her life.

The next morning she put on one of her ordinary day dresses, never happier to feel it and her shabby shawl wrap around her body.

It was a chilly morning, so she put on some pantaloons and her new boots too, for she planned to go out for a nice wander to get her mind in order. She also wanted to see if she could transform again. If she hadn't had the scrapes on her arms and the puncture on her hip, still healing below a poultice given to her by Mrs. Bellham, she would happily believe it never happened.

She thought of Magpie, and frowned. She missed that little pup so.

Her mother had let her sleep in, and she could smell fresh sugar-bread baking when she woke. Dressed for comfort, she tramped down the steps from the loft in search of the bread, only to find Lord Xanett planted comfortably at the table with Alara, sipping tea from one of their thick, unsophisticated clay mugs.

He took in Keela's long hair, flowing down her shoulders and back, her dark lashed eyes, and smooth skin and his hard lips twitched with the beginnings of a smile. She saw it and was again, overcome with confusing feelings about it.

Alara was in a good spirits for she smiled broadly at Keela. On the table between them was a swath of inky velvet Alara used to display her jewelry.

On it were her latest works, all striking. Lord Xanett had sourced some unusual stones and precious gems for this last batch, and Alara had arranged them in filigrees of gold and silver in the most artful way. He managed to tear his eyes from Keela, after draining his tea, and looked again at the jewels. "Miss Keela, your opinion," he asked.

Keela advanced with trepidation, standing over her mother, looking down at his masculine hand as it brushed over a piece in the collection. "Which one do you think is the most beautiful of the four? I have been looking forward to seeing these stones mounted, but I dare say, your mother has exceeded my expectations yet again. I can't decide which one is most beautiful."

Keela swept the items with her practiced gaze, aware of exactly how much labor was required to achieve every inch of each piece.

Alara had a particular skill in the art repoussé, which was embossing into metals, and wirework filigree. She had also learned how to create granulated pieces which—Keela was convinced—is what caused the lump to grow on the back of her neck from hunching forward. Keela knew how to do all these things too, but her artful hand was not quite as precise and tasteful as her mother.

Before her were four parure sets, each containing one resplendent necklace, bracelet, ring, a brooch that could also serve as a pennant for the necklace, and a pair of matching earrings. One set had an alternating sequence of garnet and pearl cabochons embedded in intricately bordered bezels. Another was a simpler, but no less lovely, set of emerald round-cut stones in delicate prong settings, linked together with a textured metal bead in between each to make a fine necklace. There was an artfully arranged brooch of emeralds and beads, and one bead and one stone for each stud earring. The next was a rich and garish design—perhaps a little old fashioned—with a shorter, tighter necklace with granules of gold encircling more garnet cut into baguettes. The last were dangling, pear shaped pearls hanging from little bezeled, foil-backed diamonds. It was not difficult for Keela to choose the one she thought was most tasteful.

"They're all beautiful. There's one that stands out from the others for its simplicity. This one," she pointed to the emeralds, "is about the gemstones. These others are more about my mother's skill. If I had to pick a favorite—one that balances between featuring both my mother's artful hand and the beauty of the stone—I would pick the garnet and pearl set," she said. "But the stones on the emerald set are so beautiful, that my mother chose to understate the metalwork to feature the stone. So, I have to say, if I were looking at it from a standpoint of just plainly beautiful gems, sparkling and vibrant… I'd pick the emeralds."

He looked down at them again. "Well, Mrs. Keela, I shall take these to Fisher so he can make the boxes for them. I think these are far beyond your already impeccable standard of work. It seems you do finer work when you are not distracted by the presence of your daughter," he said bluntly. Alara's brow twitched when he said it, and she frowned.

"Nonsense. I am far more productive when she's here because I have less to do about the place," she retorted. "This batch of gemstones was particularly excellent and they inspired some unique settings. Bring me good stones like this again, and we'll see more of that."

He arched his brow at her and smirked. He reached down and produced a coin purse from his belt, dropping the heavy thing on the table. "I think this should be sufficient for these sets."

She took the purse and loosened the drawstring. She looked inside, her eyes widening in surprise. "Indeed, Sir."

"Excellent. Keep up this quality, and you will have more money for it," he paused, glancing at Keela. "I wanted to mention to you something that's come up. There is a larger, better house of mine that has just been vacated. It is closer to Market Square. It is really two houses, as there's a sky bridge between them that goes over Canal Street."

"Oh yes, I know the place." Alara muttered.

"You may take it for the same rent, if you wish."

Alara's brows shot up yet again, and she seemed taken aback. "That is very kind of you sir…"

"It isn't kindness, Mrs. Dremm. It is gratitude for your daughter's heroic actions." He stood, putting on his garrick and hat—for it was pelting rain outside. He carefully dropped each set into four of the little cotton bags that Keela sewed at least a hundred of last month, and drew them closed, pocketing them each in turn. He bowed to Alara, then turned and bowed to Keela, catching her eye as he did. He then swept out of the cottage into the rain.

"Good gods, girl, what did you do?"

"I saved his baby, is what I did," Keela replied. She lifted her leg over the bench in her usual unladylike fashion, feeling a twinge on her hip from her injury.

"Oh, it's not the baby saving that this is about. Oh, no. He's never done anything generous for anyone unless he wanted something." Alara wagged her finger while getting to her feet. She went to the small cupboard where she kept some linens. She paused to reflect, her eyes dropping.

"Ugh, I don't want to hear that," Keela mumbled. She watched Alara, her eyes taking in the older woman's face. She felt a surge of love for Alara, but she also held onto a sense of betrayal that she felt since she had experienced the transformation. Alara had to know something, and she had to have concealed it. Keela had never imagined that Alara would be able to hold such a large secret for so long without telling her.

"There was this man I met at Calabras. His name was Edrick and he had a Ney wolf pup," she said.

Alara, who had come out of her reflection, tied on an apron that was stained irreparably with tar and pitch. Keela rose and helped her button the back closed, and then found her the pin cushion so she could pin the bib in place. There was no visible reaction to the mention of the wolf pup. Keela expected one, at least something subtle. But Alara was merely listening, waiting for Keela to continue while she tied her hair back.

"I missed you, mum." Alara stopped and looked at her. A soft smile fell onto her lips.

"I missed you too, my little pearl. You want to join me in the workshop today?"

"No. I would rather go and take a walk for a bit." Keela wanted to talk to her mother about the revelations of Calabras, but she wanted to wrap her mind around it more before she confronted her. "Maybe later on this afternoon? Leave me something astonishing. Like sapphires or amethysts."

Alara smiled and went out the back door to the little workshop building. She would be locked in there most of the day tip tapping on sheets of metal, mixing dangerous batches of pitch, burning it off of metal pieces, and soldering wires.

Keela found a good book on her bookshelf and then strode to her trunk, which she hadn't moved since it was dropped off the night before. She picked up the stained bonnet sitting on top of it and put it on. She opened the door, took a deep, heady breath of air, and marched down the rainy road away from town. She would go and see Loralo for a bit, and then climb up her tower.

The rain slackened to a soft mist by the time Keela reached the edge of the old wood, but her hair was dampened and the hems of her skirts were sodden with rain. This never bothered her. She enjoyed the rain, and the clean air.

Veros could have thick, acrid air some days thanks to the draught-animal droppings, street sewage, rotting produce, and the stench from the slaughterhouse stockyards. Sometimes it was more than she could bear. It was never quite so bad near the central market square, but in the vendor districts it could be unbearable. To make it worse, the jewelry making business was not without its nasty smells too, like burning pitch and tar.

The forested hills wilderness beyond town were cleansing to Keela. She often dreamt of living out there in her tower; or somewhere near a loquacious brook of clean, vivacious waters where the ground was covered in moss and the trees were dripping with old-man's-beard.

She hiked along the narrow deer path— a shortcut to the tower—that veered off the main path, up a stony incline. She saw fresh deer tracks, tiny ones belonging to a new baby fawn. She smiled, imagining it with its sweet spotted rump and bright white tail. She was so glad to be home. The deer path led to the far end of the

143

ledge upon which the tower was built. It was situated overlooking the valley. Trees rose up in front of the drop like a wall. Long ago, it had probably been fully logged and there would be an unbroken view of the foothills and the flatlands beyond the valley.

She was listening to a birdsong, lost in her head when she was startled by the sight of a massive Ney wolf standing on a fat boulder that jutted out of the ledge into the trees. She could not believe how considerably immense the wolf was.

This time she felt it before it happened. It came directly after she felt the explosion of shock in her stomach and head from the sight of the wolf. Her heart started racing. And then there was a prickling, sharp, thorny ache that started in the back of her head and spread out to her body in a wave. She watched as her skin transformed along the wave that moved out from her shoulders to her limbs, ending with her fingers fused into large, black paws. She felt her clothes slip away from her as she fell onto her forepaws.

Her mind somehow knew this body as well as her other one. She pointed her ears at the intruder, and her nose twitched as his distinct scent filled her nostrils. She chuffed his strong scent out, and shook her head, growling low and menacingly. Her hackles were up, head hunched down, and her tail low. She slinked a few steps forward and lifted her lips to bare her teeth. Unlike Keela, the intruding wolf made no aggressive moves.

He watched her warily, his burnished eyes piercing, studying her. His posture was neutral. His ears were perked forward, his mouth slightly agape. He sniffed the air as she neared. His tail was relaxed.

She shouted, "go away!" but it came out as a strange, snarling bark. The male wolf twitched, and then backed up a step. "Get out of here!" she barked, the words screaming only in her mind.

He sniffed once more at her, and then turned, gingerly bunching up his body before dropping lithely off the rock down into the trees. She walked to the boulder, and looked out to find him slinking sinuously through the trees below. When he was out of sight, she

144

heard him let out a long, plaintive howl. Before she even realized it, she too was howling. Far, far, off, an ordinary wolf responded. His song was lovely; but it had no meaning. The Ney wolf's did. It was a song of friendship and a call to follow—but she did not.

Keela wanted to explore as her wolf form. She padded up the tower steps, sniffing around, sorting out different scents of animals and people who had come to this place that Keela held sacred. At the top she propped her paws upon the crenel where she normally sat and took in a deep, heady breath of air. With it came just the faintest whiff of something familiar to her. Her ears perked, and she sniffed again.

She dropped to the floor and spiraled back down the tower as quickly as her paws could carry her. She loped over the ledge, descended to the bank and across the main path into the dense thicket. Her nose was low, following the scent. She came to one of the many brooks and creeks that drained from the high hill into the river, and crossed it, lifting her head high when she reached the other side.

She pattered ahead as the scent grew stronger, carried by the breeze blowing in from the east. She trotted along the scent trail as it grew stronger and stronger. She traveled a mile, two, three or more. She then she stopped. She had reached the main road to Veros. And there she found little Magpie, caked in muck and terrified, aimlessly wandering on the roadside.

The little dog yipped in joy and wriggled around Keela's paws the moment she arrived, rolling on her back and batting at her. Magpie whimpered in relief to see her.

"Come," Keela said with a gruff snort, nuzzling the little one. She trotted back the way she had come. Magpie joyfully leapt to her feet, and was soon galloping in her wake.

Trembling from the chill mist on her skin, Keela drew on her clothes quickly, afraid that someone would stumble upon her.

Magpie huddled against her legs, gazing up at her lovingly as she tugged the fitted sleeves over her damp arms, her teeth chattering. The large wolf had alerted her, prompted her to change so she could find Magpie. His scent intermingled with Magpie's leading her to the frightened pup. Her mind was racing. Where was Edrick?

She knelt to tie her boots and pick up her shawl, which was now dampened from being left on the ground. She bundled the puppy in it, and made her way carefully down the slope, back to the main path and homeward.

She burst into the cottage, grateful for the warmth. Alara was still in the workshop, hunched over her work. Keela could hear the tapping of the metal tools. She put Magpie by the hearth and sat in front of it, warming herself, too. Her mind was wild with questions, and the pup could offer her nothing. After she was sufficiently warmed, Keela grasped the large copper tub, and began to heat water for it. Magpie needed a bath. So did she.

Chapter 10
They Come in Threes

Edrick squinted his eyes, and rubbed the back of his head. His temples throbbed and he could only see little shreds of light in the darkness, seeping in from some cracks around a doorway. Where he was, he had no idea. Last he remembered he was riding along the Retler road which went through Veros to the great city for which the road was named. He was on his large horse with Magpie stuffed into a saddle bag, wondering if he was making a great mistake that could cost Yvrem everything. But his instincts defied him. He felt deep down that he had made the right decision to go after Keela.

He groaned and shifted about on the cot upon which he had awoken only a few moments before. *And now, I am trapped. And Magpie is gone. Probably alone in the forest, terrified, poor thing. What will become of Yvrem now?* He chastised himself, shaking his head miserably.

He stood and staggered through the darkness to the door, battering on it.. How was he going to get out of this situation? When his calls and rapping yielded nothing, he dropped his hands

147

Miranda Mayer

and turned, leaning back with a thump against the door. He raised his eyes to the dark ceiling and groaned in irritation. He simply *had* to find a way out of this pickle.

Alara squirmed. Keela watched her mother with an expectant glare as she unconsciously ran a hand along Magpie's silky raven fur. Alara wrung her washrag, trying to remove the tar from her fingers.

"It wasn't up to me to tell you anything, Keela. I know as little as you do. You were given to me as a charge when I was staying at Marlatt. I was told to come to Veros. That I would find a patron here to help me, as I was hoping to find a place to settle."

"So Lord Xanett was never an old friend."

"Not in the way I implied," Alara admitted. "We have become friends to some degree over the years, but the story of us being old friends was concocted for your benefit alone. So you would not wonder at our connection."

"Who gave me up then?" Keela asked for the third time since the conversation began. When Alara had returned from the workshop at the end of her work day, she found Keela, freshly washed, with a damp puppy by the fire. She was displeased by the pup's presence. But her protest was met with a pointed, cutting question that stopped her cold. "Who gave me to you, Alara? I want the truth this time. No more lies."

After attempting again to avoid the topic, and failing miserably, Alara finally gave in. "They were just people. Nothing special, nothing out of the ordinary as one would imagine for people of Yvrem. The lady was a sandy-haired beauty. Small, like you, with large eyes. The man—a tall, harsh-eyed fellow– was handsome, but intimidating. They said they were brother and sister, and the sister had given birth to an illegitimate child. They were of some great family, and the scandal of this news would have rocked their reputation to the ground. The girl was devastated, utterly beside herself to let you go, but her brother was not having it. He insisted that she give the child away. He would help raise the child through a friend, he said. And then they told me of Xanett and Veros. And that they would arrange for a home and for funds to assist me with your care as you grew.

"I had been seeking some kind of stable employment. Perhaps I wasn't fully prepared for raising a child, but I was concerned that I would not find the income I needed to start making jewelry with precious stones instead of the paste and cheap common stones, and I worried about renting a shop. This arrangement seemed to suit. And you were so beautiful. So small and so helpless, your little hands clutching your little goat's milk gourd. Your beautiful eyes. I always wanted a child on my own terms. And here you were... You were the answer to so many of my wishes."

"They did not tell you anything else? Nothing at all?" Keela demanded.

"No, Keela. I think Lord Xanett might know more. The identity of your mother at least." She wrung her hands and pursed her lips. "But I suspect he won't tell you. He never told me, and I've asked him many times over the years because I knew you would want to know someday. I did not want to be in this position, feeling like I've been lying to you all this time."

"Well, you sort of have, mother," Keela pointed out with no shortage of bitterness.

Alara sighed and sat down, picking unconsciously at her dirty hands. "What was I supposed to do? Put all those questions in your head to further torture you? You already had enough challenges growing up. Adding the truth that you were an unwanted child wasn't something I wanted to heap onto your little shoulders."

"Unwanted..." Keela whispered, her eyes misting up. "I've always known you as my mother. I've always taken it for granted that my mother was dead, and that you were it for me. This changes everything. In ways not even you could understand."

Alara sighed shakily. "Keela, you have and always have been my heart. From the moment I held you in my arms to this day. You are the child I always wanted, you are the person I have always hoped you would be. This does not in any way change that. You are still my daughter as far as I'm concerned. The woman who brought you into this world was willing to submit to the will of others and let you go. Were you mine, I never would have done that. Never," Alara said decisively.

"You cannot know what motivates a person to decide what they decide, mother. I aim to find out and understand it better. And it will help me figure out who I am, and what I am."

"You're Keela. My daughter."

"I'm more than that, mother. It is up to me to decide what I learn henceforth. I am not doing it to hurt you, but I have questions that must be answered."

Alara nodded listlessly. Her voice trembled. "I don't know what precipitated your desire to know. Something happened when Vianca threw herself to her death, or perhaps leaving home only prompted more questions, but know that I love you, Keela. That is all I hope you carry with you. And I am happy you are home."

Keela offered her a little smile, which seemed to have a positive effect on Alara's demeanor. She wanted to tell Alara about Lord Xanett's inappropriate behavior, about her transformation, but she did not want to discuss it at the moment. Instead she rose, and put the puppy on the floor.

"I'm going to go for a walk," Keela declared. "Keep Magpie here."

"Must you have this dog?"

"She's not mine. But if I can't find her owner, she will be. I won't give her up, mother."

"As you wish, darling child," Alara grunted grudgingly. "I'll find some scraps for her to eat." The bent down to pat Magpie's head. Keela slipped out the door without another word.

She made her way down the main road away from Veros, back to where she'd found Magpie. She'd start there.

The afternoon was just giving way to evening by the time Keela reached her destination. The clouds had gone and it was now clear. She stood on the road, exactly where her large paw prints came out from the trees to meet with Magpie's smaller ones.

She looked around, appearing lost as her eyes traced along the earth. In the late afternoon sun, the indentations of paw prints in the soil were deeply shadowed. She followed the pup's winding prints that padded quite serendipitously in the soft muddy humus on the side of the road. They then vanished into the leaves about a quarter of a mile down.. There, Keela saw horse-prints on the roadside.

She peered into the trees, her brow furrowed. She stepped down off of the hard-packed path into the thick, waxy leafed bushes, and pressed through them, forging into the underbrush. There were broken branches and crushed stems all along the path. As she forced herself through the low boughs of a tree, she saw a horse, its reins tangled in a tree branch, its eyes wild and nostrils flaring at the sight of her.

"Hush, hush…" Keela said soothingly, reaching out. The horse snorted, its sweaty flanks quivering. It pulled against its reins.

Keela gently reached up—aware of the alarmed whites of its eyes as it watched her fearfully—and began to untangle the reins from the branches. With her other hand she tentatively and gingerly reached for the panicked horse. "Shhhh…"

The horse sniffed her hand and relaxed as the tension of the reins on his bridle began to slacken. She soon had the horse freed, and she led him back away from the tree. He took a deep, long breath and released it with a snort, shaking his head and body, the saddle and packs rattling loudly.

Amongst the many things tied to the saddle was a large, leather bag in which Keela surmised Magpie had been riding. "Where is your master, horse?" she asked.

The horse merely lowered its head for her to place her hand on, and she petted around his ears and his large, wide cheek. The animal was exhausted and frightened. She led the horse out to the road, and looked around again. She knew she would have to change to a wolf in order to find Edrick, but she didn't know how to become one without being prompted to change by a threat.

She frowned and started back towards her home, Edrick's horse in tow. She stopped by Ejesh's home. She had not taken the time to bid him farewell when she left Veros with Vianca. She felt awkward simply showing up like this, in need of his assistance. She had little choice, and she led the horse through the gate to his humble cottage, and tied it to the fence before going to the door.

The house squatted under a pair of walnut trees. Some of his sheep were out in the stone-walled pasture around in the home, resting on the ground like little woolen lumps in the golden light of the evening. Ejesh's pleasure was evident on his kind face when he opened his door to her.

"Mish Keela," he exclaimed bashfully. "Loralo shaid you were gone for the shummer," he queried. Keela offered him a meek smile.

"I'm afraid the plans were thwarted by a tragedy," she replied. She then bowed her head and pursed her lips. "I'm sorry to greet you by asking for a favor, Ejesh, but I am in a quandary." His gaze moved past her to the horse tied at his fence.

"Can you keep him for me, for a day or two?" she asked.

"Of coursh," he replied. He exited his house, a sheepdog at his heels, and led the horse around the back to the byre. Keela followed, and helped him remove the horse's tack and all of Edrick's things. Ejesh allowed her to store them on the straw bales in his small, low-roofed barn. He released the horse into his field with his sheep and it ran out and rolled around in the grass almost immediately. He then stood a good long time by the water trough and took long, desperate gulps of water.

Keela thanked Ejesh. As she walked back towards the road, the horse was grazing on the thick grass, the sweat on its coat dried, its tail calmly flicking.

She reached the place where she'd found the horse. The sun was almost set, the sky orange under lighting the clouds with gold. She sighed. *How how how,* she asked herself inside her head. She stepped through the place where they'd come out of the brush and aimlessly wandered around the area where she had found the horse, looking at the hoof prints, the broken brush, the signs of struggle from the horse.

She took a deep breath, trying to smell the air, but her nose did not taste what it did when it was a wolf's nose. The frustration was building.

Change! She chastised herself.

Transform! She shouted at herself in silence.

Nothing.

The change had come so naturally when she felt protective or defensive, but now there was no threat. Magpie was safe at home. Nobody was in danger. But then she realized that someone was indeed in danger. Edrick was gone. It appeared he'd been forcibly taken, and his horse with Magpie set loose on a strange road.

She needed to find him. The idea of his being harmed or in danger distressed her further and her eyes misted up. He had been heading to Veros which meant he was coming after her. He hadn't been revolted by what he saw her become… And now something had happened to him, probably because of her. The tears and anger at her ineffectiveness overcame her and she bit her lip. "I'm useless. Why am I here?" she barked at herself. Magpie, all alone, had escaped her bag and jumped down from a frantic horse.

The sun had finally set, and the light was dwindling. Angry and disappointed, she turned back towards the road. As she did, she tripped over a root and fell. She reached out to stop herself, and found herself landing on paws instead of hands. She felt her gown fall away from her slender, lupine body, and she kicked out of the rest of it. She shook herself, and dropped her nose to the earth, Edrick's scent filling her nostrils. Other scents—those of a stranger and another horse—intermingled with that of the horse she just brought to Ejesh. She followed the trail of scents the few steps back to the road. It led towards the town a ways and then veered off onto a narrow path into the forest. She trotted silently on her paws, her nose hovering but an inch or two above the earth, the familiarity of Edrick's scent rolling in her nasal cavity, creating images of his smiling face in her mind.

Keela's hackles bristled and she twitched her ear, her silver eyes narrowing. She could see Lord Xanett clearly in the light of the candelabra, speaking to a stocky, golden-haired man in hunting clothes. The fellow had a rough edge to him in spite of his mannerisms of a high-born. He had dark brown eyes and long teeth, with ruddy cheeks and a sharp chin.

Both men drank from their ales, the bitter aroma of the hoppy beer curling into her nostrils from the window. They were in the private room at the Aydus lodge on the northern edge of the city just inside the tree line. It was part public house, part inn for sportsmen and it was owned by Xanett. The two men were the only occupants of the building at this hour. She had followed the scent trail to this place.

"He gave a bit of a fight getting him into the box dray—but he's secured. A bit soft, this fellow. But what does one expect of the ruling class, eh? He could have benefitted from a few boxing lessons with the Lion, poor boy," the stranger chortled. With a scoff, he continued: "He is on his way to Ulken. Out of your hair, Lessander, if you *had* hair." The visitor laughed. Xanett, with his humorless eyes, shook his head, drawing from his beer.

"Ulken seems a bit rash, don't you think? I just need him out of the way for a month or two." Xanett's voice had a velvety quality to it. It cut through the distance like a knife, and rung clear in Keela's ear.

"If you want him out of the way, what other choice do I have? When the Akravani invade, then you can have him set free," the stranger replied. Xanett merely grunted, drinking from his cup.

"As long as he's gone long enough for me to get what I want, I suppose it'll have to do," Xanett grumbled.

"Why do we not merely put an end to the boy?" the other man asked. "A spongy, fragile little prince like that. No direction, no use. It would do no one a disservice," the man offered callously. Xanett's eyes narrowed and he frowned darkly.

"I'm not an evil man, Effrem." Keela knew at once who this man was now. He was Effrem Kayte, a rich landowner from the rural area east of Veros. He was an infamous tyrant, and one of the largest instigators of conflict with the neighboring state. Keela was not aware of him being Lord Xanett's friend. Xanett was known to be a fair man on the most part, and she would never imagine him rubbing elbows with this creature. "I'm not a killer. I am, perhaps, self-serving by putting him away. But he is an unwanted element. He *must* go. There is no reason to harm him."

"Let's hope he doesn't come and kill you for this," Effrem warned. "I cannot be held responsible for that if he does, I have presented you with the option to prevent it, remember this."

"He has no idea it's me. That's why you are here and your men are doing their work. It will be on you if he does find out." The exchange became prickly. "Do I need to be concerned, Effrem? Is there going to be a problem between us?" Xanett asked.

Effrem shook his head. "Of course not," he snapped.

"Just make sure I get my end of the bargain, and do as you promised. *No harm*. Am I clear?" Xanett growled in a warning tone. He reached for the bottle of ale, and poured more into Effrem's cup.

"I'm a man of my word, as you are reputed to be," Effrem replied and leaned back in his chair.

Keela reared up and pivoted on her hind legs, launching silently through the brush. She broke into a full gallop down the road towards the Ulken prison, as fast as her legs could carry her, bunching up her muscles and propelling her smooth body forward in long, sinuous bounds. Her nose worked as she ran. Her mouth hung open, tongue lolling. She caught a scent and it spurred her on faster.

Edrick sat hunched in the rocking conveyance, his arms bound behind him, his cheekbone and his ear still throbbing from being punched in the face. He'd managed to land a few blows of his own in the scuffle, but it wasn't enough against the stalwart thugs that had wrestled him from his confines and forced him to the ground, tying his arms behind him. They threw him violently onto the wooden floor of the box wagon, and tied a rag around his mouth, gagging him.

He was now trying to chew his way through the sour-tasting fabric. As he did, he stopped, for the sounds around him changed. The cart was slowing, and the men had fallen oddly quiet.

"What is that?" one of them asked.

"Where is it?" was the other's reply.

"I don't know…"

There was a moment of quiet and the cart drew to a full stop. It was then that Edrick heard it: A low, bass, ominous growl. It was long and continuous, only pausing as if to take in more air. The growl got meaner, turning into the cackle of a beast with its teeth bared. It escalated to a terrifying rumble that made the hairs on the back of his neck rise up.

"Big dog…." one of the two drivers hissed.

"Get the dray moving!" the other said.

"Hup!"

The reins snapped on the rear of the large horse, and the cart jerked forward. Edrick fell painfully onto his side. The growl intensified yet again, and there was a snarling sound. There was then a yelp of pain that moved from the driving seat to the side of the cart, followed by the sound of snapping vegetation fading behind them as the cart moved.

"Darek! Darek, where are you?"

The response was but an agonized cry retreating behind them until only the sound of the rattling cart and the clattering of the horse's hooves remained. The cart sped up, the horse's gait going from trot to canter. Edrick rolled around inside, the wood scraping away at his skin. He grunted as the wheel caught a hole and he was thumped hard onto the floor.

The driver snapped the horse's croup with the reins again, pushing the poor animal into a gallop. The wagon whipped fiercely about the road, throwing Edrick around like a ragdoll. The wagon began to tip, and the top heavy vehicle began to list as the driver lost control of the horse. The vehicle turned, and there was a horrific crack as the wooden shaft snapped. The dray crashed and slid to a stop, and there was the sound of the horse continuing on without them, its hoofs battering the earth at full gallop, the wooden shaft dragging loudly behind it. Then there was only silence.

Edrick listened for the driver, but there was no sound from him. Edrick felt blood seeping from his forehead.

There was then the sound of something in the brush, and he heard the latch being toggled on the door. One side of the double-door fell open and hit the road with a deafening bang, the interior of the box wagon filling with soft, blue moonlight. Silhouetted against it was the supple, curved form of a woman, long hair brushing her hips.

"Ngg..." Edrick tried to speak through his gag.

Keela knelt under the other door, and grasped his shoulders, dragging him out into the fresh air. Her hands fumbled to remove the gag and the bindings on his wrists. He could only stare, for before him was the most beautiful thing he ever beheld. She with pale skin washed sapphire by the night, her smooth arms reaching for him, her graceful hands clutching him. He saw glistening darkness around her mouth, and realized it was blood. She was the most terrible beauty he'd ever beheld and he was never more in love with her than he was at that moment.

Chapter 11
Family

Edrick stood on the thick branch which he'd placed over a rock for a fulcrum. The cart lifted only a little, but it was enough for Keela to pull the driver's body from underneath the dray. He was still alive, but he was unconscious. Edrick helped her remove the man's breeches and his frock coat. She drew the breeches on, her skin a maze of goose bumps. Edrick lamented the disappearance of her body as she swathed it in the frock coat, buttoning it up.

She took his hand and dragged him, stumbling, back down the road in the darkness. She hadn't said a word, Her breath was trembling and anxious, her grasp cold and clammy. He followed without fear, his hold on her firm and trusting. About half a mile down the road, he pulled her to a stop. She turned, her hand still clutching his. He pulled her into his arms and hugged her tightly. She squeezed him in return, her fingers gripping his clothes, her breath fast and frightened. She let him hold her a few moments, but then wriggled out of his arms, and insisted they keep on.

It was a long walk, but in the depth of the night she led him into the cozy embrace of a tiny cottage on the edge of the city of Veros and forced him to sit by the dwindling fire. Upstairs, someone snored. The sound of paws clicked above him, and then tottered down the steps. A moment later Magpie wriggled in joy at his feet, whimpering with delight to see him again. He gathered the ecstatic pup into his arms and let her lick his face, relieved to see the little dog again.

Keela disappeared for a spell, returning about an hour later carrying clothes. Her entrance startled him and the pup from an exhausted snooze. Wordlessly, she went to the sink and pumped up some water, taking a towel and washing her face clean of the blood that still stained it. It was only then she turned at looked at him.

"Edrick, you came after me…" she said.

He smiled broadly at her through his bruises and his injuries. "As you did for me."

Her eyes softened and she sighed shakily. A sob rose up. She ran to him and fell into his arms. He held her gently while she wept.

Alara glanced sideways at Edrick, frowning thoughtfully at his scrapes and wounds. She then slid her eyes to Keela, who appeared drawn and exhausted. She put a plate of food in front of each of them. "I don't suppose either of you will tell me what happened last night," she mumbled.

Keela barely flinched, and Edrick shrugged. He picked up the rustic, two-tined fork, speared a piece of boiled egg, and ate it, wincing in pain as he chewed.

"What I know you ought to be doing now is resting. You both look absolutely awful."

"Don't you have jewelry to make, Alara?" Keela blurted.

The older woman's frown deepened and she sat down to eat. She glowered at Edrick when she saw him slide his hand down to Magpie and slip her a piece of egg.

160

"Pass me a rasher of bacon, dear," Alara said.

Keela gave her the plate with the crisped pieces of bacon. Its aroma from cooking still hung heavily in the air around them. Alara had awoken that morning to Magpie barking. She'd heard a man respond, and open the door to let the dog out. She'd sat up to see Keela looking at her with tired eyes. Keela had gotten up and went downstairs, grasping her shabby dressing gown and drawing it onto her arms before she disappeared down the stairs.

Alara followed soon after, and saw that there was a guest. They offered Alara no explanation. Alara did not ask. She knew Keela well enough to know the truth would come.

Alara focused on her breakfast, listening to the quiet taps of forks on the thick plates. The man's manners were too refined for the rugged presentation of the meal. Was this the man Keela had mentioned? She had not even introduced him. Alara put her fork down.

"If I am to suffer the indignity of hearing gossip about strange male visitors from the likes of my irritating neighbor, could you at least tell me the name of your guest, Keela?" she said overly sweetly.

Keela looked up and waved her fork listlessly towards her companion. "That's Edrick. I told you about him and Magpie when I got home."

"I see. Well, pleased to meet you, Edrick," Alara said. She then took a bite of bacon and chewed thoughtfully, her wizened eyes taking each of them in. The quiet scrutiny was interrupted by a brisk knock on the door. Alara rose and opened it, speaking briefly to someone before closing it. She held something in her hand.

"A package for you, Keela," she said. She handed it to her daughter the slim, paper-wrapped object. It felt like a book.

Keela put it on the table and pulled the twine from it, peeling back the stiff paper to reveal a fine leather-bound box with gold embossing and a little golden latch on its narrow front. She opened it, and her shoulders fell. It was the emerald parure her mother had sent off with Xanett only the morning before. On top was a small square of card that read in tiny, perfect script: *You are invited to join me for dinner and cards this evening. I have invited some friends. Please dress accordingly. Here is a gift to complete your toilette.*

Alara looked at the gift, and then to Keela, whose face was now filled with abject rage.

"He's invited me to dinner," she said with a withering anger. "After what he's done…"

"He doesn't know that you know, Keela." Edrick slipped another piece of food to Magpie.

"Carrying on like everything's fine…" she hissed.

"What do you expect him to do?" Edrick asked.

She glared at the emeralds. "His wife just died!" she snapped.

"Yes, but he is pressed to make his move, isn't he? He did what he did because of you," Edrick said. "I'm out of the way, as far as he knows."

Alara dropped her fork loudly and glared at each of them in turn. "You need to tell me what's happening, Keela," she barked.

"*Why?*" Keela suddenly snapped. "You have hidden the truth from me from the day they put me into your arms," she grumbled snidely.

"*Keela!*" Edrick snapped. This ingratitude and unkindness was not attractive, even to a man who behaved like a spoilt child before this misadventure. She peered at him wide-eyed, shocked to see this normally calm and rational man so angry. She was astounded he'd spoken so brashly to her.

"Don't take your anger out on your mother!"

"She's not…"

"Don't you *dare* say it," he growled. She balked. "She has raised you, loved you, provided for you, and supported you. She did what she thought best. This—none of this—is her fault. None of it. And the questions you have, she does not have the answers for. She

162

doesn't know about your past. Punishing her will achieve nothing except to undermine the only family you have in your life!"

Tears welled up in Keela's eyes and she picked up the jewelry box and flung it across the room. The gems glimmered in the spare morning light streaming in from the small windows before they scattered into the shadows.

"I'm a bloody changeling and I can't understand why. My mother's patron is hovering over me like a carrion bird. He's sending me gifts of jewelry my mother made only days after his wife flung herself to her death. Hours after having you abducted. How did he even know you were coming? Did he leave someone to watch you? And why? Why me?"

"I know the way a man looks at a woman when he wants her…"

"He never wanted me before."

"Yes he did," Alara's voice cut in like a knife, reminding them both that she was party to their argument.

Keela's eyes, wide and frightened peered at her mother incredulously. "What could you possibly mean?"

"When you turned sixteen, just before he married Vianca. He was here, picking up some pieces to sell as well as the bridal parure he had commissioned me to make for her. You brought them in, and then went to see to the laundry. He watched you as you worked. He looked at me…" she sighed. "He looked at me and told me how beautiful you were becoming. He lamented his promise to Vianca's father, already well aware of Vianca's caustic nature. 'Had I the foresight, I might have been able to choose for myself who to marry,' he told me. 'A gentle and useful Fperson, like Keela, would have been my choice, had I that prescience,' he said. And let us not forget, he always knew you were important to someone. He knows much more than I do. I think that he understands your true value to whomever has been supplying the funds for your supervision and keep. And that, along with the knowledge that he finds you beautiful and attractive, is enough. He was prevented from acting upon his

163

wants because he had already been betrothed," Alara explained. "He did not repeat the sentiments again, but his eyes have been on you since."

Keela remembered the coach and Vianca's seething anger. Then there was the comment in particular about how she, Keela, tempted men away. Her face grew a little paler.

"Now, what's this about abductions? He abducted you?" Alara asked.

Edrick shrugged with a look of resignation. "I think he recognized me as a credible threat to his chances with Keela. He was sending me to a prison."

Alara's brows rose and she looked at Keela for confirmation. "You must indeed be important, Keela, if he risked that kind of action."

"Do you think he knows I'm a changeling?" Keela asked.

"There is no way to know," Edrick replied.

"Changeling?" Alara looked as confused as she could be with such terms being thrown about.

"Yes, mother. I'm a changeling. I can… transform… into a Ney Wolf."

Alara stood and her lips fell open. She clapped her hand over her mouth and tears filled her eyes.

"Jessick," she blurted. "Now I know why they chose me…" She then burst into tears and scuttled away.

Alara had locked herself in the workshop. Edrick and Keela reluctantly agreed that she would have to fulfill the obligation of Xanett's invitation. As her patron, she could scarce refuse it. And she also wanted to ask him some questions. To see what he did know. So she prepared a bath to wash away as much of the soil of prior evening, and then dove into her travel trunks for the gowns she had never had a chance to wear. She pulled out a gown of cotton velveteen in monkshood blue with a bodice trimmed with silver leaves, a pair of red silk slippers, and a goldenrod shawl. Then she disappeared up into the loft to bathe and prepare herself.

Edrick and Magpie remained downstairs by the fire. It was then that Alara returned, downcast, and began to putter about, preparing food for their supper. She offered Edrick some tea, and sat down with him by the fire. There was a thoughtful silence as they listened to Keela up in the loft, moving quietly about.

"When I was much younger— a few years older than Keela—I was traveling through Mayjen. Have you been there?" she asked.

Edrick shook his head. He knew of it, a land in the southern seas. "I travel, but mostly inside Yvrem. I've never been overseas," he replied.

"Mayjen is not like any of the other sun-kissed nations. It is hot and it is rainy. It is a land that is all forest, but dense, suffocating forest—the kind where the brush returns in a few weeks after you clear the land if you're not careful. It is where you find the most dragons, for they revel in that kind of heat, and they love the thick leafy forest hills to nest in."

"Yes," Edrick remarked. "We will never see a dragon this far north. But I did read that there were many in Mayjen."

"I went there to buy dragon lapis and onyx. These are unique stones formed by dragon-fire. My mother had been jewelling for most of her life, too, but her techniques were old fashioned. She had a desire to learn new things, and to use new materials She told me of these unique stones, which are nothing like the ordinary ones. So when I first began my traveling, I made it my business to go to Mayjen."

Edrick wasn't sure why she was telling *him* all this, but he knew that Keela could hear her up in the loft. Above, water trickled, and he could not help imagine it running in rivulets down her flawless skin, as she quietly bathed above floors. There were only the creaky wooden floor slats between them. Alara was speaking loudly, and clearly.

165

"There are people who speak with dragons. They are the ones who can collect the stones and even persuade dragons to make them. They hold their secrets close, these dragon-talkers, and finding them is a challenge. There are not many of them who have managed to partner with a dragon to make these stones. So when I arrived at Mayjen, I had to find someone who could connect me with one of these people. That is when I met Jessick." She paused, and stood, taking the pot of tea that was by the fire, and filling her mug and Edrick's.

She sat down again with a groan. Edrick looked at her ragged, black-tipped fingernails and her tired face. Such a beautiful woman she must have been, he realized. Her hair was frazzled and silver, curly but pulled back into a tiny bun at the nape of her neck. Her face was a maze of wrinkles, her green eyes reddened and watery. She wore a gown with several intricately darned patches. Over that she had been wearing a tar and pitch-stained apron. She had taken it off and put it aside when she sat down. Her hands, also scarred from burns, were covered in black smudges.

"Jessick was a traveler, like me. He was the first Farkas I'd ever met. A handsome young man—tall, lean and dark. He had paused in his travels to stay on in Mayjen for a while, living with a pair of other young Farkas men. They called themselves observers, and they were tasked to journey about and to see what the rest of the world was up to, then return the news to Farkas. Of course, this was something they did not tell others—that the Farkas spy on other peoples. I was the only one who knew this, because he told me. "

Edrick was surprised by this. He leaned forward, resting his elbows on his knees. Above, water still trickled and splashed.

"I was introduced to Jessick by a jewel cutter. Jessick had just sold him a dragon onyx he'd acquired while inland. Jessick and I... our minds met in so many ways, and he was such a pleasure to be with." Alara's voice grew soft and warm, her eyes focusing far away into a distant past. "Such a beautiful soul, full of laughter and kindness. He traveled with me to a village in the north of Mayjen in the middle of dragon country. I had never seen a dragon before and to see these great, majestic creatures kiting in the winds like sea birds was beyond my wildest dreams.

"Jessick was what Keela is. He was a changeling. He transformed into an elegant wolf. One so beautiful, with a coat as black as night. He showed me one night, after we had lain together. I had disclosed in him a great confidence that I had told nobody in all my life. And in return, to show his trust of me, he told me his secret. And oh, what a beautiful secret it was." Alara's eyes misted with tears.

"Imagine how privileged one feels, to know something like that. It is a great hidden truth. One that the Farkas hold close. They are an ancient people, a conflicted people. Their invasion of Yvrem, it was a divisive action for the Farkas too, and caused a war of its own to some degree. It isn't a war of blades. It's a war of politics. Jessick chose to observe in order to escape his part in it.

"The Farkas squabbled over the invasion of Yvrem—for there are two factions who want different things for Yvrem—and this dissent has been dividing the Farkas people for decades. They say it was because of our oppressive hierarchy that they invaded. That they sought to create equality for the Yvremi people. But Jessick said it wasn't merely that. It was for something more important."

"I'd hardly call what we have here now equality," Edrick said defiantly. "We haven't had a stable government for two hundred years. City-state infighting, and—let's not fool ourselves—there is still an upper crust ruling over the common folk."

"It wasn't like it *was*, Edrick. That you cannot deny," Alara argued. "As a royal, you probably have been insulated from the hardships that the ancestors of the common folk knew." Her tone held no shortage of bitterness.

"I suppose it's not as bad, no. But who is to say things would not have improved without their interference?" he said.

"Well, what is done is done. One faction made the decision to dismantle the Yvremi peerage and assume control of the Yvremi government. There was such division over it, there was a coup at the Farkas homeland, and a new power took over. That was when the Farkas withdrew and created the Sentely. And the Farkas remained in Yvrem while they continued to struggle at home for some sort of consensus.

"The invasion served a much greater purpose because it became a warning to all the other nations with the same oppressive rule. Many of those nations feared they'd be next. There was sweeping change, almost everywhere. There are some people who are more primitive than we … war-like people who did not see the threat. But most of the nations were cowed by the utter devastation of Yvrem. Yvrem was the most powerful and greatest nation until then."

"Yes, I recall my history lessons," Edrick said.

Alara looked up, and shook her head, realizing she'd rambled on. "I am sorry. Jessick was a passionate man when it came to the politics of the invasion, and the repercussions. He did not like that his people were viewed as oppressors. His family had a legacy that was embroiled in the invasion, and they still possessed a stronghold in Yvrem. He feared that the division of the Farkas would make the presently benign Sentely a danger to the Yvremi people, but he never clarified why. He did say that many Farkas believe that those without the ability to change shape are inferior beings. He was not of that mindset. He, unlike the two men that accompanied him, spent a great deal of time with the people around him.

"I fell in love with him, and he liked me a great deal. We were dearest friends, and for a while, lovers," Alara said with a whimsical smile. "But then he fell in love. With a Mayjeni no less. A dragon-talker. She was a beautiful creature and, oh, how I hated her. So, I got my stones and I didn't stay to watch his romance with this woman grow. Before I left Mayjen, he held me in his arms, and bade me a kind farewell. That was my one great love, and he never loved me in return. Not like I wanted," she murmured.

"What makes you think he has anything to do with Keela?"

Above, the floor creaked with soft footsteps and abruptly stopped when her name was mentioned. "He and I, we corresponded when we could. It was hard when I was moving about, but I tried to keep him apprised of where I was, and where I was going. He would send me dragon stones now and again." She smiled wistfully. "After I came to Yvrem I sent him a letter and he sent a brief one in response. He was beside himself with joy. His woman was with child. Now, you must understand… The Farkas should not be able to conceive offspring with… well, with us. But after years together with this woman, it happened."

"Keela?"

"No. It wasn't Keela," Alara snapped. She gave him a glare for interrupting. "His son was born soon after. I did not hear from him for some time, but I received a letter a few years later. Jessick was inconsolable. His child had died and his wife was tragically killed. He was never clear how, but he went on for paragraphs, explaining to me how it simply must have been a murder committed by his own people, for they viewed his son as an abomination.

"I always thought that perhaps the dragon talkers had a bit of the old blood in them, and that is why it was possible for the pregnancy to happen. But Jessick dismantled my theory when he wrote to me again. He had begun traveling again and was also in Yvrem, but he was moving about a great deal. So he told me to send my letters to the chancellor of the Backrem University. And he would collect the correspondence when he could. So I did. He promised he would respond. In one of his letters he told me the purpose of his renewed travels. That he sought to find other instances of mixed children and that he had found several here in Yvrem." She paused as she sipped her tea. "He told me these children would likely be in danger, and he would not allow that kind of tragedy to befall others as it had to him.

"I heard from him a few times after that. I told him I was getting

169

too old for travel, and that I would find a place to settle down and send him the directions so that he could write at his leisure. That was my last communication with him. I found a place to live, and I sent him the location as promised, but I did not receive a reply." Alara sighed wearily, and shook her head. "I thought perhaps he'd gone back to Farkas. Or that he had perhaps died, in all honesty. I never put the two events together until now."

"The two events?"

"Well, the history I have told you, culminating in Jessick's last letters... his newfound mission. And my being given guardianship of Keela as a baby," she explained. "Until the two of you told me that Keela is a wolf changeling I hadn't realized these were connected. Keela must have been brought to me because Jessick thought she was in danger, and he knew I would take care of her. I had told him of my desire for children, of the things I wanted in life..." she let the words fade off into a whisper as she drained her cold tea.

She leaned back in her chair as she continued. "I always thought that I was chosen because to take Keela my acquaintance with the Efchels, the prominent family at Grencourt. They had children, and when I would visit there to bring Lady Efchel her commissioned jewelry work, I would fuss over them. Lady Efchel knew how much I wanted a child of my own. She even suggested that perhaps I ought to adopt a little one, but I did not have the funds or resources then to make a decent life for both myself and a child. And I knew the stigma of being without a husband would stand in the way.

"The Efschels appeared at my door one day in the company of Lord Xanett with the promise of his patronage. He would provide me the space and funds I need to raise a baby they said needed a loving home. That Jessick had any hand in it never crossed my mind. Not once." She exhaled and shook her head.

"I would love to know what Xanett knows," Edrick said.

"It does make his role in Keela's care more compelling, doesn't it?"

"What's fascinating to me is his ardent interest in her," Edrick replied.

"He's always been interested in her. She's a beautiful girl. There are many men interested in Keela, most of whom would not admit it, thanks to years of public abasement and degradation inflicted by Miss Vianca and her peers."

"Ah, the infamous Vianca. She was so vile she couldn't even stand to live with herself," Edrick snarled. There was a quiet pause.

"Well," Alara mumbled. "I doubt Xanett will tell Keela anything if she confronts him about her parentage. What you can do is to start with this..." Alara rose and walked to a small, worn sideboard that was hunched in the angled space underneath the stairs. She opened the bottom doors and pulled out a small, stylishly carved box. She put it on the top of the sideboard and opened it, digging about in a tangle of jewelry pieces, removing something shiny. She walked over to Edrick and put it in his hand.

"Keela's mother slipped it to me when I took her. She put it in my hand, balled my fingers around it, and squeezed so tightly it hurt. Maybe this will give you a clue."

"Why have you never given it to her?" Edrick asked.

Alara's emitted a shaky sigh. She did not reply. She merely turned and reached for her apron, which she'd taken off and draped on the back of her chair. She left without another word.

Edrick opened his palm and gazed down at the item. It was a tiny locket—a simple oval with delicate silver granules all around the edge. He slid his fingernail beneath the almost invisible latch and it popped open. On the bottom half was a curl of hair twisted beneath a paper thin sliver of glass. The upper half had a single graceful letter W—all curls and scrollwork— engraved in it along with a tiny songbird perched on the first middle apex of the W. All of this was contained in a circular frame of branches with little oak leaves sprouting all around the outside.

He closed the locket, and balled his fist around it, leaning back into his chair. Above, there was a marked stillness. Keela, too, had nothing to say.

Edrick watched from the window as Keela– wrapped in a gown of sumptuous velveteen–climbed into the coach. The parure she had been gifted was laced around her graceful neck and hung from her ears. Edrick already thought she was the most beautiful creature he had ever set eyes on, but seeing her dressed in velveteen and emeralds painted her beauty in a different light. He felt his heart quicken at the sight of her.

He did not like being left behind. As capable as she was of taking care of herself, he was still concerned. But he and Magpie were resigned to remain at the small cottage. He had, however, thought ahead. While Keela had prepared her toilette for the evening, he slipped out and made his way to the repository at the old academy where there was a sizeable collection of books.

Keela given him directions how to get there. He imagined, with her avarice for books, that she went there frequently. She told him exactly where to find the book he wanted, for she knew the strange system the repository used to sort and organize the books which was unlike a true library. This was a place to store texts, not a place to find and borrow them, but Keela knew the old man who oversaw the repository, and she told Edrick exactly what to say to him.

The old man let him in reluctantly, but he trusted Keela, who often spent hours helping him sort through new shipments of books and store them into their proper place. Edrick asked the old man where the annuals were, and the old man shuffled through the densely packed shelves with Edrick impatiently at his heels.

They found the shelf containing hundreds of years of annual publications of *Oyelle's Register of Landed Gentry & Peerage of Yvrem*. Edrick took the one from the sixth year of the fifth age, which was the year Keela was born, and the newest one the repository had,

172

which had been released only a few months prior. He promised the old man he would bring them back, and he returned to the cottage just in time to see Keela descending the stairs from the loft, dressed like a noblewoman, a dour, baleful expression in her eyes.

He smiled at her, and her severity melted away into vulnerability. She moved to the hearth and sat down on the shabby settee in a pleasant rustle of fine fabric. Edrick sat beside her, and put his hand on hers.

"I'm to dine with a liar tonight. Someone who harmed you. Whose jealousy sought to send you to prison. And then to top all that, I'm a murderer, Edrick. A foul killer," she whispered. It was the first time she'd spoken of what happened on the road the night before.

"You are no such thing, Keela. You are an extraordinary, beautiful creature. One of admirable strength and good judgment. You have no reason to feel any remorse for what you had to do. As far as I'm concerned, you are a hero. You were even before last night. When you saved the boy. You have lived a life of degradation and cruelty and come through it with grace and kindness still in your soul." His eyes were filled with admiration, and she felt warmth emanating from his words to a degree she had never felt before. There was love in every syllable he uttered.

She leaned onto his shoulder and shuddered out a sigh. "I dare not weep and make my face all blotchy," she said. "But that is what I want to do. I want to succumb to tears and furl myself into your arms, Edrick."

He smiled softly at her and gazed down at her lovely face. Gingerly, almost hesitating, he lowered his lips to hers, and placed upon her a gentle, tender kiss. He felt her shiver, and then her cheeks blossomed with pink. When he withdrew, a warm gust of sweet breath exhaled from her gorgeous mouth. Her eyes fluttered open and looked into his.

"You are perfection to me," he said.

"How do you not fear me? How are you not disgusted by what I am?"

"How can I be disgusted by such a beautiful thing? You have not seen yourself through my eyes. If you could, you would love what you are too," he replied.

She blinked at him. Outside, the rattle of a large coach disturbed the peace. The noise ceased abruptly as it stopped before the house.

"Time for you to go into the lair of the beast," Edrick groaned lamentingly.

She mirrored his emotion, and frowned. He bent down and pecked her again, and a smile curled onto her lips.

"Off you go."

She stood, brushing off her gown carefully, and wrapping the shawl around her shoulders. He ushered her to the door, and watched from the window as she was bundled off into Lord Xanett's coach.

Lord Xanett's eyes burned into Keela as she descended from the coach. He waited for her at the foot of the steps to his townhouse, his gaze devouring her with avarice. He took her hand and helped her down, leading her up the steps, his grip on her fingers tight and possessive. He paraded her through the house and into a lavish parlor where an entourage of wealthy people looked on with varied expressions of feigned approval, some barely withholding sneers of disdain. His introduction was met with murmurs of greeting.

He sat her down in a lovely lemon yellow chair with thin, spindly legs, and seated himself in a chair beside her. The company then sat and gazed expectantly upon Keela.

"This lovely creature is my inspiration, for it was her quick thinking and exceptional speed that prevented my child from a terrible fate. Dearest Vianca was not of her right mind, I dare say," he said sorrowfully. "If it weren't for this young woman, I would no longer have a son." He looked upon her with earnest gratitude.

Keela remained tightlipped.

"You were a friend of Vianca's, I understand?" The lady in the periwinkle blue gown asked Keela, her hazel eyes narrowing a bit.

"I wouldn't call her a friend. An acquaintance, perhaps." Keela arranged her shawl on her arms, looking upon the woman with a thinly veiled glower.

"But you accompanied her to Calabras. You were there when…"

"I was there," Keela replied starkly. She stared at the woman until she averted her eye.

"Miss Keela was, perhaps, not too close to Vianca, but I think Vianca was most comfortable with the idea of Miss Keela accompanying her in her low emotional state. She did not want to impose her sorrow or her misery on her friends. She knew Miss Keela, although not a close friend, would respect her need for discretion. I am eternally grateful for Keela's presence, as you can imagine." Xanett ended the dialogue on the matter with this statement, his eyes warning the company that this would not be an acceptable topic any further. But the guests' desire to strip Keela bare remained, existing as a prickly undercurrent that made the room bristle. It was wholly disrespectful towards their host, but it persisted regardless.

"Do you play, Miss Keela?" a younger fellow asked with a wry smile, gesturing to a harp by the window.

"No, I do not," Keela replied succinctly.

"I see. A pity. I would have loved to hear some music before supper," the young man added. "Do you enjoy other pursuits? Perhaps you are an artist? Or you are deft with the bow and arrow?"

"None of those things. I don't have much time for diversions. When I do have time to do what I wish, I like to go walking. And I read a great deal," she said. "Do you read?"

"Oh, now and again. I've never been much of a great reader. It is difficult for me to keep my attention on the words for long. And often, I'll read a whole passage and then have no idea immediately after what the content of it was, does anyone else suffer this affliction?" he laughed. There were chuckles of agreement.

Keela found this whole discussion utterly mind-numbing and tedious, and it had hardly begun. She exhaled audibly, and Xanett's gaze fell upon her. His regard was one of empathy, which surprised her. His cold eyes mirrored her expression of ennui. The exchange was interrupted by a footman who arrived to serve glasses of some viscous form of wine which Keela thought too sickly sweet. She merely handed it back to the servant the moment he came into range.

The men then proceeded to fall into a discussion about Lord Xanett's stylish new Phaeton delivered only that morning. Xanett promised to take the men out to look at it after they dined. Keela could only think how awful it would be to be left in the clutches of the five women all staring at her like... she paused and smirked inwardly. *Like hungry wolves about to leap on her like prey.*

As predicted, Keela was the focus of the discussion the moment the men filtered out of the room to look at the phaeton. Dinner had been a rather dull affair, with talk only of banal subjects such as the unusual amount of rain of late, and how one of the men's most treasured horses had foundered from a field too rich in sweetgrass and the poor thing had to be shot. That then led to a long discussion about muskets and rifles and ultimately, hunting and sport. As soon as it turned to the Akravani, Xanett changed the subject.

Xanett kept Keela close to his left, and she felt his elbow occasionally brush her arm as he ate. She did not like how he ate. There was no enjoyment in it for him. Here he presented a feast of the likes Keela had never seen, delicacies she could have only dreamt of tasting: flummeries, crèmes and jellies, roasted fowl and something she'd never tasted before—chocolate. Xanett devoured the contents of his plate, and served himself more without slowing down to taste it. When he was done, which was soon, he looked about impatiently as everyone else had hardly begun. He eyed Keela's plate, and her paced consumption of the food upon it, and frowned.

"Why does everyone take so bloody long to eat?" he hissed to her.

She paused mid-bite and swallowed, looking at him with an amused expression. "Because food should be savored. Especially good food."

"That's what Vianca said, too. I taste it. It tastes perfectly good. Does it warrant all this wasted time? I don't think so."

"The chef took a great deal of effort to make it delicious and beautiful. The least we can do is respect him and take a moment to experience his good work," Keela replied.

He frowned. "He's my chef. The people of my employ are not entitled to any particular respect."

Keela put her utensils down, giving him a dark, disapproving look. He seemed surprised by her expression.

"He could be making you swill to eat instead of this wonderful fare, he deserves some gratitude."

"I pay him to make this wonderful fare. Too much, if you ask me. So he doesn't need my gratitude. He gets my gold."

"Truly, my Lord, that is utterly repulsive to me, that you do not appreciate the gifts your staff offers you," she remarked rather cuttingly. "Do you regard me and my mother in the same light? As persons providing a service and nothing more?"

He blanched. "Of course not…"

"We are skilled labor, no different than the people in your kitchen who send up these dishes. You look at our work for what it is, artful creation. Is this not also artful creation?" She waved her hand before her where the spread of colorful, sweet and savory dishes decorated the table.

He looked at it a spell and his thin lips disappeared. "You're right, Miss Keela. I suppose that's what Vianca tried to tell me too, but not quite so … kindly."

"I was anything but kind, my Lord." Keela couldn't help but smile. "Did I not call you repulsive?"

He, surprisingly, smiled too. "In comparison to my late wife, Miss Keela, your rebuke was enchanting." His demeanor darkened a bit in remembrance.

Keela was overcome with shame for the benevolent feelings she was experiencing sitting next to this man. He was, in a strange way, charming. She had reason to hate him. He'd had Edrick taken and had withheld truths from her. A shadow passed over her pretty features. He saw it, and he looked at her questioningly.

"Lord Xanett," she said, "I have reason to believe you have some knowledge of my parentage. I cannot help but feel angry that you have kept this a secret from me."

He stared at her, shocked into silence.

"My Lord, do you not wish to partake in this? I believe Darris here is doing me a great injustice, and I am sure you would concur," one of the gentlemen called across the table.

Xanett looked away, and stammered. "I was not paying attention, Threnn, my apologies. The lady here has absorbed all my attentions and, in part, deprived my guests of discourse. Miss Keela, I am sorry, and ladies my apologies to you too."

The company smiled compliantly and continued eating. Lord Xanett then directed most of his attentions to the others, pausing only at one point to turn to Keela and say in the same soft voice they had shared in their prior conversation: "We will discuss your matter after everyone has gone."

She nodded mutely.

He disappeared soon after dinner with the gentlemen, leaving Keela at the mercy of the women. She sat down and listened patiently as one of the ladies took to a harp that was otherwise gathering dust in the parlor and set to tuning it gently before running through some bits of music. There was quiet while some listened to the strings bending their sound, and the tinklings of off-key tunes.

Then the eldest of the ladies, who Keela remembered was called Mrs. Jassa, turned her gaze onto Keela, and tilted her head. "If I recall, Lady Xanett was not a great admirer of yours, Miss Keela, am I correct?"

Keela measured her response, taking a deep calm breath, and then silently exhaling. She looked at the woman, taking in the prolific amounts of high-quality, cream colored lace tucked into her salmon colored silk gown, the detail of her cap, and the long lappets drooping onto her shoulders like the ears of a hound. Mrs. Jassa was still youthful, and quite lovely.

"Oh, she absolutely despised me," Keela replied flippantly. She tilted her head the same way Mrs. Jassa had, and smiled in the same passive aggressive manner. "Couldn't stand to breathe the same air as me."

The other ladies were immediately intrigued and the plucking on the harp fell still.

"Yet here you are, all but occupying her place. It feels a bit strange."

"I could hardly occupy her place. I'm not nearly as nasty and malicious a piece of work as she was," Keela said.

All eyes widened, mouths popped open and the youngest lady gasped audibly.

"How discourteous and impertinent! Mrs. Xanett is only lately dead, and deserves the utmost respect!" Mrs. Jassa declared.

Keela shrugged with an expression of bemusement. "I'm not obligated to treat anyone, dead or alive—who deliberately strove to make my life difficult—with respect," Keela said sweetly, smiling at each of them in turn. "I very much doubt any of you liked her much, either. Even her friends were intimidated and cowed by her. It must be a great relief to visit the manor and not be cast under her scrutiny, I imagine."

"I say…" the lady at the harp uttered. There was no attempt to disagree with Keela, which was telling.

"I thought so," Keela said with a nod. She rose and sailed across to the sideboard, where there were some ports, wines and spirits arrayed in sparkling cut glass bottles. She selected a fragrant brandy, and poured herself some into a tiny fluted glass. She drank it down, her eyes challenging the company. They said nothing. The harpist resumed plucking at the harp.

Keela had spent many years passively accepting the bile spewed by Vianca. Somewhere along the way, she stopped worrying what would happen if she talked back. She suspected it was when she stepped into the coach with her on the way to Calabras. Her sense of responsibility for Vianca's choice was gone. Edrick had helped her to realize that she was being ridiculous. And perhaps, knowing now, that she was a true predator, being surrounded by snarling imposters was but a laugh. However Xanett took the consequences of her snide interaction with these society ladies felt utterly unimportant.

It wasn't long after that, the men returned. Xanett led the pack, and he appeared aggravated. His cold blue eyes fell upon Keela. The women began indiscreetly whispering to the fellows the moment they approached. Keela rose and excused herself, a smirk on her lips. She sought out the washroom, and left them behind to stew in her behavior.

When she returned Xanett was sitting by the fire, his stare fixed upon her face and it remained there while she approached. He gestured her to sit in the chair beside him. She did, challenging his gaze with her own.

His eyes continued to bore into the side of her face while she reached for a fresh glass of brandy and drank. She then looked right back at him.

He leaned in. "They told me what you said."

180

She arched her brows and then shrugged, sipping from the delicate glass. The harp was strumming, a little more in tune now, and a soft voice began to accompany the melody.

"Did they tell you everything?" she asked, not much caring.

"I believe so," he replied. He looked over at the others and his hard profile was unreadable. He then swiveled towards her again.

"They accused you of vying to replace Vianca."

"They actually admitted saying that to me? That's somewhat astonishing. I didn't expect honesty from them to that degree."

"They did. And you did not deny it," he continued.

"I would never give them the pleasure of that," Keela replied quickly.

Xanett shook his head and a strange smile curled onto his lips. "No. You did not deny it," he said with barely contained pleasure.

Keela shook her head. "If you choose to think that I desire to take your wife's place, you are mistaken my Lord."

Xanett angled his body towards her and his cool smile remained. "I choose to believe that you do not know what you want, Miss Keela. And I will continue to do so."

"I have no interest in a man who has lied to me for almost my entire life," Keela whispered.

His smile melted, and he chewed his cheek. "I have told you no lies, Miss Keela."

"A lie by omission is still a lie."

"I have my reasons to withhold things from you, Miss Keela, but the decision to do so was not mine to make."

"Then whose was it?" Her direct gaze into his made her feel like she was falling into an abyss. Her skin flushed and a wave of heat passed through her.

"I have not been given leave to tell you, Miss Keela."

Her frustration took the form of flushing on her neck and ears. Xanett's eyes softened and instead grew desirous as he took in her spirited, passionate reaction.

181

"However," his voice softened to a low bass, and a wry, almost mischievous smile curled onto his thin, hard lips. "I will tell you what you want to know, Miss Keela. *Everything.* But only if you agree to be my wife."

"What?" Keela jumped her feet and glared down at Lord Xanett, insensible of the company. "That is simply revolting! Resorting to such disgusting tactics!"

Instead of being angry or shocked, Lord Xanett smiled at her fury, his eyes filled with fiery yearning. Keela was overcome with a rush of feelings that alarmed and confused her. Disgusted with herself and with Lord Xanett, she spun on her heel and stormed out, slamming every door between her and the street.

Keela's soft, velveteen hems were a mire by the time she got home, and her breath was ragged. She had fled through the misty rain, and her superior attire was left sodden for it. She burst through the door to find Alara and Edrick seated at the table; he in a banyan and hat with a pair of slippers. He had a large tome open before him, and a piece of Alara's rustic tea cake on a plate next to a piping cup of chamomile and nettle tea. Alara was across from him. She'd just finishing serving his slice of cake and was dressed for the evening in her shabbiest dressing gown and cap. They both looked up in surprise at Keela's entry and then concern at her bedraggled state. Magpie had no opinion of Keela's wet clothes and muddy hems. She was just glad to see her and made it quite clear by wriggling delightedly at her feet.

"What happened? Did he harm you?" Edrick asked as Keela stepped inside and shook herself off.

"No," Keela replied calmly, shutting out the cold, misty night. The fire was blazing in the cottage and it was a lovely feeling after running through the rain until she was soaked. "He did, however, tell me that if I wanted to know more about where I came from, that I would have to agree to marry him."

Edrick's eyes darkened and he glowered. "No need for such desperate measures, Keela. I've found something." He pointed to the book. "Go and change into something dry, and I'll show you."

Keela assented, and tramped up the stairs, her skirts clinging to her legs. She descended soon after, dressed almost identically to Alara in a dressing gown of the same fabric. Alara had gotten a large bolt of it for a bargain some years ago, and the scraps that remained were also purposed into the quilts that covered their beds.

Edrick had never truly experienced such a bucolic way of life, but in this house at least, he and Magpie found ease in it. There was something comforting and warm about the threadbare fabrics, the slightly bitter tea, the plain cake, the stewed meals, the wood smoke, the sharp aroma of the lye soap they used to wash their clothes, the scent of yeast and baking bread—it wrapped around him warm and cozy like the two quilts Alara had brought down for him in preparation for the night. He would sleep on their old settee, and Alara had already spread a clean, much-darned sheet over it. Magpie had climbed up on it after Keela had gone upstairs, and now dozed happily by the fire.

Keela joined him, scaling the bench and sinking down beside him.

"So, nothing more to say about your evening of delights?" he asked.

She huffed and shook her head. "What do you want to show me?"

He opened her locket and handed it to her. She had only looked at it briefly before she left for Xanett's townhouse. He held the candle near, so she could look closely at it. He then slid the book towards her. It was the one from the repository.

It was a lovely volume. The leather—a deep, forest green—was tooled with intricate scrollwork. There was an embossed cartouche in which the words: *Oyelle's Register of Landed Gentry & Peerage of Yvrem,* underlined by smaller text that read: *Published for Annum 6-5.*

The second volume was identical, except it was twenty-one years newer, the leather shinier and the gold letters still glossy. The only other difference was the publication date. The second one read: *Published for Annum 27-5*. Two of Keela's many beaded-string bookmarks protruded from each of the dense stacks of pages.

"It always makes me laugh that Oyelle's continues to follow these families after all these years," Edrick muttered. "I'm surprised the Farkas didn't put a stop to it. I suppose a publication that has been producing an annual register for over a thousand years is not going to let one invasion and occupation stop it from doing what it does."

"The peerage hasn't ceased to exist. Oyelle's still seems to think the titles mean something. According to Ilmi at the repository, the book still sells out every time it is released. As for the Farkas, they supposedly foster freedom of expression, so it would be against their values to silence the publisher," Keela said.

Edrick smiled at Keela, who still seemed remote and shaken by her evening out. It had been a long and trying day.

Edrick opened the first book in front of her, and then put the locket on the page next to a listing he had found. The intricately engraved W with the songbird on the elegant scripted letter and the ring of branches and oak leaves from the locket were replicated almost exactly on the page. The image was larger and in much finer detail. The image was also printed in color.

"Wrenn," Keela murmured. "A Marquessate…"

"Here," He reached over and pointed to the list of names of the current family members. The patriarch and Marquess of Wethlo was Drevus Wrenn. He had three daughters and two sons. The eldest daughter was fifteen when the book was published.

"She was so young," Keela whispered.

Edrick peered at the entry. "Edeera, what a lovely name."

Keela said, "Edeera Wrenn…"

"I actually know the eldest son. He's the Marquess now." Edrick reached for the newer book, and opened it to the mark. It did, indeed, list a new Marquess of Wethlo: Arius Wrenn. He was married and had children of his own, and a new heir. It showed the eldest daughter married to an Earl.

"Naturally the family no longer lives at Wethlo. It is actually now a Farkas Sentely. They are at Imbrine, about twenty miles away from their family seat. And your mother Edeera..." Edrick said, pausing, "she married the Earl of Nevin, which is west of Neyus, a long way from here. About, oh... a thousand miles."

"Good gracious!" Keela gasped. "That would be a month of solid travel, easily."

Edrick frowned and titled his head with a slight shrug.

"But Arius is not so far. A day and a half, maybe two. And I think he would speak to me, if he knew I was already party to the scandalous secret of his sister's indiscretion. And I am his king after all."

"Then we must go," she concluded.

"Then we shall."

"Your horse, it's with a friend. We need only find one for me. But I do not have the money for that, nor am I an accomplished rider."

"We will take our time then. I will supply what you need, Keela."

She gazed at him for a long, poignant moment, studying his face. She threw her head back and groaned.

Alara suspired herself, and shook her head. "I have no idea what I'm going to tell the Lord when he comes looking for you."

"He will, too. And he had better not find *you* here," Keela told Edrick.

"Then we should probably leave tomorrow. I'll wake early and find what we need to travel to Imbrine."

Keela rose. "I'm tired and I'm going to bed. Mother, shall we leave our guest to get some rest too?"

Alara finished her last bit of cake. They both bade him

goodnight and left him and his dog to finish preparing his bed.

Edrick crawled under the quilts sewn by the hands of the women above and he took a deep, cleansing breath, listening to them settle in and the low murmur of their voices. The fire snapped, and Magpie burrowed underneath the covers and wedged herself along his side, her black, shining nose peeking out from the edge of the blanket. He drew his hand over her, and released another great big sigh. In all honesty, he would have liked to just stay here and eat more cake. But there were things that needed to be seen to, and he was fairly certain now that he was meant to be by Keela's side no matter where she took him. He was convinced that the Farkas had somehow arranged all this so that the two of them would meet. For what reason, he was still unsure. He imagined the truth would come out sooner or later. He just liked it here in this little house. It felt like home, as coarse and plain as it was. The ladies, they felt like family.

Chapter 12
Homecoming

They set off by mid-day the following day. Edrick had gotten a second horse with the assistance of Keela's friend Ejesh, although Edrick did get the impression that Ejesh was not keen on helping him. It was only when Keela arrived to meet them that the man's stern and jealous demeanor melted away.

He helped Keela and Edrick apply the newly purchased, used sidesaddle and attach Keela's leather bag to the offside and rear. Keela had packed her warmest walking gowns and habits from her trunk. She wore her favorite today, a light woolen habit of deep navy blue and a heavy, woolen cloak with a hood to keep her warm and dry if the sky opened up.

Edrick wore exactly what he had worn for his arduous journey to Eyome: oiled leather greatcoat, wide brimmed hat, a wool waistcoat and frockcoat, and leather breeches with warm under breeches. He packed Magpie in her travel bag, and his personal items were fastened behind his saddle. He was so grateful that Keela had thought to retrieve these things for him after he'd been knocked off his horse by Xanett's hired thugs.

The farmer lifted Keela up onto her horse, and she slid her leg clumsily over the horn, looking a bit unnerved by the whole idea of riding. It was something she had not done much. She had learned as the Lord had insisted, riding on an obstinate pony a few times a month until she was a moderately able rider.

This horse was inordinately tall for her liking. It was a leggy, narrow sliver of a gelding with razor-sharp withers and a large head and big ears. It was a dark bay with a prominent, bowed nose and a blaze that was painted from his forehead over his muzzle to his bottom lip. He also had tall white stockings.

Edrick had chosen him because of his rock hard hoofs and his quiet nature. Keela looked a bit stricken, staring down at the men as she gathered up the reins and adjusted herself. Ejesh helped her find her stirrup for her left foot and thoughtfully arranged her cape and skirts to keep her covered. She wore a low-crown riding hat that looked much like a lady's top hat, which she covered with her hood to protect it from the mist and rain. Her riding gloves were of deep burgundy leather. Edrick thought her most elegant in her attire.

Once installed, Edrick mounted, thanking Ejesh for his assistance, which was met with a grunt. Ejesh saved his manners for Keela, whom he bade farewell, warned her to take care, and to stop frequently to stretch her legs. Keela responded with a soft smile which made the tall, ungainly man flush like a young boy. With a cluck of the tongue, Edrick's horse moved towards the road. Keela waved to Ejesh one more time before she followed on her towering horse.

It only took a half hour before Keela started feeling saddle sore. The day was as she suspected it would be: foggy mist interspersed with the occasional downpour. By the time they stopped for the night at a town called Mennandorp, they were sodden.

They found respite at the town's only inn. Edrick supplied the funds for the rooms, and before they went up to rest, they took a simple, unadorned meal of braised mutton with cabbage and boiled potatoes. As plain as it was, it was tasty and warm, and for the bedraggled travelers, a great comfort.

"I wonder," ventured Edrick, "what Xanett will do, once he discovers you are gone."

"I cannot envision what he would do. I don't think there is much he can do. I doubt he will send someone after me. I hope he doesn't worry my mother too much about it." Keela daintily sliced a piece of mutton from the bone, and ate it, exhaling heavily as she chewed.

"You seem concerned."

"I am. He holds all the power, Edrick," Keela replied with a furrowed brow. "He owns our home, oversees her trade, and provides for me."

"He does not provide for you. Someone else does, *through* him."

Keela conceded the point with a nod, reaching for the clay goblet that held a flavorful negus; a drink of spiced, warmed port. Alara could not afford good port, so it was a way to enhance a middling wine. Edrick had gone with strong grog, and was working on his second mug of it. There was a murmur about the place. It was a low-ceilinged, fair sized room set around a large open fireplace with the hefty cone shaped-chimney standing over it on four stalwart stone pilasters. There was a ring of chairs in various states of wear scattered around it, and then a variety of tables for dining and drinking. Most of which were occupied by other guests or local merchants and shopkeepers who were having a nice tipple after a long day's work.

Magpie was asleep under the table, too tired to beg for scraps. There was a tall, lanky gentleman at the table beside them who persisted in staring down at the pup until the two of them could no longer ignore it. He and his companion had been murmuring quietly back and forth until the man noticed Magpie. The conversation

189

went still and the man stared. When Edrick finally caught his eye with a questioning gaze, the man finally leaned towards Edrick.

"I beg sir, where in the world did you manage to find a Ney pup?" He was a strange-looking fellow with pale, bottomless blue eyes and a manicured beard. He wore all black, except for his stockings and his shirt, the white bright against a pallid skin. His companion had the dark, mahogany skin typical of the south mainlanders with silver hair and the same kind of clipped facial hair as his dining companion. He was also garbed in the same black ensemble, although his frock coat was fancier, with thicker pleats and silver buttons all up and down one side of the cutaway. He also had the same cool, light-colored eyes. Keela tried not to stare, and gazed at them over her cup as she sipped.

Edrick bowed shallowly from his seat, and smiled forcedly. "She was entrusted into my care, Amrait, sir," he replied with unexpected deference. Keela's brow rose in surprise.

"May I have a closer look at her?" the Amrait asked.

Edrick looked hesitant, but he assented grudgingly. Leaning down, he scooped up the sleeping pup and handed her to the man. The gentleman held her under her little forelegs, and let her body dangle. He locked his eyes on her beautiful, silver gaze and followed it as it moved, his head bobbing like a bird. He then handed her to his companion, who, too, bored into the pup's eyes with his own cold gaze. Magpie seemed to be discomfited by them, and looked away as best she could. Then she was abruptly returned to Edrick, who bundled her on his lap. She took advantage of his distraction and tried to put her snout into his food.

"She's a fine specimen. Imperial with silver eyes. Purest I've ever seen. Someone must surely think highly of you, to place such a precious thing in your care," the Amrait said softly.

Edrick bowed his head. The Amrait then looked at Keela, and his stare burned into her. She looked away uncomfortably.

"Seems sir, you are entrusted with a great deal," the pale man said. "It makes me curious as to who you are."

Edrick furrowed his brow. "I am nobody of importance," he muttered.

Keela snorted and hid her smirk behind her cup again. Edrick glared at her and then bowed his head politely to the two gentlemen before picking up his fork again.

It was only after supper that Edrick explained to Keela what the two men were. They were seated in the chairs by the fire, Keela enjoying the heat and the comforting feeling of being sated and relaxed. Magpie was draped on Keela's lap, snoring, her fur absorbing the warmth. Keela's eyes were on the two gangly gentlemen who had dined near them. The men were now seated across from them, both gazing at the fire and drawing from long-stemmed pipes in thoughtful silence.

"Those two men are peculiar," Keela murmured quietly, sipping from what was now a mug of chocolate. Edrick stuck with grog, and had his cup resting precariously on his knee, one ankle resting on the other one. His cheeks were ruddy and his eyes were a little glazed. He gazed at Keela with an unmistakable look of desire and adoration as she spoke, his eyes lingering on her mouth. He lifted his goblet up and drank, and the returned it to his knee.

"They're wizards," he replied. "Wizards of a particular priestly order known as the Awoken. You don't recognize them? They're all like that: peculiar and unsettling."

"Real wizards?" Keela blurted.

Edrick gave her with a bit of a shrug. This was nothing out of the ordinary for him. He drank again, tipping the cup back and draining it. He put his foot down, leaned forward and put the empty vessel on the stone skirt that enclosed the fireplace, where he also propped his boots, one on its heel, the other crossed over it. He leaned back and slumped down a bit in his chair, emitting a great big yawn.

"I wonder what they might be up to, wandering about the countryside like that?" she mused

"It's not unusual for them to be outside of the walls of their commonalities. They do have a purpose to serve. They can't all just exist inside their little wizard boroughs forever."

"Have you ever seen a wizard commonality?" she asked.

"Seen?" Edrick chuckled. "I have been inside many in my life. My own home is but three miles from the Revagard Commonality in Amaronna." She gazed at him in wonder and all he wanted to do was to touch her. "It's no different from any other town, except that many of the residents are magic bearers of one kind or another. There are as many ordinary people as there are magical ones because they marry, and their children are not often born magical. The real purpose of living in a commonality are the institutions that they require to hone and perfect their skills. The schools, the libraries of magical books, workshops for artisans, tradesmen, journeymen and whatnot who specialize in the manufacture of magical wares to set up shop. They would scarce do well in common communities, but in the Commonalities of Magi, their most desired customers populate the town."

"Mother told me the magi lived separately because the people once feared and loathed them," Keela said.

Edrick agreed with a bemused frown. "I suppose that's also true to some degree. I think in the past that might have been the case—especially before the days of the Hedrell Renascence."

Keela agreed. She'd read a great deal about that period. The Rebirth, as it was also referred to, was a period that was ushered in after a century of devastating war which had wreaked havoc the world over. A great portion of the population of the known world had starved after the theft and destruction of crops and livestock. That era was called the Gleaning when it seemed only the most stalwart survived. But those who had emerged from the dark times did so with a changed perspective and they brought on the

Renascence, ushering in a period of enlightenment and acceptance, of learning and progress. That vast undertaking was soon dampened by the return of the influence of wealth and power—where borders were fought over again, and the peoples were once again thrown into two castes: the poor and the wealthy with hardly anything in between.

That was when the Farkas invaded. The Farkas were known to be most respectful of the magi.

"Perhaps it was the Farkas invasion that set into motion common acceptance for the magic-bearing," Keela speculated. Edrick's brows rose.

"Yes, that is a logical assumption. You could be right on that end." He yawned again. Keela fought the yawn struggling to express itself on her lips, and she put her mug down. Rising from her seat, she scooped the dog up into her arms.

At that moment, a tower of a man entered the inn through the main door, and paused. His strange, hauntingly pale eyes in a gaunt face swept the room. His gaze fell directly on Keela. Magpie sniffed the air and whined. She raised her head and fixed her eyes on the tall newcomer.

With raven eyes, and silver-brushed hair that had once been as black as Keela's, he was unmistakably Farkas. There was something familiar about him that Keela could not place. Before she could get a proper accounting of his features, he turned to look at the magi who had both risen to their feet and were welcoming him into their midst with smiles as if old friends. The man disappeared behind the great cone of the flue, his penetrating gaze along with him.

Edrick had taken Keela's standing as a sign it was time to retire, and was not paying much heed to the goings-on in the far side of the room. He merely offered his arm, which Keela managed take with Magpie still cradled against her breast with her other arm. They left the stranger and the wizards to their own devices, but Keela could not shake the feeling that she had met that man somewhere before.

As she prepared for bed, Keela was unsuccessful in letting the train of thought go. She wracked her brain for a memory of where and when—and tried to suss out what was recognizable about him as she let her hair down and removed her outerwear. In her modest, comfortable room she mulled it over, but found no answers. For the life of her, she could not remember. Exhausted by the past few days, and more so by her inability to find a source for her sense of acquaintance with this stranger, she gave in to sleep.

The pair set off with Magpie the next morning shortly after a breakfast of diced fruits, cheese and bread. They were the only ones who had risen early, and were alone in the dining area. Keela had almost forgotten about the stranger. Instead, she'd woken up with her mind full of Xanett—imagining he might send someone to find them and interfere with their mission.

She'd donned her habit again—the wool having dried gracefully, and suffered no mud or dirt that would require her to choose another garment. It was spitting rain when they left, and the deluge did not abate all day. They took shelter two hours after mid-day in a byre, eating cheese sandwiches made for them by the inn's cook, while the bovine residents of the shed mooed at them in consternation for occupying their space.

They braved the rain again soon after, leaving the cows to their shelter. They fastened the gate and were underway. It was another seven hours of mind-numbing plodding and discomfort before they arrived at the fortification that marked the outer edges of Imbrine. The sight of two bright fires lit in braziers on the top of a pair of flanking drum towers was a welcome one, signaling their arrival.

They rode between the walls of an ancient barbican, behind which the towers and the sizable gate awaited. The portcullis was tucked up in its bed, its spiked bottom looking like sharp teeth in the gate's gaping maw. Torches lit the tunnel that led them into the city.

When they emerged, they found themselves in the dense, bustling city of Imbrine.

The main road took them through a narrow fjord of edifices built one up against the other with even narrower streets leading off this way and that—some stepped, some dark and ominous. Some streets bored right though residences, leading under low skywalks where windows shone with candlelight. The roads were cobbled and covered in the detritus of a day's traffic. They were, however, mostly without obstacles or impediments.

The city's buzz was at present, mostly indoors. Public houses were roaring with voices and laughter, conversations could be heard through cracked windows, arguments and bickering from some homes, children hollering, dogs barking, the aroma of food being prepared for supper. Keela's stomach roared at the scent of the food. The sandwiches were seven hours ago. The horses, too, were hungry and tired.

"Have you been here before?" Keela asked Edrick.

He pointed ahead, showing her instead of answering. "We'll take the left after the square. That will lead to the garden district. We'll find a nice guest house there. It's a good one.,"

She assented wearily. He felt for her. She appeared more exhausted than he'd ever seen her. She did not complain, but he knew she was in great discomfort. They had not stopped much to stretch or rest, both eager to get out of the inclement weather. The rain had stopped sometime earlier that evening and Keela insisted they keep going so they could be there before it started again.

The density of the city lessened the further they drew away from the old gate. They passed through another curtain wall and found themselves in a large square surrounded by government buildings and the like, each one as fancy as a flummery with forests of flying buttresses and nubby, pointed rooflines, ornately friezed arches and regiments of scowling gargoyles as far as the eye could see.

Keela stared like a country bumpkin, trying to make out what she could from the spare light cast from the lamps in the square. Edrick led them through to a road that drew off diagonally and that rose up steeply. Here, there were separate houses with walled gardens. Grand boxes of stone—two and three stories—bookended by flat chimney walls with decorative porticos and tall windows. They flanked up the incline like soldiers, their garden walls bursting with greenery and trees.

Edrick rode across the road to one house with particularly tall walls, and disappeared through a gate that interrupted its span. Keela followed, careful to duck as her towering horse put her head in the way of the arch. The gate led into a small courtyard where a row of horse stalls looked out into the space.

They dismounted and Keela—her legs long turned to jelly from riding—ungracefully collapsed onto her backside, with a flop and a waft of riding skirts, the moment her boots hit the cobbles. Edrick ran to her and helped her to her feet, apologizing profusely for neglecting her. He supported her while she removed Magpie from her bag.

A young towheaded fellow appeared from a doorway and greeted them politely. He took charge of the horses, and promised he would deliver their bags to their rooms. Edrick relinquished custody of the horses to the young man, and together they staggered through a corridor that led them into a stunning cloister.

"Oh, this is beautiful, Edrick," Keela whispered.

The walkway was wall and window on one side, and a colonnade on the other, looking out into a tidy garden of topiary and spring flowers with a round shimmering pool in the center. The courtyard was illuminated by iron candelabras, each taper protected by a curved cylinder of storm glass. Two paths crossed and sectioned the garden in four, the fountain marking the point of intersection

"It's an old abbey," Edrick explained. "Once housed the Medricans, I think." He watched Magpie lope out into the garden and cavort among the plants, her tail waving like a banner.

"Yes. The tracery at the top of each arch... it has the Medrican star," Keela agreed. "It's too bad they are gone. I would have liked to have some Medrican cheeses. I'm SO hungry..." she finally confessed.

Edrick was always impressed by Keela's depth of knowledge. . "We will have a nice hot meal in no time, the keeper here is a personal friend of my brother's... and he's extremely, er... deferent of my family."

"It'll probably feel nice for you to be treated as you are accustomed again, rather than slumming with the likes of us," she replied with a grin.

"I cannot be untruthful and say I do not like the idea of being in high comfort, Miss Keela, especially after today's ride. However, I dare say I never once felt at a disadvantage or lacking of comfort in your care, or your mother's," he replied. "The fact is, I found something deeply soothing being under your roof, eating your mother's cooking, and sleeping by the fire in comfort. There is warmth there that I have never known anywhere else I have ever lived. I also found my berth in the narrowboat oddly calming and pleasing to me. It was close quarters in that little boat, but it was a kind of peace that I haven't often enjoyed in my life. The broad spaces of my home, and the respectful care I received from the staff only made me feel lonely..."

Keela frowned and her brow darkened. "Sorry Edrick," she whispered.

He smiled and shook his head and gave her a warm gaze. "No need to be sorry," he retorted. "We have found one another, have we not?"

She nodded mutely. He led her away from the cloister through a pair of paned doors which opened into a round vestibule. He reached for a bell cord which he tugged vigorously.

In a few moments, the sound of heels clattering on marble could be heard approaching, and a heavy wooden door heaved itself open to their left. A rather distinctive, elegant looking man appeared before them. His smooth, manicured silver brow rose at the sight of Edrick and he bowed deeply.

"Your Grace, I am so pleased that you honor my humble establishment again. So honored," he gushed. Keela smirked, but Edrick squeezed her arm tightly.

"Mr. Ains, I am equally pleased and honored to be here. This beautiful creature is Miss Keela Wrenn, and that pup is my Magpie. I do hope both of these ladies are welcome here," he said.

The man bowed deeply again. "Of course, of course, your Grace. A room for the lady, and we will provide for the fine hound, yes. Please, I will put you in your usual room, your grace. The lady I will give her the apartments of the west corner, I think. Yes, I think it has a delightful prospect." He opened the heavy door from whence he'd come, and gestured for them to pass through.

Edrick went first, familiar with the place. He bent down and swept the puppy up, carrying her down the long corridor. On one side, large windows looked out over the sprawl of Imbrine's vast garden district, the square shining yellow with lamplight. On the other side they passed several rooms: two parlors—one next to the other—,a library where a young couple were quietly reading, and a dining room. Then the corridor turned abruptly and led back towards the cloister, circling it. The windows switched sides and now looked out into the cloister, and on the other side were doors to the various rooms and apartments. Edrick walked to a door where the corridor turned right again.

"Mr. Ains, are we too late for dinner?"

"Never," Mr. Ains replied as if the idea horrified him. "I will see to having a meal served for you in the dining room. In, oh;" his gaze wandered to a large standing clock ticking across the hall, "… half an hour?"

Edrick gave her a nod and turned to Keela. "I'll see you in half an hour, Miss Wrenn."

She curtsied clumsily and watched him disappear into his room. Mr. Ains then led her down to the other end of the hall, and there secured her a corner room like Edrick's. It was massive and far above her means. But she merely curtsied politely and went inside. Only a few moments later her bag was brought in by the stable hand, and a maid appeared behind him to help her.

The maid carried a washbowl and a decanter filled with steaming water. She unpacked and hung Keela's gowns and garments on pegs in an immense armoire while Keela freshened up with the water, a lovely lavender soap and a sponge. The maid then helped Keela into a fresh set of underpinnings and the same simple gown she'd worn in Calabras the evening she met Edrick. Her hair was pulled back tightly and wound into a bun, fastened with a ribbon. She felt so much better. Her stomach was still rattling and roaring, but being clean and dry was such a comfort to her.

She quietly made her way around the cloister and back to the vestibule, then to the corridor of common rooms. She found Edrick in one of the parlors sipping a glass of port like a refined gentleman. He walked with her to the dining room where, alone, they sat and devoured a large meal together.

After they ate, they joined the other guests in the parlor for a bit, until Keela could barely keep her eyes open. She hardly remembered ambling to her room or the maid assisting her with the removal of her gown and underpinnings and replacing it all with her soft downy cotton nightgown.

She slid underneath the crisp, fresh-smelling linens, atop which the heavy brocade blankets were piled and warm. The scent of the washing soap and the aroma left behind by the meticulous pressing made her long for home, and for peace. Sleep drew her deep, deep into dreams.

Keela was walking as snow fell all around her, but she was not cold. She only felt a chill on the bottom of her hands and feet. She looked down and saw that they were large black paws. She lifted up her moist, glistening muzzle to the wind, took a deep breath of it, and was rewarded with images of Alara ironing a pillowcase to flat perfection, the steam rising off of it, filling her nostrils with the pleasant scent. Alara looked at Keela, and smiled.

"Lovely dog," she said. She threw Keela a strip of beef short rib which Keela ate, bones and all, her teeth crushing the shards effortlessly. It was always Keela's favorite cut of meat, cheap as it was. So delicious when braised.

It was even better raw, she thought.

Keela huffed and shook herself, starting at her head and letting it spread down her body like a wave, shaking off snowflakes onto the floor. Magpie watched her from under the table, but instead of a Ney wolf, she was a little girl— beautiful, with a round face and her jet hair cut in a fringe that hung just above her large, striking, silver eyes. Before her, she had two little wooden toy knights whose heads and arms were bitten off.

"I'm trapped," Magpie complained.

Keela opened her mouth to ask why, but could only bark and growl. Magpie pushed out her lower lip and glowered at Keela.

"Now, now, Miss Keela. It isn't seemly of a young lady to speak so brashly," Lord Xanett's voice opined from nowhere in particular. "I don't mind if you bark or growl. You may do so all you please when you are my wife. But in front of company, it is uncouth."

Keela snarled and growled menacingly, and padded across the floor, her nails clicking. She saw Edrick through the window. He was climbing up her tower without her. She leapt through the window— barely touching the ground as she ran—her paws almost floating as she ran after him. The more she ran, the further away he seemed to get, the tower becoming smaller and smaller with each advancing stride. She was surrounded by trees and shrubs that were growing denser and thicker as she progressed, the snow growing deeper.

She stopped short when the path was impeded by the shape of

two wolves whose scars and scabs still oozed from Keela's bites. There was a tiny pole arm impaled in the ear of the smaller wolf.

"Abominations! Mixed bloods!" The woman in white screamed, the skin on her hands still swathed in smooth raven fur, her teeth still long canines that had filled her lupine mouth.

Keela launched herself at the woman's throat and clamped her teeth into the pale throat with a vicious bite. The woman crumpled beneath her, warm flesh pierced by Keela's teeth, blood flowing salty and delicious over Keela's tongue. The other wolf watched, whining like a puppy, tail tucked, terrified.

"Keela," a deep, resonant voice spoke. "That is enough, you've done enough."

Keela let go of her quarry. She stepped back and found herself bumping into something large, warm and massive. She turned to see a huge bear standing like a man. It dropped to its feet and lowered its head, cuddling its face affectionately against hers. There was blood on its mouth, too. Keela licked it away.

"Keela, you've done enough," the voice persisted.

She pivoted her head away from the bear, which now rolled beside her, grunting *nng nng nng* and batting at her playfully with his massive claws. She peered behind her. A great wolf stood, silver hairs dusting his snout, the ruff around his venerable face sparkled with them. His shining nose twitched, his ears pointed alertly at her. His wizened eyes were watching her. She'd seen those eyes before.

"That's him!" Keela pushed herself up from her belly onto her knees on the bed, her eyes peering into the darkness towards her headboard. "It's him..." she repeated to herself, going silent as she worked things through her mind.

Unexpectedly, she threw off her blanket, and discovered she was without any clothes. She must have wriggled out of her nightgown during the nightmare, she concluded, feeling her way around mattress until she found the little wad of cotton down at the foot of

201

the bed. She pulled it on, and padded to her door, opening it quietly. She then trotted gingerly down the corridor to Edrick's room, where she knocked gently once, and then more loudly the second time.

She heard him groan and the bed creak. There was a tired shuffle and then the door yanked open. His grumpy face was barely visible.

"You said there were killings on the way to Calabras."

"Yes," he replied in a gravelly voice.

"They were trying to kill Magpie. The people killed, they were guardians. Of that I'm certain. And now they want to kill me," Keela said. "We are abominations. Mixed blood…"

"I'm not following," Edrick murmured, rubbing his eye with his fist.

"Remember the great big wolf I told you about? The one that led me to Magpie? He was at the inn with the wizards. He was there!"

"The wizards said Magpie is pure. They're rarely wrong about that sort of thing. And we don't know if she's like you. Why would she be a wolf, and not a girl if that were the case? You weren't a pup. So she could be pure Farkas for all we know. Or just a dog…"

"Yes, but what constitutes pure to the magi? Is it different to what the Farkas might consider pure?"

"Keela, I don't know," Edrick grumbled irritably. "Can we talk about this in a couple of hours? It's almost morning." Keela's shoulders slumped and she frowned like an obstinate child. Edrick shook his head. "Go back to sleep, Keela," he mumbled before closing the door.

Keela plodded back towards her room, her eyes distant as she mulled over what her dream had revealed to her. *I'm trapped.* The words rang in her head in the voice of a child. *I'm trapped.*

She crawled back into her disheveled bed and tried to return some order to the rumpled mess she'd made, making sure her feet were peeking out from the covers as she preferred. It was only then she noticed the papery hardness against her face. She sat up and squinted at it. Her pillow was covered in something dark. She threw off her covers and got to her feet, snatching the pillow from the bed. She walked to the fire, kneeling with the pillow facing the meager light. The coverlet on the pillow was smeared in dried blood.

Keela stared at her reflection in the mirror of the vanity, her expression frozen in waxen horror. There was still blood on her mouth. There was some on her neck too. It wasn't from a bloody nose as she had first assumed. The blood had dried. In the darkness of night, Edrick had not seen it. She looked away distractedly, picking up the decanter and pouring water into the bowl, reaching for a small towel, and pressing it into the water until it was soaked. She wrung it out and placed it on her face, wiping slowly and deliberately at first, but as disgust sank in, she scrubbed faster and faster. Dunking, wringing, wiping, until the water was a sickly brown and the coppery smell she hadn't noticed until she discovered her pillow, was gone. She dumped the water out into the cloister and sat on the ledge of the walkway, her legs and bare feet dangling over a bed of flowers.

The morning had already begun to rise. All around her the light waxed until there was a deep, gold-tinted blue washing over everything. Her eyes dropped to her feet which were covered in dirt. Below them—in the soft earth of the flower bed—were two large paw prints. With a shudder, Keela began to weep.

As Keela and Edrick made their way up to the Pharos Hill district, Keela pondered her situation. She must have been in some sort of half-dream state. Aware enough to return to her room and curl back into her bed, but not aware enough to remember it. She strolled with her arm looped through Edrick's, her bonnet brim shading her tense features. The wind picked up her snowy white skirts and whipped them against her legs, and the peplum on her navy spencer fluttered. The scent of caramelized sugar and pastries filled her nose, and made Edrick mumble about being peckish.

"You seem particularly thoughtful this morning, Keela," Edrick finally said, glancing down at her from under the broad brim of his hat. She twisted up to return the glance, and smiled stiffly at him.

"Yes," she replied. "I had a strange night."

"You're telling me," Edrick laughed. "You woke me to tell me something about Magpie and her being pure… I don't particularly recall, since I was half-asleep."

"It is hard to explain," she said dismissively.

"You didn't go back to sleep, I take it. You look a little peaked."

"No, I didn't."

Edrick patted her hand gently as they walked on. The walk was almost entirely uphill. Keela was already feeling it in her calf muscles. Edrick was the first to give in to it. "Ah, look, a tea shop. Shall we stop for a quick restorative refreshment, Miss Keela?"

Keela assented with a nod. Her belly was filled with both dread and elation at the prospect of meeting the man who was her uncle. She wore the tiny locket around her neck. Clutching her reticule, she followed Edrick into the tea house.

They were met by the proprietress, an elderly lady with rouge too liberally applied to her wrinkled cheeks and bony, arthritic hands. She gestured for them to sit at a small round table and gave them menu cards.

Keela merely handed it back. "A cup of your house tea, please. And perhaps a little cake?"

Edrick gave the old woman his card too. "The same."

The old woman hobbled away. They were the only customers in the tea room. Outside people, riders and coaches hiked up and down the harsh incline in a parade of colors. It wasn't raining, so everyone was wearing cheerful ribboned hats and light outer garments.

While Edrick thoughtfully observed the passers-by, Keela pondered again on her experience the evening before. She had only just dismissed it to Edrick, but there was a little voice in the back of her head that was not allowing her to let it pass. She furrowed her brow and turned to face Edrick.

"Something happened last night," Keela told Edrick.

He looked at her in puzzlement. "Yes, I know."

"No, you don't. I had a strange dream last night. One that had many familiar faces in it, and some I did not know. In my dream, I was... well... I was transformed."

"I see," Edrick replied speculatively.

She exhaled heavily. "In this dream I encountered two people I did not recognize. First, they were Ney wolves..." she paused as the old woman brought their cups of tea. Her hand trembled and made the cups rattle and spill a bit into their saucers. Once she put them down, she placed a small plate with four tiny cakes on it, and shuffled away.

"Then one of them turned into a woman dressed all in white," Keel continued. "I lunged at her and tore her throat out."

"Well, that must have been disturbing," he grunted. "Could it be your mind working through what happened when I was captured, perhaps?"

"No. No," she insisted. "Because when I woke up, there was dried blood all over my face and pillow."

"Your nose must have bled. It happens sometimes to me when the fire dries out the room too much."

"No. It wasn't my nose. I told the maid this morning it was, but I'm certain what happened—at least part of it—was real. My footprints—my transformed prints—were in the flower bed across from my window. The only thing I don't understand is why I don't remember it except as a dream."

Edrick frowned, and picked up his tea. He slurped from it, dabbing his lips solemnly with the crisp napkin, like the gentleman that he was. "If there were any incidents, we'd have heard of it. I suspect you might have had a wander, but I don't think you killed anyone." He smiled reassuringly.

Keela wasn't quite as convinced as he was. She sipped her tea, and then drained it. They finished their cakes and then stood.

"Well then, Miss Wrenn... shall we go meet your uncle?"

Keela's uncle lived on the hilltop in a large house right in the heart of the garden district. It was set a ways back from the street, unlike the neighboring ones, and visitors had to walk through a lovely little courtyard with an elegant little pond in the center. The house rose up three stories, with a flat granite-stone face with lines of windows looking out over the city below. The mansard roof was patinated copper, making it a vivid greenish blue. It was imposing and a fairly new construct with sharp edges and modern, simple lines.

Keela and Edrick were led in to wait patiently in a small sitting room just off the main foyer. Edrick had produced a calling card with his name printed on it in a deep gold. The housekeeper took the card and ushered them into the sitting room so she could alert the master of the house to the arrival of his guests.

They were surprised to see a little girl and boy slide open the door and peer through the small crack. The girl looked to be around eleven or twelve years old, and the boy, six or seven. Edrick turned and bowed his head, and they clanked the door shut and scurried away. Only a few moments later the door slid open a bit, and the little girl was back.

"Why don't you come in, little one, and introduce yourself," Keela said. "We don't bite."

"Well, *I* don't" Edrick said. "Miss Keela doesn't bite often." He smirked at her, and Keela glared back.

"Mellie, what are you doing?" A deep voice resonated from behind the door. The door glided open and a tall man with brown hair and a handsome face entered. He was in his early forties, perhaps. He shooed the child into the room before him and smiled graciously upon Edrick. Mellie was in a white gown like Keela—a fine, light one over a pin tucked petticoat—with shining red shoes. She was a pretty girl who, at certain angles, had some features like Keela. Her nose and chin.

"Your Grace, what a surprise. I never thought I'd see you here this time of year. What in the name of the forsaken are you doing here?"

"I have a special mission today," Edrick said. "Miss Keela, I would like you to meet your uncle, Marquess Arius Wrenn.'"

The Marquess gaped at them in shock. It took a moment for the name to ring familiar, and for him to place where he'd heard it before. Keela was sure she identified the exact moment when it came to him simply by watching the various emotions cross his face. She almost reveled in it.

"I must sincerely apologize, your grace, but you must leave this house and take her with you," he exclaimed suddenly.

The little girl on the other hand, approached, a patch of defiant wrinkles crossing her brow. "You're a Wrenn?" she asked.

"Mellie, you should go to Miss Trell at once," the Marquess snapped.

"I will *not!*" the child retorted obstinately. "Tell me who she is and why you are turning a Wrenn from our house?"

Arius' face darkened and his jaw rippled. He took a moment to rein in his emotion. "She's *not* a Wrenn."

"I am sorry, but I beg to differ, Marquess," Edrick replied. "I think you owe Miss Keela the politeness and welcome she deserves as your niece." His voice was firm.

Keela shrank back in humiliation. She had an idea she would be treated by her uncle as she had been by Vianca and her like, but she had not given up hope that she wouldn't. She had allowed herself to envisage the opposite and the disappointment struck her more painfully than she anticipated. She was immediately beset with tears. The Marquess frowned darkly and shook his head.

"She has no business in this house. She is a mixed blood *bastard*," he spat. Edrick saw Keela wince physically from the word and he was immediately filled with rage

Edrick's hand flew out and his fist connected with the Marquess's face before Keela even realized it. The Marquess stumbled sideways and fell onto the ground, his hand pressed against the spot where Edrick had struck him.

"It is regrettable that I was forced to take that course of action, but your words left me no choice. That was intolerable," Edrick said, shaking his hand out.

Mellie gripped the arm of a chair, her face a mask of shock and fright. She stared at Keela, even through the nastiness between the men. When Edrick offered his hand to help the Marquess off the floor, Mellie approached Keela and reached out, taking her hand and gazing up at her face.

"You're very pretty," she said.

Keela had been so absorbed with Edrick's defense of her honor, that she didn't even notice the girl take her hand. She glanced down at her, and her face broke an uncomfortable smile, through the tears falling onto her cheeks. "You are pretty too," Keela replied with a sniffle.

"You came here to meet us?"

"To learn more about my parents. To find them even," Keela replied.

"You would be my aunt?"

"Your cousin," Keela replied. "Your aunt Edeera is my mother."

Arius, who was now on his feet snorted bitterly and shook his head. "Stop poisoning my child. I am asking you to *please leave.*"

"*No*, father. She came here for your help. To know more about her family. We will provide it," Mellie declared.

Keela gave the astute child another smile, and squeezed her hand, which still gripped hers. The Marquess stared at his daughter and allowed himself to fall into a chair. He looked upon them with a tight face, his hand still resting on his reddened jaw, and then glared at the crownless King.

"I will tell you what I can, and then you will leave and never return."

"Why do you want her to go?" Mellie asked.

"Because she's... Her father was Farkas, Mellie. She's a *bastard*..."

"I was quite clear about that kind of language being used to describe this young lady, and I will not hesitate to hit you again, sir," Edrick barked.

The Marquess frowned darkly and looked at his daughter. "Your aunt—when she was only a few years older than you—fell in with a young man from our former seat at Wethlo. He was of the great house. The one that once belonged to *our* line!" he snarled. "They call Wethlo Vederine now. Your aunt... she would sneak off to be with him there at Vederine, and she mixed with them. She danced with him at their assemblies under the guise of staying with her cousin. Until she was found out, and found with child. My father told her she would have to give the child away or she would be cast out. After she did, she was married off and went away. That is all that happened."

"The father was of the great house?" Keela asked.

"Yes. I know nothing of him except that my sister called him Lenn. Now, please leave this house at once and with all due respect, your grace, never return."

Mellie clutched Keela's hand still. She looked up at her with her eyes misting up with tears. "I want her to stay, father," she said. "She's my cousin... It shouldn't matter anymore if she's ordinary or of nobility. It shouldn't matter anymore!"

"*She leaves at once*," he commanded, "and you, young lady, have pushed your limits. If you do not go to your room immediately, I will tan your backside!"

Mellie squeezed Keela's hand, and then ran away in a flurry of skirts, weeping. Keela took Edrick's arm. Edrick put his hat back on, and they saw themselves out. Her knees were shaking and her stomach was doing flips. She could barely contain her tears. They exited the house and climbed down the stairs to the street, and turned downhill, weaving through the other people strolling along the walk.

"We should go to Wethlo," Edrick decided, taking long strides beside her. "It's only a few miles north. You could very well meet your father, Miss Keela."

Keela's stomach did another leap, and she exhaled tremulously, stopping on the corner. A coach rolled past, and she wrung the top of her reticule. "Can we just go back to the guest house today? I... It's been a mad week for me. I need time to recuperate."

Edrick finally realized just how much had been put on her shoulders. From the moment she was taken from Calabras to now. It was impossible to imagine. He took her hand, and gazed upon her gently. Her eyes were red from crying and her skin pale from the shock. He helped her across the cobbles, dashing before an old four in hand rumbled past. In thoughtful silence, they made their way back to the abbey.

Keela hoped for some peace, but that was not possible. The moment they arrived at the Abbey they were confronted by a cluster of people sitting around the table at lunch, discussing the violent death of a woman right in the city common.

"They found the corpse draped over one of the stone benches by the pond, her throat torn out!" a matronly lady gasped over her bowl of vegetable potage, her spoon hanging over the thick soup.

Keela had just seated herself and was being served soup when the woman uttered the words. Her gaze found Edrick's. His brow tightened. He shook out his napkin and spread it over his knees, picking up his spoon. He shook his head subtly, as if to defer her concern until after lunch. They ate quietly, sitting across from one another, listening to the talk and speculation.

It was only after lunch, when Edrick led her out into the cloister that she was able to emote and react. "I hate this, Edrick."

"I think we should probably make our way to Wethlo immediately, Keela. Only a Farkas can explain all this to you. Perhaps show you a way to control it."

"I thought I already could. But it has a mind of its own and it does things without my leave, like savage a woman!" Keela hissed. She tried to bite back a sob and failed.

Edrick strode in front of her and gripped her shoulders, shaking her once. She gaped at him in shock. "You will not succumb to this, Keela. You are stronger than that, I've seen it. You are letting your fears consume you. There's no evidence that the woman who was killed was killed by you. The blood could be anything. It could be from a fight, you don't know!"

She sniffed and tears fell from her eyes. "I've become a bloody murderer, Edrick," she sobbed.

He hugged her close, and let her weep against his shoulder. She clutched the collar of his frock coat. Two guests emerged from the main corridor and began to circle the garden. They gave Edrick and Keela a lingering stare as they walked toward them. Keela kept blubbering, and Edrick gently consoled her.

"The news of the murder has upset her," Edrick told them.

The woman mouthed 'oh.' They sailed past. Keela stepped away, her face a moistened, ruddy mess. Edrick tugged the kerchief from his pocket and gave it to her. She patted her face dry, still hiccupping.

"Let us set out in the morning for Wethlo. I think this is the only course of action we have," he said.

She quietly apologized for her outburst. "It has been biding its time, building up since this morning. Since I saw my paw prints."

"They might not even be *your* paw prints, Keela. Maybe you need to put this to use." His finger snaked out and touched the tip of her nose.

She realized he was right. She nodded, tightlipped and offered him just the tiniest shade of a smile.

"Come on then. If we are to set off in the morning, we will need our things packed."

"I have never been inside a Farkas estate," she said. "Will we even be welcomed at an inn there?"

"Well, we have no way of knowing. I've been inside one, just before I met you. And it was not too greatly different than here, except perhaps cleaner, with no visible poor or unwashed. I can't imagine they would turn us away."

Keela's brow rose and they made their way back to their rooms. Keela still clutched the kerchief in her hand, her puffy, red eyes still lost in contemplation.

Wethlo was not a particularly large borough. Before the Farkas took possession of it, there had been two towns, one lesser house, and one great house.. It had changed significantly in two hundred years. To Edrick, it was less surprising to see the strangeness and undeniable beauty of the communities that resided within the borders of the Farkas settlement. Keela, on the other hand, could not stop staring at the scrupulously clean cobbled roads, the drains and gutters, the flowered window boxes, and the buildings hugging the unused canals. The idyllic pastures, healthy livestock and horses, and handsome conveyances and coaches of refined design and apparent comfort were all a wonder. As were the strange, smoothened lines of the architecture with the extraordinary and fascinating details and carvings, the shape of the arches, and the sharp rooflines. There was so much to look at.

Although Keela was ogling everything with fascination, they themselves did not draw too many stares. Keela's coloring and features were so close to Farkas that the people puttering to and fro in the towns largely ignored them as they rode by.

"We are going to have to stop somewhere and speak with

someone. Find out where this Lenn is," Edrick said.

She turned to look at him from her tall horse, her brow knit with nerves. Edrick drew his horse up to the front of a public house, and dismounted. Keela remained on her horse, as he tethered his to a ring and vaulted up the two steps to the double, colored glass door. He disappeared inside.

Keela was watching the window for him when suddenly something struck her violently from the offside of her saddle and sent her to the ground with a painful thud. She heard Magpie yowl from her bag. She glimpsed only a blur of black fur before she was on her paws, her clothes left in a pile behind her. Hackles raised and jowls drawn back into a hideous grimace, she circled her bronze-eyed attacker, who also responded with a lowered head and a menacing growl. Keela was dismayed to be so soon faced with more violence. But there was no hesitation, only a sense of the inevitable as she braced herself for the onslaught.

Chapter 13
Fight or Flight

In broad daylight, in the middle of the town, the wolf attacked Keela. It threw itself at her throat only to be kicked away as she reared up and punched at it with her hind legs. She then bore down on it, and they latched onto one another, heads shaking violently as soon as their teeth took purchase. Then three more wolves appeared and hurled themselves into the fray, all of them focusing their violence onto Keela.

Edrick came out of the public house the moment he heard the scuffle, the rest of the patronage at his heels. He cringed whenever he heard a yipe or a whimper, but Keela did not look to be slowing down. Meanwhile, more patrons of the inn poured out, and to Edrick's astonishment, several of them transformed into wolves as well—all closer to the normal size of a Ney wolf than Keela. Others shouted for assistance, and some wolves ran away. Others stood gaping at Keela in awe, murmuring remarks about her immense size and her power. Keela and her assailants tumbled on the cobbles in a snarling tangle of lupine limbs, frightening the horses and, in one case, knocking a lady over. Magpie struggled to escape her bag.

Edrick shouted in alarm, but his voice was lost to the din of the growls and snarls. There was a confusing moment when another colossal pack of wolves arrived on scene and jumped into the fray. For a second he thought Keela was in greater danger, but to his astonishment, the new pack was focusing their attacks on the assailants. Edrick could see now which one was Keela, for her wolf had eyes like Magpie: a soft, pewtery silver. The eyes of her assailants were a pale copper. The wolves that arrived were like Keela, all silver eyed and larger, but not quite as large as she. Keela was the largest thing there, and her body seemed denser and stronger.

With such numbers, the assailants were soon forced back, all tangled in a ball of thrashing raven limbs and flashing teeth. There were a series of yelps of pain emitting from the tousle of twisting lupine bodies, a final agonizing cry, and then silence.

Keela was lying on her side, her ribs rising and falling, her eyes open and alert, but her body exhausted and injured. Her leg was bleeding and twitching. There was a gash under her chin, and another at the top of her neck.

Edrick went to her without thought, and knelt beside the raven colored wolf that he loved, removing his frock coat and wrapping it around the top of her leg where there was a clear set of teeth marks puncturing her. She still had scabbing from her previous encounter in Calabras to boot. She tried to lift her head to look at him, but he shook his head.

"Don't move, Keela. I will get your cloak... In case you change." He twisted to reach for her cloak and found himself face to face with a massive wolf.

The wolf stared at Edrick with dark, silver eyes as it circled him. Edrick didn't brook the hindrance. He circumvented the animal and went to pick up Keela's things. He carried them to her, and put them down beside her, shaking out her cloak and then letting it fall gracefully over her.

The large wolf sniffed at Keela, and peered into her pained eyes. He then and lifted his head, and the whole square was filled by the power of his howl. It resonated in Edrick's ears and made them ring. Keela whined and whimpered along with it, and then emitted a wavering facsimile of it, too. Soon they were all howling, even Magpie, who now had her two front legs free of the bag. The only one not participating was the wolf they had killed, which lay lifeless on the ground, blood pooling beneath its gored throat.

The howling was plaintive and even beautiful to Edrick. His skin rose up into myriad bumps. It was then that a woman and three men arrived from the main road on horse, and dismounted. They left their horses untethered and approached, the woman muttering something to the large wolf. The pack dispersed on silent paws, vanishing into side streets as quickly as they had arrived.

The woman strode towards Edrick and Keela while the men went to the dead wolf. "Can you lift her?"

"She's larger as a wolf. If she transforms back to her human form, yes," he said.

Magpie plopped hard onto the ground and scurried over, wriggling up against Keela and licking her face. She looked so small next to Keela's massive wolf form. The woman looked on with curiosity, her eyes on the pup. Keela took a deep breath, and the fur began to retract into the skin. Her body shrank, the air wheezing hauntingly from her as she returned to her human shape. Edrick had never seen it so close and in such detail—the way her muzzle melted back into the flat of her face, and how her hair flowed out of the follicles like water.

Reduced to her frail human form, her injuries looked much worse. Edrick was immediately worried. He wrapped her up in her cloak and lifted her in his arms. "Where do I take her?"

"To the physician. At once," the woman replied. "Follow me" She reached down, scooped up the puppy, and swished past him in a flare of scarlet muslin.

Edrick did not feel Keela's weight. He felt only worry for her. The woman led him down a side street to a lane where there were several flat-faced edifices lined up one next to the other. The one she led him to had a sign with a great blue eagle and a doe: the symbol of a physician and healer. The woman opened the door so Edrick could enter swiftly, and he was met by a tall, gaunt looking woman with black eyes and black hair wearing the robes of an Arcamite healer.

"Put her on the table directly," the healer commanded.

He did as he was told.

"Now get out," she said bluntly.

Edrick, in his shirtsleeves and waistcoat—both stained in Keela's blood—looked up in alarm. "I can't leave…"

"Out!" she barked.

Edrick stumbled out to where the first woman stood holding Magpie. The door slammed behind him.

"Best you come with me, young man."

Edrick stared at her in shock, and took a moment to process what she had said. "I must go and fetch…"

"It's taken care of. Come with me. The coach will meet us at Musket Street." She petted Magpie's head as she spoke.

Edrick could only do as he was asked, and with one confused look behind him at the now curtained window of the physician's shop, he fell in step beside the woman.

Keela groaned, and smacked her lips. A bitter taste still lingered in her mouth from the elixir that physician had forced into her after Edrick had left. The woman was severe and humorless, with a hard touch and a rather brusque manner about her. She was more like a butcher preparing meat than a healer. She was at present touching up some wrappings over Keela's various cuts and injuries, her hands offering no gentleness or softness. Keela grunted in discomfort, alerting the woman to her wakefulness.

"You took quite a beating, little one, but nothing too horrendous. Your old wound here opened up again. I've stitched you up and applied poultice to the wounds. You will be a sight for a few days. The bruising will fade quickly. They usually do for the imperials. Now, let's get you dressed, shall we? I have to deliver you to the great house post haste. One does not ignore the wishes of the big house," she intoned through her nose, as if she found the whole idea distasteful.

"Why must I go there?"

"Because the lady wishes it," the Doctor replied succinctly.

Keela frowned. "I would rather return to my horse and to Edrick. I don't know who this lady is."

"They are all waiting for you at the big house. Please get up," the healer said impatiently.

"My clothes…"

"They were collected No worries, dear. Now on your feet."

The physician removed her white and blue robe to reveal a simple black round gown paired with a bright white, stiffly ruffed collar and crisp chemisette. She also had lace cuffs on her long sleeves, which had been pushed up underneath her robe.

Keela tightened her abdomen and the pain exploded out from every source at once, causing her to keen from the ache. The healer turned and looked at Keela critically, tugging her cuffs down. Her thin lips were pressed into a straight line and her slim, harsh brow arched.

"Do I need to administer you something for pain, child? I imagined as an imperial you'd power through it, but if you're of the fragile sort, I *suppose* I *could* provide you something to dull the pain."

Keela really thought that transforming into a wolf and ravaging this woman would be the best remedy for her pain, but she fought her desire to do so. Instead she sat up and slid off the table, hobbling to where the woman's thin, bony hand pointed. Her riding habit and underpinnings were folded neatly in a stack on the counter of a cabinet containing an assortment of pharmacopeia.

The curtains were still drawn, so Keela was able to dress in the space provided. She tried not to show her discomfort. The bandages covered drying poultices that felt as if they were pulling on the wounds. As she tugged on her chemise, she noticed a little row of neat stitches drawing together a rather long gash underneath her arm. She could not deny how tidy the work was, and she'd never seen stitches closing a wound before, so she took a long stare at them in curious admiration.

"Something wrong?" the doctor asked as she slipped a crisp, plain little cap with a flurry of ribbons hanging from each side onto her head.

"Not in the least. I confess I've never seen anything like this before. It's ingenious and well… kind of beautiful," Keela replied with an awed smile.

The woman's hard frown almost appeared to soften for a moment and her eyes looked away in discomfort. "Finish getting dressed. I imagine you are able to do so with assistance?"

"Yes, or course," Keela affirmed. She lowered her arm, and reached for her stockings, drawing them up onto her legs. She slid her loosened stays over her head, and adjusted herself into them. These were her new ones, which hadn't quite gotten as comfortable or molded to her as the ones she had before her journey with Vianca. She did not tighten them too much—only where they needed to provide support—as her wounds made it painful. The chemisette with the standing collar went next.

She drew on her petticoat and then put her boots on. Her beloved new boots, now already scuffed and muddied and the right one had a cake of sweaty horse-hair on the right side where her foot rested against her horse's neck. The habit went on quickly. The skirts fell over her, long and luxurious, the simple little shoulder straps holding the high waistline in place. Once she fastened the waist closed, she drew on the spencer jacket with its charming peplum and military style cording and buttons laddering the front.

The doctor watched with prickly, heavily silent impatience, her hands folded primly against her chest, her elbows pointing sharply out. Keela wrapped her hair up onto her head and pinned it into a loose bun. Then she picked up her riding hat and pulled it on in turn while approaching the lady doctor.

"Good. Let's go then," the doctor snapped. She opened the curtains and then the door, ushering Keela out to the street.

Keela waited for the doctor to lock the door, and the two of them walked up the street. Keela was hindered by the injury to her hip and thigh, still stinging and smarting with each step. She did her best not to show her discomfort, for the doctor seemed to have little patience for it.

"I've never known a woman to be a physician before," she muttered, trying to distract the stern woman with idle chat so she could suffer more freely.

The doctor peered at her from the side of her eyes, her lips pursed in disapproval. "That's because you've lived amongst savages your whole life," she replied maliciously.

Keela winced at the acidity of her tone, but she merely peered ahead and bit her way through another stride of hurt. "So it is common for women to be doctors? Among the Farkas, that is…"

"It is common for women to be anything they want, Miss. We are, in many ways, the dominant gender amongst our people," the healer replied. "It is impossible for me to understand how it isn't the case anywhere else, as females are vastly superior to males in *every* way. They might have one advantage, and that is of size and strength, but that evens out amongst the wolf-kind. At least amongst the imperials. Men, although they are stronger as humans in their physicality, have many weaknesses that come to the surface if they are left unchecked. Pride, aggressiveness, inherent greed. Those things need to be managed, not allowed free rein to grow

221

unhindered. It inevitably becomes a pattern of injustice and inequality if men are left to their devices, always scrabbling to be top of the heap. Women are oppressed and taught that they are useful for little more than male gratification and for procreation. They create inequitable hierarchies of power where only the smallest number of them control the society and thrive on the backs of others. They create conflicts and destroy, destroy, destroy." The bitterness was almost palpable as she spoke, a deep seeded resentment seething from her words.

Keela grew waxen. The conversation harkened her back to the conversation she had with Alara before this whole mess began and Alara's laughing opinion on men and destruction. They walked along the road, riders passing by, some tipping their hats genteelly at them. Keela bowed her head in return, her eyes on the dark haired, pale skinned characters milling about amongst the native Yvremi that lived and functioned inside what was once Wethlo. Keela had forgotten its new Farkas name.

"So, men are controlled by the women amongst the Farkas," Keela concluded.

The doctor sighed impatiently, and shook her head. "No, not *controlled*. The people of Farkas are governed by a fully *equal* rule. But when it comes to the structure of the pack, and the pairings, women are the dominant gender. They do not oppress the men as it is done so easily in your society towards women. It is the natural state of the changers, for the females to be dominant. And as we watched other societies around us, we quickly learned that each gender has its failings, and so it was agreed that the rule must *always be equal* so that none of those weaknesses can overtake our society as it does with those like yours."

"You know I am a… as you call it, a changer, but you speak of the society of Yvrem as if it is mine…"

"Oh, dear girl, look at your mannerisms. The way your carry yourself. Your sheepish, indirect glances, your soft spoken nature.

You are not a woman raised in Farkas. It is as clear as that sign." The doctor's hand swept up to a sign carved with a corpulent pig and cow facing one another, encircled by words in a language Keela could not read.

"That sign is not clear to me at all," Keela said with a smirk.

The doctor looked up at it, emitting a single laugh. "Yes, I suppose it wouldn't be for an Yvremi wolf." She shook her head. "What an idea. An *Yvremi* wolf. So much speculated, so much disbelieved. But here you are." She shook her head and looked at Keela. "It is a difficult thing to accept. So much hope bundled up in such a lesser being."

"I'm many things, but I am not a lesser being," Keela retorted with a touch of fire.

"The Yvremi are lesser creatures than we are, Keela. Mark my words. Their knowledge is limited. They are barbaric in so many ways. Only a notch above primitives."

"There's something about the *primitives* your people must admire, or desire, or you would not still be here," Keela snapped.

The doctor peered at her sidelong as she walked, and pushed out her chin. "We have our reasons. It certainly isn't for the vibrancy of your culture or the depth of your knowledge as a people." Her words oozed with sarcasm. "You must get used to this perception of your kind, Keela. For to be an Yvremi wolf is to be impure in the eyes of the Farkas."

"All the Farkas living in Yvrem would be Yvremi wolves, would they not? They are here in Yvrem after all."

"Well, you also have Yvremi blood in your veins. There is a marked difference, my dear. As for our attachment to our Sentely, you see how this place has been transformed into something better. It is a part of Farkas in many ways. It lacks the dark forests and the soaring mountains, but inside the borders, it's a Farkas town with *some* Yvremi influences. We may have adopted Yvremi fashions and some Yvremi norms, but we are not wholly raised like Yvremi. For one, our females are not raised to be a woman like you, with all your bashfulness…" the doctor paused at a corner, waiting for a couple with two Ney Wolves at their heels to pass. A lady with a broad bonnet brim looked Keela up and down with a critical eye, and then sailed on in a swish of forget-me-not blue walking skirts.

"I will give you this," the doctor said, crossing with Keela to the raised walk that skirted another row of shops. "You certainly don't fight like an Yvremi. You fight like a Farkas imperial through and through, judging by your wounds."

Keela looked mystified. "Yes. But this power scares me."

"*It should,*" the doctor replied quickly. "You are a deadly thing, Miss. A deadly, beautiful thing."

She gestured for Keela to follow her down a street that broadened into an attractive avenue, wide enough for two coaches, lined with great old trees that created a tunnel with their branches. As they walked, the pain seemed to dull a bit. The air smelled lovely, and the pavement made for a smooth, clean stroll. Only two horses passed: one carrying a lady sidesaddle, the other, a man of Yvremi descent. They cantered past on their high-stepping, thickly fetlocked Farkas horses.

"It *is* beautiful here," Keela admitted, looking past the avenue of trees, over the low stone wall that contained a field of thin, wispy spring stalks of what looked like wheat of some kind. It was a dry day, but it was grey. Not uncommon for Yvrem. Wind whorled across the crop, making it move like ocean waves. Far in the distance there were two copses of trees under which some fine, flat-faced farm houses were hiding. Three large, dapple-grey drafts grazed in the field. They looked like boulders, their heads buried in the tall pasture grasses, their tails switching as they grazed.

Behind them, the town was hidden at the rear of another gathering of deciduous trees covered in the bright, pale green of freshly unfurled leaves. The occasional roof peered up above them, the cylindrical and domed spire of a former Hevlett temple standing tall like a beacon over the smooth, rolling hills. On Keela's left, across a cultivated field, was a vineyard striping the sides of a hill, and beyond that, another community of trees and rooftops. The temple began to emit a noise. A smooth, ululating melody played on some kind of horn. Its song carried far over the countryside.

The doctor frowned. "Hurry along girl. The evening horn has called. We'll arrive at dinner, and it would be unseemly to interrupt dinner. The Lady doesn't tolerate that sort of inconsideration."

Keela bit her tongue and swallowed her discomfort, trying to keep up with the tall woman's long strides. They turned down another tree-lined avenue that had two large stone pilasters holding an open gate. The avenue that it opened to was capped by the large face of an elegant building. They walked as quickly as they could without breaking into an undignified run. For that Keela was thankful, for she hurt terribly.

Keela was flushed and out of breath, tears stinging in her eyes from the ache. She looked up as they reached the door, and found two sets of eyes gazing down at her with unmistakable astonishment.

"Doctor, is there a reason we have a girl who looks like she's about to faint on our threshold?" the lady asked.

Keela could not look at them, for she was busy trying to catch her breath and not cry at the same time.

"We were hurrying. You told me to have her here as soon as she woke. I worried we would interrupt the dining hour," the doctor blurted defensively. "If you had sent your coach we would not have been subjected to the walk. She had only just woken from the soporifics I gave her."

The lady in the doorway bristled, and an angry fire lit up behind her eyes. "Was it my imagination that she was gravely injured? Because I believe she was. She is in no condition to be traipsing across the countryside. I didn't envision a need for a coach a mere *four* hours after she was brutally attacked! She should have remained until she was well enough to travel."

"She's well enough! She's here isn't she?"

"How could you make her walk all the way here?"

"She's an imperial, she can handle it," the doctor retorted boldly, her tone viciously sarcastic. "I am a doctor, and *I* am the one with the qualifications to determine whether a patient is strong enough to walk or not, not *you*!"

"Get out of my sight!" the lady of the house shouted. She turned to a man standing in the doorway behind her. "Get her, Iram. Help her into the house, for Eyleth's sake!"

The older man, Iram, looked startled. He hurried down the four steps to help Keela climb them. She heard footfalls approaching and Edrick appeared. Keela was never more relieved to see his face.

"I'll do that," he grunted. He rudely shoved the man aside, slid his arm around Keela's back, and hoisted her up the stairs.

The doctor stood aghast, having not moved since she'd been scolded by the Lady. The four of them squeezed through the open door, and the lady shut it in the doctor's face.

"I cannot stomach that woman, Iram. I cannot say it enough! She needs to go. Damned perfidious dog!"

"Dear, we can discuss it another time," Iram said soothingly. "-Llet us make this girl comfortable first, shall we?"

Keela listened to the exchange with no small measure of discomfort. She wondered if they argued in her language for her benefit.

The Lady was about sixty years old by the look of her, a graceful creature. Keela remembered her voice from earlier, when she had come into town to assist after the fight; but she had not seen her face until now. Iram was about the same age. Both of them had dark hair that had gone steely silver. They took her into a parlor and helped her down into a delicate little chair with spindly saber legs.

"Thank you," Keela whispered, embarrassed.

Edrick pulled another, similar little chair of pale blue to the spot next to hers and sat down in it. Magpie wasted no time in climbing into Keela's lap. She gathered up the puppy's gawky limbs and stroked her on the head.

"You look pale, Miss. May I offer you something for the pain? I have leafbitters, which will dull it down a bit. Did the doctor not give you anything?" the Lady asked.

"She did not," Keela replied sweetly.

"Let me guess… Imperials don't need such a thing, for they are superior, correct?" The older woman did not wait for an answer. She rolled her eyes and sailed over to a cord which she yanked numerous times with great vigor. "I would love to dive into the purpose of your presence in Vederine right now, but I think we should allow you to rest. That unforgivable harpy… Imagine. Making her *walk* from town!" The door opened and a servant peered into the room. The lady snapped out orders in her native tongue.

Her partner on the other hand was supremely calm. While his spouse ranted, he was moving purposefully and unobtrusively about the room, fetching a pillow for Keela to recline upon, serving both Keela and Edrick a tiny glass of sherry each, and—when the Lady finished her final complaint—he silently slipped a glass of the buttery sherry into her hand, which she accepted almost unconsciously and sipped without once even acknowledging her husband.

Keela was shuffled off to a lovely set of rooms where a shy little girl of Farkas heritage tended to her. She was stripped down yet again, and then re-dressed with care in clothes that were not her own. The stays were left comfortably loose around her painful ribcage and the day gown was neither fussy nor elaborate, a perfect round gown in which to recline in the chair and relax after the painful walk.

Edrick and Magpie were on their own downstairs in the company of the hosts. Keela did not fret. She merely nodded off into a light nap, allowing herself to forget the pain and the questions that were waiting impatiently at the back of her mind.

She was awoken not too long after by the servant girl who brought her a pot of tea. She was helped up and her dressings were studied for their cleanliness. She was wrapped up in a shawl so large it could cover a bed and brought downstairs again where Edrick, the Lady and the Lord were comfortably quiet, each reading a book. The men stood when Keela entered the room.

"You look much better," Edrick said, noting her much less bedraggled appearance.

"I *feel* better," she admitted. The Lady indicated she should sit, so she did.

"Now, young lady, Edrick has explained to us why you have come here," the Lady said. "We heard rumor that you were on your way. Sadly, we also expected the reception you received. Some nasty types followed you."

"It was not my intention to arrive trailing a pack of violent wolves," Keela replied.

The Lady shook her head. "Your companion here said you came looking for your father who you know only by his first name, Lenn. I'm sad to say that your father is no longer here. But your arrival is significant. And important. And we've been awaiting it." The lady looked at the older gentleman who remained markedly silent.

"I don't understand," Keela muttered in reply.

The lady looked to her husband, who now spoke. "You are a creature of mixed blood. Something that will capture the attention of the people of the Sentely no matter where you are."

"Why should it matter?" Keela asked, realizing that she had no formal introduction to these people at all. But the conversation had taken a turn that was more pressing, considering her epiphany in regards to her strange dream which had been confirmed by her conversation with the doctor.

"From the perspective of the Farkas people, you are either one of two things: a miracle or an abomination. Your arrival here has stirred up reactions from those that stand on both sides. Those that want your kind dead and those who think you are the salvation of the Farkas people." The lady spoke clearly. The words hung heavy in the room. The four adults and the pup remained quiet for a moment. Keela's brow furrowed.

"So... Magpie here, and I... we are being followed and attacked because we are seen as abominations?" Keela asked. She already knew this but it was necessary for her to hear it.

"Indeed," the lady replied.

Keela frowned. "And these people with opposing views coexist in this Sentely?"

"In most Sentelys there are those that represent both ideologies. Most represent the one that would protect you. This one is one of the few exceptions. Your arrival has... provoked the factions, so to speak. You are in a dangerous place, my dear," Iram said, his brow set in a grave line.

Keela shuddered a little, and clutched her elbows. "Why would I be the salvation for some?"

"Because you represent the rebirth of a dying people, Keela. Or at least, that's what the Conclave believes. The Nall—the ones that view you as polluted—do not think the same. They believe that the Farkas are not dying, but are becoming purer. That the weak are being weeded out. They think that the common Farkas Neys, the copper-eyed ones you saw, are inferior and should be bred from the bloodline. They believe it is the time of the Imperials."

"Imperials..." Keela repeated.

"The wolves of the silver eye," the old man intoned. "It is as like..." He paused. "Think of a common mixed breed horse ... the imperial is to such a horse as a Doreal Hack, or a Setta Destrier."

"So the Imperial is the warmblood, if you will, of the Farkas kind?" she asked, "the higher form of wolf," she posited.

"I suppose we are," he laughed.

They were interrupted by a knock on the door, and two servants entered carrying a large pot of tea, some cups, and a tray of refreshments. They patiently waited for the service to be completed before they continued. Everyone was served a cup of tea, and then left to go on. The lady sipped the steaming cup of tea, and gazed benevolently upon Keela.

"Imperials are generally known to be more graceful, stronger, of better stock, more intelligent, and larger than their counterparts. There are several types of Farkas *breed*, if you will. The bronze eyed ones are the smallest. There are the Fesh. They are of white eyes and small in number. Then there's Eeru, they are of black eyes and they do not leave Farkas, for they remain in a small … what? A nation of sorts, of their own. The Bronze wolves and the wolves of Farkas rarely intermix. Each one thinks it is the superior *breed*."

"The Doctor?"

"A bronze. They don't much care for Imperials," the Lady replied with a sneer. "But don't take her nastiness as any idea that she is on the side of the Nall. All her detestability aside, on the notion of the survival of the Farkas, she has good sense. I may not like her, but she is to be trusted."

"Because of our size and our strength, we tend to top the hierarchy," her husband added. Edrick, who had been listening intently, and keeping quiet as to not hinder this intriguing conversation, shifted in his seat, moving to the edge of it, furrowing his brow in intrigue.

"I see," Keela muttered. "She called me an Imperial, in spite of my mixed blood."

"You are an Imperial. Your silver eyes are the proof of it. But your lineage is known to us. You *are* a child of an Imperial. Your father is such. That little one is one as well… Although her white mark is unusual, and it will assure her of a future of many difficulties if she remains amongst the Farkas," the lady informed her. "She will persevere through it," Keela replied. "I am well familiar with that kind of childhood. As long as she is surrounded by people who care about her, she will come through it." There was a pause. "But you were saying... The time of the Imperials, what does that mean?"

"The problem we are facing is, at present, mostly affecting the lesser wolves, if you will, but Imperials are certainly not excluded from it," the older woman explained, sipped her tea again.

"Problem?" Keela asked.

The older couple looked at one another for a moment, and then the Lady proceeded. "The Farkas changeling is becoming a thing of the past."

It was bewildering for Keela to hear this. She furrowed her brow, but did not speak. Edrick remained quiet and watchful the whole time, his eyes on each of their faces, Magpie in his arms.

"I don't understand... Are your people dying?" Keela asked.

"No. They are merely remaining wolves—born as wolves, and unable to change when they come of age," Iram explained.

"I'm sorry, I know this may seem forward of me to ask, but... your people are born as wolves?" Keela was astonished.

"Yes," the Lord replied. Edrick's eyes widened, and he gazed at Iram expectantly. "At the age when we are able to breed, our ability to change into this human form manifests itself. For several generations, this ability has been inconsistent. Each generation produces fewer and fewer full changers. There have been markedly few these past four decades. If this continues, soon there will be no Farkas at all. Only wolves."

Keela sat up, wincing a bit as one of her wounds twinged with pain. "I understand this is a terrible thing—I do not mean to diminish it—but what does that have to do with me?"

"Everything," the Lady replied quickly. "Amongst our people there are two schools of thought on this sickness that has taken our people. There is one faction that believes that mixed breeds like you are what will save our people. That your people—the Yvremi—will

231

be the salvation of the Farkas.

"The other school of thought is that the wolves that are not changing are merely a weakness in our kind, and that only the strongest and purest will remain. There is an idea that the impure—as you are thought to be because of your Yvremi blood—are abominations and that any further mixing ought to be stopped immediately."

"This is the interesting part, Keela," Edrick interrupted. Keela peered at him as if surprised to see him there.

"Again, I fail to see how my presence matters at all in all this," she said. "Yes, I might be impure and an abomination to some, but what does it matter in the greater scheme?"

"The Conclave of Sages of the Rathama temple are the ones that support the idea that Yvremi blood is key to renew our bloodlines and infuse it with strength again. And your existence is proof that theory is true," the Lady asserted. "My existence?" Keela asked.

"Yes. It is believed that all babies that are produced as mix breeds are successful changers when they grow up," the Lady replied. "It has only been proven twice, as only two that we know of have reached the age of change. But there are other signs that these are mixed babies are successful changers. Only the Mages can tell for certain that early on. The wizardly folk have been crucial in the fight for our people."

Keela frowned with thought.

The Lady continued, "The sages believe that the people of Yvrem are unique in the world. Yvrem was once home to the ancient people—the Amali—who left behind their beautiful ruins and forests of great oak. Some say they disappeared, but others say that their people were merely absorbed into the cultures that arrived later.

"Farkas have never been able to cross breed with any other people. But it was discovered that Yvremi are able to do so. The sages deduced that whatever it is that allows us to be changelings is slowly breeding out of our lines, and that in order to restore this special ability, our bloodlines require a fresh dose of ancient blood to make the people strong again.

"The Nall claim that the failure of our changers is merely a symptom of our people becoming purer. That the ones that still can change are the ones that are meant to lead the Farkas into the future, and that those who remain Neys are merely the weaker strains of blood that should be purged from the bloodlines."

"This has been a growing problem for a long time, but it is what ultimately led to the occupation of Yvrem," the old man said. They all took pause for a moment, to refresh their teas and eat a little bit. Edrick looked positively charged from all this information. His eyes were alight with excitement over it. The lady slid her tea and saucer onto the small table between them, and dabbed her lips with a napkin, folding it thoughtfully into her lap as she began to speak again.

"The Imperials are still strong changers. We always have been up until about two hundred years ago. Then our own family lines began to fray and drop away. The civilization we had spent so many centuries building began to crumble and became much like Yvrem is now: factions and city states fighting amongst one another.

"The Sages were the ones that prompted the move to Yvrem. They believed that the Farkas had a moral obligation to not only subdue the savage people and to civilize them, but to create strongholds where our people could find the best of the Yvremi to couple with in order to strengthen our peoples' bloodlines."

"You invaded Yvrem to breed?" Keela was aghast, her eyes cast with incredulity on the Lady

"To preserve our people. Our changers," the Lord explained.

Keela blanched. Edrick was speechless, clinging to Magpie.

"Farkas is a shadow of what it once was. The people who believe that the invasion of Yvrem was but an act of disgrace are at war with those that supported the idea. There is little left to fight for back home. The strength of our people now resides here in Yvrem. Most of the imperials live here. We have not been successful in replenishing our lines because from within our own Sentelys the factions opposed to mixing blood have been killing all the offspring they can," her ladyship added. His lordship continued:

"But there are those who have made it their life's work to protect these mixed children. As happened with you. You, and the pup, and only a few others have managed to survive through this. But your coming here has endangered you both further."

Keela frowned. "Where is my father?"

"Your father has been returned to Farkas. I must tell you…your father is our son," the Lady said.

Keela's eyes widened. "You are my grandparents?"

"Indeed," the Lady replied, her eyes misting over.

"I don't even know your names," Keela said through fresh tears.

"I am Lady Leesa Vederine. Your is Iram Wellis. Our family founded this Sentely and it was named for them."

Keela's hands began to tremble. *She had grandparents!* "My father, Lenn Vederine. And my mother, Edeera Wrenn," she recited. "I wonder what they were like," the Lady smiled broadly and said:

"Your father was besotted with your lovely mother. He adored her. She adored him. Such pairings, since the Sentely were incepted, have been viciously embattled for the Nall have continuously fought to stop them. But since Vederine was a fully Conclave-dominated Sentely at the time, the pairing managed to escape the notice of the Nall for a spell. There was, however, not *only* the objection of *her* family, there was that of the Farkas of the Nall. They heard rumor of your mother's acceptance into our circle and they began to threaten our son. When your mother was with child, he sent her to her family, for he feared she would be harmed by the Nall. Her family sent her away for other reasons, and she, along with you, was lost to us completely. We decided it was best for it to remain so, for your sake."

"But there was Jessick," said her grandfather with a smile. "Jessick had been blessed with his own child by a woman who was not Farkas. His child was tragically murdered by the Nall. His grief was vast, and his purpose then became one of protecting the children that were born of mixed blood. His resolve was taken up by others, and he built a small society of sorts whose entire purpose is to watch over the babies like you and the pup there. They've taken some losses protecting you, from what I understand. It was one of them that alerted us that you might be coming.

"Jessick continued to seek you out after we had given you up, worried that you would be found by the Nall if he did not intervene. He found you and your mother and convinced her family to adopt you into someone's care. That way you would not be found until you were old enough to defend yourself. He arranged for our funds to be sent for your support in a manner in which they could not be traced and he made sure that you lived a life that was a humble one and didn't draw too much attention, with unseen protectors watching over you."

"But *I* was not born a wolf…" Keela exclaimed.

"No," the Lady laughed gently. "You were born the creature your mother was. As was little Magpie."

Edrick nodded knowingly but Keela looked even more shocked. "So she *is* a changer?"

"Yes. She must be if Jessick is involved. She has surely been confirmed a changer by the wizards. And looking at her, one cannot escape those knowing eyes," Lady Leesa said, smiling at the pup which was at present draped over Edrick's knees. "She is still very young. Just a baby. She has another fifteen years or more before we see what she looks like as a human. But she is watching, and she is learning as all Farkas babies do. They emerge from their wolfhood quite rounded."

Keela's mind went back to her strange dream where Magpie was a child. Her eyes flitted about as she explored the fading memories of that dream.

"My question is, why was Magpie given to me?" Edrick asked.

The Lord Wellis sighed and shrugged. "Those were not our decisions. We did not know about Magpie until you brought her here. All we heard was that our son's child might be looking for him as she was moving towards Vederine. We expected there would be trouble, so your grandmother set some of the men out to watch for your arrival in case there was an attack. The message that warned of your arrival also noted that you were followed by Nall."

"*I* have been followed by Nall. I led them to Keela," Edrick said.

"Yes. The Nall must have felt it greatly convenient that there were now two such creatures together," the Lord agreed. "Until we can come to some sort of peaceful resolution with the Nall, you should remain here Keela. There is some notion that you'll be safer here with us than on your own out there, in spite of the possible Nall presence in this Sentely," her grandfather said. Keela frowned. She was not so confident of her safety as they were. She had been helped by the pack of wolves, but she had still been attacked. It could happen again. "Many new wolves have been arriving, escaping the conflict at home. And we suspect a good portion of the new wolves are Nall. I wish you'd have remained safe where you were—and your Magpie to be where her parents are, if they are still alive," her Ladyship murmured lamentingly.

Keela reached out and caressed the pup's face, her eyes sad. She could not help but feel sorry for the little thing. How lost she must be, if her parents are lost. Her Farkas mother, and human father, possibly dead. Could she understand all this? Behind her silver eyes, was there the loss and pain Keela now felt?

"It seems more than coincidence that you were brought together. We suspect that perhaps it was done for a purpose. Perhaps even orchestrated by Jessick in some way or another. I think it's because the Conclave of Sages needs you. Our people are at a fragile stage in our conflicts right now. The more changelings born without the ability to change, the more overt and violent the Nall become. Their brutal philosophy is beginning to degrade their credibility with the people, and many purists are now beginning to sway to the idea that the Conclave of Sages are right.

"If the Conclave can show them healthy, beautiful changelings born from Yvremi blood, there is the belief that the Nall could become merely a vocal minority. You are literally the hope of a people, Keela. And perhaps Jessick and his connections have decided that it's time to bring you both to Farkas, to show the people that there is indeed nothing more to fear." After pausing, the lady reached for the teapot and poured herself a fresh cup.

"The society that Jessick created—the message they sent—asked that you wait here for them," his Lordship added. Keela's eyes fell on his face and her brow furrowed. "Then I imagine my usefulness has been served," Edrick muttered.

Keela turned to peer at his face, and he looked lost for a moment, as if his sense of purpose had all but evaporated.

"We can't know what your purpose truly is, until someone from Jessick's group tells us," Lord Wellis said. "He is a ghost. The Nall despise him. He has made it his life's work to keep the children of the Yvremi Farkas out of their hands. And a hard job of it, it has been. You are only the second one to reach full adulthood, Keela. *The second one old enough to transform.*

"The first was a young man by the name of Nettos. He is legendary but nobody saw him but Jessick. Nettos was magnificent, by his account. Large, stalwart, powerful, vibrant... Jessick was sure this would be all the people would need to see to end the madness, but the Nall got to Nettos first. Had the boy been given the chance, he could have taken his killers. He was like you, from what Jessick said. But the Nall assassinated Nettos in his human form as his slept, and they left him for Jessick to find. Since then, Jessick's resolve has been further inflamed. He is determined to weaken and destroy the

Nall. Until yesterday when you arrived, we did not believe any of this."

"From what I saw," the lady added, "the Conclave will be more than astonished by you. You are larger than a common Imperial, Keela. The wolves that came to you were all astonished by your tremendous strength and power—and for such a young, inexperienced thing. You are no abomination, you are the ideal," she exclaimed with pride. "That is probably why the Nall are now so desperate to harm you. You represent the demise of their claims that mixed bloods are inferior."

Keela blushed and shook her head. She didn't think she was all that much bigger than Jessick, and he was the largest wolf she'd seen. But she couldn't judge for herself. She looked at Edrick, and his eyes were full of meaningful things.

"We will stay until Jessick's people arrive," Keela agreed. "It's not as if I have anything pressing to keep me from staying. Father gone, mother a thousand miles away. I at least have the answers I needed. I now know what I am, and where I come from. I now know that I have grandparents." She smiled, but it faded as she continued. "And an uncle that hates me."

"That is tragic indeed," Lord Wellis answered. "But we are here for you. And we are so delighted to finally meet you."

Keela's sigh was tremulous and thin. She looked pale and drawn, and this fount of new particulars had taxed her.

"I do hope you will make yourself at home, here, Keela. For this *is* your home," her Ladyship assured her.

Keela bowed her head shallowly and swallowed. She managed to eke out a warm regard for the kindness. So much information swirled in her head. She thought she was going to faint from it all.

Night fell with a steely, bristling sort of unease for Keela. She shared her meal with the family and Edrick, and vanished to her room with an excuse of feeling unwell. She climbed the stairs in the darkness of the old stone halls, guided only by the small sphere of light cast by her candle. She stood by the fire while the servant girl helped her get undressed and changed her wound dressings before helping her into a nightgown. She watched the girl leave and crawled into the enormous bed, looking out the large window at the sky, filled with a large three-quarter moon of silver.

Through her mind wound all the thoughts that plagued her from the beginning of this journey, Now she was in the home of grandparents she never knew she had, looking at her existence as something more than just the bullied girl from Veros. She wasn't sure if she was better off for this knowledge or not.

The dense row of tall, lancet windows across from her bed peered out over the darkened earth, the navy sky and its bright jewels. The moon hung like a pennant on a chain of stars. In spite of the serenity, there was a sharpness to the night. An edge to the cold that fought against the pressing force of warmth radiating out from the hearth, where the fire chewed its way contentedly through a large round of oak.

What should have been cozy felt stark. What should have been embracing felt hollow. Her instincts were tingling and she couldn't suss out why. Perhaps it was being in this new, secure place, surrounded by potential enemies who would love nothing more than to see her die. There was one thing Alara had drilled into Keela's head the moment she could speak and understand: to trust her instincts. Always.

Keela had learnt the hard way on more than one occasion that this was valid wisdom. She let her body sink down into her pillows, and stared out into the night.

Morning came with more quiet. The servant girl brought her breakfast to eat in her room. After Keela was dressed, she sipped tea while the maid arranged her hair into a stylish coif. Keela watched the girl as she worked. Her eyes were quick, her extraordinarily long lashes always low and fluttering to cover them from Keela's direct gaze.

"I was to understand that there were no such things as servants in the Farkas world," Keela said.

The girl's eyes dropped to her task, her fingers twisting a skein of Keela's raven locks into a little knot. She reached for a pin and slid it into Keela's hair, freezing the little twist against the bun of them that she was making.

"I am well-paid for what I do," she replied shyly. "I am neither indentured nor enslaved as so many of your people were before we arrived."

"But the Lord and Lady are without a doubt of higher status than you."

"There *are* classes amongst the Farkas," the girl replied matter-of-factly. "However, they do not govern us all. All of the classes are represented in our government." She twisted another strand and pinned it against the bun. "That is the difference between us. Our society is not so different than yours except there is no such oppression as has existed, and in my eye, continues to exist in Yvrem. I'm astounded that the Conclave has not ordered a renewed reprisal against those that haven't halted the practices of enslavement and indentured servitude."

Keela remained as impassive as she could, and calmly bit the inside of her cheek as she measured her response. "I find it difficult to understand what justification or qualification exists amongst my father's people, that they possess the right to impose their values on other nations and peoples…"

"Their values are righteous, My Lady. That is inarguable," the girl replied quickly. "Is there something wrong with equality? Is there something wrong with liberating those who are oppressed, and giving them the means to better themselves? If we did not intervene, the lives of the disadvantaged would remain unchanged, or worse!"

Keela could not argue that yes, the people of Yvrem had a

society that had been designed to benefit only the elite. Where most of the people had existed in abject poverty, and—if born to such a life—would hardly ever rise to anything greater.

That had, indeed, changed with the arrival of the Farkas. The poor were given new opportunities to learn a trade or to have access to education—at least early on after the invasion. When the Farkas retreated to their Sentelys, many such options dried up for some people. Keela, had it not been for the patronage of her family, would probably never had obtained her schooling. She would have been a trade jeweler as Alara had been. One that would be less successful for her deficiency of talent in comparison to her mother.

But there was the darker side of the Farkas invasion: The instability it left behind. They had withdrawn without giving any further support, leaving only a mandate for change and the threat of war should it not be implemented. But there'd been no instructions on how to sustain or build on the so called improvements to their society's structure. The government—having been dismantled and its leadership removed—was in disarray and there followed a succession of failed governments, one after the next. Skirmishes over independent city states sprang up, followed by full-on civil war, and insurgencies against the Farkas which ended only in death..

Like most Yvremi, Keela had never understood the perspective of the Farkas, but she was learning more about it with every passing moment. The opinions of a common chamber maid seemed out of place and even offensive to Keela. Perhaps it was the tone of her voice as she spoke of Yvremi people, which sounded to Keela to be imbued with disdain.

She did not prompt any further conversation from the girl, allowing her to finish her work. After she pinned the final twist into place and laced the length of silken ribbon around her crown and up do, Keela said in her best impression of Vianca, "This will do. Thank you. You may go,"

The girl's irked expression as she bustled out was all Keela needed to feel a little satisfaction.

Keela heard muffled sounds of bickering through the doors of the drawing room. It stopped when she pulled open the large pocket doors, and slid them back into place after entering. Her grandparents stood and faced her, her grandfather's face looking particularly flushed, his ears a hot red. They both bowed to her and curtseyed, respectively, welcoming her quite stiffly.

There was a third person in the room. A rather imposing woman, black of hair and eyes, with a lofty height and a broad, sturdy body. She was not graceful like Keela's grandmother, but rather coarse looking. An expression of unmistakable disgust washed across her face as she looked at Keela.

Keela's instincts flared up again, but she kept her poise and reciprocated the greeting, her eyes passing over the woman and falling on her grandfather's. "Is Edrick not awake yet?"

"Oh, I believe the young fellow and the dog have gone out for a walk together," the strange lady replied tersely.

Keela was growing increasingly suspicious of her with every passing tick of the magnificent clock on the wall. She was suddenly worried for Edrick and Magpie. "Well, I should like to join them. Which way have they gone?"

"Oh, you needn't. They left at least an hour ago, so I wager they'll return shortly," the interloper replied. Keela could see quite plainly that the woman was lying.

Keela looked not at her, but at the face of her grandfather, who was looking away with his jaw muscles rippling. "Grandfather, at the risk of sounding forward, who is this lady that is answering my questions in your stead?"

"This is Miss Edra Kell.," he replied.

"What transpires here?" Keela asked, her eyes locking onto Miss Kell's. There was a terse silence as the woman seemed to order her thoughts.

"There's a disagreement as to whether there's any real use for you," Mrs. Kell replied sharply.

Keela's brow wrinkled and her eyes narrowed. "I'm sorry?"

"The deposed king—he is protected by his importance to the Yvremi, and the little pup, her mother is someone of particular importance, especially for the Conclave. These are valuable assets to have in our efforts against the Conclave and its followers."

"I don't understand…"

"Miss Kell is Nall," Lord Wellis interjected with no shortage of disgust.

Keela took her in, her skin bristling, hairs rising up along her arms and the back of her neck. Her grandparents were intimidated by Miss Kell's broad presence, and they seemed almost afraid.

"There is question as to whether you belong here," Miss Kell said haughtily.

"I am a member of this family," Keela snapped.

"Bloodlines only matter when they are pure, my *sweet girl*," the woman retorted. The last two words were laced with sarcasm.

"I will leave, if I am not welcome here. But you will not intrude upon this household or persecute my grandparents!"

"No. I think *we* will decide where you belong, child," the woman sneered.

"It is not up to the Nall to decide any such things," Lady Wellis interjected.

"The Farkas think themselves entitled to decide what others ought to do." Keela frowned darkly. "And you continue to presume you can do so with me as well."

Mrs. Kell merely looked on with a smug arch to her brow. Keela fumed inwardly.

"Where are Edrick and Magpie? And tell the truth this time," Keela insisted.

"If you mean that useless man and the half-blood pup, they are going where they can be useful to us."

"You will take me to them immediately!" Keela roared.

"Dearest child, I would not be posturing so, if I were you," Miss Kell snarled.

The air in the room prickled as they faced off in razor sharp silence. Keela actually felt herself measuring her transformation, initiating it with a fleeting lament for her lovely, hard-earned coif. Her body first stretched long, her ribcage narrowing, her arms and legs tightening and contracting. A painless thing, Keela briefly mused, as large, shining black paws fell soundlessly onto the splendid pile rug before her, accompanied by the song of myriad hairpins scattering about her. Her clothes crumpled around her; her wound dressings flaking off of her skin as the fur extruded quickly from the follicles. Her wounds were still painful, but not so much that she felt inhibited by them. Her gaze washed over the intruder.

Miss Kell was slower to change. Her thick, stalwart body was still lighter and less substantive compared to Keela's. Her eyes were a bright, haunting silver. Keela's grandparents did not transform, but their postures showed their readiness.

Keela's stance remained tense, but she did not snarl or invite aggression. She merely stood with her hackles high. Keela was a solid, more muscular version of her counterpart, and her shoulders stood a good two hands higher than those of the interloper. There were some marked differences in her shape and her size, and they had nothing to do with health or age. It was evident that Keela was a different breed. Miss Kell in wolf form was clearly gauging her.

"I don't believe this is a prudent way to act, Miss Kell," Lord Wellis said. "Keela clearly has a significant advantage in size and strength, in spite of her injuries. I've seen her fight. She is a monster. She tore up two wolves with a few snaps of her jaws." His voice was imbued with pride.

Miss Kell's response was a menacing growl. For a few fleeting moments, Keela was certain the woman was going to lunge at her.

Unexpectedly, Miss Kell relented and stepped back, swinging her head away. She growled and snorted before padding to the door. Lord Wellis let her out, returning to pick up a little wool throw from a chair, and holding it out in front of himself while averting his gaze.

Keela recalled her anger—her sense of danger—and collected it into what felt like a little ball inside the front of her head. She could almost feel the weight of it. In doing so, her wolf retreated as well, as if it belonged inside that little orb of instinct. She was in but a few moments kneeling on the floor, her skin and all its cuts and bruises exposed. She stood and accepted the throw, covering herself while she bent to collect her things.

"I don't have any idea what's happening," she confessed. She began the tedious routine of dressing herself, donning her underpinnings quickly so she could discard the little coverlet. Her grandmother wordlessly helped, her cool hands moving purposefully over the laces and hooks to help enclose her granddaughter in clothing again.

"How is it that this person could stroll right into this house and intimidate you both? Are you not wolves? Could you not drive her away as I did?" Keela was incensed. She trembled with anger.

"Miss Kell is a principal of the Nall. She moves between the Sentelys. I suspect she came at the heels of your attackers, who were likely under her orders," her grandfather explained. "We did not expect her. We are at a particular disadvantage because it was she who took your father, and sent him to Farkas to be tried for treason., His arrest was contrived, and under whose authority, is still unknown. Until his case is annulled for lack of evidence by our courts, he remains imprisoned. And with the instability with our government, he could be in their custody for much longer than he already has. This was his punishment for the crime of fathering you—whether or not the Nall care to admit it.

"There is a delicate balance, dear girl. They stand to harm Lenn, if we step over their lines, and the Nall must be careful as most of the Sentely are Conclave held. We cannot harm her, or our son could die. She cannot harm us, or there will be full-on war inside the Sentelys, and that is something both sides have striven to avoid since the beginning." He looked at Keela apologetically.

"Miss Kell wants to kill you. She just saw that she is not able to do this alone. I suspect she will summon assistance from the Nall dissidents that live here. I propose we take a little stroll," Grandfather suggested nervously.

Keela's brow darkened, and she stopped dressing. "I'll be fine on my own," she replied, fidgeting with her gown closures.

"I promised my son I would watch for you, my dear. He knew you would eventually find us—and he understood that you would have to be protected from the Nall presence in the Sentely. That fight in the square should have been warning enough to the Nall that such things are not tolerated here. But Miss Kell's presence has made our offer of a safe place seem like a terrible lie."

"It's not your fault. If what you say is true, their need to intervene is indeed more desperate, if I threaten to demolish their cause." Keela drew her gown over her now loose and disheveled hair with her grandmother's help, and once her head and arms were through, and she was closing the stomacher, she looked at her grandfather.

"I still don't understand how she could just walk in here and do what she did," Keela grumbled, looking at them with anger. Yes, the woman was strong, but her wolf form was no more threatening than her grandfather had been when he'd come into the square. "You could have taken her. And nobody would have been the wiser. She had nobody else with her."

"Her brethren would know. And for your father's sake, and also for the people of the Sentelys, our hands are tied.. There are enough Nall here to harm the Yvremi that live among us. That has always been the threat, and that was how Lenn was removed without a confrontation. Those of us here that are Conclave, we must protect the Yvremi that live here—and maintain peace as best we can. The Yvremi have, in many ways, become a liability to us against the Nall," her grandmother said. Keela could tell that her grandmother was ashamed for not being able to act to protect her.

"The Yvremi are in danger?" Keela asked.

"Very much so. All Yvremi are as long as the Nall continue to seek power. They are intent on their goal, dear Keela. They want to control Yvrem, and Farkas. They want to squash the Conclave's movement for unity and, in essence, control the source of the new blood. The only thing that's stopped them so far is the presence of the Conclave, and their dubious numbers."

Keela shook out her skirts over her petticoat and peered at the older couple, seeing perhaps a shade of herself in the shape of her grandfather's brow and the tilt of his beautiful eyes.

"Oh, damn, I forgot my boots," she snapped. She bent down huffily and snatched them up, sitting down ungracefully and drawing them on as best she could as her stays were now snugly wrapped around her.

"I will go to the Conclave's stronghold," Grandmother said. "They will need to know what is happening. I will find you after I have done that." Leesa turned to her husband. "I will speak to Ederil first, to make sure peace is kept here at home." He nodded, preoccupied with his granddaughter.

"You should not travel alone, grandmother," Keela supplicated.

"I will not be alone. We have our allies here. I will seek them out and ask them to accompany me. You must go with your grandfather."

"I am going after Edrick and Magpie," she said decisively. "I won't be stopped."

"Your grandfather will take you to some members of Jessick's society. They will be able to help you. Please, Keela. You need allies with you no matter where you go from here. Be discreet and move quickly. Your grandfather knows how to reach me if he needs to."

She stepped forward and embraced Keela. "I'm sorry this was so brief. I had envisioned more time to get to know one another. However I can hope that someday we can."

Keela put her hand on her grandmother's. The old woman blinked out a tear.

"You look so much like Lenn. He had the same little widow's peak…" Lady Leesa reached up and caressed Keela's cheek. She then gathered her wits about her and sailed out of the room quickly.

Keela turned to her grandfather. "Well. On the run again eh?"

"I'm sorry, Keela," he said compassionately.

"I don't know why I bother getting dressed, honestly."

He laughed. "I have a solution to the clothing problem. Go and fetch some of your things from your room. Some traveling clothes perhaps. Then come find me here."

Keela nodded and vaulted up the stairs, gathering a few essential items. She included outerwear, and a few utilitarian pieces, including her stained bonnet. She bundled the items into her arms and returned downstairs, to find her grandfather holding his own stack of neatly folded items.

"If you'll follow me," he told her.

Keela frowned and fell into step at his heels. They crossed one corridor into another and meandered down a narrow service stairwell. They emerged in the belly of the great house—the domain of the servants—which was at present mostly quiet. There were two housemaids darning linens at the common table, speaking quietly to one another as Keela and Wellis passed. Someone was clattering about in the kitchen where delectable aromas spilled into the corridor and reminded Keela how hungry she was and how long it had been since she had eaten.

Lord Vederine brought her to a linen closet where he reached in and pulled out two rough cotton washing bags. He put his clothing in one and handed her the other. She crammed everything in without a care. He then gestured her to follow him and they slipped out into the kitchen's garden. There he pointed to an arbor heavy with berry vines and told her: "Disrobe, put everything in the bag and then effect your transformation."

She and vanished into the leaves. She undid everything she'd put together only moments before, and—now nude— knelt and put the bag on the ground. Shed changed smoothly and easily with only a small effort, releasing again all the collected feeling that had been knotted up in her brain. Once she was a wolf, she snapped up her bag in her jaws.

She was met by the same gangly black wolf with silver fur around his eyes and whiskers she'd seen in the square. He held a cotton bag heavy with boots and garments.

He pivoted on his rear haunches and cantered away. Keela broke into an easy lope and found a pace by his side. The bag swung from her mouth and her ears perked forward. In spite of the grave situation, she could not help but find pleasure in being a wolf.

Miranda Mayer

Chapter 14
On the Hunt

Keela could not help but try to find a scent trail to follow. But Edrick and Magpie's scents were well concealed. Keela imagined that a race of wolves would know how to avoid leaving a trail as obvious as Xanett's accomplices so clumsily did when they took Edrick. She was left with the conclusion that she had to do as her grandmother asked, and rely on her grandfather and Jessick's allies to help her.

Poor Edrick, she thought. She worried for him, but not as much as she worried for Magpie, who was truly helpless. She had to find her.

Lord Vederine and Keela slid through the fields of swaying grain towards town again. The two wolves skirted the residences. They padded down a long hillside between the walls of grapevines. Keela's grandfather then stopped suddenly, dropped his bag and lifted his head, emitting a deep menacing growl.

Keela stopped too, and let her garments fall in front of her paws, her nose up in the air. It was a familiar scent. It was that of the wolf that had led her to Magpie—she remembered it distinctly, because it had been her first benign encounter with a wolf while she herself

251

was in wolf form. She now connected his scent to Magpie's. Keela wound around her grandfather and sniffed again, lowering her tail, her ears flattening back onto her head as she gingerly advanced ahead of her grandfather, her black, shining nose sniffing.

She made a little noise, a half-whine, half yelp. A slender muzzle appeared around the end of the row of vines, followed by a pair of deep, burnished, trustworthy eyes. The body soon followed, and Keela tucked her tail against her leg and lowered her head in submission as the elegant wolf approached. She whined quietly in relief as the great canine picked up her bag and then trotted away. Lord Vederine followed, with Keela loping behind them.

The big dog led them a long distance. Two hours of walking and trotting until they left behind the borders of the Vederine and arrived at a picturesque house at the foot of a hill, nestled a lush copse of trees by a fast-moving river. It was a two story stone building bookended by a pair of chimneys. Someone opened the door before they reached it, and the large wolf padded right up the steps and into the house, followed by Keela and her weary grandfather.

Awaiting them was a young lady of Keela's age. Her hand rested possessively on the large wolf's head. She was a vision with strawberry locks with perfectly buffed side curls, and a demure ensemble of modest roll-printed calico of pale green and soft pink, and a thick fichu ruched around her neck and into the front of her neckline. She pointed up the stairs. Keela picked up her clothing bag from between the large wolf's feet. Her nails clicked on the wooden floor as she scaled the stairs to one of nearest available rooms, where she transformed again.

She felt heavier and clumsier as a person. Her senses felt dull too, after so many hours being able to smell even the most subtle scent her human nose would never even detect. A young chambermaid came in just as Keela pulled on her wrinkled chemise and offered her a washcloth and a pitcher of warm water, which she poured into a washbowl in the corner of the room. Keela thanked her and quietly washed herself while the girl shook out her creased garments and aired them out.

She helped Keela into her clothes, and quickly arranged Keela's luscious raven locks onto the top of her head and a simple bun. Adorned in a white muslin day gown and walking boots with no tucker or jewelry, Keela returned to the room where they had entered, left of the entranceway, where a formal parlor of humble furnishings awaited her.

The young woman with red hair awaited her when she alighted onto the ground floor. She stood when Keela entered. "Hello," she said.

Keela curtsied clumsily and complied with the girl's gesture to sit. She gazed at Keela curiously. "My name is Edda," she offered.

"I'm Keela." She arranged her wrinkled skirts as best she could, conscious of them in spite of the girl's most evident unfussy tastes.

"Yes, Jessick told me about you," Edda said.

Keela tilted her head and her brows rose.

"That's my name." A tall, lean man entered the room. This was the man that Alara had fallen in love with but never manage to keep. His head barely cleared the doorframe as he stalked in. His face was handsome. His head was mostly bald, but the semi-circle of locks still persisting on his scalp were close-trimmed and tidy, like his long sideburns that rolled out low onto his chin, trimmed into sharp little points. All of it was a salt and pepper blend. His olive skin still had a youthful glow, however his face, like Alara's, had earned its lifetime of lines and wrinkles. His showed a brow that was often worried, and lips that were frequently tense and hard. The angles and arrangement of his features gave Keela a good idea what Alara might have found attractive about him.

He flashed a bright smile with flawless white teeth, and his pale gray eyes sparkled. He was fussing with a cravat that had been haphazardly tied in a knot under his chin. He was busy tucking the

253

long ends into his waistcoat.

Keela stood and curtsied, unable to tear her eyes from his face, trying to somehow see him with Alara's eyes. Her mother had always been alone. It was intriguing to meet the only man Alara had ever mentioned in regards to romantic interest. He seemed to sense her train of thought, the way her eyes were devouring his presence with great curiosity.

"How is the lovely Alara?"

"Last I saw her, obstinate and loving, as she always is."

He smiled broadly and plopped down gracelessly into a chair across from Keela. "I'm glad to hear this. I hope to go see her soon—if some of these little problems I have to contend with are finally resolved."

"Little problems?" Keela blurted incredulously. "Edrick has been taken… Again. And Magpie!"

"Magpie?" he asked, his brow arching in puzzlement. "I hope you don't mean Ellayne?"

"The pup? Yes, Magpie."

"Good gracious who would dub such an elegant little creature such a ridiculous name?"

"Edrick did," Keela muttered.

"Ah," he huffed, shaking his head. "That idle, worthless fellow *would* choose a name of so little imagination."

"He had no idea what she was. She was but a Ney wolf to him. A dog," Keela replied. "And Edrick is neither idle nor worthless."

"You've only known him for a little while, girl. Before all this he was a purposeless ne'er-do-well," Jessick murmured. "And Ney wolves are not dogs, dear child. Ney wolves are people. All of them. Well. They used to all be people, but that has been changing for some time. Nevertheless, we must find Edrick and Ellayne, and I cannot do it without you. That is why I came looking for you."

"You know they were taken?"

"Of course. I have my sources and my friends. I have been

following … *Magpie*," he said with no shortage of disgust, "for some time, intervening with attempts to harm her, fighting off Nall killers sent to take her. Someone got wind of her movements, and it's been a battle to keep her alive. Your arrival on the scene changed that quite a bit. It was intended for you to assume her protection. It was important that you did because you are stronger than the common Neys, and stronger even than the Imperials. She's important, the little whelp. They want her—and we need her. She must be kept safe and protected until she is of age to transform."

Keela's eyes remained locked on Jessick. The girl, Edda, sat impassively, her hands folded in her lap, quietly listening.

"I knew Magpie would be safer with you, but I never planned on Xanett interfering. It ruined everything," Jessick muttered. "The three of you were meant to come to the Conclave stronghold where they could see the truth for themselves. We had arranged an envoy and an escort to collect you once you'd effected your first change, and the three of you were together in earnest. But Xanett interfered before they arrived. He was never told to remove you from Calabras or separate you from the pup."

"Why is Edrick important?"

"Edrick is a King, Keela. Not a King with any official power, but he still holds tremendous influence over the Yvremi who may no longer overtly have a peerage-based hierarchy, but still honor the bloodlines in spite of the mandate against them. He was summoned to meet with a Conclave elder who is staying with her daughter, the Navray, at Eyome. Tales of his slothfulness and lack of conscientiousness preceded him, and the elder wanted to see for herself if Edrick was a worthy soul.

"Edrick met with them, although he thought he was meeting the Navray. He was watched by her as she was transformed. He interacted with her daughter. He was a pleasant surprise to both mother and daughter. He did not exemplify the idle fool he was said to be. There was already a rumor going about that the Nall were

255

going to attempt to use the King as a means to persuade the Yvremi that they were trustworthy. They would coerce him to be a smiling, reassuring face of Yvremi leadership, while the Nall quietly assumed power over Yvrem. It was determined that Edrick was not such a gullible, careless cur and that he could still be worthy and useful if he was given the chance. A little responsibility perhaps would bring the better qualities to the surface.

"I was at Eyome to speak to the Navray and her mother about your coming of age, and the necessity of finding a place for you to safely transform with Neys nearby to help you through it. But it happened much sooner than I had anticipated, because of the animals hunting little Ellayne.

"Moving her was vital as she had been discovered by the Nall, and they have plans for her. I was there when Edrick came. I and the elder transformed and allowed the elder's daughter to interact with him. One of our most trusted Yvremi allies was there too, and he was impressed by Edrick's comportment. And he had been a critic of his from the start. After Edrick left, we decided that both Ellayne and Edrick were of value in different ways.

"We knew there were two certainties. You would form an immediate attachment to the pup, as she would you, because of your wolf-blood. It would be a natural attraction. And you would transform the moment you felt that she was in any way threatened. What we did not expect, and are utterly intrigued by, is that you are much stronger than a full blood Farkas wolf, Keela. I witnessed this the first time you were assailed at Calabras. If I had not seen it, I would not believe it. You, a mere juvenile, defeated two high bronzes with minimal effort."

"Am I the only one you've seen?" Keela asked. She accepted a glass of port from the young woman with a polite nod, her attention riveted to Jessick. Lord Wellis entered dressed in trousers and his shirt and nothing more. He accepted a port from Miss Edda as well, thanking her politely.

"There was one before you, who I knew, he was large like you. But I never saw him fight. I never got the chance to. You are what the people of Farkas need to see. You, my dear, are the future of our people.

"We have always suspected that the mixed bloods would be different and a stronger breed. I do not wish to disparage you, my dear, but it goes with the truth that mongrel dogs possesses few of the weaknesses and deficiencies that are often inherent in purebreds."

"Mongrel. Add that to the many degrading monikers I've endured in my life," Keela laughed uncomfortably.

Jessick smiled thoughtfully. "The new blood has bred out all the weaknesses we have accumulated over the centuries. Weaknesses that are causing us to lose our ability to transform."

"Yes, yes, I know all that," she interrupted him. "Go on, please," Keela insisted. "We don't have much time."

Jessick laughed once and drained the port Edda had put into his hand. "We arranged for Ellayne to be brought to Edrick. He was to be watched to see how well he cared for her. We sent him to Calabras, where we also arranged to send you. Farkas are drawn to Farkas. We counted on that to bring the three of you together, and it worked. However, somehow someone got wind of the pup's journey and I was tasked with keeping her safe along the way until she reached you.

"You transformed and protected her, but in doing so also made yourself vulnerable, for you are the thing they fear. Proof that the Conclave of Sages was right. You were managing well enough... until Lord Xanett intervened." He shook his head in frustration. "He has always been a reasonable person in our interactions, and he is particularly fond of you. I never once imagined that the fondness he fostered for you was anything other than that of a benign benefactor. It has added unnecessary complexities to our situation. He has been invaluable, has Xanett. But that is behind us now. As for you, you have learnt of your abilities most expertly. Far beyond our expectations, and without guidance, as we had hoped."

Keela pursed her lips, but remained silent. In her head, the information of the past day consumed her mind. She was glad to learn that Jessick's goal was the same as hers. The talk of Xanett only discomfited her. She peered at her grandfather, who seemed almost aware of her state of mind, and he gave her a kind, understanding look, and put his hand on her arm. She moved in to his side and cuddled up against him. He wrapped an arm around her. "Well… everything is upside down. We must retrieve the idle king and the little Magpie," he muttered. "You can help us with that task."

She exhaled shakily. "I'm so tired."

She did not mention how sore her wounds were either. She did not need to speak of her hunger, for her stomach roared in the coarsest way that resounded about the room, to which her grandfather, responded: "Good heavens someone please feed that darling wolf!"

Finding Edrick this time would be more challenging. It would not involve using her nose, but instead, using the information that Jessick had provided through some of his sources. He had intelligence that the Nall were taking Edrick and Magpie back to the capitol, Kireen, where Jessick speculated that they would use him as a pawn to gain influence over the current unstable Yvremi government.

"A royal face—a royal that still commands respect in spite of his lack of power—is all they need to prompt the old guard to rise up and demand their place. If somehow they destabilize the interim government and the senate, they could possibly spark a coup… Edrick will be put in as a figurehead and the Nall can assume power in the Senate with Edrick's assurances to the people that they can be trusted. And whether there's a revolt of the traditionalists or a revolt against Edrick and the Nall, insurrection would be ideal either way, for the Sentely would be able to set loose the Nall army that are now quietly amassing," Jessick said. "They will use Yvrem's need for help with the Akravani to do this. They know it was his mission to secure assistance from us—they know it will be what the Senate wants to hear. And they will use that to their advantage."

They sat both in the cozy drawing room, shortly after breakfast. Keela was swathed in a woolen day gown the color of evergreens, her favorite boots on her feet, and a rustic clay mug of tea clutched in her hand. She had only brushed her hair out and left it loose over her shoulders, the dark locks shining against the matte of her linen bodice. The fire popped and snapped in its dark little hearth.

Keela's brow furrowed as she absorbed what Jessick had said. "Army..."

"The Nall have been at it for almost two centuries, my dear. Undermining our Sentelys, replacing the supporters of the Conclave wherever they could. They've been massing their forces within them for a long time for a moment like this. The Conclave is aware of it. It has been matching the Nall efforts, and staging its own forces to stop it, but now that the Nall have Edrick, they will also have the royalists of Yvrem beside them, fighting for what amounts to their own enslavement."

"Edrick would *never* submit to that!" Keela exclaimed.

Jessick frowned and shook his head. "They still have *you*, as far as he's concerned. He has no idea you're safe. There's no doubt that Edrick is attached to you. And he now knows that Magpie is more than a mere pet, but I suppose that wouldn't matter much, as he was much attached to her before he knew this."

"He does love that pup," Keela laughed with lamentation. "Then what can be done? I must go to the capitol."

"Indeed. I will accompany you."

"The Yvremi must be told what is happening, Mr. Jessick," she said.

"The Yvremi have no trust of the Farkas, my dear. Yes, telling them might serve to stop the Nall, but it would also serve to destroy the presence the Conclave has worked so hard to build and to harm the efforts to unite our people in peace. How confident would the Yvremi be in us, if they knew our people suffered such division and unrest?"

"The invasion was a bad plan," Keela ventured.

"Invasions are always a bad plan. But we can't change what is done."

Keela drank from her tepid tea. "Now there lies the challenge of finding Edrick. I cannot allow the Nall to manipulate him as they are, nor allow him to continue to believe that I am in harm's way. I am concerned that this could all end in disaster if I do not work quickly."

"Don't over think it, my dear," Jessick muttered. He bent forward, put his elbows on his knees and looked at her. "I think we all add unnecessary complications to the challenges that face us. When a person stands before a great maze in a garden, for instance, they look ahead. They run into all the dead ends, repeat turns, and backtrack. But if they were smart," he tapped his temple with his long finger, "they would merely look down. For the path most worn will lead to the way out."

Perhaps he was right, Keela mused. She should keep looking down for the worn path, and not forward at the obstacles. She sipped again. "Then it is to the capitol," she said. Her companion agreed with a nod, and smiled ominously.

Edrick sat on his horse, chewing his lower lip. Magpie was secure in her bag. Beside him, the lean, gaunt man by the name of Harden and his stalwart companion, Elmar, sat on their own steeds. They looked down at the city of Kireen from the Skyline Hill which stood tall over the bustling city, and the shimmering plane of ocean beyond the bristle of Kireen's piers, marinas and stone cobs.

Edrick was harshly divided in his mind. On one hand, his desire to eliminate the Akravani threat was strong, as it would be for anyone with the slightest sense of responsibility and love for their nation. But a selfish part of his heart wanted to leave the wars and the invasions to fall as they may and turn his horse back with Magpie in tow to find Keela.

He felt as if he were but only a hair's breadth from telling his guardians go and hang themselves, and to ride off at full tilt. But there was the small complication of the men carrying flintlock pistols, and Elmar had already demonstrated his skill for the shot, killing an unfortunate squirrel right of its tree some miles back. Such an attempt would leave Edrick deuced.

He reached down and patted Magpie's head. He would simply have to play it by ear. Perhaps an opportunity would arise that could change the course of events and allow him to secure Keela's safety on his own terms, and not of those of his captors.

They did not speak of themselves as captors. They described themselves as the peacemakers. The Farkas who were most motivated to take the necessary steps in order to stop an invasion. However, there would be a price.

"If you want the Farkas to help with the Akravani, this is what you must do: You must give us a place in the government of Yvrem. You will not be without reward for this. The Farkas will restructure the government to include the peerage again, and the Monarchy can be restored along with a parliament. You, Bethranorn, could be a king again."

Edrick tried to explain to the woman who had asked this of him that he was perhaps titled, but that he lacked any influence in the government. But the daunting woman, whose name remained a mystery to him, insisted that his title did indeed have influence and it would help the public accept that the Farkas were part of their lives now. He would represent his people and theirs, she told him.

The prospect of such was not as appealing to him as the woman likely imagined. That implied a plethora of responsibility he was not prepared to accept. He preferred to be the 'idle waste of space' his father once acrimoniously described him. Or at least something of the like, as long as Keela was part of his days in one capacity or another. And Magpie, of course.

His gaze wandered to Elmar's musket, which was holstered onto the front of his saddle—his pistols tucked away in the saddlebags behind his thighs. Edrick had only fired a rifle for shooting clay pigeons, and had never been particularly apt at it to begin with. He chastised himself for even considering he could do anything with those weapons.

The men pressed their mounts forward onto the road, Edrick between them. There would be more people to meet them at the townhouse where Edrick was being led. The traffic increased significantly as they merged onto a main throughway, and they remained in single file. Harden first, then Edrick, with Elmar taking the rear, his wrist resting idly on the butt of his pistol, his eyes almost burning a hole on Edrick's back.

They entered the thick of the city about three quarters of an hour later, wending through the dense congestion of downtown coaches, riders and walkers. There was a great celebration going on, and the crowds were thick. Nearly impossible to forge through on horse. Edrick realized it was the Manthrane spring festival. This boded well for him.

Edrick's eye fell upon a storefront and an idea came to him. A bright surge of hope glowed in his chest. He wasted no time. His hand slid slowly to the bag on the front of his right thigh in which Magpie was bound. He loosened the strap, and pulled her out against his stomach as stealthily as he could, disguising the movements by steering his horse around a large ox and cart that were stopped in the middle of the street. As his horse navigated around it, Edrick let himself list to the left and slid off onto the ground.

Once he was down he clutched the puppy close, ducked under his horse, and bolted in front of the dray, crouching down low so that he would be invisible underneath an undulating canopy of parasols, bonnets and hats. The din was so that he could barely hear the shouts of his captors as he slipped away. He circled back around, and crossed behind the riders, peering up now and again to glimpse them. Elmar tried to dismount but was impeded by a horde of laughing ladies.

Edrick slid into the eye-wateringly fragrant shop of a perfumier. There, he pretended to interest himself in some scents while his eye remained fast on the riders frantically peering about in search of him.

He grasped a tiny vial of pure lavender oil, and he paid a great deal more than it was priced. Putting some on his hands, he rubbed it all over Magpie. He then shook it over his coat until he reeked of the concentrated essential oil.

With a wry smile he turned to the befuddled perfumier, a lovely old lady as tiny as a child and as frail as a bag of bones. "Is there a way to get out the back?"

She pointed to the door leading to her private apartments. He slid through a shabby sitting room that smelled of sour apples mixed with a riot of other scents, and out a door that led to a small garden. He crossed to a gate which opened to a lane which backed many other such gardens and gates. In long, easy strides, he and his odorous dog slipped away into the capitol, leaving his lupine captors in his wake. He hoped that the lavender oil would keep their noses off of his trail.

He knew exactly where to go. He'd been to Yvrem's capitol of Kireen more times than he could recall, and had connections aplenty here. He used the back streets, keeping to alleyways and lanes between residential areas as much as he could until he found Aster

Lane, which was a far sight finer than the one he'd escaped from. Here the garden gates were made of the finest ironwork, and the rooflines peering up over the garden plots were tall and lovely. He entered the one marked with the name 'Evam' and closed the gate behind him. He crossed between beds of new vegetables and herbs to the set of stairs leading down to the kitchens. He shocked a chamber maid, who curtseyed low at the sight of him, her nose wrinkling at his strong aroma.

He vaulted up the narrow stairway that led to the butler's pantry and emerged in a dining room which had just concluded a late lunch meal for the residents. A footman was at present clearing up the stemware, and he looked up in startlement at the intruder before bowing in greeting. Edrick stole a leg of cold pheasant as he walked through, and bit into it, devouring a good portion before he gave the pup the rest, discarding the bone into a potted plant in the foyer. He made his way to the parlor where he knew he would find the people he needed. They were just reclining in their chairs and groaning from their full tummies when he entered.

"Edrick!" a lovely lady blurted, vaulting to her feet. She dashed to him and threw her arms around his neck. He felt the firm bulge of her pregnant belly press against him. She then withdrew and clamped her hand over her nose. "Oh gods, why do you smell like a brothel?"

The young man in the room with them laughed heartily. "Indeed. I can smell you from here, man," he said.

Edrick bowed with a smile to the man in greeting. The man rose and bowed in return, advancing, but not too closely.

"Keeneck!" Edrick roared in greeting. "Now, perhaps you can explain to me dearest sister and your elegant wife, how would you know what a brothel smells like?" he asked the girl with a mischievous smirk. She smacked his arm and waved the away his reek. "I'm in a bit of a pickle, Dayna. Had to escape some changeling wolves."

She laughed at him, thinking it a silly joke. "Why didn't you send a note ahead to let us know you were coming?"

"I wasn't planning on coming to Kireen until just before you left for Ajental for the summer. I just ended up here. I don't even have my things."

"Well, our man Avorno will scrounge something up for you. I beg you go upstairs and ring for a bath and some clothes. I cannot bear your aroma."

"Of course, my dearest sister." Edrick bent down and pecked her forehead.

She reached out and patted Magpie's head. "At least you redeem yourself by bringing me my own Ney wolf pup," she said with a wry smile.

Edrick shook his head. "Fat chance." He left the room and vaulted up the stairs to the apartments he often occupied when visiting his sister and her husband.

One long, satisfying bath later—for first him, and then Magpie—the lavender scent had been mostly washed away with a strong soap and hot water. Edrick dressed in the clothes borrowed from his brother-in-law. He carried the damp pup downstairs, and was greeted in earnest by the residents of this familiar home.

"You look lovely. You are aglow, sister," he exclaimed warmly.

She took his hands and embraced him, leading him to sit by her. She quietly served him tea while he watched her. "Why are you truly here? Not that I am displeased by your sudden appearance, but I would have liked a little notice. We could have prepared better for your visit," she chided him.

Edrick shook his head. "It's a long story, Dayna, and I am confident you would think it all madness."

Dayna looked down at the dog. "She is lovely." She reached out and borrowed Magpie, folding her limbs up into her arms and kissing her fuzzy head. "How long will you stay? Tammin and Areya are to visit in only a week. I hope you will stay to see them. Areya means to remain until I've delivered. It will be nice to have someone close by who knows what they're about when it comes to babies. It's not that I don't trust the midwife, but it's not the same as family."

"That's wonderful of her to do that. And Tammin will stay too?" he asked.

"No. Your brother will stay only a fortnight, and then he will travel on to Daradell, where there is to be some gathering ordered by the Senate in regards to the Akravani armies at Hellebos. He was a bit concerned that you were not on the list of those invited, but he was informed by the Senate that you had been dispatched for more important duties in regards to this crisis," Keeneck said.

He stood and moved closer to them. He sank down into a chair across from Edrick, throwing out his tails in a flamboyant manner as he did. He crossed his legs and reached into his pocket for a snuff box, which he quickly opened and served himself of a pinch of the white stuff.

"Yes. My mission to the Sentely has concluded. I am now on another task, in a manner of speaking. I cannot stay long. Not even a few days, I regret to say, dearest Dayna. I have obligations elsewhere."

"Sentely? You mean to say you went inside a Farkas settlement?" His brother-in-law's leg unfolded from the other and he scooted to the edge of his seat, his brown eyes full of intrigue. He clutched his hands together in eagerness. Keeneck was from Armion, a southern island nation a week's sail from Yvrem. His skin was an elegant walnut brown and his hair, scrupulously coiffed, was a riot of ringlets that were tied back into a queue and coiled most elegantly in two side curls on each temple. He was a fully titled man, the Armion equivalent of a Viscount.

"Yes, I did indeed go to a settlement of Farkas occupation," Edrick replied. "It was…" he paused, "an experience."

"You mean to say that this is all you will tell us about it?"

266

Keeneck demanded.

"Right now? Yes. It is all I can tell."

"Well," Keeneck blurted poutily, throwing himself back into his seat dejectedly. "That is most disappointing, brother. Most disappointing!"

"There is nothing stopping anyone from riding into a Farkas Sentely, Keeneck. They won't harm you. And many of the residents are Yvremi. Go see one for yourself. You will find only normality there. Perhaps a slightly better, finer normality, but that is what you will find. Houses, farms, orchards, crops, cheese makers, the lot. Better dressed, better cared for, better off." Edrick did not mince his words. He leaned back into his chair, picking up his teacup and saucer, thoughtfully sipping the warm infusion. It was his favorite tea. The one his sister preferred. A deep dark tea infused with elderberry and the subtle hint of nettle.

"I see," Keeneck muttered softly.

Dayna cooed over the pup, and patted her quietly. "So what is next for you then, brother?"

"I don't know," he admitted. "I must ride back towards the Wethlian country. There's someone I must find. Someone who needs my assistance. Someone who has become quite important to me."

Dayna's face lifted and her eyes widened. Her brows arched in immediate interest. "Oh? Do I hear what I think I am hearing?"

"Dayna…"

"Oh, no, I heard it. You *like* someone? Really!? At last!"

"She is somebody our family would certainly not choose for me," he said.

Dayna scoffed. "Edrick, at this point, the family would be happy if you settled down with a scullery maid! Who is she? What's her name? Is she lovely? Of course she's lovely. You wouldn't look at anything that wasn't perfectly lovely. Oh, Edrick, I do want to meet her!" she babbled.

"You might meet her sooner than you think. I may have to bring her here until I can figure out what can be done," he said reflectively.

"She is welcome here. Is she not husband?"

"Of course, my dear, of course!" Keeneck replied solicitously. They both looked upon him expectantly.

"I am wondering if you could be so kind as to loan me a horse," he asked.

Keeneck's mouth pursed in thoughtfulness and he shrugged. "As if you have to ask…" he waved his hand to dismiss the question, and then flopped back into his seat. "I say, Edrick. Care to accompany me to Marden's this evening? Join us for a few rounds of Speculation with the fellows, along with a dram or two?"

"I would love to, Keeneck, but I am tired. I would like very much to go to bed early. I might want to leave before dawn. I'm not certain yet."

Edrick questioned the wisdom of leaving and heading back to Wethlo for Keela. The Nall would surely know that he would go there, would they not? He sunk further into his chair, allowing his body to relax in this familiar environment. He pondered what he ought to do—he did not wish to endanger Keela, or Magpie. Or himself, for that matter. He watched his sister coo and fuss over the puppy who had grown so much already. What would he do?

Keela and Jessick moved with lithe, chilling silence through the brush that edged the road, the darkness of the night making them virtually invisible with their jet black coats. Keela's body moved like a smooth vessel over still water, her legs compensating for the variations in the terrain, her head hanging level and low, tail balanced out behind her like a rudder. Jessick was in front of her, his silver eyes catching the merest glint of light and reflecting it hauntingly whenever he looked back at her. Much further ahead, another Imperial of Jessick's network led the way. The large wolf blazed the scent trail for the two to follow. His scent grew suddenly stronger, signaling that he had stopped. So they did in turn, keeping their distance as best they could.

Jessick and Keela both wore little packs on their backs sewn of black wool, with straps that looped around their front limbs and belts that constricted around their chests. The girl, Edda, had strapped them on after they had transformed.

Keela had bidden her grandfather a hasty farewell, for they would meet at the capitol in several days if all went according to plan, and Edrick was found. Keela was convinced she had picked up traces of Magpie's scent a few times near the road, but she chided herself that it was probably her imagination, for it had rained since she had left the great house at Wethlo and the road was awash with all sorts of strong aromas, from wet animal to evergreen pitch. The occasional waft of cooking food, or the boozy breath of a drunkard stumbling home from the public house also intruded upon her palate.

What is the delay? She thought to herself darkly, her impatience manifesting in a large lupine sigh, which Jessick turned to admonish with a flash of his reflective sterling eyes. He lifted his head. The other wolf had started moving again. They discovered that the hindrance had been exactly what Keela had caught in her nostrils: a pair of drunken men barely managing to balance themselves on extremely well behaved horses.

The lead wolf waited for them to pass before crossing behind the pair as they wavered back to their homes. The horses caught the scent of the Ney Wolves as they slipped like shadows across the road and into the trees, and became agitated. The drunken men grumbled at them, and one yanked the tense horse's reins, making it shy suddenly from the side of the road. That was more than enough to send him sliding out of his saddle into a crumpled, inebriated heap on the ground. The other man cackled loudly with laughter as the wolves moved away.

Not long after, there was a long, piercing howl that cut through the night somewhere a mile or two away. The reply from the lead wolf startled Keela, for it was much closer and extremely loud. As soon as he began, Keela felt an impulsive bay rising up into her throat, and before she knew it, she was howling along with them.

Jessick nipped her shoulder, and she yelped. *Sorry!* She shouted inside her own head, snuffing at him. The lead wolf huffed and snorted. He was only a length or two ahead now. He broke into a run and darted across a large open field filled with radishes, their watery, peppery fragrance filling Keela's nose.

They traversed the field, past a farmhouse where the scent of wood burning and fat drippings made her hungry and tired simultaneously. Down another road between a windbreak of poplars they turned abruptly onto a drive leading to a modest house of unassuming proportions and style. A sturdy sort of house, of good size for a decently well-off family with few pretentions. There, a smaller wolf with copper colored eyes waited on the stoop of the entryway. It whined in excitement at the sight of lead wolf and she ran to him, bouncing like a house-dog, tail wagging, and snorts of happiness escaping her. She stopped when Keela and Jessick came nearer, and lowered her head and tail at the sight of them. She quietly turned up the steps of the house and nosed the door open.

As soon as they entered the house, Keela released the binding of her pack with a tug of her teeth, and wriggled out of it. She was directed by a young Farkas man through the open door of a study off the foyer towards a dressing gown draped over the back of a chair. She and the copper eyed she-wolf went in, not bothering with the door, merely using the wall of separation to obtain the privacy needed to quickly cover themselves once they receded into their human forms. Keela exhaled loudly as her body constricted around her organs, and her cuts and wounds were contorted by her body's efforts to shrink to her normal size. She noticed the others made that same tortured wheeze too. Her blunted sense of smell was the first thing she noticed, breathing in air that now seemed heavy and stale.

She knelt for one moment on the rug, getting used to her new boundaries again, feeling almost suffocated by her own tiny being. She braced herself with one hand on the chair and got up, grasping the dressing gown and pulling it on. She pulled back her voluminous hair and twisted it up into a knot.

"I'm glad you are here, all of you. I have news!" a young lady's voice exclaimed from behind Keela loudly enough to be heard from the other room.

Keela turned to see that the former copper-eyed wolf was now standing behind her, clutching her own garment closed, an excited twinkle in her eyes. The gentlemen were around the corner of the corridor. They stepped out once they were covered, Jessick in a banyan, clutching his pack, and the lead wolf, now a lanky, young man, examining Keela as he drew a shirt on to accompany the breeches he'd hastily tugged onto his legs. "I'm Adrom," he said quickly.

"Keela," she replied curtly. They had only met as wolves, so introductions were necessary.

"Tell," Jessick said impatiently to the unnamed girl.

"They're scrambling at Kireen. They lost your man, you see! *And* the little whelp with him! I don't have the details as to how, but they lost him in the city. The Nall guardians have been sent to Irino. You know what that means," the girl said.

Keela's gaze took her in. She couldn't have been more than twenty—close to Keela's own age—petite and delicate, with unusually wavy, lovely black hair with a red tint that was brought out by the low candle and firelight. She gestured for everyone to sit. "I am Ameera," she said in a soft voice. Keela reciprocated the introduction, and they both curtseyed to one another.

Keela had gotten used to the state of perpetual undress that

271

seemed to permeate the Farkas lifestyle, and was no longer bashful to sail about in a loose dressing gown, completely à poil underneath. She sat down, but her limbs were tingling, the muscles in her legs were experiencing little bursts of nervous energy, and she was restless. News of Edrick only made her more so.

"So what does that mean?" she asked.

"Oh, Irino is the Nall stronghold here. It's the only Sentely that has been fully overtaken by the Nall, and it's there where the leadership for the Yvrem-based Nall reside."."

"They're not chasing Edrick? He will undoubtedly head back towards the safe house outside of Wethlo!" Keela said.

"Oh, there's no doubt there are wolves out there searching for him along that route," Jessick intoned. "We also will have wolves out there too."

Kella frowned darkly and shook her head. "How long ago did he go missing?"

"Only a day," the girl replied. "They arrived yesterday afternoon, and they lost him before they even got to the house where the Nall contingent was waiting."

"So he could still be in the city," Keela rationalized. She stood. "I can't stop here. I must go to Kireen immediately before he decides to head back, into the hands of the Nall."

Her hosts Adrom and Adeera frowned in thoughtful disagreement, but they did not protest.

"I will go alone if I must," Keela insisted.

Jessick frowned and shook his head in disappointment. "As if I would allow it," he murmured in annoyance. With a great big sigh he turned to the towering young Imperial upon whom the young woman gazed lovingly. "Fancy throwing us a bit of food before we go? I could hear that one's stomach roaring since we crossed the bridge at Amadyne."

The strapping young man smiled, looking back at his young wife. She preceded them out of the room to scrounge up a quick dinner for the guests before they departed.

The capitol was thick with revelers as the city celebrated the Manthrane spring festival. Jessick and Keela had chosen to take Adrom's coach rather than enter the city as Ney Wolves, as there was a report of a strong Nall presence in the city. Keela spent the five and a half hour trip in quiet contemplation, mulling over questions as Jessick snored across from her; his head lolling with the movement of the coach.

The first thing she pondered was how she was going to locate Edrick in the capitol. The question became more pertinent as they approached the city and were immediately bogged down by the nearly stagnant flow of traffic clogging the road. She imagined it was the week-long festival that had allowed Edrick to escape his captors to begin with, because the scene was all chaos, even several miles out from Kireen. Catching the slightest scent trail would be impossible. What might have been a blessing for their escape would turn out to be a detriment for their recovery.

Secondly, and more direly—which Keela could scarce admit—was the question as to how they would curtail the Nall. She understood that there was no option but to try. Neither she, Edrick, the pup nor any mixed blood would be safe unless the Nall were stopped. It was a daunting notion, to consider this her lot too. It was a responsibility she would rather pass onto the wolves of the Conclave, but she could not in good conscience do nothing. Not when so many were in danger. And if Jessick was right, and she was stronger and larger than her purebred counterparts, they would certainly need her amongst their ranks.

The how, that was still an unworkable dilemma. She scarce believed she alone would conjure up a miraculous solution that would resolve the crisis and bring enough normality to their lives that the Conclave could focus on the problem of the Akravani. But she had only time to bemuse herself over it as the coach inched its way towards the center of Kireen.

The idea came to Keela as she was gazing out of the coach window, half-watching the hordes of people milling about, hindering the wheeled and hoofed traffic. She saw several gentlemen dressed as the Manthrane King, enrobed in flowing scarlet velvet capes capped with capelets made of snowy rabbit fur painted to look like ermine. Their ridiculous, comically large crowns were adorned with glistening jewels made of sugar or glass, their cheeks painted as bright as apples. They threw tiny citrus fruits and sugar coins and gems into the crowds from large baskets they carried in their arms, all the while shouting spring blessings to the people who reached up to catch the treats. Small children darted between the people, collecting from the ground the projectiles that had been missed.

The coach passed by one of these men. He shouted loudly into the coach through the partially opened window, and tossed in a couple of little yellow-orange citruses and some candy coins. "Spring bounty to you, young lady!" he barked. Jessick was startled momentarily by the noise, but resumed snoring only a moment later.

Edrick is a king, Keela thought, as the painted face moved out of view and another spray of fruit and candy arced into the air. *This is the capitol. He surely has a riot's worth of connections here, would he not? He does not live here, but he would unquestionably come here frequently. So he must have apartments somewhere. Friends for certain. Or... or family.* Keela's brow rose. *The book.*

The book they had peered into to find her father. That same book could help her find Edrick. She doubted there would be an open library to be found, with all the festivities. She reached across the short span between her and Jessick, and shook his knee. He snorted awake again, his eyes sleepy.

"Hm... we arrived?"

"I've a notion," she said. "Where do you think we could get our hands on an up-to-date copy of Oyelle's?"

Jessick's shaggy brows furrowed together and he pondered it a moment, sitting up straighter and raking his fingers across his bald head, then scratching the back of it. "Well, let's see. Public libraries would be closed for the week, but the university libraries are never closed."

"Where's the nearest one?"

"That would be Neecham. That's over in the Laurelwood district. It sort of *is* the Laurelwood district," he added. "At this pace we'll get there... well, never."

"Let's walk. The coach can go to the Conclave house without us."

Jessick picked up a cane he borrowed from Adrom. He used the knob on it to pummel the wall of the coach. With a few shouted words they were pushing open the door and exiting the coach, immediately swept away by the crowds pouring around the conveyance.

Keela rode in Jessick's wake as he was used his cane to brusquely prod his way between people. They moved off of the street and onto the walk, sliding close to the buildings. They wove in and out of the never ending stream of people who seemed to hardly notice them as Jessick and Keela elbowed and shouldered their way through. It was a hectic way to travel, but seeing how quickly the coach receded behind them, Keela knew it was the best choice.

Neecham was like an oasis of quiet in the middle of a city in full celebration. The university's tall stone walls encircled the ancient campus, flocked in thick mantels of ivy and cascading vines. Great old trees bowed out over them to create a canopy of greenery that shaded the otherwise sunny street. Outside, people congregated in the shade. Inside, it was quiet and mostly devoid of citizens. They entered a secondary entrance near the Evrel temple and it was as if the bustle and din of the city immediately disappeared.

"What I would give to be changed into my other form right now," Keela snorted to Jessick.

He glanced down at her in amusement, and smiled, offering no response. Keela, in a thin linen walking gown of an orange-red, struggled to keep up with him, her skirts flapping around her fast-moving legs. Her bonnet, the one with the stain that made her think of Edrick, with its feather flouncing. Jessick did not slow to accommodate her. Had they been in their wolf forms, it would be Jessick having trouble keeping up.

They moved through the shaded pathways of the university's dense, leafy gardens. Only once did they come across a student strolling along a small grassy area near the path, holding some sort of device with lenses and a clear glass flask of water. They did not stop to ask what he was up to.

Jessick's cane tapped as he strode with gentlemanly purpose down the tidily cobbled walkway towards a cluster of colonnaded buildings. He lifted the end of his cane and pointed it at the building on the far left. "That's the one we want," he said.

They crossed the broad park, Keela slightly winded from the effort. There they found the library open, the large double doors agape to let in fresh air. The attendant was a petite middle-aged woman in a day dress of periwinkle blue with soft yellow lines and a work apron over it. She was all ruffles: a ruff about her neck, ruffled lines down the front of her delicate chemisette. She had a large older style cap with long lapettes drooping over onto her shoulders, also edged in lace ruffles. She smiled when she saw Jessick.

"Good day, Sir," she said with a flush of her cheeks. Jessick smiled down at her from his lofty height and bowed shallowly.

"You may call me Mr. Kole, Madame," he exclaimed with no shortage of flirtatious energy. Keela realized that Jessick was a bit of a cad. She imagined that perhaps there was a string of broken hearts like Alara's left in his wake. *Poor mother*, thought Keela.

"Thank you Mr. Kole. I am Mrs. Jakane, curator of the

university archive." She smiled and curtsied genteelly. "You are not of the university, I see. What brings you to visit me today?"

"Ma'am, we've come in search of a book which we have a particular need to see. Most shops and libraries are closed for the celebration days," he explained.

"Yes, of course," she replied. "What book do you seek?"

"The most recent Oyelle's," Keela blurted.

The lady seemed startled by Keela's presence, as if she hadn't even noticed her. Her gaze returned to Jessick. "I will allow you to look at the university's copy." With a coy smile she spun on her heel and flounced off through the work tables towards the archway to the books.

Jessick seemed quite content to keep Mrs. Jakane busy by indulging her interest in him. Only the subtle little black tear-drop pennant nestled in her flounced décolletage gave clue her status as a widow. Had she been married, it was unlikely she would be a book curator, as most curators were expected to live on site of the archive. She was well past the mourning period, as indicated by her soft, cheerfully colored gown and trimmings. Grey or black would have been the norm for at least the first year after her spouse's demise. Some ladies wore their grief much longer.

Keela was left to pore over the book, and it didn't take her long, nor did she have to leaf far into the book to find Edrick's name. He was in the first grouping of the highest born Yvremi royalty, his name almost on the first page. His family was listed below him with their current connections by marriage.

He had only one close relative living in Kireen and that was a sister. She was wed to a southern gentleman who owned vast properties throughout Yvrem, but who kept his primary residence in the city. She knew at once that is where Edrick would be. She looked up from the book and caught Jessick's eye. With a little nod, she let him know that she had found what they were seeking. Jessick quickly made his polite thanks and a gracious bow to Mrs. Jakane, who waved delicately to him.

"Now we only need directions," Keela whispered as they remerged into the sunny afternoon.

"Let's hope the Nall aren't as clever as you, Keela."

"Indeed. Or if they're about at night sniffing around, they could find him. We must move quickly and find someone who knows where the Princess Royal lives."

"That should be easy enough," Jessick replied with confidence. They crossed the campus again and exited the peace into the chaos of the celebrations.

"There. They will know," he said, gesturing towards a small huddle of people who were idling about the entranceway to a tea house, watching the river of humanity flow sluggishly by. Jessick was right. They were most noticeably high-born, rich folk. The three ladies wore gowns of the muslins so spare and light they would be nearly invisible, and embellished with such lace and silk ribbons of the kind few could afford. Stylish and regal, the two gentlemen were as pretty as peacocks in their sweeping cutaway frock coats and their bold, bright waistcoats of striped silk. They both held canes with silver tops. One wore a slightly tapered topper, and the other in a broader brimmed hat with a shorter crown. They both wore white silk breeches, one with stockings of scarlet and the other of mustard, with navy clocking up the ankles. Both wore little thin black slippers.

Keela slipped across the road before Jessick realized it, and worked her way to the nearest lady who appeared to be no more than sixteen. Keela positioned herself beside the young lady, and pretended to watch the promenade pass by.

"Good gracious!" Keela sighed dramatically. "This city is almost too merry for me to bear!" She put on all her airs, channeling perhaps a bit of Vianca in her accent and her manners. Her plain walking gown and her stained bonnet did her no justice, but her mannerisms on full display as they were, would have fooled anyone.

The lady was standing slightly apart from her group, and was a tiny thing, with mousy brown hair and bright, flashing green eyes. She immediately looked at Keela, and her brow arched at the sight of this young woman who was well-spoken, if not slightly shabby in her appearance. The girl also appeared intrigued by the fact that Keela looked so much like a Farkas.

"Have you never visited the capitol during a celebration before?" she asked.

Keela shook her head, and laughed. "I've never visited it at all until today. I wasn't expecting all this!"

"Well, a pleasant surprise, then," the girl replied, smiling shyly. Her other companions were taking notice of the conversation, and their expressions were ones of disapproval. But the girl forged on, not noticing the silent disdain of her peers. "There is much to see in Kireen. It is replete with diversions to please everyone, young and old,"

"I hear that the Princess Royal lives in Kireen. Is that so?"

"Oh yes. She lives on Dellbury Street in the finest town house one could ever desire. You cannot miss it. It's the one with the half-moon window over the door.," the girl replied.. "I met her this winter at the Ymlym Assembly Hall at the Doreks' Ball. Oh, she is lovely, and her husband so distinguished and handsome."

"You met her?" Keela feigned awe.

"Indeed," the girl replied.

"Miss Valla, I am loathe to interrupt your conversation with this lovely young lady, however we must depart from here soon if we are to join our party for the evening," one of the young men interjected in a nasal, stiff-lipped tone. He tipped his hat to Keela, and reached out to claim the girl's arm, leading her rudely away. The girl smiled at Keela and waved. "Goodbye!" she called.

Keela returned the kindness, and then looked at Jessick who had taken a place beside her. With a nod of approval, he gestured for her to precede him up the street, indicating with only this gesture that he knew exactly where Dellbury Street was.

With a smile, she fell in beside him, and they forged their way westward through the crowds to the finest part of the city.

Edrick had only heard of Irino. It was another one of those places that had been absorbed into the blank parts of the map and now belonged to the Farkas. He knew only what it once was. As Elendra, it was a seaside county where the richest people from Kireen would spend their summers in the semi-circle of elegant townhouses that faced Elendra Bay. The city had been an architectural wonder with plazas and circuses of townhouses, stately homes overlooking an assortment of parks, and a variety of gardens and commons that once hosted many a promenade in the days before the Farkas.

Now, he had no idea what had become of the city, its infamous architecture and its many gardens. He would soon discover it, he rationalized, whether he liked it or not. All his efforts to escape and he had ridden right into their hands again like a dolt. He should not have headed back towards Keela. Not in such an obvious fashion, but his worry for Keela had overwhelmed his common sense. There were wolves awaiting him along the road.

All he knew was that he was being taken to Irino, and this time he was tied up inside another box cart with Magpie huddled up against his side, whimpering. She did not like the scent of these people. She somehow knew that they were the enemy. Edrick worried for Keela. He wasn't sure why, in all honesty. He'd seen her fight, but she'd been so battered by the last attack, he was concerned they'd kill her if they came at her again en force.

He listened. There was a lingering hope that he would hear the same sounds of violence that had once freed him from such a predicament; and he imagined Keela again, that fateful night in the moonlight. How he missed her. But no such sounds of her attack arose. There was only the silence of the box cart's guards who rode in front and behind the uncomfortable conveyance, and the impossibly irritating screech of the cart's axle, which rubbed on something with each revolution. All he could do was dwell on his regrets: that he had taken a horse from his brother in law that he would likely never see again, that Keela was lost to him, and that Magpie was frightened. He cursed his misfortune in brooding quiet, while outside the landscape changed in a slow parade.

They arrived at Irino without interference, unfortunately, and he was allowed to enjoy the peace of the stopped cart momentarily before the door was opened and he and the pup were yanked from the interior into a bleak, rainy night. He was towed by his captors up the steps of a building and into a softly lit foyer, the pup pushed into his arms.

He and Magpie were guided to a shuttered room with a bed and a hearth, and locked inside. He remained there for an undetermined amount of days, interrupted only by the arrival of food, the delivery of more firewood, and the removal and replacement of chamber pots. Magpie was forced to relieve herself on some brown paper that they had thrown on the floor for her. There was little noise except the sounds of a seaside city.

And then one evening, he was pulled from the room, his puppy thrown into his arms, and shoved down the stairs, left to stand in the same foyer where he had arrived. He tried to open the front door, but it was locked. Before he could test the other doors, a voice cut through the strange silence.

"Well, if it isn't the crownless king. You gave us a bit of a chase, didn't you? But not for too long, thankfully. It was a laudable effort, so you can be proud of that," a deep male voice mocked. A young fellow of about twenty-five slid into the reach of the candle-light and stood before Edrick with a look of amusement crossing his handsome brow.

"You may call me Vigo," he introduced himself. "I already know who you are." He had the appearance of a Farkas through and through. Smooth, pale skin. Dark, shining eyes. Hair as black as night, fashionably coiffed forward towards his fine, aquiline features. He wore the highest fashion: a smooth cutaway frock coat of evergreen and cream pin stripes with an impressively high collar that framed his face stylishly. Inside were the layers of the equally high collar of his cream waistcoat, and the bright white of his shirt collar, all held fast by a fancy cravat of snow white tied in an attractive knot under his striking chin. He wore cream breeches, forest green stockings and shining black slippers. It was an impressive presence he held, in spite of his youthful appearance.

"Come, and bring the child with you," he said. He swiveled on his heel and his tails flared out behind him as he moved into the darkness. He opened a pair of doors into a brightly lit room, cutting the shadows apart.

Edrick followed him in, squinting against the constellation of candlelight sprayed along the walls, doubled by the reflecting mirrors. There was an ample appointment of fine furnishings about the space, all arranged in small groupings. The young gentleman chose the one closest to the hearth and gestured for Edrick to sit.

"Now. I believe her ladyship has outlined what is required of you in order for you and I to have a productive and equitable relationship, Mr. Bethranorn," the young man intoned in a haughty, condescending voice. He was clearly referring to the woman that had arranged Edrick's capture.

Edrick merely rolled his eyes and sat down without leave, cuddling Magpie on his lap. She whined quietly, her little flanks trembling. "The pup needs to go outside," he said.

The young man, who was prepared to go on with his condescending missive, looked put off by the interruption. He opened a large, tall windowed door which immediately wafted in a gust of humid, sweet-smelling air from the dark night. Edrick stood and Magpie followed. She slinked outside and ran out into the darkness, leaving a dark trail in the dewy grass, as if someone had run their finger against the pile of fine velvet.

"Magpie!" he called. "Magpie come back! Magpie!!" He ran out after her. In the doorway, the perfect silhouette of the gentleman remained poised, his details obscured by the shadow. He sighed audibly and called for a servant in frustration. Edrick did not bother to look back. He kept his eyes on the path the pup had forged into the darkness, relying on the decreasing light to remain at her heels.

Keela smiled inwardly at the memory of Dayna, and how like Edrick she was in appearance. The same smooth, broad brow, the same deep eyes and the same smile. She was better humored than Edrick, more affable and open. Keela really liked her. In all her worry for Edrick, she could not help but feel the residual warmth of their meeting, and how much Dayna overtly liked her too. She'd been received so warmly, in spite of her shabby bonnet and her rough linen gown. Jessick looked far more presentable.

Regardless, when they rapped on the door they were ushered in by an elderly gentleman with a dusty queue and eyes blurred by cataracts. He walked with a hunch, and shuffled in a pair of inexcusably worn slippers and some droopy stockings that rumpled at his ankles and feet. He led them to a lovely little morning room where the evening sun shone through a row of gallery windows that looked out over the small garden space on the narrow city plot.

Doused in the golden light and looking as sweet as a doll was Edrick's sister. She looked up from some intricate paper quillwork she was making at a round table by the windows. She had a tall glass of cool water beside her, a scattering of scissors, strips of paper in some different colors, a clay pot of glue with a tiny brush handle sticking out of it, a quilling needle with a turned ivory handle, and a boxed frame in which she was carefully placing the little curls, spirals and shapes she was forming from the paper coils. She looked up at the old man, and then at her guests, having not been notified of

283

their identity before being led into the room. Dayna was most markedly surprised.

"Well, good evening." She stood and curtsied, her eyes wide, taking in the two personalities that had just entered her refuge.

Keela took in her rounded belly and she smiled. The old man did not say a word. He merely turned in a shuffle of feet, grasped the two doorknobs, and pulled the door closed as he exited.

"I'm sorry, we were not announced," Keela blurted, embarrassed. "I'm looking for the sister of Edrick of the Bethranorn. I assume because your man merely led us here upon our query, that you must be her."

Dayna's head tilted. "I am. I am Dayna, formerly of Bethranorn. Now Evam. May I ask who is inquiring?" The question was posed with a playful smile.

"I'm sorry." Keela curtsied hastily. "I am Keela Dremm. This here is my companion Mr. Jessick Kole. We are searching for your brother, Mrs. Evam."

"Do call me Dayna, Miss Keela. I beg both of you sit. You look positively exhausted."

"We have been trudging about the city in our quest to locate Edrick," Keela said, complying with the lady's request, moving with little grace to some chairs arranged for intimate discussion by the small fireplace. Jessick followed. They sat while Dayna frowned, still standing by her work.

"I'm sorry to say that Edrick left early the day before yesterday. I believe he went out in search of you, Miss Keela." The young lady wove around her table and moved to the sitting area where they were now seated. She alighted on a chair across from them both, and puckered her brow with worry. Keela reflected the sentiments, and for a moment, nothing was said.

"I suppose we should go to the Conclave house," Jessick said.

"What will that gain us?" Keela asked.

"A meal and a change of clothes for one. A moment to find

one's bearing perhaps?"

Keela glowered at him. "If he's gone, we don't have time to go larking about the city again," she snapped.

"If I might interrupt. I can at least offer you respite here, Miss Keela. The gentleman as well, of course, if this Conclave house you speak of is too far to go."

"Did Edrick have the little wolf?" Keela asked, wringing her hands.

"Yes. He took her with him."

"If we leave from here, there's a trail to follow," Keela stressed to Jessick, her words pointed and imbued with hidden meaning.

Jessick's brow rose as he realized that this was true. There would be a scent trail to follow from this house, Keela was sure of it. In the crowds of the celebration, she wasn't sure how long it would last. She didn't want to dawdle, but Jessick was right. They were bedraggled, hungry and tired. But Jessick still seemed reticent.

"I should go to the Conclave house, Keela. You remain here. You can begin your journey on your own, I will join you soon after. I think the Conclave needs to know what is happening. They can send assistance with me to help find them both."

"You trust me on my own, Jessick?"

"I do. But if you do find his trail, you must only follow. You must not engage. Not alone," he murmured. "Wait until we arrive before you do anything, am I clear?" Keela did not reply, but she looked impatient.

Dayna merely listened, brow arched in curiosity. Keela nodded shallowly, and Jessick stood. "Madame, I will embark for my own destination. I will see to it that your things are sent here by messenger at once, Miss Keela." He bowed deeply to Dayna and then to Keela.

"Do you require a carriage sir?" Dayna asked.

"No, my fair lady, I do not, but it is thoughtful and kind of you to offer. I will catch a hired chaise where I can. I thank you." He bowed again, and returned his hat to his head, seeing himself out.

"There won't be a chaise to be found in that mess out there," Dayna said to Keela as soon as he was out of the door.

Keela shrugged easily. "I'm sure he knows that too." She smiled wanly.

"So you are the infamous Keela. In spite of your travelled state, I can appreciate what Edrick sees in you for certain." She smiled, folding her hands prettily on her lap. Keela merely blushed. "Well, let's dispose of that atrocious bonnet, shall we? It's seen better days. And we'll get you out of that gown. You can borrow something from me until your trunk arrives."

"Oh, I have no trunk, Miss Dayna. Only a small bag to carry with me when I travel. My things are presently at Vederine."

"Edrick was not forthcoming about what exactly he's embroiled in, but I suspect it has been a bit of an adventure for both of you, from the sounds of it." Dayna shook her head. "I will see to it that you have something other than your walking dress to wear, Miss Keela. We'll get you outfitted with some useful, versatile garments if you're to embark from here again. We are similar in size, thankfully."

"There is no need for much fuss, Mrs...."

"Dayna, please," the lady interrupted, standing. "Come, let's get you out of that thing and into a nice bath. We shall get you a gown and then feed you. You can tell me what your plans are while we do this." She took Keela's arm and pulled her up.

As they exited the room they were met by a large long-haired, attractive tabby cat which was padding smugly across the floor towards them. However once it caught sight of Kella, it abruptly came to a halt, skidding on the slick marble floor in an effort to scamper away, tail puffed out like a bristle-brush.

"I hope you don't have this effect on *all* cats, Miss Keela. It would be a tiresome thing to have everyone's cats scurrying away at the sight of you every time you enter someone's home," Dayna laughed.

Keela chuckled too. "I don't have much experience with little house pets, Mrs..." She stopped and sighed. "Dayna. I'm sure it is quite evident to anyone, including you, that I haven't spent much time in homes where there are pets."

"Oh la!"

"In fact... I only know one pet. And it's not really a pet. It's a dog who spends all of her time with the flock and looks very much like one of the sheep." Keela added, "My occupation is not one that would justify having a dog."

"And what occupation is that?"

"I am a jeweler of middling skill," Keela replied.

Dayna laughed easily and gestured for Keela come with her. She followed the lady up the stairs, eager to get moving, but also glad to have a moment to breathe. And to laugh again, even though Edrick and Magpie were alone out there, and possibly in the hands of the Nall.

Morning rose bringing with it a heavy fog that choked the city. Keela, too, felt suffocated. The city's celebration had gone to bed, and the revelers were still slumbering when Keela rose. She dutifully filled her little pack with the garments she thought she would need, leaving with only one pair of the two sets of slippers that Dayna had so kindly given her. Once everything was packed, she stripped off the night gown loaned to her by her hostess and folded it tidily on the bed, placing the slippers on top of it. She cracked the door and shouldered her bag, fastening the belt that hung loosely around her slim body. With a sigh, she closed her eyes and let her arms drop down, filling her mind with Edrick and Magpie. When her palms fell onto the soft pile of the rug they had become the pads of large paws.

Immediately, the panoply of aromas washed into her nasal cavity, and rolled across her palate. There they were, the scents she was so familiar with. Edrick and Magpie and —inexplicably along with

287

them—the most horrendously strong stench of lavender. Dayna had given clue to her of what that was about the night before as they had finished their supper and retired to a little sitting room where Dayna embroidered and her husband—who had late arrived—snoozed quietly in a chair after a day of work.

"It was such a surprise to see Edrick. He has a habit of just popping in for a visit whenever the mood takes him. But there he was with such a lovely little pup in his arms. What wasn't as lovely was the reek of lavender all about him. Even the dog smelled of it. I've always loved lavender water and enjoyed it in my lemonade, but goodness me, lavender oil in heavy quantities is absolutely intolerably strong. And they both reeked as if they'd been soaked in a tub of the stuff!" Dayna giggled.

"He never explained what that was about, but I bade him to bathe at once and remove what had become a stink, and he did. But the lavender didn't quite disappear after that. It was still lingering around them. It will probably take several hot washes for both of them to finally be rid of the stuff." Dayna shook her head with a bewildered smile on her lips. "My brother is a character that is for certain."

Keela had sat and quietly listened, her hands folded in her lap, watching Edrick's sister work the embroidery frame. The needle punched through the taught fabric, the thread singing as it was pulled through. Keela knew the reason for the lavender oil. It was a good idea in concept. But also seemed a little bit of an obvious tactic to escape from those that hunt by scent.

Now, with her nose hovering over the floors of the house, the lavender was overpowering. She had not smelled it at all in her human form. She pattered down the quiet stairway, passing Dayna's room where she could hear the deep breathing of slumber. She slipped by the servant's door, and behind the old man who was walking about in his shirtsleeves, carrying an ash bucket, brush and pan. Keela found the servant's entrance and used her paw to scratch the latch open. She nosed her way out and slipped into the foggy morning.

The fog was a deep cobwebby grey, barely lit by the rising sun. She was able to move freely thanks to the fog. The moisture seemed to intensify the scents of the city and those of the recent past. There was a strange odor near the house that filled her nostrils and confused her. She could not identify what it was, but it was strong, and musky. It was neither wolf nor human. It was nothing she was familiar with. It was strongest in the area outside of Dayna's home, but it did not completely overpower that of Edrick and Magpie, which led away west towards the countryside.

She bounded down the streets, flitting past the morning traffic of merchants and journeymen. The lavender made following Edrick and Magpie quite easy—especially after the strange scent faded away altogether. There was another confusing moment when the scent trail brought her to a small shop, but she realized she might be tracing an older path.

She backtracked and found the trail leading her to a tall building near the city center. She did not approach it, for the aroma of Ney wolves was almost as strong as the lavender. But he wasn't there anymore. There was a thread of lavender intermixed with horses, wolves and people. She dropped her nose and trotted along the foggy streets.

His scent remained strong and detectable. The noise around her faded as she moved and she only realized after a bit that she was now outside the city. She paused and looked up from the road, her head pivoting about as she surveyed the foggy landscape that rolled out below her.

To her right, there was a stone plinth with words etched into it: Dulan – 6 miles. Genna 11 miles. Irino frmly Elendra – 14 miles. She huffed. Fourteen miles to run. With a laborious sigh, she took off running, stopping only to lap water from a stream before resuming her long marathon towards Irino.

Miranda Mayer

 **Chapter 15**
To Not Wait

Keela's paws found the cobbles of a Farkas Sentely in less than an hour of leaving the capitol. Edrick's scent was growing stronger, and the presence of other Ney wolves began to intrude upon it increasingly as she neared the Farkas territory. It became overwhelming once she entered the Sentely, and she had to rely on the dwindling lavender smell to keep on the trail.

By now the daylight had fully broken and the fog had burned away. She kept to the trees knowing her larger size would call attention to herself. She would dash into the road occasionally dropping her nose to find the hint of lavender. Unlike the other Sentely she had experienced, this one was small, and centered around a large, old city. One that was built many years before the Farkas invasion. It was one of classic, Ghenthan period style. It was no surprise the Farkas took it. It was, in comparison to other Yvremi settlements, surprisingly civilized and well-designed.

It became impossible to hide well once inside the city. She

dashed about, trying to appear smaller than she was, hunching down on her bandy legs, skulking between alleyways while still struggling to keep on the trail of lavender. The city was surprisingly busy. It seemed residents took loose Ney wolves in stride here, and the fast-moving dog was largely ignored. Nobody seemed particularly alarmed to see a large wolf, which surprised Keela. This was a fully Nall Sentely after all. Perhaps, she thought, the people who were looking for her did not believe she would boldly breach a Nall-populated Sentely.

She forged on, catching glimpses of the occasional wolf that passed by, some at the heel of a stylish lady or a peacockish gentleman. There was a strong presence of Yvremi people here, as there were at other Sentelys, but in this one the Farkas also made up a large percentage of the population, including tradesmen and merchants. She felt boldest when there were only Yvremi people, counting on their lesser knowledge of Farkas wolves to keep undetected.

Keela found herself heading towards a semi-circle of fancy townhouses overlooking the ocean. There Farkas ships—mind-bogglingly large—created a forest of swinging masts along the north side of the cob wall, the south side being left open for an uninterrupted view of the water-washed haystack and arched rocks off the still waters of the harbor.

Keela slipped quickly into the narrow park that spanned the space between the buildings and the harbor wall where graceful couples and groups strolled. She dove into a leathery-leafed shrub in the garden where there was shade and concealment, and sank down to the ground. Her long front legs stretched out in front of her. Her hind quarters squatted down. She pointed her head towards the houses and watched, ears perked, nose twitching. Nobody paid her any mind. She remained there for hours, ignoring her thirst, ignoring her hunger, her entire being focused on the front of the building where she knew by the scent trail, Edrick and Magpie were being held. Morning faded into afternoon, and then the day wore into evening, and she remained fast until the dark finally concealed her.

Fatigue had overcome Keela and she dozed off sometime in late afternoon. She awoke in the evening when the buildings' windows were brightly lit and the coaches still rattled along the throughway in front of the houses. Farkas and Yvremi alike were visiting and dining. The aromas of cooked food rolled over the ground towards her, and her wolf-belly bellowed, waking her from her slumber and reminding her where she was and what she was supposed to be doing.

She stood, bowing down low and stretching her sore back, yawning out a high-pitched whine and shaking her wolf body. Her pack rattled against her body. She verified that the park and cob were now abandoned and slid out of the shrub, trotting off towards the buildings. She moved around the back of them and trotted through the shadows along the lane, looking for the gate to the garden belonging to the correct house. As she neared it, she was overwhelmed with the scent of Edrick and Magpie intermingled with that of sweaty panic and more Ney wolves. The trail veered off into the darkness down the lane. Her instincts flared and her back hairs hackled. She broke into a full run, forgetting her need to be unseen. He was near and he had escaped again.

Edrick clutched Magpie to his chest, his breath ragged. He had managed only to grab her after they'd run through several streets. She was fleeing west, her nose high in the air. There were no easy solutions to throw the wolves—now taking chase—off of their trail. He knew he was literally leaving a path for them to find him with every step he took. He could hear their yowling and yipping as they pursued him. They were so close!

He darted across the park and towards the ships, his body

protesting his every stride, his lungs burning. He could hear their panting gaining on him, but he could not see them in the darkness, only catching glimpses of coppery eyes flashing in the meager moonlight.

Just as he was about to lose hope and leap into the water, he heard a terrifying growl. Something that moved with enormous speed came from the right. He saw a flash of silver, white teeth, and then heard the sound of one body hitting another and the wind being knocked out of a creature. Then there was the unmistakable din of snarling and fighting, keening and the occasional piercing yip of pain.

Edrick huddled against the edge of the water, sidling along it, moving further from the tousle. He wondered with optimism who it was that interceded with his pursuers. Magpie wriggled with all of her might to escape his grasp, whimpering and straining towards the fight. He knew now it was Keela. For Magpie only reacted in such a way for her. He grappled to hold the pup, fearful and confident all at once.

He had no idea how many wolves were in the fight, but there were many. The noise, however, was attracting more wolves from the ships and the shore. And then people began to arrive, running with wavering lanterns, shedding light on the scene.

Keela was literally covered in wolves. Her size against her attackers was easily double, but they still swarmed her in droves. She savaged them in turn, throwing some off and shaking them like rag dolls. Some rolled off into the water, others fell prostrate on the ground, whimpering. But as she neutralized one, another would arrive.

Edrick had seen her fight before, but he had never seen her so feral and violent. Her savagery was astonishing, her teeth awash in the blood of her attackers. She was, however, losing ground, it seemed. But the attackers were also wary of approaching her now that there was a ring of dead and dying around her.

294

For a brief moment, they stopped. She stood head down, ribs rising and falling raggedly, drool and blood dripping from her mouth. She looked like a monster. A beast. Her silver eyes glinted malevolently as she stood between the wolves and Edrick. And then the next wave of arrived, led by a large wolf. They lunged at her without hesitation, leaping onto her back, latching onto her ruff and biting at her. She reared up and snarled, her mouth falling on the throat of a small wolf and ripping at its skin with ferociousness.

Another clamped onto her leg. She fell and was immediately covered in writhing, snarling bodies. Edrick called out something indistinct, his voice filled with raw terror, his hands gripping Magpie so hard, she whimpered.

And then a great beast appeared. A massive blot of fur and bone and sinew with white teeth and glinting eyes of black. The animal rose up to enormous height, and then fell onto the pack of dogs, sending one flying with the bat of its massive claw. It was a bear. A mammoth, towering bear. It picked up wolves by the ruff and tore their throats out with one bite, throwing them meters away into bleeding, twitching heaps. As the wolves were reduced violently in numbers, Keela was able to regain her footing and her tall shoulders were once again lofting over her attackers. She renewed her attacks, sending her assailants fleeing and crying. She threw the large wolf flat under her feet and savagely tore out his throat.

The attack stopped. Keela only now seemed to become aware of the enormous bear that stood beside her with bloody jowls and nary a scratch. He balanced back and forth on his large front paws, challenging the witnesses to persist.

Edrick let Magpie go, and she ran to Keela, whimpering and crying, twisting in joy and relief to see her. Keela's nose dropped and she licked the pup's head, then moved her body over Magpie protectively.

A cohort of wolves appeared, all silver-eyed. Along with them was the Vigo. He was a handsome Farkas man with smart clothing and an air of arrogance and confidence that could only represent a leader. He looked utterly beside himself at the carnage of the scene. Enraged even, biting it back behind a red face and wide, glaring eyes.

"*You mongrel!*" He blurted at the top of his lungs, "*Bloody mongrel!*" He looked to his wolf compatriots and pointed at her. "*Kill that abomination! That atrocity against everything Farkas!*"

The wolves hesitated, looking warily at the bear. Keela was in a rough state. Covered in patches of seeping, shining darkness over her fur, a tear on her jowl. Someone had taken a knick out of her ear. The leader, whoever he was, merely commanded the wolves to attack her, and they advanced. Keela lowered her head and her hackles rose. She stepped forward, and nosed the pup back towards Edrick, who hung back with the onlookers. She then slinked towards the growling cohort, lifting her jowls into a black snarl. She dove into the fray. The ferociousness of the fight was magnified by the presence of the large wolves.

The bear—who had been watching with interest—merely strode forward and snatched a wolf by the rear leg with his mouth. He dragged it out and then climbed over it, slashing its throat with his great claws. The wolf fell instantly still.

Keela was in encased in ball of flailing wolf limbs, the noise of it was startling and terrifying: snarls and growls, cackles and snaps of teeth. Tears rolled from Edrick's eyes as he knelt beside Magpie and watched with horror as a pack of wolves tore at Keela. The bear methodically helped remove her attackers, and Keela had dispatched two on her own. It was hard to discern her from the mass of violent ebony limbs as the battle waged. Edrick was sure she would be killed. He was terrified for her.

But the bear—that massive creature—gave her the advantage she needed. And while she fought off her lupine assassins, the bear systematically claimed a wolf, and killed it. The repeated this one by one until they had killed the last wolf, and Keela stood wavering on her long, chewed up legs, blood and saliva hanging in glistening strings from her fearsome lips. Her eyes locked with almost palpable hatred on the tall young man. His pale, livid face seemed almost illusory against the darkness, his hatred and disgust flowing from him like an oozing fog. "I will *kill* you for this. *Kill you!*"

He transformed in a fluid movement, his body slipping from the many layers of his silken, fashionable ensemble. His front end landed with a graceful whisper on the grass as he fell immediately into a challenging posture. His hind legs were still in his shoes, his stockings in a puddle around his paws. He stepped out of them and moved in a circular approach to Keela, his hackles high, his growl enhanced by a row of sparkling ivory teeth.

Keela was in no state for another fight. She could barely stand, and wavered on her rickety legs. She was bleeding profusely, and having trouble holding her head up. Edrick watched with horror as the fresh, healthy opponent leapt at her, mouth agape.

Without hesitation, or a moment's thought, Edrick threw himself into the wolf's path. Its paws landed on his shoulders, throwing him back as its teeth snapped into his tender neck. Keela howled out in fury and threw her body at him, colliding with the wolf and rolling them both away from Edrick. With every shred of her remaining strength, she savaged the dog's face and ears, biting at his throat the moment there was an opening. She ripped into him, biting down with every inch of force she could muster until she felt her teeth pop through his skin and sink into his flesh, the salty blood filling her mouth. She tore away with all her strength and ripped his throat out. The wolf fell still. She stepped away and watched the blood rush out of the gash in his neck. Her breathing ragged, she wavered.

She turned and saw Edrick lying on the grass. The blood pouring from his wound was gushing, shimmering with moisture, steam rising up from the heat dissipating from his being. The life in his eyes were fading.

She transformed, falling heavily to the ground, her body riddled with cuts and gashes, blood and bruises. Tears were flowing from her eyes and she keened and sobbed in sorrow, crying "No, no, no, no, no….." Her voice raw and hollow as she crawled towards him, naked and vulnerable, falling over his form and clutching at his clothes. Magpie whimpered and licked his face, her body trembling. The bear rose up on his hind legs and emitted a massive roar, sending the people scattering, leaving them in darkness again.

The bear stood, his snuffles and breaths quiet and respectful, as he watched Keela weep over the now still body of her crownless King.

 ## Chapter 16
Ally

The Conclave arrived at length, a large contingent of wolves and people who had followed the murmurs and mumblings to the place where Keela rested naked, her upper body lying over Edrick. Her hands clutched his face as her tears flowed. Her body was battered and bleeding. Beside them was a Crested Bear—a species of thought to be extinct—resting quietly on its belly. Its large, brooding eyes rested on Keela. Magpie trembled and whimpered beside it.

Jessick knelt beside Keela and took her hand, which she tore away in anger and glared at him. "*You*! You did this. *You* involved him. This blood is on *your* hands!" she sobbed, her beautiful face a mask of blood and viscera.

"Keela, I am sorry. I wish you had waited. I wish you had waited so we could have prevented this..."

She then fell weeping onto Edrick again. "I couldn't wait. They were after him… Oh Edrick…"

A lovely, willowy woman in a silver gown approached and removed her shawl. Kneeling next to Keela, she draped it over her shoulders and then pulled her to sit up.

"Can you stand?" she asked.

"No," Keela sobbed. "We can't leave him here alone."

"We will not leave him," the woman replied. "I promise." She turned Keela's blood and tear soaked chin towards her. Keela did not see the beautiful, fine features of the woman, or her stunning curls of silvery black hair. She saw only her steel grey eyes.

The bear stirred and the newcomers made way for it. The beast lumbered towards Keela and rose up on its hind feet, bowing down and lifting Keela like a doll. He walked like a man, carrying her slight human frame. The army of wolves converged around him, flowing like a river, leading and following both, back to the house Edrick had escaped from. The tall woman carried Magpie. Jessick and a few of the Conclave people remained behind to tend to Edrick's body.

Keela allowed her grief and her pain to carry her into a cloudy fugue that eventually faded into unconsciousness. She felt only the brush-bristle fur of her bear friend, its grunts as it walked on its hind legs, carrying her like a bundle of kindling. And then there was blissful nothing.

Keela awoke to darkness, her body riddled in a web of soreness and pain. She remembered and her grief returned in the form of a massive sob which bubbled up from her raspy lungs. The moment she stirred, there was a shuffling and the sound of feet approaching. A snap of a fire twig, and brightness filled the room, fading into the mellower flicker of candlelight. Highlighted by the soft luminescence of the flame were the harsh angles of Lord Xanett's face. His piercing eyes looked weary, but relieved. He lowered the candle and put it on the table by the bed in which Keela rested, and climbed up to sit on it beside her.

"What are *you* doing here?" Keela murmured groggily, her nose stuffed, her words clipped.

He reached into a pocket of his waistcoat and pulled out a

kerchief which he gave to Keela. She took it, wiping her eyes and her nose, noting the dried grains of blood that came away onto the smooth, soft pressed cotton. The whole catastrophe returned to her in its grisly and horrifying reality, and she felt again overwhelmed with misery.

"I've been following you for some time," Xanett confessed.

She sniffled and turned onto her side, her back facing him. "Go away."

"I'm sorry you lost your friend, Miss Keela."

"No you're not."

"I might have seen him as a threat, but I never would have wished him dead, dear girl."

She did not reply.

"The pup is fine. She has been standing vigil outside your door for over eleven days."

Keela only sobbed again, and her sore shoulders shook. "I killed him. I should have waited for Jessick," she cried.

"There was a good chance he would have died regardless, left in the hands of the Nall for as long as that. He did invite the situation by attempting to escape again. That was not a well thought out plan. But ultimately, what value did he have to the Nall after that first escape anyway? They knew he would not cooperate with them. The only thing I can think of is that they knew he would be a viable lure to bring you in. I don't want to sound callous, but he was a liability to you, in the end. It almost cost you your life."

Keela turned over specifically to glare at him. This was a painful process—to turn her body like this in the bed—but she did it anyway. "What do you know?" she snarled.

"I know everything, Keela. Jessick and I, we *are* friends. He has informed me of most of what I didn't see, and I know what I was present to witness. If I had not been following you, I imagine you, the Bethranorn and the pup would all be dead," Xanett said with finality.

Keela frowned darkly. "If it weren't for *you?*" she replied incredulously.

"Aye, me. Your ursine friend. One of the few remaining Yvremi purebloods," he retorted. "I who has kept you safe and alive for your whole life. You cannot imagine the number of times I've had to remove Neys from my lands throughout the years, sniffing about looking for mixed bloods like you."

Keela blanched, and was rendered speechless.

"I have always been looking after you even before you knew what you were. Always." He turned away and glared into the darkness.

Keela's eyes shifted away as she recalled a dreamlike memory of the great crested bear rising up and swatting wolves off of her like they were but rodents. She furrowed her brow as a succession of other memories trickled into her mind. The bear that she'd seen close to the tower. The bear that had chased off the young boys who'd started throwing rocks at her. The bear with what looked like eyes of buffed silver. The bear by the river, watching her at the tower. Her gaze fell on the man, and she was without words. He did not turn to look at her.

"I, perhaps, pursued you too fervently and have disgusted you. But you understand why you are a beauty of such fascination and interest to me.."

Keela fell back into her pillows, wincing from the pain of it. They shared a silence between them. "What of the Nall?" she finally asked.

Xanett took a deep breath and his eyes seemed distant. How different he seemed to before. Almost downtrodden. "Between the two of us, we neutralized most of the Nall in Yvrem in one fell swoop. Your choosing not to wait for the Conclave had one benefit and that was we caught them all together, so infuriated by your infiltration of their city, that they threw caution to the wind and came after you en masse. You and I, we killed all the imperials and most of their bronze wolves. The Conclave and many of its wolves took care of the rest and secured Iromi. Without its leadership, the Nall can be flushed out of the other settlements, and at last their resistance will be squashed.

"Edrick's death was what the Conclave needed to mobilize the Yvremi Senate. They told the Senate of the insurgent factions who vied to harm Yvremi interests, and that they were hindering the Conclave's efforts to send assistance for the Akravani problem. The Senate ate it up. They supplied the Conclave with armed forces to breach the various Sentely that were Nall controlled. There's been a great deal going in the past days. Jessick keeps me informed. I have been here."

Keela sniffled and reached up to rub her face. She looked worse for the wear. Her body was a riddle of poultices and bandages, scratches and cuts, dark blemishes and bruises all wrapped in a clean nightgown. Her hair was plaited into a long rope. Where she was, she had no idea.

"So you can congratulate yourself. The incepted the beginning of the end the Farkas civil unrest after so many years. The talk of your feats has been spreading like wildfire amongst the Farkas. My existence too. Jessick says that many Nall are now changing their minds about the conclusions of their leaders. There were too many who witnessed your superior makeup to continue believing that you are an abomination. And my presence, Jessick says, shows them that the Conclave's theory of the old blood is valid. It gives them hope where there was none. They desire to be a strong people again. So... if the Conclave does its job, half-bloods like you. Magpie will no longer be in danger."

"That's a relief." Keela didn't bother to veil her bitter sarcasm. There was a marked silence between them. He huffed out a weary sigh. "How long have you been here with me?" she asked, staring at the opposite wall.

"I have not left your side, Keela. I've been hovering over you so long, it is a habit I could scarce break now, I'm afraid. I'm sorry for stealing that man away. He irked me. After all this time I had hoped, and then Vianca did what she did, and just as I was allowed to hope again, I find you have acquired an admirer. I was rash. I've always been rash."

Keela continued to stare, impassive and now hollow. She lifted her hand and wiped her face again. Xanett straightened.

"I will be taking you home, if you are amenable to that," he said.

"Yes. Home. To go back to my life knowing all that I now know, having lost what I have lost. I will never have that normality again."

"There will be change, Keela. A new house, the one we discussed. And perhaps… Perhaps a friendship. With me."

Keela did not reply. She merely continued to look away.

Xanett stood and—without looking back—moved to the door. Magpie squeezed in the moment he opened it and leapt up onto the bed, immediately curling up against Keela and huffing out a sad, trembling voice. Keela lifted her arm laboriously and wrapped it around the pup. The door latch closed and there was silence in the room.

"I'm here, Magpie," she whispered. She drew her fingers along her precious face, and kissed her nose. She then cuddled her up onto her chest and turned over onto her side, still clutching her. They both emitted deep, wavering, sorrowful breaths, and went to sleep.

The End

About the Author

Miranda Mayer lives in the Mount Hood territory of Oregon. A polyglot, artist, avid historic costumer and lifelong equestrian; her interests are broad, and edge on geekery most of time. She is married with one child.

Miranda's stories range from Science Fiction to Urban Fantasy to Fantasy. She writes from her heart, imbues her writing with her quirky humour, and tries very hard to make her characters as real and three-dimensional as possible. Her unpredictable and rather Attention-Deficit-Disordered nature guarantees that her stories will take readers to unexpected places.

Other titles by Miranda Mayer

The Trilogy of Tinna:

Tinna's Promise

Tinna's Might

Tinna's Reign

Red Slipper series:

The Wizard King

A Problem of Ghosts

The Witches of Tirdonne

The Belletrist

Blackroot

www.ingramcontent.com/pod-product-compliance
Lightning Source LLC
Chambersburg PA
CBHW030648260626
47157CB00007B/2544